LEXI J. KINGSTON

IN THE
MOON LIGHT

Published by L. Kingston Books, LLC
Edited by Susan Barnes
Cover Design by Lexi Kingston

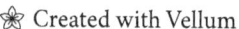 Created with Vellum

IN THE
MOON
LIGHT

For the daring.
The timid.
The lionhearted.
And the wild hearts looking for
their something more.
The world is only as wide as your mind perceives.

PROLOGUE

*T*his town is a poison. It seeps through your skin and into your bones, courses through your veins, and alters your blood so you become something other than you were before stepping foot within its borders. It kills you slowly, and at the beginning, you don't realize you've been infected. You don't realize it has sucked you dry of every ounce of life left in your vacant body until your soul is fractured, and the fragments of your face look cracked and mangled in your reflection. And at a certain point, things begin looking up. You think that maybe you're being restored, that you were too strong to be overtaken by the evil flowing strong and rapid through your bloodstream, but that is a false hope. It lifts you up, raises your spirits only to crack through your skull with the knowledge that you will never survive, and believing you could was a foolish delusion. Because in truth, the disenchanting and unfortunate truth, your life was lost the moment you arrived.

CHAPTER 1

ater drips down my arms as I stand beneath the rain-soaked tree, branches creaking softly against the chilly air. There's no movement in sight except for a small group of kids creeping steadily up the hill, as far as they dare wander for fear of being seen. The girl leans in close to one of the boys, softly whispering in his ear. He snickers giddily, nodding in approval. The girl then turns to the other boy, looking ahead.

"You should touch it," she says, cupping a hand over her mouth in a silent giggle. They can't be more than twelve—maybe thirteen.

The second boy turns, glancing between his friends hesitantly, and then shakes his head. "You mean the gate?"

A sly grin stretches across the girl's face as her gaze travels up the iron posts glimmering in the moonlight. "Better yet... ring the doorbell."

"Maria..." he drags out her name, fumbling with the hem of his t-shirt and glancing over his shoulder at the tall mansion ahead. They're hidden in the night's cover for now, but a few more feet and the spotlights shining on the length of the Manor will bathe them in light. "You can't be serious."

She rests an elbow on his shoulder. "I mean, if you're too scared…"

"I'm not," he says immediately, clearing his throat.

"Then do it," she coaxes, and the other boy lets out a strangled noise.

"I'm not sure that's such a good idea. The gate is one thing… but what if they're awake?"

"Then we'd better run like hell," Maria responds, egging him on. "I dare you."

The boy facing the challenge looks behind him once again, assessing the height he must climb in order to fulfill his dare. "I'll need a leg up."

The three stumble to the gate, crouching down to avoid being seen. Just as they begin to hoist him up, a fourth shadow appears behind them, towering over their thin bodies.

The kids turn slowly, eyes wide and fearful. The girl shoves the two boys in front of her, then dashes back down the hill faster than her feet can carry her. She trips, stumbling and rolling the rest of the way. The boys stand, shaking in fear as the figure closes in on them. Cracking his neck, he moves closer and his deep voice cuts through the silence like a knife.

"Leave."

"Y-yes, sir," one of the boys stutters, latching on to the arm of the other, pulling him in the same direction as Maria.

My eyes slice through the dark, taking in the man as he smirks darkly, watching them retreat, tripping and shoving, stumbling over each other and their own limbs. Then he turns, and in an instant, he's in front of me. His sinister smile stays cemented in place until his eyes travel to my bare toes, submerged in a shallow pool of muddy leaves and rainwater.

"What are you doing out here?" Miles asks finally. Leaning against the tree, he crosses his arms, eyes roaming over me.

"Watching," I say simply, looking back to the path the kids used to run away. Now they have their own stories to tell. Their own contribution to the town's plethora of tall tales about the Draven family and the horrors that lie beyond the safety of town. I scoff at that thought. *Safety.* Whoever believes such a lie must know better than to go into town after dark, because I know firsthand the true horrors that lurk in the shadows of this damning place.

Miles breathes in, tracing a warm finger down my cheek and across my jawline where he pauses on my bottom lip, triggering a wave of goosebumps that travel across my damp skin.

"You'll get pneumonia," he whispers, entranced by something about me that I can't see.

I roll my eyes, even as I rub my hands over my arms. "No, I won't."

I thought becoming a vampire would make me numb, cold, heartless, and immune to all of the weaknesses humans are programmed with. But I can still feel the cold and the warmth of another's skin. I can feel pain, although it dissipates rather quickly, and hunger so intense it burns in my gut and claws at me from the inside out until I satisfy it with the blood it craves. Most people are ruled by love, envy, or hate. The lucky few have minds so strong they can keep themselves from becoming overwhelmed by all of those emotions—they can compartmentalize and decipher them rationally. Logically. But me? I'm ruled by the utmost desire to devour anything that stands between me and my next meal.

I don't get sick, though. I'll never age, nor will I ever die so long as my life isn't stolen from me first. Eternity sits before me on a pedestal, and I don't have the first clue of what to do with it.

"I'll never have kids," I say abruptly. "I mean, I never knew if I wanted them—I'd never really given it much thought to be honest—but now I know I'll never have kids."

The choice was made for me, like so many others.

I meet his eyes then, bright as the stars above us, their color resembling that of the moon's. Yet, there's an abyss of darkness there as well, an inhuman part that stays hidden behind the light. He closes them, momentarily snuffing out their glow. "I never wanted this for you."

"I'll never make new friends, either," I continue absentmindedly, turning into the breeze to remove the hair from my face. "I can't. After so long, they'll realize I'm not aging. And the friends I have now, and my family—I'll be forced to watch them grow old and die. Leaving me here. Alone. I potentially have more life ahead of me than every human in this world combined, and I feel like it's already over."

Well, either that, or I'll die before my life has even begun. Because in this twisted world, there are no assurances.

Miles dips his chin, lowering his gaze to find mine in the dark, and takes my face gently in his warm hands. "So long as I'm alive, you will never be alone, beautiful."

"You don't know that," I whisper, feeling a burn in my nose. Before I turned, one of my biggest fears was losing myself to the monster within. But now I am the monster.

"I do." He presses a kiss to my temple, pulling me in until I'm wrapped in his arms and my entire body is pressed so tight to him that it suppresses my trembling. All of my apprehensions melt away in his embrace as I focus on the sound of our hearts beating as one. "I promise you, Aspen Troy, no matter what happens in this lifetime, or the next, loneliness will never find you."

"Unless Vanesa locks me in a cage and siphons venom from my veins," I say without humor.

Vanesa is still angry with me for refusing to build her family an army to fight the other clans, and once the Twelve discover I've broken the curse that was placed on the Dravens, they'll attack with the sole purpose of wiping us out.

Miles' shoulders shake with laughter, and he pulls back to look at my face, placing a kiss on the bridge of my nose, then each cheek and my chin, before his cold lips find mine. He brushes them temptingly, allowing his bottom lip to scrape across mine before molding them together and sliding his hands down my stomach and around my back, pressing me into him.

He breaks away with a sharp breath and lifts me onto a low-hanging tree branch so I'm slightly above him in height. His fingers play with the holes in my jeans, worn from long and tiring days and nights of fighting, training, pushing myself to the brink of death, sleeping, then starting all over again. I'm luckier than most newborns since I had a little bit of self-defense training before I turned. If only it had been enough to keep me alive.

Miles slips his hand beneath the ripped fabric on my knee, tracing around the hole with his thumb. "You know, just because you can't have kids doesn't mean we can't help young vampires find their way."

I nod solemnly, unable to let go of all the things this life was supposed to bring me before death. Instead, it brought me death before I'd hardly lived.

CHAPTER 2

The floor creaks beneath my feet as I tiptoe across the living room, reaching carefully over my father's snoring figure for the remote to turn down the TV. A quick chill races through the room and I tremble, looking for the source. This time, unlike most of the others, there's a reasonable explanation for the draft, and it's the open window over the kitchen sink. Since I killed Ambrose Draven, the paranormal activity in my house has stopped, but no matter how many times I scrub the floors, he's still here, still watching me, still waiting for the perfect moment to strike. I don't think I'll live a day of my life without remembering the feel of his fingers on my skin or his tongue tracing the line of my veins.

My stomach churns at the memories, and I reach for the window, preparing to close it when it slams shut on its own. I jump back, spinning around and checking every dark corner for glowing eyes. I wait to feel his breath on my neck, or his voice to whisper my name, but it never comes. The only thing I hear is my father groaning as he sits up, rubbing his eyes.

"Aspen?" He peers at me through the dark. It's almost

impossible for him to see me in this light, but I can see him. He twists around, looking for the flashlight that never leaves his side, almost as if he's afraid of the dark.

Elliot made sure my parents wouldn't remember a thing about what happened the night Ambrose attacked, and they don't. But they must know something bad happened, something worse than what we told them so they'd be able to sleep at night and allow us to leave the house without worrying. Because now they're always paranoid. Almost like they can't see what it is they're supposed to be afraid of, but they know it's there, watching, waiting.

"I'm over here." I give in before he turns on his flashlight and blows my cover. Our power went out last night, and even Ted, the town handyman, can't seem to figure out why. Now only the TV and kitchen appliances are connected to a small generator out back.

Father's head swivels in my direction, and he flinches, clicking on the flashlight anyway.

"Sorry, did I wake you?"

He shakes his head, looking at me strangely. "No, I don't think so." He purses his lips, shining the light on my face before shaking his head again, running a hand over his face. "That was weird. For a minute, it looked like your eyes were glowing."

"Probably a trick of the light." I gesture toward the TV, shifting so my dirty feet are hidden from view. I rummage through the pantry in search of something sugary to curb my cravings. The only reason I left my house tonight was to get something to eat, but I was distracted by the kids sneaking up to Draven Manor, and then by Miles, and I didn't realize until I walked through the door that I'm still absolutely famished.

"Shouldn't we at least talk about what happened?" he asks,

taking a few swigs of water from the glass sitting beside him. Apparently, it was Ambrose's influence that drove my father to drink and made my mom retreat into herself. When we took away their memories of him, it also took away their memories of who they became during that time.

Ambrose told me once that he couldn't make a monster out of a good man... does that mean the people my parents became is something they're truly capable of? Is it possible for my father to really be *that* mean all the time?

"What's to talk about?" I shrug him off, grabbing a box of something that looks like a chocolate dessert—cupcakes maybe? I know he won't let it go. Almost every time he sees me, he brings it up. "A man broke into our house. Tried to kill me. You and Mom ran. Dallas and I scared him away. There's nothing left to say."

I walk quickly to my bedroom, slamming the door before he has the chance to say anything else. It's hard enough having to lie, having to downplay everything bad that's happened to me over the past few months, but what's worse is constantly worrying about slipping up and revealing a new piece of information that we haven't programmed them to know. In order to make them forget Ambrose, Elliot had to *make* them remember something else. He couldn't just erase such a traumatic experience and convince them they were sleeping the whole time—which I would have preferred. He had to implement parts of the truth. Personally, I wish we could ship them back to Colorado like this never happened. But nothing is ever that simple.

"You're awake?" I mumble, noticing my brother sitting up in bed, sketchpad in hand, flashlight in his lap. I move away from the empty doorframe between our rooms and strip out of my wet clothes, throwing on an old nightgown and slipping under my covers. I then unwrap a mini cupcake and plop it in my mouth, savoring the sweet chocolate.

Dallas doesn't flinch, hardly acknowledging my presence. "I don't sleep anymore."

Guilt pricks in my heart, expanding in my chest. Dallas used to have horrible dreams, so bad that I'd have to stay up the entire night just to make sure his screams didn't wake up our parents. But now... now that my brother has had a glimpse behind the curtain, a peek into the world of blood and horror, he can't sleep at all. Ambrose invading his dreams didn't do him any favors, but I can't help but feel like everything that's happened is somehow my fault. The only reason I don't resent Miles for finding me, saving me, and turning me into what I am, is because if it weren't for him, I'd be dead. Dallas likes to pretend he's angry, that he's terrified that his life has forever changed. But if he had lost me, too, after our own brother tried to kill us because drugs were more important to him, it would have quite literally ruined him.

"I think Father is starting to remember." I sigh, pressing my face into a pillow. "Or he just knows something feels wrong."

Elliot originally used a temporary memory potion to make them forget what happened with Ambrose, and then eventually used his compulsion, which doesn't seem to be up to par.

Dallas grunts, and I hear his pencil drop to his sketchpad. He's quiet for a long while until he finally speaks. "Everything is wrong."

"Dallas—"

"Why couldn't you make me forget, too?"

I clear my throat, staring up at the ceiling as his words

strike me. I let them seep into my skin, wrap around my bones, and suffocate my heart. "I didn't know you wanted that."

"I don't, I guess. I'd just much rather go back to being afraid of the dark—*only* the dark."

"Not what lies beyond it," I whisper. "I'm sorry. All I ever wanted was to protect you."

"Maybe that's the problem," he says without a trace of emotion in his tone as he shifts on his old mattress. We decided to keep the crappy ones for the time being, at least until the more pressing issues with the house are tended to. Although, no amount of fixing is going to make this place livable again. We'd probably be better off tearing it down and building a new house from the bottom up.

I don't respond to his offhand comment. With Derek unhinged and on the other side of the world, and our parents basically incapacitated, the two of us only have each other. But lately, I feel even our relationship is dwindling. How long do I have until my own flesh and blood becomes a stranger I faintly recognize?

An odd smell drags me from sleep. I scrunch my nose and attempt to roll on my side to see if I left the window open, but when I try to move, I notice a heavy weight pressing down on me. I shift, left then right, but I'm pinned in place by what feels like another body molding me to the bed.

The smell grows stronger, burning my nose and souring my stomach so much so that I feel as if I might puke. And then the tapping starts. I can't see where it's coming from, but it's consistent and grows louder each time I struggle to sit up.

I cry out, the air in my lungs growing thinner and thinner as the heaviness increases. The pressure builds until I'm wheezing.

"You can't escape," a voice growls. A finger drags across my collarbone to the collar of my shirt, then up my neck to the permanent mark reminding me of the day my life forever changed. I can't see him, but I can feel him—and not just physically. He's in every fiber of my being, in my pores and my veins like a drug. I feel his hot breath and then the stroke of a cold tongue across my ear. "You will never escape me."

CHAPTER 3

"*A*spen. Aspen, wake up."

I jolt up, banging my forehead off whatever imbecile thought it was smart to lean so close to me while I was having a nightmare.

Dallas stumbles backward, clutching his nose.

"What the hell?" he yells, baring his teeth.

"Are you all right?" Elaine asks, but I'm not sure if she's speaking to me or my brother. I blink slowly, trying to see through the sleep-fog coating my brain and focus on where I am. On what's happening.

"When did you get here?" I ask, shifting to pull the sheets up to my shoulders. Like everything else in this house, the heater is barely functioning, and we can't light the fireplace because of all the ash it will produce—ash that will weaken me beyond comprehension.

Elaine sits at the edge of my mattress, looking at me like I've sprouted three heads. "I was tapping on your window and heard screaming. I thought..." her voice trails off, and she bites her lip, inspecting her short nails.

"Bad dream," I explain, staring a hole into the sheets. Elaine eyes me, disbelieving.

"Just a bad dream, though? Nothing... *else?*"

The tapping I heard in my nightmare must have been her, but it was like I couldn't wake up, like I was being forcefully held in my subconscious.

I swallow, avoiding her gaze. The last thing she or my brother need to worry about is the man they thought I killed three months ago coming back from the dead—again. "More like post-traumatic nightmares. Nothing to be concerned about."

She purses her lips, shooting a worried glance at my twin. "Are you sure it's not Amb—"

"Don't!" Dallas warns, moving between us with a frantic look in his eyes. His hands tremble nervously at his sides, but I'm not sure he notices. "Not in this house."

Elaine nods once, and I finally remember that it's the middle of the night and she's been knocking on my window. "Wait, what's wrong?"

"I was going to wait until morning to tell you," she starts, looking around like she's expecting someone to appear out of thin air. "Remember how I told you I put up cameras around the area to keep an eye on things?"

I roll my eyes. Elaine has taken this "watcher" title literally. What her ancestor must have forgotten to write in the journal she found of his, is that she's allowed to let us out of her sight. Well, more like *me* since it seems I'm the only vampire in town she's tasked herself with protecting. The only reason she bothers with the Dravens is because she knows if they're in danger, I've probably already been kidnapped. So far, things have been calm, though. She's had nothing to report—no new vampires sniffing around town, and the hunters have been uncharacteristically quiet, which in itself is a cause for concern. Especially after the bonfire incident. Since that night, we haven't seen a single one. "Has something come up?"

"More like someone." She pulls out her phone, and I sit up to make room for Dallas on my bed. As much as he hates the world I dragged him into, he'll be damned if he doesn't know every single thing about it. "Look familiar?"

Her phone screen is bright at first, and it takes a few moments for my eyes to adjust, but once they do, my blood runs cold. "No, I've never seen him before."

"Me neither." An unfamiliar face wandering through town at night is not a good thing. We get very few new faces around here, much less ones who surface out of nowhere.

Dallas yanks the phone from her fingers, and I can tell it takes everything in her not to yank it right back.

"Hold on—can you zoom in?" I ask, and he obliges, pinching the screen so we can better inspect the tall man standing in the dead center of town. On the back of his right hand is a small, circular tattoo. Just like the one that's behind Adrian's ear.

"He's one of Adrian's," I say, and a chill rushes through me.

"Talk about blending in," Dallas comments, and it makes me realize something.

"You're right," I muse, taking the phone from him. "He's standing out in the open. Almost like..." I trail off, searching the background for anyone suspicious, someone else to identify. But there's no one.

"It's almost like he wanted to be seen," Elaine finishes, looking uncomfortable. "It must be a warning."

No good could possibly come from a vampire purposely making himself known.

"We have to tell Miles." I stand quickly, throwing on a hoodie over my shirt, and rummage in a rickety drawer for my phone, which of course, I must have misplaced again. "We're not safe anymore. The hunters managed to catch us off guard last time—we wouldn't stand a chance against an entire clan of vampires."

"He could be the only one." Elaine grabs my arm and I let her. I could have easily avoided her grip, but I'm trying to remain as human as possible, and using my speed to avoid touching my best friend seems like a waste of energy. Using my abilities also tends to drain me more than it should.

I shake my head rapidly in disagreement, eyeing Dallas over her shoulder.

"Where are you going?" He shifts his feet, messing with the long strings hanging from his old beige pajama pants.

I'd hoped once things settled down a little that he'd come to terms with the insanity that now and forever will be my life. Instead, he's continuously found new ways to freak himself out over what goes bump in the night.

I walk to him, throwing my arms around his neck and squeezing. He's stiff for a moment, before he places a hand on my back, only halfway returning my hug. He's been this way for three months. He only halfway smiles, halfway hugs, halfway acknowledges me... he's only halfway my brother, and I miss the whole thing.

"You can't worry every time I leave the house," I tell him, moving back so I can see his face. "I'll be okay."

He gnaws on his inner cheek, trying his hardest to look indifferent and not like he's so overwhelmed he doesn't know how to deal with it all. "You don't know that. Anything could happen to a normal person when they leave the house. Bad things happen all the time. But worse things happen to you. People seek you out because of that family, and I'm afraid one day you won't be able to outrun their demons."

I am a demon, I think to myself, but refrain from repeating that out loud. I've tried really hard to convince Dallas that I'm still me, just frozen in time, so admitting that his fears are also mine wouldn't help the situation any.

"I'll be careful," I say, hating that I don't have better words to console him. I can't deny the dangers I face. I can't promise him anything. I can't swear to be safe, because so long as I'm the only thing standing between eleven clans of vampires and the key to the Draven family's survival—the Draven family, who believe in preserving humanity and are the only ones who can keep the Twelve from ultimate control of the vampire population—it would be a lie.

"Come to the Manor with us," I insist, still looking around for my phone. I'm leading him into the exact danger I've spent months trying to keep him away from, but the only way for Dallas to get over this fear is to see the good the Dravens bring into my life, as well as the bad. Only then will he understand why I've stayed. I could go anywhere in the world. I could be absolutely anyone my heart desires... but I chose to stay in the town that condemned me to eternity.

Dallas runs an unsteady hand through his thick hair, then scratches the stubble shadowing his chin. He hasn't shaved or gotten a haircut in two months, which for my brother is completely out of character, but something he can control. He even tried sleeping with his lamp off one night, but that only ended with him screaming in his sleep.

"Ambrose is dead." I grit my teeth, fisting the sheets in my sweaty palms before I smooth them out, feeling the lump of my phone beneath them. "He's gone, so stop giving him reason to be remembered. Don't let him rule your life."

"Aspen, if you want to warn them, we should go now," Elaine interrupts whatever Dallas was about to say. She shrugs apologetically and crosses her arms with a shiver, examining the walls of my room. "You should also invest in a new house, just saying."

I ignore her. "Are you sure you don't want to come?"

Dallas shakes his head, disappearing into his bedroom and taking the dim flashlight with him.

"Well, that's brilliant," Elaine remarks, and I shake my head, laughing when she walks into something by the door. "Goddammit, Aspen. I don't know how you live here."

"Maybe I'll come live with you. At least I'd have heat. And lights. Hot water... Or you know—" My sentence is cut short by her yelp, and she stumbles backward into me. I clasp her shoulders, using my bodyweight to keep her upright.

"What's wrong?" I ask, voice high and panicked. She stands up and clears her throat, looking all around us. I do the same and see nothing but Dallas lying on his bed, reading by flashlight.

"Nothing." She shakes her head, the light catching her eye. "I just thought—never mind. It was just the coat rack."

I swallow, whispering goodbye to Dallas before leading Elaine out the front door and into the light drizzle of rain. She hops over the front steps, having figured out by now that they're in no way structurally sound and should not be walked on. I follow suit, my feet landing softly on the patch of loose gravel that we call a driveway.

"Do vampires have to be invited in?" Elaine questions randomly, making me laugh. Sometimes I think her hilariously short attention span is the only reason I survive the day. Without her and Miles, I would have probably gone insane by now.

"No. That's just a courtesy. They're not technically supposed to enter a residence without being invited, but they're not physically constrained to the outer regions of a house." Oftentimes, I realize I know more about vampire etiquette than I do humans. With vampires, I know where I stand—whether they hate me or want me for their own gain. There's no second-guessing their intentions, no worrying if they're being fake.

"Oh, interesting," she says, seeming unsatisfied with my response. I don't blame her. I'd feel a hell of a lot better knowing vampires couldn't just waltz into my house whenever they please too. Though I suppose that makes them no different from normal people. Still, they're quite a bit more dangerous than the average person.

The hairs on my neck stand up at a sound in the distance, and I latch on to Elaine's wrist, yanking her a little too hard. She stumbles, whipping her head in my direction. "What are you doing? My house is just a few more blocks, and then we can take my car. Well, actually, I need you to push it onto the road so we don't wake my parents up."

"Someone's there," I say softly, still holding her thin wrist. Suddenly, I'm wondering if she really did run into something in my room that wasn't the coat rack. My back had been turned before she yelled, so it's possible someone was there that I didn't see.

I close my eyes, listening as the footsteps speed up, faster and faster, until they're running at a pace that's humanly impossible. The sound echoes in my ears in slow motion, and I leap to the side, trying to pull Elaine with me, but not before someone rips her from my grasp, sending me spiraling into the hillside.

I try to shift so I land on my feet, but I'm too slow and instead land on my ankle, twisting it in an unnatural position. It throbs as I stand, but I push through it, lunging at a second vampire before he, too, can get to Elaine.

"This is not your territory," I growl, grabbing a branch from the grass and breaking it in two. I hold the halves in my shaking fists. No amount of training could ever take away the panic that fills my gut when I'm attacked. Every single time, I'm reminded of the first one. My brother and his fiancée Rachel, and then here in the field where a hunter beat and left me for dead. I never thought I'd miss the days when these sorts of situations were saved for my nightmares.

The man smiles, and his eyes darken as he turns away from the moonlight illuminating the scene. He grits his teeth, kicking me in the stomach and sweeping my legs from beneath me. As he leans over me, the stench of stale blood on his breath burns my nose, sending chills across my skin. "It will be."

I shift my weight and press a hand to his throat, then arch my back so that I can roll him over, positioning myself on top of his stomach. I shove the branch into his chest, and he chokes. His skin darkens to an oily black before it begins oozing red from his pores, dripping down his skin like a thousand tiny rivers and soaking into the earth. I gag at the sight of his body, dried and shriveled, as every drop of fluid sucked out of him like his life force. I've been told what happens when a vampire dies, but I've never seen it firsthand.

Legend says, when a vampire is killed, he or she bleeds the

blood from all of their past victims, returning them to the earth and leaving the vampire as he leaves his prey—sucked dry.

Erasing that image from my mind, I scramble to my feet to find the other vampire simply watching. He's holding Elaine in front of him by the neck, bending it at just the right angle for him to attack at any given moment—assuming I'm not fast enough to stop him.

"Let her go," I warn, twirling the other half of the stick between my fingers as I listen for further movement coming from the trees. As far as I can tell, it's only the two of them, which means now it's just him, alone in another vampire's territory.

"I'll make you a deal," he offers sweetly, quirking his head to the side as he sizes up the vein pulsing beneath Elaine's skin. He drags a thumb down the length of it and her eyes widen, her nails digging uselessly into the hand clamped below her chin. "Come with us, and she lives."

I bite my cheek, pretending to ponder this option, when in reality I know Elaine would die the second I agree.

"I propose she lives." I attempt a low voice, but it comes off as strained and scared instead, not at all matching the threatening tone I'm trying to convey. "And you die."

CHAPTER 4

The vampire tsks, throwing Elaine to the side like she's disposable, and taking slow, deliberate steps toward me, licking his lips with a smile. His feet slosh sloppily through the mud until he stands in front of me, close enough to touch, and so tall I have to crane my neck to see his face. He watches me, oozing power, knowledge, and age.

I check on Elaine out of the corner of my eye as she crawls to her knees, mud smeared all over from her harsh landing. She backs away slowly, glancing between me and the vampire, and I pray she's as smart as I think she is and will sneak off to find help. Unfortunately, the man in front of me holds his hand in the air, never taking his eyes from me.

"You won't get far," he warns her, then grabs me around the neck. He holds me above him, leaning in to take a whiff of my long, blonde hair. I squirm, scrunching my face and remembering the last time someone unwanted got this close to me. I was unwillingly frozen in place by fear then, but not anymore.

I spit in his face and my saliva lands directly in his eye,

which squints in reaction. A low rumble sounds from his throat, and it becomes apparent that it's taking every ounce of his willpower not to snap my neck like a twig. For whatever reason, he needs me alive. I can work with that.

"Now," he growls, clenching his fingers around my neck. "Tell me who you are."

"Why do you care?" I rasp. The effort it takes to speak scrapes my throat raw and the metallic taste of blood finds its way to my tongue. If he's here to kidnap me, shouldn't he already know who I am?

He bares his teeth, losing patience as I stall. "Because one look at you tells me you're not who you claim."

"Adrian," I choke. He raises his chin, eyes hardening. "He sent you."

"He's not the leader of the American clan because he's ignorant." He lowers me to the ground but continues to hold me by the neck like some sort of prize. "He will be very happy to know I've tracked you down. He has been quite... *entranced* since he met you. Although, I'm afraid I don't see the appeal."

"I'm no different from you," I lie, hoping his reaction reveals how much they know about me and my role in the Draven family. Do they know the curse is broken? And that I'm responsible? If they do, then I'm in more danger than any of us realize. But judging by this man's lack of response, Adrian didn't tell him why he's here.

He takes a long breath, and I see Elaine moving slowly behind him, a wooden stake in her hand. "No, you're not like me. You're..." He pauses, dragging out his words and assessing me with fascination. He searches the night sky for words, until his gaze levels back on me, so intense I could swear it burns a hole straight through me. "Something different. Something... human."

"Aspen!" Elaine yells. I act on impulse, clamping down on his arm and kicking his abdomen so hard he chokes. He falls away from me and straight into Elaine's outstretched arms. The second he's in her grasp, she raises the stake and brings it down with as much force as she can muster, stabbing the wood into his heart. She backs away rapidly, tripping over her own feet and watching until all of the blood pours out of his skin to be sure he's dead.

"Does that happen a lot?" a voice squeaks from the shadows and I jump, heart spiraling out of control. Elaine doesn't look the least bit fazed, and my eyes travel to the stake deep in the vampire's chest, suddenly understanding how she got it.

In retrospect, it was idiotic of me to leave the house without a weapon, even though the woods themselves hold all the weapons in the world.

"I thought you weren't coming!" I hiss, trampling over the limp legs at my feet and pulling the stake from the body.

Dallas moves to my side, eyes searching the area wildly for any more unwanted company as his hand finds my elbow. "I wasn't." His voice sounds hollow and small. "But then you were gone, and the house makes a lot of unnatural noises. It occurred to me that I feel safer *there* than at home, and especially out here, so can we go before any more vampires come along?"

By "there" I assume he means Draven Manor, given the shudder that vibrates through his body when he says the word. I heave a sigh and wipe the rain from my face as I trudge toward Elaine. She's bent over, rolling up her pant leg to assess her knee. A trickle of blood runs down her calf like a small river, twisting and turning, melding with the streams of rain that stop at her ankle and absorb into the fabric of her white socks.

My lips purse to silence my sharp intake of breath, a dangerous sign of my growing anticipation. I swallow hard and turn away, keeping my eyes on the road ahead and not at the scene behind me. It's torture. My friend is hurt, and I have the incredible gift of healing, but I can't quench my hunger long enough to ensure I won't be the one who hurts her further. Blood pools on my tongue as my teeth cut through my lip. I release the skin, dabbing it with my sopping coat sleeve and press the material to my nose so the only thing I can smell is rainwater and my own blood—not the intoxicating scent of Elaine's.

"You're hurt." I clear my throat, pushing past the ravenous need clouding my brain.

Deep breaths, in and out, in, then out.

"Yeah, it's just a scrape." She huffs, unfolding her pant leg which slightly masks the scent—but not nearly enough.

As we continue toward Elaine's house, she and Dallas walk ahead of me so I can keep an eye on them at all times. Once we get there, I make sure they're safely inside Elaine's car with the doors locked and engine running before I tell them I'll meet them at the Manor, taking off down the winding trail.

Within seconds, I'm on the front steps of the Draven household. My eyes scan the concrete, images of Miles and Vira lying helplessly below me flash through my mind— Vanesa's eyes pleading with me to help them, even though that would have required strength beyond my capability at the time.

I quickly step back as the front door swings open and take in the person before me. Raven black hair brushes the edges of her hips, flowing effortlessly over her shoulders. She stares back at me with eyes deep enough to swallow an ocean, and dark enough to lose your soul in.

"Leave." Vanesa's sultry voice is inviting as ever as she squints her eyes and crosses her arms over her chest like an unmovable wall. In fact, she probably is. The Dravens have been vampires for the better part of two hundred years, which means they're strong and capable, whereas I'm struggling to learn and adapt to the new abilities enhancing my body and mind. I know I'm new and that learning takes time, but we don't *have* time. We have a war coming, and I need to be ready when it gets here.

I wince. Her hatred of me still stings more than I'd care to admit, even after all this time. I suppose three months isn't that long when forever is stretched out before you, but in this dangerous world time is, quite ironically, a fickle thing.

You never know how much of it you have left, but that hasn't stopped Miles's older sister from hating me with every inch of her cold, dead heart.

I had always thought Vira would be my biggest obstacle to overcome in being accepted by the Draven family, but she has turned out to be more of an ally... well, most of the time, anyway. I'm almost certain she's only civil with me because some twisted part of her feels that she owes me for saving her life, even after she left me to die. Honestly, I'd love to hate her, to despise her with every piece of my darkening soul the way Vanesa does me, but at the end of the day, Vira was only trying to save her family, and I am not, nor will I ever be, that.

"Where's Miles?" I ask tiredly, not in the mood for her games or meticulously thought-out insults.

She winks, condescension bleeding through her pores as

she wraps a delicate hand around the door, moving to close it again.

"You knew it was me," I remark, raising an eyebrow. We don't have time to waste on her petty issues. "You knew it was me, and you still opened the door, to... what? Close it in my face? I doubt that." I take a step forward, up on the ledge so we're face to face. Normally, Vanesa has a good four inches on me, but she's in bare feet now as opposed to her usual sky-high heels, which levels the playing field. When she's not towering over me, she's not quite as intimidating. "Let me in, Vanesa."

She looks me up and down, squinting her eyes as two small dimples form in her cheeks. "Or what?"

"I'll scream." I shrug, knowing that will wake up her entire house, if they're not already up. Miles says that because I'm still adapting, I'll continue to sleep more until my human urges fade away, at which point rest will only be a suggestion, not a necessity. Though, it will still replenish me when I'm worn out.

"He's not here." She smiles sweetly, and if I were anyone else, I might think she's being genuine. But I'm me, and she's Vanesa, and there's not a genuine bone in her thinly sculpted body. As if to rid any doubts I might have in her honesty, she calls for him. "See? Not here."

"Really?" I cock my head. The sound of a vehicle approaching reminds me once again that we don't have time to waste, and somehow Vanesa always seems to distract me with her greater-than-thou attitude.

"Miles?" I call out over her shoulder, and she shoves me backward—once, then a second time off the two-foot concrete porch before she's yanked back and a hand grabs on to me.

Miles turns to her, hardly acknowledging my presence. "What did I say?"

"We don't need her," she says almost immediately, teeth clenched, fists tight at her sides. "She served her purpose and now it's time she goes, Miles. The sooner you unwrap her noose from around your neck, the better."

"She's like this because of us," he reminds her, his chest rising and falling with controlled breaths, his hand still glued to my wrist. "Is this the type of person you want to be? Where's your humanity, Vanesa?"

She scoffs and narrows her eyes, looking pointedly at the way Miles positions himself slightly in front of me.

"There is no humanity," she spits, her face a contortion of disgust. "There's only loyalty, and mine is with my family, brother. Which is where yours should be, too."

"Everything all right?" The sounds of Elaine and Dallas's footsteps slapping the wet pavement shatters the tension, and within seconds, Vanesa has vanished. I should have warned her about the new vampires in town, but she's made it perfectly clear there's nothing I can offer her, so I suppose I'll do just that.

I turn, forcing a smile to my lips as Miles's hand finds my back, pressing lightly between my shoulder blades. Dallas looks around worriedly, bouncing his eyes between the two of us.

Soft raindrops drip off the edge of the roof onto my forehead, and I tuck my chin, shuffling closer to the door for shelter and giving Dallas what I hope is a reassuring smile. "Everything's fine."

Miles nods his head toward the light spilling from the doorway. "Give us a minute?"

Elaine bites her lip, nodding curtly before walking past the threshold, eyes turned up at the height of the cathedral ceiling. Her lips part in a short inhale as she takes in the immaculate detail and precision of the design, disappearing down the haunting hallway.

Just like Dallas, Elaine avoids Draven Manor at all costs. In fact, she's never been inside at all.

Dallas reluctantly follows her, less enchanted by the Manor's architecture and more concerned with leaving me alone in the dark when there seems to be danger lurking around every corner we turn. He shakes his head, disappearing down the hallway as he tries to catch up with Elaine, no doubt uncomfortable being in the house without a companion.

Miles turns, and his full attention is on me at last. Lines crease his forehead, scrunching the usually smooth skin, and it takes a moment for his gaze to travel over me. When it does, the gold flecks in his eyes darken to a shade of black so deep it's unbeknownst to the rest of the world, lingering on the tender skin of my neck.

"Who did this to you?" His hands are on me in an instant, carefully grazing the bruised skin around my throat.

I shake my head, hair falling in my face. "He's dead, it doesn't matter."

His eyes widen as the ghost of a smirk paints his lips, torn between the need to rip someone's head off for hurting me and being mildly impressed at my indifference. Rough fingers follow the curve of my jaw and my eyes flutter closed, the sounds of crickets and raindrops meshing into a peaceful background noise.

Miles leans in close, wrapping an arm around my shoulders. "He hurt you," he says, voice gruff and thick with emotion. "It matters to me."

CHAPTER 5

"*R*emind me again why I'm awake?" Vira blinks rapidly, sucking on her teeth. She's sitting on the arm of the chair Elliot occupies, looking no happier to have been bothered at this hour.

The lights are off, save for two lamps on either side of the room that seem to be permanently lit, casting all five of their faces in unwelcoming shadows. Miles and Elaine are on either side of me, and Dallas is hovering by the door, so quiet I almost forget he's here.

"Because Aspen Troy is here, and God knows the entire universe revolves around her," Vanesa snarks, tossing a clump of hair over her bare shoulder.

I insisted it wasn't necessary to wait for her return to have this conversation, but Elliot and Vira agreed that she should be here.

Biting my tongue, I cross my ankles and allow Elaine to do the talking. It was, after all, her brilliant surveillance that alerted us to the problem to begin with, so it should be her who tells them—that, and I know if I open my mouth, I might just bite Vanesa's head off.

"When I was combing through the security footage from tonight," Elaine begins, scowling at Vanesa when she fake yawns into her palm. "There was a vampire standing right in the dead center of town."

"And you know it was a vampire because..."

"Because people don't just show up unannounced around here, Vanesa," Danielle sighs from the couch, resting her head on Lucas' shoulder and closing her eyes.

"Anyway," Elaine continues, unfazed. "It was like he wanted to get our attention. We were on our way to tell you when two vampires attacked us."

"Was he one of them?" Lucas asks, knee bouncing nervously.

I shake my head. "No, which means there could be more of them. They were sent by Adrian."

I hadn't realized until I said it, but if we saw one vampire on Elaine's footage and two more attacked us... who knows how many may have infiltrated our town overnight.

"You're telling me none of you sensed anything unusual?" Elaine blanches, unbelieving.

They shake their heads, looking equally baffled.

Elliot stands, always the first to leave our group conversations. "For now, we should lay low. Keep a low profile, don't make any... ruckus." He looks at me on that last part, making my blood simmer. As if I thought going for an innocent walk one night would upend their entire universe. "We'll let the hunters take care of Adrian's people."

"We should inform the clan. About Adrian, the curse—everything," Vira says, sliding down into the seat Elliot vacated.

"I know it's risky, that some may want a war for our freedom and others may wish to stay bound in order to keep the peace, but they're in more danger if they're sheltered from the truth."

Elliot grunts, shoving his hands in his pockets as his sharp eyes burn holes through the carpet. "A clan meeting is not laying low."

"They wouldn't be here if they didn't already know something," Danielle points out, shifting to her knees and turning around to pick up a decanter of blood on the sofa table behind the couch. She pours the red liquid into a short cup, then reaches over to place it in my hand. "You look hungry," she whispers, and I thank her, taking a long sip.

"And if they want to fight?" Vanesa raises an eyebrow, and in an instant, all eyes are on me. "If our people want to regain their natural rights as vampires instead of fake smiling into complacency for the sake of peace? Is her Moral Highness okay with that?"

I swallow, knowing very well I can't keep the Draven clan from exercising their right to feed and live freely, but if the American clan is sniffing around, there is no chance of them allowing us to do that peaceably. "We don't know Adrian will fight us. We don't even know who he's told or what he wants. My guess is only a few of his most trusted members."

Lucas shrugs at my logic. "She has a point. We can't stop the inevitable."

"Are we done now?" Vira asks, biting at a purple nail and looking bored.

I start to say yes when Miles puts a hand on my thigh, meeting my gaze.

"Actually," he begins. "If we're coming clean, there's

something else we should tell you. The rest of the clan can't know. Not yet."

"Hold on." Vanesa raises a hand, looking between us with a scrutinizing gaze. "How the hell does Adrian know you exist to begin with?"

Danielle opens her mouth, then pauses, leaving her jaw hanging in midair. "Actually, how does he know who you are? I mean, he knew to send his people after you and everything."

Suddenly I understand what Miles wants to tell them and why he's so apprehensive. We never told them where I really went with Elaine at the end of summer, just that I needed a few days to myself. None of them had been particularly happy about it, but I'd had Miles on my side, so it hadn't mattered.

"When I went away a few months ago, it was to my hometown," I say. Five blank stares strip me bare and hang me out in the cold. Not only are they going to be angry, but I've also only ever told Miles the truth about my older brother. Even Elaine, who went with me, doesn't know the full story. It's not something I like to think about, much less relive for anyone else's benefit.

Dallas moves across the room into my line of sight, watching me carefully. We swore to one another that we'd never, ever go back there. No matter what. We also made a pact to never tell anyone what happened so that no matter where we went, we'd be free of our demons... or at least, free of the judgment passed because of them. I've already broken both promises, and recounting all of the horrifying details in front of him would only make matters worse, so I make my next words as vague as possible without leaving room for too many unanswerable questions. "I went there to try to turn someone."

Everyone sits forward at once, bottoms scooting to the edges of the white furniture.

Vanesa is the first one to speak, looking especially intrigued by this new development. "Did it work?"

I fist my hands between my thighs, shifting anxiously in my seat. "I-I don't know."

"What do you mean you don't know? How could you not know?"

"I let her go." My words come out in one fast, fluent breath, but I have no doubt she caught every syllable. "She was still coherent though, so I think it worked. I told her to find me when she's ready. Adrian tracked me down as I was leaving. He must have sensed me somehow."

"So let me get this straight." Vanesa bites her lip, looking two fuses away from bursting into flames. "You went all the way to America to turn a vampire and then set her free without guidance or knowledge before even knowing if the transition was completely successful? She'll kill every soul in sight if it wasn't, and *you're* the one who claims to care about humanity? You just sicced her on the humans like an all-you-can-eat buffet!"

"I didn't sic her on the humans, I sent her to kill my brother!" I snap, losing every ounce of control over my emotions. The half-empty glass tumbles to the floor with my jerking movement, splattering blood across the hardwood.

Danielle is next to me in seconds, placing a hand on my shoulder before I can stand to clean up the mess. "I've got it, keep going."

Everyone but Miles shifts their attention from me to Dallas. Vira points at him half-heartedly, finger limp and mouth open to form the shape of words she can't seem to find.

"Not him." I shake my head, tears prickling at the corner of my eyes. "My other brother."

"There's more of you?" Vanesa's voice deepens, and somehow, I think I've just transformed her worst nightmare into a reality.

Dallas grabs my shoulder, whipping me around to face him. "You turned Rachel?"

Vanesa wheezes, pressing her pale fingers to her temples. "Who the hell is Rachel?"

"I had to." I reach for him with a shaking hand, but he pushes me away. "Derek ruined her life. I had to make it right. I had to help her if I could."

"Help her? You call turning her helping?"

"What happened to her—wouldn't you do everything in your power to fix it? I have the power to do that. I couldn't just leave it be." I reach for his hand, and tears blur my vision as he wrenches it away, clutching it to his chest like he's been burned. "Dallas."

"Just—don't." He backs away from me, almost running into Danielle as she makes her way out of the kitchen with a clean towel.

I stand to go after him, but Lucas' smooth voice stops me. "Just give him a minute. He'll come around."

I nod solemnly, wishing I had his confidence. I've put my brother through so much. I'm beginning to wonder at what point it will become more than he's willing to handle. He tries to accept it—*accept me*—but I know a part of him is scared of what I've become, and turning Rachel wasn't a remotely good start to gaining his wavering faith in me.

Dropping my head into my hands, I listen to the rest of the conversation without giving any input. Opening your mouth in front of the Draven siblings—it's like I'm a glutton for punishment. Lucas suggests the three of us spend the rest of the night here since the vampires were already lurking around my house, and Elliot doesn't look happy, but doesn't argue. To my surprise, Vanesa doesn't either, just shakes her head and struts out of the room with a scowl on her face, as if she already knows it's a losing battle.

"And this, little brother—" Elliot pats Miles on the back, giving him a tiny shake, "—is why we don't get involved with humans."

CHAPTER 6

*L*ooking in the mirror is hard. It's never easy to acknowledge who you really are, but it's abundantly harder to do when you don't have the slightest clue as to who that is.

How can I confront my demons, separate them from my heart, when I have no idea what the me beneath the carnage and the bad things looks like?

How can I repel the demons hunting for my soul when the worst of them are caged away beneath my skin?

"You should sleep," Miles whispers, although he makes no effort to rest his wandering eyes either.

I scoff, tucking my arms beneath my chin for warmth. "*You* should sleep."

There's so much bad in the world that I imagine I'll never sleep again. How can I when I'm actively aware of everything that could go wrong at any moment?

For the first half-hour, I really did try to sleep, but the best I could do was close my eyes. My restless mind took care of the rest.

I can't stop thinking about everything that's gone wrong in my life, stemming from the day we hung the mirror that Ambrose's soul was attached to. I can't help but wonder what my life would be like if Mom hadn't discovered it in the attic. Would I even be here right now? Would our family still be whole? Or were we always destined to wind up splintered and hollow?

Nothing but death and pain has come from that day—between the curse, the hunters, the other clans, and the police investigation that's still at large.

"Have you heard anything?" I lower my voice, the words coming out on a soft breath. We shouldn't be talking about this with Elaine so close by, sleeping on the opposite couch. She has enough to worry about.

Cool air kisses my skin as Miles shifts under the blanket. His hand searches through the material for mine. I meet him halfway, threading my fingers on top of his.

"Not yet. If they found any evidence, they're keeping it quiet."

"And the girl?" I ask thickly, unable to utter her name. Nadia Porter. The girl who lost her fiancé—a man who claimed he was in the military when he was really a vampire hunter getting a thrill out of beating me senseless. Until I ended his life to save Vira's.

Miles is silent. I've learned over the past few months that he's naturally quiet. Not loud like his siblings, but calm and benevolent. But this is not that—this is him diluting his response to protect me.

I purse my lips. "Don't lie."

His thumb traces slow circles down my pinky finger, lulling me into a state of relaxation. "She's out for blood."

"My blood."

"She just wants to understand."

"And she never will." Nadia can never know the truth. Unless a human has a specific purpose, exposing yourself to them has proven to be disastrous—or so I've been told countless times by Miles's overbearing family. Mostly by Vanesa, who believes allowing my brother to remember is a mistake. I believe keeping him in the dark would be a bigger one because then he'd be like Nadia, obsessed and forever seeking answers he can never find.

"Knowing the truth isn't always better than wondering. Wondering provides hope, possibility, the chance of a better outcome in the future. The truth can be deadly."

"I understand that." I look to the side, needing to see something other than the deep brown trusses on the ceiling. An incandescent glow flickers from the candles rounding a chandelier above, bathing Miles's face in a soft golden light. "I just wish understanding was enough to erase my guilt."

Miles rolls toward me, moving until I'm near enough to feel the heat radiating from beneath his shirt.

"Don't tell me it will get easier," I urge, sliding my cold fingers across his abdomen for warmth, teasing the edge of his shirt. "I don't want it to. Guilt keeps me human, and staying human preserves my humanity."

If I don't feel horrible for killing a man, albeit a bad one, then who have I become? Who am I to claim morality if I'm as unfeeling as the rest of them? Well, all except a select few.

My eyes refocus on Miles. Half of his face is in shadow as he watches me detangle the mess of emotions in my mind, and he plays with a short piece of hair that angles my face. "You did a terrible thing to a vile man. That doesn't justify it by any means, but you can't let it eat away at you like this. Our lives are only going to get more complicated from here, and I don't want you weighed down by this extra guilt."

I scoot closer so my legs can tangle with his, and I wrap my arms around his stomach as he brings his lips to mine, gentle and deliberate, drawing out his movements in a steady rhythm.

Even with his hands wandering across my bare skin I can't help but worry about what comes next, and I know, despite his efforts at hiding his concerns, at keeping his features indifferent and expressionless, he's worried about the same thing.

"This thing with Adrian." I break away breathlessly, pressing a light palm to his chest. "We'll figure it out."

"I know." He kisses my forehead, bringing my cheek to his chest and resting a hand on my back so I'm trapped between his arms.

"No, you're worried." I blink rapidly, fisting his shirt in my palm.

"We've never faced anyone like him before. We haven't had to. For the past two hundred years, no one has bothered us—but we've also had no hope. All we had to worry about was the hunters, and even they've grown stronger since you showed up."

Shivers spread through my body in memory of all the times I've come face to face with the hunters—none of them good.

Miles touches the chain around my neck, holding the heart pendant between his fingers and thumbing the small vines that snake around the design. I've tried several times to return it, but he claims it was fate that led me to his late sister's necklace, that she must have wanted me to have it. I fear my discovery of the artifact was Ambrose's doing, in which case I want even less to do with it. Regardless, wearing a piece with such history doesn't feel right no matter how I came across it. I'm not family. It does not belong to me.

"Try to get some sleep," he mumbles into my hair, allowing the necklace to fall back and slide until it rests between us on the blanket.

Even after all of my internalizing, I'm still not sure how sleep is possible when there are demons lurking in the shadows of reality and in the pores of my consciousness. But I can't just lay here, stuck in a time loop in my brain, thinking of all the things I wish I could go back and change. Miles is right. Things are only going to get more complicated, and if I'm lost in my head over the past, drowning in guilt over my actions, I don't stand a chance in this world.

So I close my eyes and do my best to wipe my mind of these worries, even if just for tonight.

CHAPTER 7

*E*laine and I sit alone in the empty library. Blankets from the night before are wrinkled and sitting in a heap behind us on the floor, and we're both lazily stretched out on the couch Miles and I shared, which conveniently pulls out into a bed. He got up early this morning when Elliot called a clan meeting. They want to inform them about me and our friendly new guests in town as soon as possible. I insisted I should be there, but this time Vanesa got her way. I can't say I don't feel slightly betrayed that even Miles voted against my presence in the name of my safety. He has such unending faith in his clan, yet won't allow them to see my face out of fear.

"Thanks for staying out here with me last night." Elaine taps my thigh with her hand. Her eyes are trained on the immaculate bookshelf resting behind a large oak desk that I presume belongs to Miles's dad, Edgar, who I have yet to meet. From what I've gathered, their parents are hardly home, which leaves the six of them alone in the house most days. They have no idea what's happened or that their ages-long curse has finally lifted. When they leave on vampire business, it's indefinite and they're always uncontactable. Though, I suppose with the curse making them practically powerless in the face of eleven other clans, there's no need to be around all of the time.

I look at her, knowing I wouldn't have wanted to sleep alone in a mansion full of vampires who dislike me either. "You stayed with me when I needed you."

She rolls her eyes, most likely thinking back to the night she discovered that the stories her ancestor meticulously wrote in his journal were true, and not the ramblings of the madman she believed him to be. "Yes, but I'm sure there was somewhere else you'd have much rather been." She eyes me, mischief sparkling in her eyes. "You stayed, though, so thank you."

"You were awake?" I choke, feeling my cheeks flush.

"Awake? I thought I might have to make an excuse for the bathroom so you two could be alone," Elaine quips, scrunching her nose playfully. "Besides, it's Draven Manor. Do you think I'm stupid enough to let my guard down?"

"Fair point," I say. I'd felt the same when Vira and Vanesa came for Miles after he'd been poisoned. I was certain they'd sink their teeth into my carotid while I slept. "I think I might walk into town. Do you want to come?"

Elaine gives me a bland look, not at all fooled by my ruse. "I'm sure Dallas is fine. Vanesa said she took him home."

"Precisely." I roll my eyes, stretching. Is it so horrible that I'm concerned about him? Especially when Vanesa is involved? "I can't just sit here and wait for the others to return, anyway. I'll go out of my mind."

"You go ahead. I think I'm going to take advantage of the empty house and give myself a little tour." Elaine waggles her eyebrows, bouncing off the couch and sliding her socked feet across the hardwood. Her eyes roam the bookshelf hungrily as she drags her blue nails across the spines, tapping them thoughtfully. "I wonder if there's a secret doorway hidden here somewhere... or trap doors beneath the hardwood? Aren't you curious what they have locked behind closed doors?"

"Honestly, I don't want to know." I laugh. I've had enough surprises for a lifetime. I'd rather not start searching for hidden corpses in Draven Manor. I wrap an arm around Elaine, giving her a squeeze. "Let me know when they get back?"

She nods, her attention split between me and a locked desk drawer. "Be careful."

I shake my head. As if being careful has ever done me any good before.

Something is noticeably different the moment I emerge from the woods at the edge of the town square. There's an unusual hush replacing the chatter and small talk I've become accustomed to in my short time here. Sure, it's getting colder out, and no one wants to gather outside for fun, but it's been cold for a while now and this is one of the warmer days in late October. Very few people mill around, and those that do keep their heads down.

Seven police officers stand around the perimeter, between stores and some in places less obvious to the average naked eye. The townspeople scurry from place to place without a second glance at anything but the brick pavers beneath their feet.

A young girl with dark hair and deep brown eyes adjusts

the scarf positioned loosely around her shoulders so each end drapes over an arm, defeating the purpose of the added warmth. She talks purposefully with an elderly woman shivering in the cold, her voice coaxing and smooth. With a shift of her weight, I recognize Edna, the old woman who runs the jewelry stand where I bought a bracelet for my mom. Her eyes lock with mine, and her already harsh frown draws tighter.

Edna moves around the girl, ignoring whatever she's saying, and comes to stand before me, reaching a hand out to touch my necklace. Her frail lips stretch into a thin line as she uncurls her shaking fingers, releasing my pendant.

"Such a shame." She tsks, shaking her head faintly. "Darkness can find even the brightest of souls."

My eyes widen, and with that said, she hobbles away, her hair seeming grayer than the last time I saw her. The girl she was talking to watches me, and my breath hitches when I take in her face. The soothing voice she spoke with is replaced by her shrill screams in my memory.

I swallow hard and start to turn before she can move toward me. But she's fast and touches my arm almost immediately, cementing me in place with the mere tips of her fingers. "I was just asking Edna if she knew anything about the death of my fiancé... I'm Nadia Porter."

I blink, willing my face to remain blank, and force every ounce of recognition or familiarity to blow away with the wind.

"Aspen Troy." I nod curtly, offering her the slightest of smiles.

She turns her chin up, eyes narrowing so little that most people wouldn't have noticed her expression changed.

"Aspen Troy..." She mulls my name over her tongue and crosses her arms over her stomach. "You live in that old house at the edge of town."

Rolling my eyes for show, I match her stance, rubbing my hands up and down my arms for warmth. "I mean, you can hardly call it a house."

"Funny," she muses, and I quirk an eyebrow while her eyes travel me up and down to take in my appearance. They linger on the necklace, which is much nicer than anyone who lives in my house should be able to afford. "You'd never know it."

"Right, well I should be—"

"Aaron was basically my only family," Nadia interrupts me, pushing forward with the subject.

I clear my throat. "I'm sorry, that must be—well, I can't begin to imagine."

"He was murdered." Her voice hitches, but she does an impeccable job hiding it and glides into her next point like she's skating on ice. "Not long after you moved to town, actually."

"That's awful. I remember hearing about that." I glance around for an escape—any excuse I can use to get away from Nadia and out of this conversation. "Why the police presence?"

"I finally... *convinced* them that they weren't taking the investigation serious enough. They were about to close the case, actually, but there was too much evidence of multiple people at the scene to close it so soon. And the fire? Seems like a cult thing to me. Anyway, they've started questioning people in town the way they should have from the beginning. I just hope it's not too late."

"Me too—for your sake. Anyway, I've got to run, but I really hope they catch the bastards."

She attempts a smile, but it's strained. "You and me both."

I back away from her, waiting until I'm sure no one's looking at me to speed to my house, where I stumble into the grass. I clutch my chest and roll so I'm flat on my back, staring straight up at the treetops. Deep breaths filled with cold air and rising panic expand and contract my lungs until I'm breathing so quickly I think I might have a panic attack.

Miles was right. Nadia Porter is out for blood—my blood. She wants justice for Aaron's murder, and that means putting me behind bars. Or worse. Judging by the skeptical look in her eyes, knowing I moved to town soon before he died is not helping her suspicions. I'm a strange face in a town full of people who have lived together their entire lives—there's no possible way they're going to look at someone else, someone familiar, before me.

As if things weren't bad enough with Adrian's clan in town and the hunters undoubtedly planning their next attack. Then there's Rachel, who I sent to kill my brother because I thought it's what she needed and what he deserved. Now I don't know if either of them are dead or alive, and I can't find out without risking my life by crossing territories again—a chance I can't take. If I got caught, I'd be putting everyone in danger.

The shed door bounces open behind me. I sit up, running a hand down my face and fixing my windblown hair.

"I didn't know you were home," Father says, arms loaded with fresh-cut firewood. "What time did you get up this morning?"

"Five," I lie, hoping he stuck with his routine of waking at six-thirty. "What's with the wood?"

He sighs, rubbing the sweat on his brow. "Well, I can't find the problem with the heat. Until we can get that sorted out, I'm afraid we'll have to rely on the fireplace."

"The—are you sure?" I choke, chest constricting at the mere thought of a fire burning all winter long—all the ash it's bound to produce. "Dallas will probably get really hot, though, being that close."

"Better than freezing to death." He toggles with a small log that's sliding off his arm. It falls, and I catch it thanks to my reflexes, then quickly drop it so as not to look too coordinated.

"Dallas home?"

"No. He went with the police to help with their investigation."

"Investigation?" I ask, rising to my feet. "You mean that military boy and his friends that died?"

"That's the one. I guess it happened close to here. They wanted to question him."

Anger swells in my chest, but I force it down, keeping my feet rooted where they are. "You didn't think that was odd? Or that maybe you should have gone with him?"

"They said it was fairly routine. Nothing to worry about. Besides, he's over eighteen."

"Right." Except between Nadia and the police, I'm starting to get a pretty good idea of who they're suspecting.

My phone buzzes with what is probably a call from Elaine to tell me the Dravens are back, but I can't move to look at it or zip away without my father having questions I can't answer. He was supposed to get me a new phone months ago, but in his drunken stupor, he didn't care. If he knows I have one now, he's going to question where I got it and how I could afford it.

"Come help me clean the old ash from the fireplace," he

orders, trying to shift some of the wood into my arms. I step away, pushing it back at him.

"I can't—plans. Sorry."

Father shakes his head, looking less than pleased with my refusal. Before he can start an argument, I jog away from him, back the way I came.

CHAPTER 8

*D*raven Manor is buzzing with nervous energy when I return, slipping through the door Elaine left cracked for me—though I'm sure they noticed I was gone. No one explicitly said not to leave, but judging by the looks of irritation I receive when I walk into the living room, they didn't want me to.

"What part of 'laying low' did you not understand?" Vira pounces the second she sees me, and the rest of their chattering voices quiet.

Miles gives her a pained look. "She's not our prisoner."

"She should be," Vanesa says dryly.

He sighs heavily, ignoring her snide remark. "Where were you?"

I raise an eyebrow at the continued line of questioning. "I was looking for my brother."

Vanesa rolls her eyes. "I took him home. You knew that."

"Did you watch while the police took him in for questioning, too?" I snap, clenching my fists at my sides. Her eyes widen. "Didn't think so. Good job though. You got him home alive, at least."

"You're lucky I did that much." She bares her teeth. "I'm not his babysitter."

Vira puts a hand on her sister's wrist, directing her question to me. "Do you know why?"

Biting my lip, I pour myself a small glass of blood. My morning hunger is acting up again. "I think it has something to do with Aaron Anderson."

"Who the hell is that?" Vanesa shakes her head. "We're wasting time. Don't you think we have more important—"

"That's the hunter you killed," Vira interrupts. She folds her arms over her chest, crossing her ankles. "Why would they want to question Dallas?"

"I ran into Nadia," I admit, then take a long gulp of my drink, feeling my body regenerate as the thick liquid glides down my throat. "She seemed suspicious of me and kept looking at my necklace. I assume that has something to do with why they wanted to talk with him."

"The cops are the least of our problems right now." Elliot runs a hand down his face, appearing from somewhere behind me. Danielle and Lucas are nowhere in sight. "The clan has agreed to protect you—for now. But if you don't start helping us soon, things could get ugly. They never thought they'd have the chance to live again, and now that they do, they won't let you stand in the way of that."

"So then do your job," Elaine says, surprising us all. "Keep them in line. Because you know very well that Aspen dying might jeopardize any chance you have at freedom. Make sure they remember that."

"She's our test dummy at this point. We don't really need her," Vanesa says almost immediately.

"Van," Elliot warns. "Criticizing her every chance you get isn't going to help get her on our side."

"She'll never be on *our* side. She'll never be okay with us turning people."

"I don't care what you do as long as the people you do it to agree." My voice rises considerably, and I hate that once again my anger is getting the best of me.

"Sometimes we don't get what we want. I don't expect *you* to understand that."

"Aspen has given up everything for you," Elaine argues, her voice taking on a tone of disgust. "She died for your pathetic agenda, and no, it wasn't her choice, but it still happened and she's still here. So maybe you should come back to Earth because you're no better than the rest of us, no matter who you think you are. If it were up to you, you'd turn everyone in town into bloodsucking freaks. You could use someone like her on your side, if only for morality."

"Their lives don't matter. If we don't turn them now, they'll just die in the clan war. Aspen said so herself." Vanesa moves toward me and gets in my face. She doesn't intimidate me, though. Not like she used to at least. Vira was always more frightening in my opinion. "And if it weren't for your *purpose,* yours wouldn't either."

I stand straighter so she doesn't seem quite so tall. "You can't deny life to those you don't love. You'll only suffocate yourself."

She scoffs, backing off but maintaining the same razor edge to her voice. "You really are the worst thing that's ever happened to our family. Why don't you take your pathetic brother and incoherent parents back to where you came from? Or is it brothers, plural? I can't keep up anymore."

"Vanesa." Miles grabs her arm, pulling her away from me, but I'm already storming out of the room and onto the balcony. They can't see me since the living room curtains block their view outside, but I know they can still hear my erratic heartbeat, which mirrors the overwhelming emotions that threaten to slit me open from the inside.

Someone else joins me, but I don't turn to see who. I already know.

"You agree with them," I say softly, pinching the bridge of my nose. I can't get angry every time someone says something I don't like—but Vanesa brought my brother into it, a topic she knows next to nothing about and has absolutely no right to comment on. She's always mean, but this time she made it personal, more personal than just insulting my intelligence and unimportance.

Miles moves next to me, resting his forearms on the railing that overlooks the mountain in the distance. The one he took me to the top of when I was first bitten. "Of course not."

"You just stood there."

"What?" He looks up at me.

"You always intervene when she gets out of hand." My throat constricts, and I blink rapidly as if doing so takes away the pain. "Elliot had to, and he never defends me."

It's a toss-up between the two of them for who hates me the most. Vanesa is more vocal in her hatred, whereas Elliot is the strong-silent type. Regardless, he's made his opinion of me known on several occasions.

"I did intervene." He touches my cheek, and his sorrow washes over me in waves.

"Not until the end. Not until you were sure I was going to punch her."

He laughs deeply, pulling me to his side. "If I had known you might punch her, I would have waited."

"Shut up." I roll my eyes, some of my anger dissipating. "I'm sorry, I know it's not fair of me to ask you to choose between me and your sister."

"You've never asked that of me, and I know you never would. I should have said something sooner." Miles presses a kiss to my temple, melting my frustration. I allow myself to lean into him, my legs rubbery with nerves.

"Seeing Nadia has me on edge," I say, gripping the railing to stop my hands from trembling. "I'm afraid she knows something."

"She couldn't possibly," Miles assures me, resting his chin on the top of my head.

"We left the body, Miles. My DNA has to be all over it. My saliva is probably—" I stop short, suffocating a gag.

"Vira broke into the morgue. She wiped any trace of you, I promise."

"You don't know that. Not really. Why else would they be investigating my family if they didn't find evidence of my involvement?"

"Aspen." Miles chuckles and turns me to face him, eyes drifting over my face. "It's a good thing you're not human anymore because you'd probably have a stroke. You worry too much."

"This is serious." I close my eyes, taking a deep breath to calm my raging heart, when something else occurs to me. "The vampire that attacked us last night said I was different. That I was something human. What does that mean?"

Miles searches my eyes intently, pondering my question. "It's possible he just meant that you seemed new. I mean, you do reek of humanity. Vanesa's not wrong about that."

"You're the least helpful person I know." I shove him halfheartedly. "I'm trying to understand."

"There's nothing to understand, beautiful."

"There's so much I *don't* understand," I counter.

He raises his eyebrows, probably the most emotion he's ever displayed on his face. "Well, for starters, you're incredibly sexy—probably the most beautiful immortal to walk the earth, besides my last girlfriend, of course."

"Oh, of course." I roll my eyes, knowing very well his last girlfriend was over one hundred years ago. And she tried to kill his family for Adrian. They didn't have the numbers to fight back, and I think part of the reason this fight is so important to Miles is because of her. He wants revenge. "My only competition is a dead woman. How do I one-up that?"

He pulls me to him, wrapping his arms around me in a tight embrace. I bury my face in his neck, his scent mixing with the sweet smells of rain. "You don't even have to try."

"We should probably go back in before Vanesa devises a plan to siphon my blood to create new vampires," I say, dragging him to the door and preparing myself for what we might be walking back into. I shake away images of Vanesa bolting me to a chair and drawing my blood with long tubes, and head back inside.

The air is thick, and all their faces are red with anger. Elliot stands off to the side, per usual, looking exhausted. Vira and Vanesa are staring at each other, and Elaine is watching them with intense loathing.

"There's something off about her! Something isn't right

and you're all too infatuated to see it!" Vanesa throws a vase across the room, and it shatters against the wall, shards flying everywhere. She smooths her hands down her shirt and stands up straight, collecting herself and normalizing her voice once again. "I just hope we're not all dead before you realize it."

"They're here." Elliot changes the subject, heading downstairs.

"Who's here?" Elaine asks, following him with her gaze.

Vira speaks up. "Two clan members. I think you guys have already met Gwen—she brought you the berry basket after you arrived in town." Vira nods at me, then her gaze travels to Elaine. "And you already—"

Elliot reenters the room with two young vampires following behind him, right as Vanesa leaves.

Gwen I recognize instantly by her bright blonde hair, but the boy I don't. He's about Gwen's height—which is tall because she's Vanesa's size *without* heels on—with rich brown hair and a gray jacket half-unzipped to reveal a black t-shirt beneath.

"You must be Aspen," he says, with an American lilt to his voice. He extends a hand, but my attention is on Elaine, whose head snaps away from her phone the moment he speaks.

Her mouth drops open, and she's paralyzed in place with a wide-eyed stare.

I squint at her, looking haphazardly back at the boy in front of me. "I—yes. Uh, I'm Aspen. And you are?"

He takes my hand, shaking it politely. He begins to tell me his name when I notice Elaine is beside me. Her voice is as venomous as I've ever heard it.

"His name is Owen. Owen Ayles."

Owen is rendered speechless, his warm eyes soaking in Elaine. "Elaine. What are you doing here? I didn't see you."

"You're good at that," she says casually. I snort. "I'm here for Aspen. And because I'm a watcher now. So. You know."

Elaine is most definitely taking this whole watcher thing to heart. "But I thought—they said your ancestor wished for his family to stay out of the legacy?"

"Yes, well, that didn't work out so well for him." Elaine tilts her head ruefully. "Everyone in my bloodline knew of our purpose but stayed away. My grandfather chose to stop the tide of information once my father was born, but I found my ancestor's journal hidden in my house. Your efforts were for nothing."

"Right." He bites his lip, looking uncomfortable. "So, how are you?"

"Look, I hate to interrupt," Gwen cuts in unapologetically. "But this can wait. Elliot invited us here as proof to the clan of your existence. It is my understanding that if you can successfully turn a human, then we can as well?"

"That's the theory," I say.

"You're hesitant, though." She assesses me, walking in a slow circle. "You're worried about what we'll do."

I shrug, uncommitted. "Could you blame me if I was?"

"I suppose not." Gwen bites her lip, inserting herself between me and Owen. "I understand your apprehension, but if we don't do something fast, Adrian's clan will strike us down. You don't want blood on your hands, right?"

I quirk an eyebrow.

"If you wait any longer, then you'll have ours on your hands, too. Adrian will murder us all, then your family. Everyone you've ever met will be in danger. You think a turf war is dangerous for the town civilians? Think about everything else you'll be losing instead."

I hadn't wanted anyone to know what I'd done to Rachel—if I can turn one person, they'll expect me to turn more. But I shouldn't have left her to fend for herself while searching for my brother. Now I'm afraid Adrian may have gotten to her. She could be dead for all I know. In helping her live again, I may have shortened her lifespan.

"And if it doesn't work? Then what?" I ask, worried her answer will describe the way in which I'll die.

She breathes out through her nose with a slight shake of her head. "Then we figure something else out. Though, whatever it may be, I have a feeling you will play a major part."

Her words release a knot in my chest, unwinding the bounds of tension tangled around my heart. Not everyone thinks I'm disposable. That's a start.

"I'm great, by the way," Elaine says suddenly. Her attention is still solely on Owen. It's as though this entire conversation never happened.

He nods shortly. "I'm glad. I wanted to tell you the truth, but they said to keep you out of it."

"Because of my ancestor?" she asks, her voice softening a bit.

He nods.

I can tell she wants to believe him, but the cynic in her denies this notion. "Likely story."

CHAPTER 9

*D*allas waits for me on our front porch later that day with his hands clenched between his knees, face sweaty and pale. He stands immediately and engulfs me in a bear hug. I hesitate before hugging him back, unsure of what brought on this sudden burst of brotherly love.

Things between us have been tense lately, and though they're getting better, I still miss the days when we were normal kids with average issues. Everything was so much simpler then.

"I feel like the walls are closing in," he says, voice barely a whisper.

If only I could tell him he's wrong. "What happened?"

"The police questioned me for hours, but I insisted I didn't know anything."

"Did they believe you?" I ask hopefully, though I know that's doubtful given how long they kept him.

He shoots me a look, and I follow him back to the front steps, where we sit side by side. "No. They said they have evidence. Something from the crime scene. I don't know what that has to do with me or if they were bluffing to make me talk, but they wouldn't leave it alone. Kept asking about my shoe size. I think they're trying to figure out who the other hunters were."

"You said nothing, though?" I need to know he didn't accidentally slip and reveal more information than he should have. If they found a footprint, it could be anyone's. Besides, Dallas wasn't even there, so he has nothing to worry about on that front.

"I called them crazy a lot, but that's about it. You think they're trying to get to you?"

"Probably. I don't know." I pause for a minute, choosing my next words carefully. "Look, I know you're mad at me—"

Dallas cuts me off and drops his matted head of hair onto my shoulder. "I would have done the same thing."

"With Rachel? Really?"

"Yeah. Besides, we were different people when we made our pact. Different circumstances. Different—"

"Different lives."

"Different lives? Different *worlds*. We didn't know anything about ourselves much less the world." Dallas picks up a pebble and tosses it into the dirt mindlessly.

"Thanks for not hating me. God knows you have every right to."

My brother sits up, looking at me with glassy eyes. "All you've ever done is look out for me."

"We look out for each other." I squeeze his hand, staring absently at the ground. "I told Rachel to find us when she was ready."

"You think she'll come?"

"Is it weird that after all of that—everything I did—I don't want her to?" I peek up at him through my hair, bouncing a knee. If she follows through with my request, she won't be the only one with blood on her hands.

He lifts a shoulder, looking as unsure as I feel about everything these days. "No? I don't know. It's not the worst thing to want to keep her away from all of *this*." He gestures with his hands, and I know exactly what he means. I had wanted to keep him away from this, too, but I failed. And now I've probably failed with Rachel. "Do you think she'll do it? Do you think she'll kill him?"

"Am I a terrible person for wanting her to?" I could have easily tracked him down myself, but facing Derek wasn't something I thought I could do at the time—still isn't.

"I don't know anything anymore," Dallas says.

Disappointment weighs on my chest. I wanted him to tell me I'm not a terrible person, to take away some of the burden so I can feel better about my mistakes. It's times like these when I wish I would have taken Miles up on his offer to leave. He'd offered and I made a stupid joke about being back in time for college classes—which I never enrolled in anyway. A vampire in college? The mere thought is ridiculous. Neither of us have mentioned running away since, and a part of me wishes he would suggest it again so I don't feel so horrible for wanting to abandon everything and everyone we love.

"How'd the clan thing go?" Dallas asks, and I know he's been patiently waiting for the right moment to bring it up.

"Good, I guess." I blow out a puff of air. "I mean, they know about me now, but I'm not sure that really changes anything except the burden I'm under. Now I not only have the siblings from hell pressuring me to turn someone, but I have an entire clan depending on me for their continued survival."

"And now Adrian is in town," Dallas adds, making my stomach sink further.

I roll my eyes. Of course Adrian won't just attack. He's biding his time, staking out the area—the competition—and making us squirm in our boots until he's ready to make his move. It's a predator-prey game with him, and I hate to admit we don't come out on top in that scenario.

I scoff, digging my heel into the dirt roughly. "No. Adrian is not in town, he's *near* town. A safe distance away, but close enough to keep an eye on things. He's not the type of man to fight his own battles. He has henchman to do it for him."

"And you're sure of this because...?"

"Because I met him. His hands are too clean, his hair too well kept. He's cruel and calculating—meticulous even, but he's not a fighter. Not anymore, at least."

"Maybe you can use that," Dallas suggests.

"Maybe." My mind is already wandering to something Dallas just said—Adrian didn't have any other vampires with him when we first spoke. Miles said it was probably because he wanted to scope out the situation on his own. If that is true, there's a chance he sent very few vampires to watch us... only the ones he trusts completely. Which means it's more than a war he wants.

"Hey, did Father light the fireplace?" I ask, thrown from my train of thought by the faint smell of smoke coming from inside.

Dallas drops his head, an apology forming in his eyes. "I tried to talk him out of it, told him I'd get too hot. He ended up screaming at me."

"Guess he really is back to normal," I say snidely, remembering all the times he used to yell at Dallas for no reason. If my poor brother blinked wrong, he would launch into a ten-minute lecture on how to do it properly and most effectively. Derek was always the perfect one, so in the eyes of my father, Dallas was always lesser.

Dallas is quiet, and I know he's thinking about the elephant in the room. After I killed Ambrose, we all slowly went back to normal. Dallas wasn't as irritated, my father finally managed to stay sober and awake for more than thirty minutes a day, but... "Mom isn't."

Mom. Her emotional spells haven't lessened, and she's still frail and quiet as a mouse. She was once a soccer mom, in charge of the middle school events committee. The do-it-all-mom, and the don't-stop-until-you're-crawling-mom. I had hoped once Ambrose's influence diminished that she'd go back to normal like the rest of us. She hasn't. She's actually less talkative recently than she's been in a long while, like she's still trapped in the shell she cowered in after Derek hurt us.

The last time I remember her being remotely herself was when Dallas and I were in the hospital, and she was trying to cheer us up by reading passages out of a scientific discovery magazine in funny voices. That day feels like a lifetime ago. Actually, it doesn't even feel like part of my life anymore.

"I'm going to get something to eat," I say, standing and breaking the thick tension of self-pity. Dallas stands, too, turning toward the house. He pauses with the door open when he discovers that I'm not following behind him and am instead going in the opposite direction.

He bites his lip, looking away from me as the realization sinks in. "Right. You're going to—" he lifts his hands in air quotes "'—eat.' What should I tell Father? He's pissed at you for bailing on him earlier—I got an earful of that, too."

Shaking my head, I back away from him slowly. "You know they won't notice for at least a half hour. I'll be back by then."

My phone buzzes fifteen minutes later, and I answer it mid-dinner with the blood from my meal dripping down my chin.

"Hello?" I slurp, wiping my hand across my lips and licking off any excess.

"Whatcha doing?" Elaine asks, then stops suddenly. "Never mind. I think I know. Gross, that slurping sound is worse than talking with your mouth full."

I can only imagine what I look like at the moment, and I smile. "Sorry. Juicy squirrel."

"Aspen, *please.*"

"I'm only kidding," I relinquish. "It's a rabbit."

She gasps and I have to refrain from laughing out loud. "You're a monster."

"Hey, it could be you," I remind her.

She sighs. "Gee, how lucky am I that you've chosen to consume a furry animal instead?"

"That's what I've been saying." Elaine doesn't say anything else, but I know she wouldn't have called me if there wasn't a reason. "Have you talked to Owen?"

"How'd you know that's why I called?" she asks, positioning the phone between her ear and shoulder. I can tell by the way her voice becomes muffled and distant—luckily, I have impeccable hearing.

"Because for the first time since I met you, you're not talking my ear off." I tuck my own phone between my head and shoulder, looking around for something to wipe off the sticky blood from my fingers. I settle on a clump of wet leaves since my options are limited and my clothes are entirely out of the question. The last thing I need is to go back home with blood smears on my pants.

"Are you sure it's safe to be outside alone?"

"Nice try. Owen."

She grunts, the sound echoing due to the poor reception. "He cornered me in town after you left. He's ignored me for so long, and now, when I finally want him to stay away from me, I can't seem to escape him."

"What did he say?"

"Just that the Dravens thought it would be best if he stayed away from me. I mean, we all know they don't fraternize with humans unless they don't have another choice—besides you, of course—but that doesn't make up for him disappearing. He says my ancestor asked the Dravens to never involve another person of my bloodline in their affairs, and they respected him enough to honor those wishes. Can you believe that? They respected a human. The *one* time! Of course it just had to screw me over."

"I wonder why?" It seems odd of them to respect his request hundreds of years later.

"You know why. It was a convenient excuse to keep their secret out of human clutches. I doubt they had any respect for my ancestor, much less me. Also, I still can't believe Vanesa turned out to be the wicked witch, and not Vira."

Elaine's ability to jump from one topic to another never ceases to astound me. "Vira thinks she's in my debt. That's the only reason she isn't clobbering all over me, too."

"Isn't she, though? In your debt, I mean. She left you to die and then you wound up saving all of their lives."

In a way, I suppose. Sure, I blame Vira for abandoning me, and I'll admit I get the tiniest sliver of satisfaction knowing she would have died if not for me—but above all, I don't view it as if she owes me. "No, I don't think so... I'm not about to tell her that, though. Her continued cooperation is fine by me."

"Good to know." A voice startles me, and I yelp, accidentally dropping my phone.

I clutch my chest, breathing heavily. So much for my impeccable hearing. "Vanesa. What are you—"

"Here's the deal," she says, irritation flaring in her eyes. "I won't tell Vira she doesn't need to feel indebted to you if you can keep your tongue clipped about what I need your help with."

I bend over hesitantly, retrieving my phone and ensuring a panicked Elaine that I'm still alive—unless Vanesa has something to say about that.

"You want my help?" I ask, doubting her intentions.

Vanesa sucks in her cheeks, shifting her weight awkwardly. "No, I don't *want* your help—aren't you listening? I *need* it. I can assure you I wouldn't be here if I didn't."

Immediately, I'm scared for an entirely different reason. If Vanesa Draven is asking for my help, something must be horribly wrong.

CHAPTER 10

Our shoes slosh through the muck and remaining debris from the ongoing thunderstorm, only slowing when we near a flickering porch light. It occurs to me that I should have told Elaine where we were going—just in case—but it's too late now. We're in a part of town I've never dared venture through before—the cul-de-sac. It's where the vampires live, separated from the human side of town by the town square and Draven Manor, which sits above it all on a slight hill. There aren't many houses, and just as well, I don't think there are many clan members—part of the reason why Vanesa is so desperate to multiply their numbers.

Vanesa veers off the path before we reach the first vampire residence and leads me back into the woods to where a small cabin sits.

She pauses, ear pressed to the door for a second before she pushes it open, walking through and allowing it to slam on me. I catch its heavy weight just in time and ease it closed behind me. Her head swivels around as she scans the tiny space.

The room is dark, lit only by a small lantern on a far shelf.

My shoes crunch against dirt and other scraps as I walk farther inside. Several erratic heartbeats fill the silence, unsteady and sickly sounding, along with rasping breaths that make my lungs hurt by association.

"Vanesa, what is this place?" I ask quickly. Three beds sit farther in the room, two on the left wall and one on the right, all with ratty white sheets and thin blankets that cover the long lumps lying on them. "Vanesa?"

When I turn around, I'm surprised to find her staring at the ground, defeated. The sight is disheartening. Her eyes lift. "I screwed up, okay?"

"S-screwed up?" I gape, moving to get a closer look at the people lying before me—still as rocks. "You screwed up? What did you do to them?"

Their discomfort wafts through the air like the stench of death, leaving me nauseous in its wake. Vanesa crosses her arms, refusing to look at the bodies.

"I thought," she starts, growling in her throat when she can't bring herself to force out the words. Her lethal fists clench at her stomach and her knuckles whiten. "I thought I could turn them."

Irritation flares like a bolt of lightning. "You tried to turn them? You were supposed to wait!"

"For what? You? Come on, Aspen, you know you've never had any intention of helping us. You don't have the stomach."

"Oh really? Don't I? Then why the hell am I here, Vanesa? Because I don't think you brought me here for an I-told-you-so," I spat. My anger is spiraling uncontrollably. The longer I stare at her hardened face and controlled temper, the harder it is for me to control my rage.

This is exactly, *exactly* what I was trying to avoid. The lives of people who haven't lived several lifetimes, much less their own, are hanging in the balance so the girl who has survived two centuries can ensure her continued existence.

I thought I was protecting the humans by refusing to make more vampires. Instead, my hesitation pushed her to make a rash decision, and now these poor, innocent people might die.

"You're here so you can fix them," she says, as if that was supposed to be obvious.

"What are you talking about? Vanesa, I don't know how to fix them." When a human is bitten by a vampire, they become a transitioner—a sort of limbo between human and vampire—and are presented with a choice. Sacrifice themselves for the clan to which they would have been born into or take a human life so they can live. There's no other option, and with a transitioner's drug-like blood, no one has ever lived long enough to know if that state is survivable. A lot of radical vampires seek out transitioners. Some do so because they don't believe in the Twelve and want to refuse them new life, and others—*most*—are simply addicted after stupidly tasting it once for an unparalleled high.

"Clearly there's something wron—*different* about you. You were able to turn. You survived as a transitioner and became a vampire—albeit a lousy one, but here you are. That's only possible if the curse was lifted." Of course, even when needing my help, Vanesa can't abstain from insulting me. "They were fine at first, but then they just… deflated. I've tried everything I can think of except you. If you were able to turn, then maybe you can help them."

My jaw clenches. So many questions bang at my skull—how long have they been here? How long did it take for this to happen? How could she be so completely and utterly impatiently idiotic? "The only thing that's going to help these people is death."

"There has to be another way. Without them, we're basically defenseless against Adrian and the hunters."

I stop in my tracks, hand inches from the door handle. "You don't care about them at all," I say, unsure of why this revelation surprises me in the least. Here I thought Vanesa felt remorse, guilt, desperation to save the lives she stole. I was naive to think she could ever care about something as *frivolous* as human life. "You just care about your stupid pissing contest."

"Please," she begs. "Try your blood, your venom, something. You have to be the answer. I may not care about these people, but I know you do. I know you won't leave them here like this without at least trying, so please."

Gritting my teeth, I slide off my coat sleeves and walk back across the room to peer at their blank eyes and dull complexions. Sweat gleams off their sickly skin. I refuse to look at Vanesa, to acknowledge her existence much less warrant her request with a response.

I hover my hands, afraid to touch the first man. He's lying still, and if I couldn't hear a heartbeat, I would think he was dead and has been for a while. A twitch in his eye is the only acknowledgment I get when my fingers press to his skin, searching for a pulse as if I know what I'm doing. As if I can't already hear how weak it is. How do I go about helping them when I have no clue what's wrong? No clue if something I try could make their condition worse?

"I need a knife," I say, then glance up when she doesn't respond. Vanesa stares at me until I snap my fingers in the air. *"Knife, Vanesa."*

Her eyes narrow, but she does as I ask, bringing me a knife

with a rusted tip and jamming it into my palm point first, instead of placing it there by the handle.

"As you wish," she says sweetly.

I remove the tip from my skin. Blood pools rapidly in my palm as I hold it above the man's mouth, allowing a small stream to spill over his lips and down his throat. The wound on my hand closes slower than I expect it to, and I watch as the skin reseals itself cell by cell.

Vanesa stands over my shoulder like an overbearing mother, and I stick my elbow into her ribs. She grunts. Before she has the chance to retaliate, the man coughs—once, then twice, and on the third cough a spew of red erupts from his mouth, spraying us from head to toe as he vomits blood all over himself.

"It didn't work. What do we do?" I ask. His body seizes uncontrollably, white foam builds in his mouth, and he shakes so hard the entire cabin vibrates. The lantern on the bookshelf crashes to the floor, erupting into hot flames.

Vanesa curses, looking around for something to put it out with. I toss her the man's sheet.

"That's not thick enough," she chokes, covering her mouth. We don't have time to find something heavier because this tiny cabin is made entirely of crumbling wood.

"Figure it out, he's dying!" I turn him onto his side, but it's already too late. His body grows still, writhing slightly until there's one less heartbeat in the world.

Vanesa's on her knees, smothering the flames with the sheet and cursing as they burn through it. When she finally gets it under control, she stands. Soot covers her cheeks and raw burn marks crease her milky skin.

"Goddammit," she yells, kicking the bedpost nearest to her

and shaking her arms like they need to cool down. "Try your venom on the next one. See if we get a different result."

"No." I blink, unbuttoning my blouse to reveal a ratty sports bra, then discard the shirt on the floor. There's no salvaging it now. Reaching for my coat, I slide my arms in the sleeves and zip it up, ready to brave the chilly evening with one less layer of clothing. "It won't work. We'll just kill her, too."

My eyes dart between the woman in the next bed and the boy in the one across, and I pray they have no one, that there's no one looking for them or worrying themselves sick over them. Because thanks to Vanesa, I highly doubt they're ever going to make it back home.

"They're going to die anyway. Look at them. If we can find a solution—"

"This trial-and-error thing of yours isn't going to accomplish anything but killing more innocent people." They have a better chance of surviving if we stop and logically try to figure out a solution as opposed to testing each of my superhuman gifts on them. "You'll do anything at the expense of someone else if it benefits you, won't you?"

Her eyes harden, glowing golden in the darkness that surrounds us. "You don't know a thing about me."

"Maybe not," I agree. "But I do know one thing. Vira may not owe me, but after this? You sure as hell do."

CHAPTER 11

I hate Vanesa. I despise her with a burning passion— but still, I wish I'd have forced her to walk me home. Two vampires are better than one, after all, and right about now I'm feeling especially stupid for walking alone in the dark. Flashes of last night dance through my mind as I keep my eyes peeled, but they soon shift to images from three months ago when I was graciously introduced to the vampire world by a hunter who mistook me for something I wasn't. Most days I try not to think about it. Not about him, not about how I got here, but if I let my guard down, I can still feel his hands grabbing me, the feeling of his foot jamming into my knee, and the look of satisfaction in his eyes.

I've been attacked three times since that night, all brutal, and none an experience I ever want to relive, but it's that first one that sticks with me—that leaves a sour feeling in my stomach and a metallic taste in my mouth. I'm not sure why that night in particular scarred me more than the ones that followed. Maybe it's because I was completely alone, or because I didn't know what I do now. Whatever the case, it haunts me almost as much as Ambrose Draven did himself.

Someone in this great big, entangled web of a world must be watching out for me, because I make it home in a record time. I couldn't use my speed until I was a safe distance away from the cluster of homes in case anyone was watching, but even that isn't enough to get me away from potential predators.

I rush into my house, dropping my gloves and boots at the door and unzipping my jacket until I remember I'm not wearing a shirt underneath. Warmth hits me immediately, along with an odd queasy feeling that makes me want to vomit. I shake it off, nose tingling as I trudge into my room, abandoning the jacket and sliding into a black tank top and flannel sweatpants.

Being a member of the Draven clan has its perks—such as receiving a sort of allowance for being under the clan's thumb. The Twelve siphon money from the economy by doing business with humans. Many of them have the power to do so discreetly, and then they distribute it to their clan members as payment. I was able to put a little of it toward myself once the worst of the house was taken care of. At least the roof doesn't leak anymore… for the most part at least. Sealable windows are a battle I've yet to win.

"Why do you insist on torturing me?" Dallas appears in the doorway with a towel around his neck and torso. Wet curls drip onto his forehead.

I raise an eyebrow, tying the strings on my pants so they don't fall over my small hips. "What do you mean?"

"You swore you'd be back in less than a half hour. You've been gone almost two." He's trying to come off as annoyed, but the worry in his eyes is unmistakable.

Vanesa insisted we walk normally to the cabin so we'd know if we were being followed. Sometimes in the intensity of our speed and the head rush it brings, it's easy to miss someone trailing us when we're moving at the speed of light. "Something came up."

"You couldn't text? I was about ready to send out a search party. Things are crazy right now. You can't just disappear on me, I don't know what to think."

"I'll call next time," I say, biting my lip sheepishly. His face is lined with stress, and I feel bad for being the cause of it. "You have to realize, though, if anything happens to me—"

"No, stop," he grits, ripping the towel from his shoulder and throwing it at my head with terrible aim. "I don't want to think about anything happening to you."

"But if it does—"

"*No.*" He breathes out unsteadily, shaking his head like a child. "Just… no. You're immortal. You are going to live a long life. You are going to watch me grow old and die, and then you're going to live some more. You are not going to die now, do you hear me? You won't. So just—tell me where you are from now on."

"Okay."

Dallas nods, and my eyes follow him as he walks around me to his room. The motion makes me dizzy, and I tilt, reaching for something to grab on to. Except there's nothing around me but the hard floor. I let out a strangled sound, and my legs give out beneath me.

A voice calls for me, but it's soft and far away, and I can't quite see straight. There are hands on me, and suddenly I feel like I'm moving. It's too hard to tell when I can't lock my gaze on anything.

Then fresh air fills my lungs like a drug, and I close my eyes, feeling it sober me as Dallas drags me up the stairs, through my mom's room, and into the study. Mom's small frame follows behind him, tentatively looking over his shoulder at me as he deposits my body on the couch.

Dallas touches my face gently, smoothing back the hairs matted to my skin.

"You're burning up," he says, then quieter, "The ash?"

Of course. The ash. The fireplace. I'd completely forgotten Father had lit it today. That explains the nausea I felt when I walked through the door. But the fireplace isn't close enough to my bed for my reaction to have been so severe. Sure, it would have weakened me, but knocking me to the brink of unconsciousness is intense.

"I'm so sorry," Mom whimpers, tears streaming down her cheeks. The nightgown she wears is in need of a wash, maybe several, and the lines wrinkling her face are much deeper than they should be for a woman her age. She rushes toward me, eyes wandering my face.

"It's okay, Mom, it's not your fault." I touch her wrist, and she smiles sadly, bringing her hands to my cheeks. The sensation tingles, intensifying the longer they linger on my skin, and soon her touch is searing with unimaginable pain. "Mom?"

I squirm beneath her grasp, tears blurring my vision as I try to signal for Dallas to help. Her thumbs rub up and down my cheeks, burning like acid. "We will purge the devil from your soul."

"Dallas!" I choke, struggling to peel my mom's hands off of me. Dallas is on her in an instant, trying and also failing to pry her away from my face. "Mom, please. *Stop.*"

My skin is on fire, and for a second, when I meet her wild and erratic eyes, I see Derek.

Just when I think I'm going to pass out from the pain, Dallas yanks her shoulders back, and she slams into the couch across from mine. Dallas drops to his knees, hastily wiping the grit from my cheeks until my breaths come easier. He turns on Mom then, roughly taking her hands in his. Gray powder is smeared across her palms and fingers, darker in the creases where sweat has formed.

"What is this?" he asks, voice teetering on the brink of rage. Tears spill over her cheeks, and I think she knows just as well as I do that the question was rhetorical. We all know what her hands are covered with. "Why would you put ash all over your hands?"

She chokes on a sob, and snot runs down her face, intermingling with her tears. "I have to burn the devil. He said he must be stopped."

"Who?" I sit forward, momentarily distracted from the minor fact that my own mother just tried to-to I don't even know what. Kill me? Hurt me? Burn a hole through my soul? I don't think I can die from ash, even if ingested, but it packs one hell of a punch. "Who said the devil must be stopped?"

Her frightened eyes look away from me, and a deep flush rises on her face. "He said the devil must be stopped." Her finger points, spasming uncontrollably in my direction. "The devil—he's inside of you."

Dallas collects her in his arms, eyeing me over her shoulder as I try to stop my own hands from shaking. "Shh, let's get you cleaned up and in bed, okay, Mom?"

She nods somberly, lips quivering as he guides her back to her room. The moment the door is closed, I drop my face into my hands, letting out a loud sob before clamping a palm to my mouth. My head shakes in disbelief as the tears writhe my body so hard I can barely get a breath in. Curling in half, I rest my forehead on my knees, keeping my mouth shut with my hands as I attempt to regain control of my emotions. I've worked so hard at keeping them in check. So, so very hard at maintaining a straight face even when a knife is being dug into my back, and it's exhausting. I hear a pair of feet jog down the stairs and then back up a few moments later, nearing the study door. I sit up, wiping the snot from my nose and pressing my knuckles beneath my eyes to deter my tears from escaping without permission.

"There was ash all throughout your room. Mostly lining the walls, but there was a lot under your bed as well." Dallas's throat bobs when he swallows, and a pair of shorts now replaces the towel that he had been wearing.

This isn't the first time a threat has not only been in our home, but a member of our family. The last time something like this happened was Derek, and if I said what Mom just did to me didn't tear open a lot of old wounds from that night, I'd be lying.

My brother looks stricken, pale, and petrified. That's enough to tell me he's thinking the same thing as me. We lock gazes, neither one of us brave enough to say it out loud.

"I think you should stay somewhere else," he whispers, voice thick. I nod and wish I had it in me to be mad at him for kicking me out, just to feel something other than betrayal. "She didn't mean it."

I nod again, this time fighting hard to hold back more tears. "I—" I take a breath, swallowing. "I don't know who she is anymore."

Dallas closes his eyes but doesn't say anything. He doesn't have to. "Just figure out who compelled her to do this." He hesitates, watching me as I stand, and probably hoping just as I am that someone did compel our mom to hurt me, and that this wasn't leftover from the memories Elliot suppressed. "Where will you go?"

I shrug, pulling my hair up into a high ponytail. "Probably Elaine's tonight, and then... I don't know. Draven Manor. That's my safest bet."

His face scrunches at that, despite knowing I'm right. I would go there tonight, but it's too far and too dark for me to travel alone with who knows how many vampires creeping around every corner. I don't particularly want to walk to Elaine's either, but at the moment, the biggest threat may be inside my own home. I suppose some things never change. "Are you coming, too?"

"No." Dallas pulls me in for a long hug. "I'm going to stay and make sure Mom's okay. Dad slept through everything so we don't have to worry about him."

Numbly, I shuffle my feet to the door, debating how safe it is to walk through the living room in case there's more ash hidden somewhere. My phone is still in my pocket and whatever else I might need Dallas can just bring me in the morning.

"This yours?" he asks, picking something off the floor and examining it. Then he brings it over for me to see. "It was sticking out from under the baseboard."

Shrugging, I take the small, faded square of paper. It's torn around the edges, stained with watermarks, and has four words written in black ink. They're each on their own line, scribbled messily on the rough parchment.

Whole.
One.
Two.
Undone.

"That mean anything to you?" Dallas asks.

My brow furrows in thought. This house is over two hundred years old, and I've been messing with some of my ancestor's old files to try to learn as much as I can about this world and his life—he was family after all. It most likely fell out of one of his boxes. "Not a thing."

Dallas shrugs. "Be safe, okay?"

I rub his arm, giving his biceps a squeeze. "Of course."

"And—"

"Text you when I get there—" I punch his arm "—got it."

Seconds later, I'm standing on Elaine's front porch, shivering in the cold night with nothing but a tank top and thin pants on while I eagerly wait for her to get the door. I texted first to make sure she was home. If she hadn't been, I probably would have broken in just so I wouldn't have to run across town to Miles, though I'm sure if I asked, he'd be here in a heartbeat.

"Hey, everything okay?" She opens the door wide, stepping aside for me to come in.

"That depends." I draw out my words, quirking a brow in her direction. "How do you feel about a slumber party?"

CHAPTER 12

"Your mom did what?" Elaine's jaw hits the floor. She quickly recovers, clearing her throat and pouring us each another glass of wine. I'm not much of a drinker, but it's been so long since I've allowed myself to unwind, I figured I deserved it.

Ever since Derek was arrested and my father began drinking, I've been scared to indulge. As a vampire, though, alcohol doesn't affect me the way it does humans.

I take a swig, enjoying the sweet warmth as it spreads across my tongue. "I don't want to talk about it."

"But your mom just—how did she know how to hurt you?" Elaine swishes the liquid around in her glass, twisting the spine. She's only had two glasses, but it's obvious she's feeling the effects more than I am.

"Are you sure your parents won't mind me staying here?" I change the subject, knowing her quick attention span will eat it right up.

She snorts into her glass, taking a large gulp. "You could sit at the kitchen table for dinner and they'd think you've lived here for years." I raise an eyebrow at her comment. "What I mean is, they don't pay attention to or notice anything. Anyway, they're out of town for the week. They left early this evening."

"I'm sorry, I know how horrible that feels." I offer her a smile, then snag the wine bottle before she can pour herself a third glass.

"Yes, but unlike your parents who were drunk, traumatized, and under the possession of a two-hundred-year-old serial vampire, mine don't have an excuse. They just don't care. I always had Oliver, though. His parents used to buy me a cake for my birthday just in case mine forgot. He was my family."

Elaine's infamous best friend Oliver, who I still have yet to meet. "How is he?"

She snorts again, this time softer than the last. "Don't know. He's busy. He went on vacation last month. I've tried to get him to take a break from school and meet up with us so I can introduce you, but his summer courses ended right around when everything with you went down, and then his fall ones started. I'm kind of worried about him, honestly. He's working himself too hard and is always stressed. This is the longest we've ever gone without hanging out since we met."

"I'm sure he'll come around," I assure her, finishing off my glass and setting it on her nightstand. Elaine decided to take a gap year after graduating high school, and now with this watcher business, she thinks human milestones and priorities aren't as important. "Speaking of mysterious men."

"Don't. No. Don't think you can get me tipsy and I'll spill all my dirty little secrets."

I roll my eyes. The plan was good in theory. "Come on, I need a distraction from my mom trying to mutilate me."

My fingers brush my cheeks where her hands pressed into me. The skin is still uneven and raw.

"There's nothing to tell." She tsks, flopping into bed and snuggling deep under the covers. "I'm still mad at Owen, and he still abandoned me. Maybe that's the same issue... I don't know, but I do know that I don't forgive him, even after a couple glasses of wine."

"Whatever you say." I lay back on the floor in the makeshift bed Elaine made for me. If I'm being honest, it's more comfortable than my bed at home, but it's still not *home*. Oddly enough, the one place I always dread returning to is the place I miss most right now.

A large hand wraps around my throat, squeezing and crushing me as I grapple the air to find the source of my pain. There's nothing but darkness, not a soul in sight or a heartbeat for miles—not even my own. The pressure spreads from my throat to my chest, and then through my abdomen like water in a river, stilling and freezing to ice, pinning me in place. I can still breathe. I can still scream. But I'm frozen. Rooted in a moment. Stuck between life and death like I'm in an invisible prison cell.

Hands are on me, roaming over me. Stroking my neck like I'm the most fascinating creature alive. I want them gone. I want them off. I want to be free—except I don't know how to *break* free when I had no idea I was trapped before this very moment, when it's too late.

Hands press to my shoulders, pushing me deeper, deeper until the ice in me explodes, releasing the pressure and flooding my body until every ounce of liquid leaks from my pores and out through my nose. I cough, thrashing, sputtering, gasping for breath, but they keep pushing me down until I'm submerged and—

"Aspen, wake up. *Wake up.*"

Coughing, I claw at my throat and roll onto my side, breathing in the stale air. I dry heave until I'm sure there's nothing in my stomach that could possibly come back up. Elaine kneels at my side, rubbing my back in soothing circles. Her entire face is drained of color. I reach for her nightstand, and she jumps up, rushing to grab me the glass of water that's there. I lift my head to take three long gulps.

I wipe my mouth, a few droplets having dribbled out before I could swallow.

"Thanks," I rasp, still gasping for air.

She opens her mouth, then shakes her head rapidly. "I don't know what question to ask first."

"I told you I get nightmares." I shrug off her concerned gaze, downing the rest of the water as a buffer.

"Most people have nightmares and wake up frightened, not like they've just been strangled to death and reborn." She pauses, pursing her lips. "And you're sure you killed Ambrose?"

I sigh, bringing my knees to my chest to stop their trembling. "Positive. This was different. I was conscious and aware, not paralyzed with fear."

"Have you told anyone?"

I look at her plainly. "Like who?"

"Your all-knowing vampire boyfriend, maybe?" She returns my plain look. "He might be able to help."

"He has enough to worry about, Elaine. We all do."

"He worries about you. He's only doing any of this for you. So when stuff like this happens, what's the harm in telling him?" Concern replaces her hard features, her sharp eyes turning soft.

"Then call him." I roll my eyes, feeling especially agitated for no reason. When she doesn't move for the phone, I glance up, removing my fingers from where they're massaging my temples. "You already did."

There's a soft noise from downstairs, and I bang my head against her footboard. Miles has his clan to take care of, the hunters to protect his family from, and the intruding vampires to worry about—a little bad dream doesn't constitute a late-night visit.

"You weren't waking up. I didn't know what else to do," she says defensively. I feel bad for snapping at her, but ever since I woke up, I've still felt... caged. Strangely suffocated.

"God, I know. I'm sorry. This has just been the longest day in a lot of really long days."

Miles looms in the doorway, shoulders relaxing when he sees that I'm awake. His dark hair is tousled, and a few thick strands fall onto his forehead sexily. I've changed my mind. Miles Draven can drop everything when I have a nightmare any time he pleases.

Elaine excuses herself, giving Miles a once-over I don't miss, so we can have a minute to ourselves.

"Why didn't you tell me you were still having nightmares?" He lowers himself to the floor, resting a forearm on his knees while his other hand reaches for mine, threading our fingers.

I lick my lips, refusing to meet his smoldering eyes. "I've had nightmares since I lived in Colorado. It's nothing new. I'm fine." Miles doesn't look remotely convinced. I twist toward him, tucking my feet beneath my bum and turning his chin to face me. His eyelids lower, fluttering closed when my fingers drag along his lower lip, teasing it with my thumb. "I'm fine."

His lips curl up in a soft smirk, and he presses a kiss to the tip of my nose. "That, you are."

Miles pulls me into him. My knees rest against his thigh, and I reach so my arms slide all the way around his waist until my cheek is pressed against his stomach. His breath warms the top of my head when he presses his lips against my hairline, taking in a long, unsteady breath.

"Can I stay with you tomorrow?" I start to lift my eyes, but then look down sheepishly, staring at the seams in his pants. "I can't go home."

"You never have to ask. The answer is always yes." Warmth floods my chest, and for the first time since last night, I can breathe again. Actually breathe without a sharp sting in my chest or the pressure I've felt weighing me down for the better part of three months. For the moment, I feel... safe. "Elaine told me what happened."

A sigh escapes my lips, and some of the bliss I felt moments ago escapes with the breath. "Of course she did."

"Don't blame her. I asked why you weren't at home."

Just then, the door opens, and Elaine pops her beautiful face around the corner. The dim light highlights the splash of freckles on her cheeks.

"You guys don't need your own room, do you?" she asks, eyeing the comforter that she left crumpled in a ball.

"Elaine." I practically choke, and I feel Miles heave a laugh from beneath me.

She smirks. "Just checking. Do you mind if I go to bed? I'm really tired."

I nod and start to sit up, assuming Miles is about to leave anyway, but he holds me in place. "Go ahead."

Elaine slides under her covers, pulling the lamp cord so the room falls dark. "You guys can still talk, I'm a heavy sleeper."

Within a meager three minutes, Elaine's heartbeat slows, and her breaths come out heavier and longer as she drifts off. Miles and I remain silent, listening to the rhythm of our hearts beating in sync as he strokes my hair, rocking us back and forth on the carpet. My chest feels tight again, all of my worries intermingling and forming a ball of fear.

A sick feeling settles in my gut when a thought occurs to me.

He said the devil must be stopped.

I'd been so preoccupied with what she'd done and who "he" is, that I completely overlooked one important factor: Someone told my mom to weaken me. Someone wanted me immobilized, and after last night, when we killed two of Adrian's vampires, he probably didn't want to take any chances by sending more. What if he had my mom compelled to hurt me, and then planned to abduct me quietly? I don't know how else she would have known about the ash. They must not have banked on Dallas getting involved—though I'm not sure why hurting him to get to me would be an issue for them. I suppose Adrian wants to keep things clean—the fewer bodies the better. His goons last night didn't get that memo, but now they know brute force isn't the best way to capture me.

"Do you ever stop thinking?" Miles murmurs into my hair, tearing me from my thoughts.

"Not even in my sleep." I attempt a bad joke, but it falls flat in the recent revelation of my nightmares. At least this time I don't think I'm being haunted by a centuries-old vampire.

A phone vibrates somewhere between us, and I shift, feeling around for mine. No notifications. Miles works his out of the pocket between us, sighs, then shows me a message from his sister.

My eyes widen, and I start to stand. He grabs my wrist and pulls me back to the ground, holding me in place with a tender kiss. "We have three hours until sunrise, and you need rest. Let me worry about this."

There's no point in arguing with him. I'd love to rest for a while, but I'm not sure if that's possible. "Be careful."

His fingers squeeze mine. He pulls me to his chest before releasing me and disappearing down the stairs.

I fall back, staring at the fan on Elaine's ceiling, wondering what scares me the most—my recurring nightmares, or that Vira's text said she thinks the American vampires struck a deal with the Ichorye hunters to take us out.

CHAPTER 13

First thing in the morning, Dallas brings me a few changes of clothes, my toothbrush, and a plethora of apologetic glances. He feels guilty that I can't stay at home, and I know he worries when he doesn't know exactly where I am. If I'm not coming home each night, he doesn't know that I'm okay.

I know this is necessary for my safety, but a small, jealous part of me feels like Dallas chose our mom over me.

"I promise I'll keep you updated. Just be careful, and let me know when you leave the house," I say, equally as concerned about being separated. The two of us don't spend a ton of time together, but enough that when the other doesn't return home before midnight, we know something is seriously wrong. That's why he was so worried about me when I first started spending time with Miles. He knew something wasn't right but had no idea what it could be. I think we'd both prefer if he still didn't know. "Are you sure you don't want to come?"

"Mom is a mess and Father is clueless. I can't leave them alone just in case something happens. Don't worry, I know how to take care of myself." Dallas whips out a wooden stake, twirling it between his fingers.

I raise an eyebrow, mildly impressed. "Where did you learn to do that?"

"Vanesa." He pockets the stake and pulls his t-shirt down to conceal it from view.

I blink, trying my very hardest not to get mad at him. "Vanesa? As in hates me with a burning passion, cares about no one, wishes me dead, Vanesa?"

"She's not that bad, Aspen." He leans in and gives me a peck on the cheek. "Stay safe."

He walks down Elaine's front steps while I gape after him. When in the world did Vanesa and my brother find time to perfect parlor tricks? And since when does he think one of the Dravens isn't "that bad?"

"I'll look in on them, don't worry." Elaine touches my back, dropping her chin to my shoulder.

I reach my arm around and pat her on the head. "I really appreciate that, thank you. And thanks for letting me spend the night."

"Are you kidding? You're the closest thing to family I have right now, it's no problem at all." Elaine pinches my arm, the both of us still watching Dallas walk down the road. "I'll see what I can do about cleaning up the ash in your room, as well."

"Aspen Troy." A voice from behind startles us, and Elaine and I turn in unison, staring down the man who somehow managed to get into her house unnoticed.

Elaine's fingers find my forearm, digging into my skin so hard I'm sure she's drawn blood. We stare up at the tall blonde with a wicked smirk and eyes darker than an abyss.

"Adrian." I gulp, wishing Dallas would return with his handy wooden stake.

"Did you really think I'd believe your little story?" He quirks an eyebrow, tongue skating over the tips of his teeth. The movement reminds me of Ambrose, and I shiver.

Telling him I knew Ambrose two hundred years ago was never meant to stump him. I just needed a good enough story to keep him from kidnapping me on site.

"I'll admit, you had me perplexed after our first meeting." He comes a step closer, and Elaine's grip tightens on my arm. She's silently asking me what we should do, and I don't have an answer for her. "What I couldn't figure out was how it was possible. Until I learned your name. You see, your ancestor was a *friend* of mine. He helped me with our little Draven issue back in the day."

So I was right. It was because of my ancestor that I was able to break the curse—well, I suppose the curse isn't exactly broken. I guess I have Vanesa to thank for something. If it weren't for her experimenting, we might not have known for a while.

"How did you manage to find your way back to Ichorye?" he asks.

I hesitate, then decide there's no point in lying about everything. Adrian has been alive a lot longer than the Dravens, and since the Twelve were involved in the making of the curse, it's safe to assume each of them knows how to break it. Lying only makes me disposable. I need to pick my battles, save up my lies until I can make them count. "Ambrose Draven led me here. I did know him, that much was true."

Adrian blinks, clearly not understanding how a dead man found and led me to his hometown to save his family.

"The curse isn't broken," I say. "I'm not the key."

Elaine's head snaps in my direction, and I can see the wheels in her head turning.

"I know," he says, surprising me. The condescending gleam in his eye makes me uneasy. "Still, I have been trying to speak with you, but you've been... less than cooperative."

"Just for future reference, compelling my mother to harm me isn't the best way to do so," I say, becoming agitated.

Adrian doesn't bat an eye. "I sent my men first, but it seems they got lost on their way back."

My jaw tics, and Elaine's breath hitches. "Strange town. It happens."

Adrian takes another step forward, towering over the two of us like the Empire State Building. He draws a finger across my cheek, lingering on the burn from the ash. I'm beginning to wonder if that gesture is a vampire thing, because even Miles does it to me.

"Just for future reference," he mocks me, face hardening, "when I want to speak to you, you come. Or it might be your brother's pretty face that gets burned next time."

In the blink of an eye, he's gone, and Elaine is slamming the front door and running through the house to check the remaining doors and windows—not that doing so will keep him out. I don't tell her this though. We all need a taste of sanity time and again.

"Why didn't he kill us?" She stands on her tiptoes, peering out of a small window on the door. She's already launching into her next question before I get the chance to process the first. "Why would you tell him about the curse? Now he thinks there's a fault in it, *and* that the Dravens are weak. How is that helpful?"

"He already knows, Elaine. That's why we're still alive. For some reason, he doesn't want me dead yet. Besides, the curse isn't broken. Vanesa has been trying to turn humans and they're dying almost instantly. Well, not dying but—" I search for the word she used, unable to come up with anything better. "—deflating."

Her eyes pop open and red anger flames in her cheeks. *"She what?"*

"She took me to them last night. She thought I'd be the answer to completing their transition, but—" I pause, running a hand through my hair. "One died when I tried to help."

"Oh God." Elaine drops to the couch. "I can't believe she went behind their backs. I mean, yours I get, she hates you—"

"I'm aware, Elaine."

"—but her siblings? Elliot? I just don't believe it. You don't think he told her to, do you?"

"All I know is one thing is abundantly clear—I don't know anything anymore."

"Wait, you said that your parents seemed off, right?" she asks, twisting a ring on her middle finger.

I nod. "More than usual, yeah. It's like they know something, but they're not sure what it is."

"If Vanesa can't turn anyone, then maybe that explains why the compulsion Elliot used on your folks is having side effects? The memories are gone, but the trauma was left behind."

Elaine's suggestion has me looking at the situation in an entirely new light. It's incomplete—the transition, the compulsion, everything is incomplete.

"You're a genius." This warrants me a satisfied smile. "I have to go warn them. I promised Vanesa I wouldn't tell anyone about what she did, but this is too important."

Elaine makes a judgmental sound, scrunching her face in disbelief. "You can lie to her, but not me. You were just waiting for the right moment to screw her over."

Licking my lips, I raise a shoulder, uncommitted. "Now we'll never know—oh, and if you want, I'm sure Dallas wouldn't mind if you stayed in my room while I'm gone. It might be better if the two of you aren't alone. He'll never leave my parents to stay with the Dravens."

Technically, Dallas won't be alone, but with my parents' growing suspicion and lack of knowledge about the vampire world, he essentially is on his own.

Elaine nods thoughtfully. "I'll think about it."

ost of my day is wasted on the Draven's luxury couch. Ever since I said my piece about the curse, the siblings have been hurriedly running back and forth between the house and wherever else their clan duties take them. I've requested to come along more times than I can count, but Miles wants me kept out of harm's way, and the rest of them are reluctant to defy him. Besides, it's not like any of them would want me around anyway.

"Where the hell is Vanesa?" Vira stomps into the lounge room—that's what I'm calling it because there's already a living room in the Manor, and I don't think this counts as a second one.

The fates were kind to me today—Vanesa wasn't home when I told her family about what she'd done. Danielle and Lucas went to the cabin to collect the other two transitioners— if you can even call them that—and took them to the armory in the basement, where they have thousands of remedies, poisons, and potions on file, all concocted with herbs and natural elements. It's truly a fascinating place to see, but Elliot was wary about letting me near some of the more potent poisons, so I was banished here. Apparently, not even their clan members have access to the armory, so I feel slightly included at best.

Sitting up, I check my phone for an update from Dallas or Elaine, but there's nothing. I grunt, setting my phone back down. "She hasn't been here."

"I'm going to murder her," Vira says. Her plum lips curl into a scowl. "We told her to wait for a reason, this *exact* reason, but she had to prove she was superior."

I wait for her to continue, not quite sure whether to join in and insult Vanesa or allow her to continue ranting without interruption. Vira and I haven't been alone since the night the hunters attacked us. We've been together plenty, but there has always been someone else, a buffer between us. I prefer that to this. She's talking to me as if I'm someone she trusts, and I'm not sure how to do the same, or if I should. So I wait.

"I just hope she didn't have to compel any witnesses, because that could get ugly." She draws her eyes to me, face fallen and flat with slight irritation in her eyes, almost as if she can read my mind. "I don't hate you."

This brings a rueful smile to my lips. "Anymore."

Her lashes flutter as she rolls her eyes. "You made it nearly impossible, so thanks for that."

"Does Vanesa disappear a lot?" I ask.

Vira shrugs, unconcerned. "Honestly, we aren't all together often, but recent events have made being apart risky. Besides, we have too much to worry about to wander off on our own. Vanesa always does, though. I swear, she has no regard for anyone else."

"Miles told me your theory. About the hunters working

with Adrian." I shift the subject from Vanesa, afraid the moment I say something bad about her Vira will change her tune.

"Danielle saw a vampire she didn't recognize talking with one of the hunters we know of. Most of them keep their identities hidden so we can't pick them off in their sleep, but there are a few we've seen before that haven't ended up dead." Vira quirks her lips in a *it happens* smirk. "That would explain why the hunters aren't all over the intruders. They hate us being here, much less allowing more vampires to flood our little town without a fight. My guess is Adrian offered to get rid of us, and in return, promised to never again allow any of our kind to step foot in Ichorye. It's just a theory."

"A pretty good one," I admit. Teeth gnawing my lip, I watch her stand, amazed that she didn't once snap at me or regard me as worthless. That's progress if I've ever seen any.

Miles peeks his head around the door, expression softening when he sees me. "Are you ready to go?"

A glance out the window tells me it's almost sundown, and I'd prefer to get out of here before Vanesa returns. Maybe Vira will manage to talk her down before she rips my head off, but I know if I'm here, I'm as good as dead the second she finds out I snitched. In my defense, I didn't have much of a choice. They need to know if the curse isn't broken, and again, I kick myself for not dragging Rachel out of her bed and back to Ichorye with me. We didn't have that kind of time, though. Elaine and I almost didn't make our flight as it was. It's bad enough Adrian tracked us here but being trapped in his territory would have been ten times worse.

I say bye to Vira and am acknowledged with a grunt as she's clearly lost in thought, staring at her nails.

I was surprised when Miles told me we'd be staying at his house instead of here at the Manor. I hadn't realized he sleeps there most nights, and not at home with his family like I'd thought—though, I suppose I'd do the same if I lived with them. Time alone would be a godsend.

Danielle is standing by Miles's truck, giggling at something Lucas said when we get outside. She looks up almost immediately, and her smile broadens at the sight of us. "Aspen, I have something for you."

My eyes flick to Miles, but he just nods toward his sister, a smirk playing on his lips. Danielle pulls a garment bag through the half-open window, rising to her tiptoes to avoid it catching on anything inside. Lucas reaches beneath the bag to help her with his height advantage.

Her ballet slippers slap on the ground as she floats over to me, untying the bottom of the bag and lifting it to reveal a sheer, deep blue dress with a nude slip beneath it. The plunging neckline draws my eyes almost immediately. Small gems line the entire V. The dress is long, cutting straight up the front of the thigh, so much so that I fear you'll be able to see under it when I walk.

"Do you like it?" Danielle gnaws on her bottom lip hopefully. "If you don't, I can take it back, but..."

I gape, utterly speechless. "Like it? Danielle, it's—oh my God."

She giggles, and I touch the soft material, shifting the bag to admire the strappy back of the dress.

Miles reaches to see the dress, but Danielle swats his hand away. "No peeking."

Lucas stifles a laugh, stepping up behind her.

"Where in the world am I going to wear this?" The dress

is… otherworldly. Definitely not bought anywhere around here.

Miles slides his hands across my hips, pressing a kiss to my forehead. "To dinner. With me."

Lucas rests a hand on his girlfriend's shoulder, giving it a squeeze. "Danielle thought you could use a night off from, well, everything."

"After the clan meeting the other day, Lucas took me shopping because it relaxes me, and we started talking about how overwhelmed you must feel—though I have to say, you're good at hiding it." She gives me a pointed look, and I wonder what gives her that impression. If anything, I thought my emotions were written all over my face. "Then I saw this dress, and I knew you'd look amazing in it. And of course I had to *beg* Miles to spend time with you in order to pull it all off, but he eventually gave in and agreed to dinner."

Reaching out my arms, I pull Danielle into a hug, touched that she went to all of this trouble for me. I don't even want to know how much the dress cost. Even if her family is well-off, that's still a lot to spend on someone you don't know all that well.

"Are you sure we should be going out, though? With everything going on?" The last thing I want is to ruin this gorgeous dress in a fight.

"You will be eating in." She scrunches her nose disapprovingly at that. "Miles ordered from a fancy Greek cuisine restaurant in the city, so you don't have to suffer his cooking."

"My cooking is not that bad," he says. I get the impression this is not the first time they're having this conversation.

"If you like dry and burnt," Danielle mutters.

"Seriously, Danielle, this dress could not have been cheap. Are you sure?" I interrupt them so Miles doesn't get the chance to further the argument.

She bites her lip, glancing up at the Manor. "Actually, Vira paid for it. She offered when she found out our plan, that way I wasn't paying for both the dress and dinner."

She paid for dinner, too? I hadn't even thought about that.

"Anyway, all the two of you need to worry about is enjoying your night. You both deserve it." She pauses, then jogs back to the car. "I almost forgot the shoes."

"The shoes?" I breathe.

Miles chuckles beside me. He leans in, pressing his lips to my ear. "Enjoy it. She doesn't do this for just anyone."

Danielle bounces back to us with a silver shoebox in hand, dumps it in Miles's arms, then takes the dress from me and drapes it over his shoulder.

"Have fun, you guys." She places a quick kiss on her brother's cheek, then pulls me in for a bear hug. "Oh, and I didn't buy that dress to not see pictures of you in it, okay?"

"Understood." I return her hug, feeling excited for the first time in a while. "Thank you. So much."

She shakes her head, as if this, planning our evening, buying us dinner and me a gorgeous dress and shoes, is nothing. "Thank me by having a good time."

CHAPTER 15

I rise up on my toes as I bend, balancing myself on the counter while trying to put on the heels Danielle gave me. Flats are more my speed, but for her sake I thought it would be nice to get at least a few pictures with them on before I discard them in the living room.

I turn to the side, admiring the crossing straps on the top of my back, leaving my skin bare all the way down to where the fabric sits low on my waist. My hair is atrocious, though. I didn't have time to do much with it before I left Elaine's this morning. I also didn't think I'd be going on a seriously formal date at the time, either. Grunting, I pull my hair up into a messy knot and splash some water on my plain face.

A text from Danielle tings on my phone in response to the picture I sent her, but before I can respond, Elaine's name appears on my screen with a video call.

"Hello?"

"Of course, you get the sexy vampire who plans romantic dinners and whose family buys you fancy dresses, and I get stuck with the mute avoider from hell. You look really nice by the way." She adds that last part as an afterthought.

"Thank you. Have you heard from Dallas?"

"I stopped by your place earlier," she says, voice muffled. "He's fine. Worried about you. Your mom slept all day, and your dad was cutting more firewood."

"Good." I breathe a sigh of relief. Nothing has changed.

"Dallas actually offered for me to stay in your room so I wouldn't be home alone." She giggles. "I let him think he was the one doing me a favor. I'm going back once I eat dinner. Also, did you know he taught Vanesa how to paint?"

"Don't remind me." How is it that Vanesa hates me so much and yet doesn't mind my brother? I didn't think much of them painting before. It was only once during the cookout they had when I got back from America, but the stake tricks, too? Did she teach him those the one time she walked him home?

"Oh, remind me to tell you about something I found in my ancestor's journal. I'll tell you tomorrow, though. Enjoy your *date*," she singsongs, ending the call.

My date. Who would have thought?

After taking a long breath and one last weary look in the mirror, I pull open the bathroom door that sits on the edge of the living room and large kitchen. Miles looks up from the counter where he sits with a crazy amount of food and two wine glasses holding what I'm almost certain isn't red wine. The carpet is hard to navigate with these shoes, but once my feet hit the hardwood, I don't feel as though I'm going to trip anymore.

Miles stands, eyeing me from head to toe as he reaches for my hand and guides me to an already pulled-out chair. "You look… ravishing."

I drop my gaze to the china dish in front of me, so shiny I can see my own reflection. Miles tugs on my fingers, and my small hand fits perfectly inside his. "You do."

"So do you." I eye his dress shirt, surprised to find that it's a deep burgundy and not his usual black staple, though he makes up for it with his dress pants. Something tells me I have Danielle to thank for the color change.

He licks his lips, eyeing his shirt sheepishly. "Danielle wasn't happy with me for messing up our color scheme. It's all I had that wasn't black, but evidently I should have worn blue to match your dress."

"It's perfect," I say, reaching for my wine glass to find that it is, as I thought, not filled with wine, but blood. I take a slow sip, savoring the flavor on my tongue and taking my time so as not to fill the silence with conversation.

Strategizing and theorizing the moves and motives of everyone trying to kill us comes easily to me. It's life or death, a problem that needs to be solved. I can hardly recall having any normal conversations about anything else in the past few months. When there isn't an end goal in sight, a finish line, or a course of action, my words just feel as though they're floating aimlessly through the air without a purpose.

"You're always in your own head," Miles says, touching my arm lightly to draw me out of my thoughts, before serving himself.

I bite my lip, taking the spoon from him and placing a helping of what I think is tzatziki on my plate, as well as two Souvlaki skewers. The heavenly scent makes my stomach groan in anticipation. I swallow, glancing at Miles, who watches me with patience. "I'm not good at this."

"At what?" he asks, breaking eye contact to move the food around on his plate before he dives in.

"Being normal."

We fall into a comfortable silence while we eat, and I'm thankful that Miles isn't the type of person to push me to explain what I mean or try to force conversation when there needn't be any. He knows my past, about my older brother, and everything following that had to do with his uncle Ambrose, so he's very aware that normalcy isn't something I'm attuned to anymore. And everything about this evening is so foreignly ordinary.

Once we finish eating, Miles abandons our dirty dishes on the counter and leads me from the bar into the living room, where he places a vinyl on a record player. He turns the volume all the way up, sliding his fingers down my arms and leaning in close. "Dance with me."

"Do I have a choice?" I eye him, teasing.

His hands find my waist. A sinister smile plays on his lips when he says, "No."

"I didn't think so." My elbows rest on his shoulders as his head drops to the crook of my neck, breathing me in. I'm almost as tall as him with these heels on, but he still has me by a couple inches. "You're always so warm."

He chuckles, the sound vibrating through his body. "Am I supposed to be really cold or something because I'm dead?"

"No." I roll my eyes. "I still get cold, though, and kind of tired when I don't sleep, but you're always hot."

"It's so I can keep you warm." He locks his arms around me, lifting me up and spinning us in a semi-circle as the first song ends and a new one begins.

"Do you ever get cold, though? Is that normal?"

Miles drops his forehead to mine, shaking his head tiredly. "Can we not discuss this tonight? Let's just... pretend to be normal. Call it practice?"

I twist my fingers around the dark hair at the base of his neck, resting my chin on his shoulder. "We will never be normal. It's why we work."

"We can try." He pushes me away just to spin me back into his arms, dipping me low to the ground. I let out a laugh that echoes throughout the room, keeping a hold on his arms so I don't fall. "See." He smirks, picking me back up and rocking me in his arms. "Normal couples laugh."

"We have something going for us then."

"Normal couples dance," he adds thoughtfully. "They also..."

"Sing?" I suggest, nodding toward the record player, knowing very well Miles Draven doesn't sing. "I love this song."

He gives me a dubious look. "I'm not quite that normal. You know this song?"

I grin, and he spins me again, this time to the couch where we drop down on the cushions. "Heaven" by Bryan Adams warms my ears and soul. "Of course. And I admit, it does feel nice to be normal."

He leans close, touching a warm hand to my hip, the heat burning through my thin dress. "It does."

He kisses me, and the music fades into the background—for all I know it's not even playing anymore, because I can't seem to focus on more than one thing at a time, and right now, my attention is otherwise occupied.

His lips part when I move, sliding a leg over his lap to be closer, pulling him to me by his shirt. I swear he's like a furnace, constantly radiating heat through his skin. His hands slide up my hips, thumbs traveling along the plunge of my V-neck, which cuts below my breastbone, and around to my bare back, teasing the edge of the fabric on my hips.

"You should only ever wear this dress," he says, breaking away. I frame his face with my hands and place a kiss on his nose.

He kisses me again before I speak.

"It would get ruined in our line of work," I say breathily, only imagining the blood, dirt, and tears the poor thing would have to endure.

"Danielle can buy you more. A lot more. Maybe in different colors."

"Shut up." I slip off of him and grab my phone from the bar. "Speaking of, we should take a picture for her."

He doesn't look entirely enthusiastic, but he agrees anyway, pulling me onto his lap and holding the phone high enough to appreciate our outfits.

"One more." I smirk, milking this for all it's worth. I use a vase on the coffee table to prop up my phone, setting the self-timer to three seconds. I move between his legs so my back is to his chest. His hands rest on my lap, and our faces press together sweetly as the camera flashes.

"I've always preferred Polaroids," he says upon examining the image, and I have to agree. Digital will never be the same as a tangible photo you can hold between your fingertips. "You should get them developed."

The record stops, and Miles leans over to replace it with another, moving the tonearm so it begins on a specific song. "I love this song, it's—"

"'If.' By Bread," I finish, kicking off my shoes.

"You know it?" He seems surprised.

"I may not be as old as you," I tease, "but I know a classic when I hear it."

When the song is over, we continue to sway as it transitions into the next.

"You seem tired. Do you want to go to bed?"

My heart flips. I nod hesitantly, breaths shallowing and heart speeding up.

I follow him up a set of stairs that leads to a short hallway, my insides doing somersaults as I take in the lack of decorations. It's a small space, but nothing like the downstairs area, which is furnished nearly as perfectly as the Manor. He leads me through the first of two doors, drops my hand to flick on the light switch, then moves to his bed. The room is nice, mostly black which doesn't surprise me given his daily wardrobe colors. The walls are gray, but not a cold, frigid gray—a warm, almost silver tone that accents his dark comforter beautifully.

Miles busies himself undressing the bed and throws the comforter on the floor to reveal (of course, black) silk sheets with red accents cutting across them like cracks. He slides his shirt over his head, revealing more of his insanely toned body than I've ever seen. His family crest is outlined on his chest, stretching over his shoulder and across his arm like spiderwebs. He pulls his phone out of his pocket, setting it on the nightstand and running a slow hand through his curls.

I stand awkwardly, sliding my fingers in and out of each other as sweat coats my palms.

"What's wrong?" Miles stops what he's doing, tossing aside a throw pillow once he realizes I'm still standing in the doorway. He moves to me, watching uncertainly. It only takes a moment for him to understand. His brow furrows, and he touches my neck, thumb brushing over my scar. *His* scar. "I'm not expecting—we don't have to."

A little bit of tension releases from my chest, and I nod, thankful he can read me as well as he can. Words don't always come so easily to me—not when they matter. Not about my feelings.

The knot in my stomach shows no signs of dissipating as he hands me my bag of clothes and points me toward a bathroom across the room. I change quickly into shorts and a long t-shirt, figuring it's too warm for sweatpants.

Exiting the bathroom, I toss my bag in a corner and collapse onto his bed, shifting so I can pull the sheets from under me and slide my body beneath them. Miles is already laying down, so I scoot across the mattress and curl into his side, but no matter how hard I try to relax, my body remains rigid. This is no different than last night, or when I fell asleep against him in his truck when he was nothing more than a stranger to me. Yet somehow it feels different because we're in his house, in his bed, completely alone, and I have no idea how to act.

"Miles, I—" I clear my throat, tongue dry as sandpaper. "I'm just, I don't—"

He interrupts me, pressing a thumb to my lower lip tenderly. "We have forever, beautiful. We don't need to rush."

I huff a laugh, hooking my leg around his. "You make forever sound so easy."

Miles talks about forever like it's not a question, like that's just what it is, what we are. Like it's our undeniable future. Most days I worry my life is going to end before it's even begun, and here he is, thinking all we have is time.

"Forever with you is easy." He shifts so his head is farther down the pillow, directly next to mine. "You are all I want. All I will ever want, don't you see?"

"What happens when all the bad catches up to us? Avoiding death so many times… eventually it will find us," I whisper, feeling his golden eyes boring through my soul. I've been sidestepping death since before I met him. I never should have lived this long, but I did. I miraculously survived, and every time I do, it feels like a reminder that I won't always be so fortunate. "What happens if I die?"

Miles stiffens, eyes flaring bright as he grabs my chin, voice clouded with emotion. "Don't say things like that."

I shake my head into the pillow as all of my earlier reservations resurface. "It might happen."

Miles pulls me close, kissing my lips with pure passion. Every ounce of regret and fear, worry and love, is poured into such a simple gesture, and I know now that this, him, is all I want, too. He touches his forehead to mine, heat from his breath coating my lips like a blanket. "The mere thought of losing you makes living unimaginable."

"You lived plenty before me," I argue, but it's tepid. There is no fighting his words. No dissecting or denying them when I know in my bones I feel the same. That I'll never feel this way about anyone else. It's unexplainable.

"I did," he agrees. "But having you, knowing you, feeling your heartbeat against the palm of my hand—there is no after."

"No?"

"There is just… *you*."

～

Sleep doesn't come for either of us. We just lie in bed, staring at the ceiling, or at each other, sometimes talking, sometimes sitting in comfortable silence.

After a while, I shift to my elbows so I have a better view of his face, lit by the stars outside. "Tell me about Elijah Troy."

He traces my skin absently and turns his head toward me, so close I could kiss him with a mere tilt of my chin.

"He was a good man," he says at first.

"You didn't like him." I know that conflicted look in his eyes all too well.

Miles shifts, pressing his lips together. "I didn't trust him. I thought he'd betray us if he had the chance. He disliked our presence in Ichorye, and always knew exactly when the council would be in town for meetings—it would be too easy. I feared he would make the same deal the hunters may have made with Adrian. He never did, though."

"He sort of did," I counter. "He was part of the reason you were cursed."

"I think about that all the time," he admits. "How Emile must have felt knowing her betrayal of Ambrose was the reason we were suffering. She was different after he went mad, but we thought she was just brokenhearted. It wasn't necessarily that, though. She knew what he'd done, and she knew she was to blame for what came after. It must have eaten her alive to keep that inside."

"I think she kept in touch with Elijah when he ran. He had a bunch of newspaper clippings about Ambrose in his boxes, and I think Emile was trying to warn him he may have found a loophole to the curse."

Miles touches my necklace—Emile's necklace—and sighs. "That sounds like her. She always had a soft spot for humans.

That's what drove her to Ambrose. He was fighting for humanity—God, it must have broken her to find out he used the cause to gain power. That he was willing to harm the humans to overthrow the Twelve. And Elijah, the only person who knew the truth, who she could confide in about it, left."

"Do you think he left because he was afraid, or because his bloodline was the key?"

He mulls this over for a minute. "Both. No one thought Ambrose would kill himself. Elijah probably wanted to make sure that if he ever escaped, he couldn't find him."

I snort. Ambrose didn't need to be alive to find me, much less break out of the house he was locked in. "Some good that did."

"He meant well."

"What was he like, though?"

Miles shoots me a look. "Very inquisitive. Determined. Asked way too many questions. He was really close with Elaine's ancestor, Timothy. Actually, the two of them and Elijah's girlfriend were best friends. That's why we were all surprised when the Graves family stayed behind. In fact, they were so close that when Elijah left with his love, Timothy named his own daughter after her. Her name was Elaine Bridgewell. Our Elaine was named after her."

So our Elaine was essentially named after my ancestor's girlfriend. "She would die to know that her name has meaning. I can't believe our families were so close only to never speak again."

"It was strange," he agrees. "When you first arrived here, I was sure there had to be some mistake. You were a Troy? Then you told me you'd changed your name before you moved, and I was even more confused."

"Elijah must have changed his last name in order to remain hidden from your world. Ambrose influenced our choice to pick Troy when we left Colorado. He influenced a lot of our decisions, actually." I find it ironic that my ancestor changed our surname when he fled from the Dravens, and my family and I unknowingly changed it back when we fled from our own home—straight into Draven territory. "I'm sure Elijah's name is all over the paperwork, but none of us really looked at it that closely. It brought me here, though."

I'm not entirely sure if that's a good thing or not, but as of this moment, it doesn't seem too tragic.

"He did one good thing in the end."

CHAPTER 16

*S*erenity is too much to ask for when you're constantly surrounded by people who are two steps away from closing in on you, and you're not sure how exactly to stop the inevitable from happening.

At seven in the morning, someone bangs incessantly on Miles's front door. He groans, rolling away from me and tugging on the strings of his sweatpants, which are hanging low on his hips.

"Stay here," he says, sleep clinging to his voice. His hair is messy, but it looks intentionally so, tousled to the perfect degree of sexy.

I hear the door open, and a female voice is talking at him before he can get a word out. "Where is she?"

"It's seven o'clock," he mutters tiredly. "Go home."

I strain my ears to hear her lowered voice, sitting up in bed. "Miles, I am done being nice. I did what I had to do for our family, and if you have a problem with that, then maybe you should rearrange your priorities. I will do what's necessary to protect my family, and right now she's the only thing standing in our way."

In the next second, I hear Vanesa's footsteps pounding up the stairs, Miles cursing after her. She throws open his bedroom door and marches to the bed, grabbing me by the hair and shoving my back against the wall. I grab her wrist, digging my nails into her skin and staring her down with malice.

"I owe you, huh?" she spits. "You couldn't keep that pretty little mouth of yours shut for five minutes."

"You're not the only one affected if the curse isn't broken." Her fingers are lodged in my hair, and I tighten my grip on her wrist. "Your compulsion won't work. They had to know."

"No, *you* were supposed to help me. You didn't even try." She slams her fist into my stomach, the force quaking the entire wall.

Miles grabs her arm before she can hit me again, but this just makes her pull harder on my hair, and my nails can only do so much damage.

"Vanesa, enough," Miles growls, his eyes blackening.

She drags her gaze to him, anger flaming in every movement.

"It's okay," I say, drawing her attention back to me. What's worse than Vanesa beating me? Vanesa getting into a fight with her own flesh and blood over me. She'll see it as him choosing sides, and that won't be good for anyone. "She's pathetic." I spit her words back at her, and her dark lips quirk to the side in an ominous smile.

"This isn't a game. This is our livelihood, and pardon me for believing someone such as yourself shouldn't come along and dictate whether or not we can finally break free." She tears her arm from Miles's grasp and wraps her fist around my throat with a squeeze. "You have one more chance. One more chance to figure out a way to save those people or start turning people for us."

"Or what?" I challenge.

Her tongue scrapes across her teeth, and she dips her chin so her face is directly in front of mine. "You will regret it for the rest of your life."

Vanesa releases me and turns to strut out of the room. Miles surprises me, and I can tell by the look of pure disbelief on Vanesa's face that what he does next surprises her too.

He reaches out, grabs her by the hair like she did me, and tugs her backward so she stumbles on her heels. He growls deep in his throat, bringing his face dangerously close to hers. "You need to watch yourself."

He shoves her away, and she stumbles again. The malice on her face is replaced by a look of betrayal. She blinks rapidly, trying to hide the tears springing to her eyes. "You would hurt your own sister to protect her?"

Miles says nothing, turning his back to Vanesa and reaching for me. She shakes her head in horror and disbelief, staggering out of the room.

"You shouldn't have done that." I press a hand to my stomach, sharp pains stinging my right side. I'm pretty sure Vanesa broke a rib—possibly multiple—when she punched me. I ease myself onto the edge of the bed, massaging the side of my scalp, which is also sore from how hard she yanked my hair.

He shakes his head, lifting my arm slowly so he can feel my ribcage. I suck in a sharp breath when he presses his fingers toward the middle, and pains shoot up my side. "She crossed a line."

I don't point out that Vira attacked me once, too, back when Miles was poisoned and she wanted me as far away from the situation as possible. Her attack wasn't so much physical as it was a warning, a threat—although she did lift me by the throat and pin me against the coffee table. Ironically, Vanesa was the one who convinced her to let me go.

"Miles," I say as he feels his way across my stomach for further damage. I touch his face, and like a magnet, his eyes are on mine. "Don't choose me over them."

He drops to his knees so for once he's not towering over me. He lines his arms up with the sides of my thighs, holding my hips in his strong hands. "There is no choice."

"I need you," I whisper, tears clouding my vision. "But so do they. When Adrian decides to attack, you can't be divided."

His fingers tighten on my skin, urgent and distraught. Wild eyes meet mine with a desire I can feel humming beneath my skin. "None of this would be possible without you. You are everything to me, Aspen Troy. Everything. So don't you dare put anyone in front of you." His hands slide up my waist, then shift to my elbows where they explore down to my fingertips. He pulls them to his chest, safely trapped between his hands and his heart. "Vanesa is not being rational. I love her. I love my family. But I love you, too."

CHAPTER 17

For the first time in almost four weeks, the sun isn't obscured by the eternal gloom that hovers over our town. Halloween is only a few days away, and something about its proximity makes my skin crawl in anticipation. Every minute of every day it seems as though there's a clock ticking down the minutes until I run out of time—or life. Despite my much-needed night with Miles, it's not long before the sinking in my stomach reasserts itself after Vanesa's lovely visit—God forbid I have the chance to feel normal for even a few hours.

Everything in the Draven's world is entirely intricate and bewildering, and most days I'm just trying to keep it all straight. Miles and his siblings grew up here, they know the town, they know their world, they know the rules. In three months, I've been dipped into the crazy and forced to swallow more than I can comprehend at once. It also doesn't help that most of what I have to deal with is substantially unprecedented. I've been forced to rely heavily on the Dravens for guidance, but even they don't understand half of what we're dealing with, although they're reluctant to admit it.

Elliot has been keeping a close eye on Vanesa's transitioners, but there's no change in their state, which I suppose is a good thing because that means they're not getting worse. As far as I know, they're not being experimented on, but between him and Vanesa, I wouldn't put it past them.

"Don't be nervous." Danielle touches my shoulder, a look of sympathy in her eyes.

I shake my head shortly. "I'm not."

Vira scoffs, eyes glued to my bouncing knee. "You're shaking the entire car."

"Look, some of our people are still skeptical of you. They need proof. Hope. And as much as we want to keep you out of danger, you're the only proof we have."

Naturally, the clans are skeptical of my existence after going so long without the ability to use their gifts. The last time they had one of these meetings, I was begging to go with them and officially cement my role in society, but now, knowing Adrian is in town, I can't help but consider the recklessness of giving the rumors a face.

"And Miles is okay with this?" I raise an eyebrow, noticing his absence.

The two girls exchange a look.

"Are you kidding me?"

"Look," Vira begins, puffing out her lips. "You were right the first time. We didn't think you needed to be at the clan meeting, and Miles wanted to protect you, so we made you stay away. But you can't dangle a blood bag in front of a vampire's face and not give it to him."

I don't know how comfortable I am with being the metaphorical blood bag in this scenario, but I understand where she's coming from.

"All you have to do is stand there. You don't have to talk or explain yourself. We will handle that part," Danielle says, opening her car door as another vehicle with Lucas, Elliot, and Vanesa pulls beside ours.

"Vanesa attacked me this morning," I tell Vira.

She looks away from the window, gradually leaning forward to rest her elbows on her knees.

"I'm not telling you this because I'm angry or because I want to be consoled. She knocked on Miles's door, stormed upstairs, and attacked me. In front of him. Needless to say, he didn't take it well." I twist in my seat, lowering my voice as I do so, double-checking that Vanesa is still in the other car so she can't overhear. "You guys need each other now more than ever, and I really don't want to be in the middle of his anger toward you, and I especially don't want to be the reason for it. I'll go out there, stand beside you, and I will play my part, but if you don't tell Miles first, you're going to have one more problem on your hands."

Vira's jaw clenches, and she eyes me warily. "Of course you couldn't have been a witless or discourteous girl. At least then I wouldn't feel so bad about wanting to side with Vanesa and force you to turn someone." She runs a finger along her bottom lip, staring intensely at the back of my seat, or maybe trying to burn a hole through it. It's hard to tell whether or not she's thinking, or just so impossibly pissed that she can't stand to look at me.

"I know you only keep your mouth shut because you think you owe me, but I really do appreciate you giving me a choice." In actuality, I'm under more pressure by holding out and refusing to change my mind than I would be by suffering the consequences of finally giving them what they want.

She shakes her head. "You don't get it. Every second you waste fighting us, we get closer to the day Adrian decides to make his move. There is nothing we can do to prepare other than acknowledge that he's coming. Our numbers are small, as you'll see, and he has command over the entire American territory. Even with an army of newborn vampires, our chances would be slim—they'll be clueless and untrained. But Aspen, we have to try. We're open targets, and I know you don't want this responsibility, but you are the *only* one standing in our way. Vanesa will be a dream compared to an entire clan of vampires calling for your head because you refuse them their birthright. When they realize you're actively choosing not to help us, Adrian's vampires will be the least of your concerns."

"How many people would I need to turn?" I ask, staring at my hands. And how many people would actually be willing? And how do we find out who is and isn't without compromising the existence of the supernatural?

"As many as it takes." She gets out of the car, typing something frantically on her phone before strutting over to where her siblings stand in a circle.

We're parked at the end of the cul-de-sac on the vampire side of town, which is apparently a mile walk from where the meet is taking place in a remote area—if you ask me, this entire town is remote.

We're silent for a few minutes, listening and scanning the perimeter for anyone who may have followed us, then take off into the woods, speeding faster than a bolt of lightning. I try my best to keep up with them, but my legs don't move nearly as fast as theirs do, and I end up lagging behind a bit.

We arrive at the site within seconds, slowing our pace as we near a group of maybe three dozen vampires. They seem to vary in age, most looking to be between seventeen and thirty, some older, and very, very few younger. I shiver when my eyes find a girl who looks no older than thirteen. I don't want to know what tragedy turned her into a vampire so young. I can't imagine living the rest of my life as a thirteen-year-old.

"We know you've been anxiously awaiting this day for two hundred years." Elliot steps forward, spreading his hands like a preacher. "I know you're impatient, and I know that you are anxious for your freedom. I am, too. But this is not as simple as breaking a curse and resuming life as we once knew it. There are a few"—he glances at me unintentionally and I wince—"*snags*, but I can assure you that we're doing everything we can to understand this new development and make it so we are all free to feed again. To live again."

"You asked for proof." Vanesa steps next to her brother, raising her chin high. "This is the girl we told you about. Against all odds, she completed the transition, and as soon as we sort out these complications my brother mentioned, we will multiply our numbers and prepare to face the American clans."

"And if they attack tomorrow?" a woman asks. She has long, dark hair and black outlined eyes that look like they could electrify you if she stared hard enough.

Vanesa falters, no doubt cursing me in every language she knows. There wouldn't even be an attack yet if I hadn't stupidly brought us to Adrian's attention.

Luckily, Elliot picks up where she falls off, keeping his voice doubtless and assuring. "Then we fight. We make the most of what we have and hope it's enough."

Written on every expression in the small crowd is exactly what I'm thinking: this mediocre group, no matter how mighty, will never be enough to beat an enemy such as Adrian. Nausea rips through me, causing any and all assurances that what I'm doing is the right thing to recoil. I'm in the exact same place I was three months ago when I was deciding whether or not to become a vampire—in saving one group of people, I'm essentially killing another.

"We discovered that our venom no longer makes a transitioner go insane, but that it does weaken them beyond physical ability. Our compulsion has also been restored, but it is not at full strength. So please, if you must use it, do so sparingly and thoroughly. This is not what we hoped for, but it is progress, and—"

"And there is a chance that Aspen may be the only one who can turn others for the time being—an avenue we will begin pursuing tirelessly within the coming days," Vanesa interrupts her brother, and several starved eyes turn on me. I can almost feel their need as my own, and if I reached out to the air, I'm positive I could clutch their desires in my hand.

Vira stills, face paling. Danielle clenches her teeth, and Lucas's jaw tics. Elliot looks impressed, but not surprised or angry at Vanesa's untimely reveal.

I breathe in slowly, trying my hardest to keep my face still and expressionless. She's backed me into a corner, all but giving me no choice. Now every person here knows that, sure, there's a snag, but there's another possible option. Now all of these people are expecting me to be their solution, their salvation, and I seriously doubt they will accept any outcome without complete confirmation of my success or failure. They wanted proof of my existence—they'll want proof of whatever happens next.

"In fact, Aspen has already—" My heart stops. Rachel. She's going to bring up Rachel. She wouldn't dare.

"Aspen has already expressed her desire to help us in any way she can," Danielle speaks up, earning a look of pure disgust from both Vanesa and Elliot. This was the plan all along. To make it so I had no choice but to help them. Now it's not just the Dravens pressuring me, relying on me, it's their entire clan. How am I supposed to refuse them now when everyone knows I can help? A few confused looks are shared, and Danielle glances meaningfully at Vira.

She clears her throat, and without even stepping forward, every eye is on her. I'm a little impressed, actually. Vira commands attention, as does Vanesa, but Vira has a way of doing so with an air of power and assurance. All it took was a slight sound from her to quiet the hushed whispers that were rising.

"Truthfully, we're not sure what, if anything, will be able to fix our current problem before Adrian attacks. We don't know if Aspen holds all the answers, or if she is part of a chain of events leading to our freedom. We do, however, know that we are strong. And though we may be small in comparison to our enemy, we will fight them with vehemency just the same. We will match their strength and multiply it. Our answers do not lie with one woman alone, they lie within all of us." This time she does step forward, moving in front of Vanesa in the grass. "So we called this meeting to ask for your help, for you to lend your brains to help find a solution. This is unprecedented territory, which means we need anomalous ideas, unique solutions, and incited theories pertaining to the curse—what makes Aspen different from everyone else? What separates her blood from the commoners'?" She pauses, her eyes softening as she takes in all of the fretful expressions before her. "These changes may be unexpected, and not quite what we hoped for when we envisioned the unlikely event of this day ever seeing the light, but regardless, things are evolving. We may not be where we wanted, but we're further than we were yesterday. Thank you all for taking the time to meet with us, and be sure to stay alert."

With that, Vira walks away from our small group, away from the crowd and down the small hill we're positioned atop. Her face is taut, and her hands are clamped in front of her as she moves swiftly in the direction we came.

Elliot starts to speak again before the crowd can disperse—it seems he doesn't like anyone but himself dictating the events of a clan meeting. When I'm sure no eyes are lingering on me, I back away, jogging to catch up with Vira.

"Thank you," I breathe, lungs aching from the cold. "You didn't have to do that."

They would have hunted Rachel down. Or terrorized me until I made more vampires, since whatever I did to Rachel may have worked. She was still coherent when I left her room, and from what Miles has told me, those they turned in past years have gone insane almost immediately.

"I wouldn't have had to do that if you would just get off your high horse and try to turn someone. If it works, great, then we go from there, and if it doesn't, we can stop giving our people false hope. The only reason you left Rachel behind is because you were afraid it would work, and that once it did, your defense of being scared to accidentally kill a human would no longer be valid. You have unfinished business with your brother or whatever, I get that, too. But my clan—we have unfinished business here." She blinks a few times, her eyes clouding over before she sits me with a look I'm not fond of. "You can consider us even now. I won't defend you anymore. I don't owe you." She pauses again, looking strained. "We're even."

Then she disappears before my eyes.

The clan meeting breaks up, and the siblings make their way toward me, looking satisfied with the results of today's meeting.

I'm prepared to dig into Vanesa for undermining me, and confront Elliot for possibly encouraging it, when a glimpse of movement catches my attention. Miles stands off to the side, looking all but pleased with what his siblings have done. They follow my gaze, and Danielle immediately looks guilty, dropping her eyes and glancing at Lucas, who also looks remorseful. Even Elliot stops mid-stride. Vanesa, however, continues walking. Miles moves toward us, heat flaring in his eyes. He's almost to me when Vanesa passes by, bumping my shoulder. I grab her arm just as Miles reaches us.

"I won't do it," I grit. The stubborn, spiteful child in me wants nothing more than to watch her rot after what she's done. But I know that's not realistic, and it's certainly not fair to make everyone else suffer for her insolence.

She raises an eyebrow, a sly smirk tugging at her full lips. "You will."

"I will never help you," I growl, matching her flare and stepping into her personal space. "Any chance of me doing so vanished with your lack of consideration for my wishes."

Anger radiates off Miles like fire in the pits of hell.

"There's more to life than what you want, Vanesa," he says darkly, and I can tell just how hard it is for him to hold himself back from ripping out her hair.

She rolls her eyes. "Oh please, you want this, too. You're simply not man enough to admit that you want something she doesn't believe in. You're too whipped to realize she will never put our needs above her own, above her family's. She may be like us now, but she's still human where it counts." She touches my chin with her sharp fingernails. "She will never know loyalty."

"Maybe," I admit, though I hardly believe that since all I do is worry about everyone else and how what I do affects them. "But you will never know decency or sacrifice so long as you continuously choose yourself over those you love."

Vanesa lifts her arm to strike me, but Elliot intervenes, snatching her wrist out of the air. "Not now, and certainly not here."

She contains her anger, however poorly, and allows him to lead her away from us. Lucas follows behind sheepishly, shooting several apologetic glances at Miles.

Danielle touches his arm gently, and he doesn't so much as flinch. "It needed to be done, Miles." Then, as an afterthought, "Don't hate me."

"The only one I don't hate right now is Vira," he bites. Danielle purses her lips at his tone, nodding solemnly as she backs away, mouthing an apology to me.

I'm trying really hard not to be mad at Danielle since she went to all that trouble to plan our date night, but I can't help but feel a little betrayed. I expect this from the others, but not her and Lucas.

If Miles wasn't so protective, if he could see through his desires and stop pushing his family away by trying to defend me, they would have had no reason to lie today. They only went behind his back because they knew he would never put me in harm's way to do what was necessary.

"You have to choose them, Miles."

He tries to take my hands, but I turn away from him, wrapping my arms around myself. The only thing keeping me rooted in place is knowing that if I try to leave, he'll chase after me until I listen.

I can feel his heat behind me, so close that if I shift back an inch, I'll be leaning against him.

"Do you want me to choose them because it's the right thing to do for my people... because it's what you want... because I'm not what you want?" He pauses, his hands wandering my stomach until they find each other, moving so his entire front is pressed against me. "Or are you scared of what it means if I choose you?"

I'm silent as he whispers that last part, his lips dangerously close to my ear. A shuddering breath escapes my lips as he presses his own on the tender space between my neck and jawline.

"I told you I loved you. You didn't say it back."

This time I turn, staring at the place where my fingers cling to his shirt. My tongue is thick with words I'm dying to say, but can't bring myself to speak.

"I lose everyone I love," I utter, voice sounding as fragile as my bleeding heart.

Miles lowers his forehead to mine so the tips of our noses touch and our breath intermingles as one. "That is not true."

I shake my head, shivering—not because of the cold, but because of his warmth, of his need. His love. "I lost Derek. Rachel. My parents. If I lose anyone else... if I lose you... I'm not sure I could survive it."

"You still have your parents. Rachel is still out there because you saved her. You have Dallas." He strokes my cheek, brushing his lips to my forehead. "And you won't lose me."

My parents may still be here, only fifteen minutes away in our cursed house, but they're gone. The father I believed in, the mother I admired—they're no longer with us, and that sort of mourning is worse than death. I'm watching the shells of the two people I loved most in the world walk around as if they're my family, as if they birthed me and raised me and taught me everything I know about life, only it's not them anymore. Everything that made them who they are is gone.

I'm not in the mood to argue with Miles, though. With everything else, this should be the least of our concerns.

"I've let you choose your path, have never pressured you one way or the other, and I will ultimately accept whatever you decide. So now you must allow me my choice. I hope it never comes to this, but I will defend you against my family if I have to."

"I'm going to go see Dallas," I say, instead of commenting. "I know I shouldn't go home, but I need to see him."

Miles's phone rings before he can respond, and he looks at it strangely.

He holds it out to me, and I take it upon recognizing Elaine's phone number. "Hello?"

"Thank God," she says breathlessly. "Where are you? I've been calling."

"I'm actually on my way to see Dallas." I start walking, and Miles follows, leaning in so he can hear the conversation.

Silence fills the line, and I stop midstride. Miles continues walking but stops when he realizes I've fallen behind.

"Dallas isn't at home," Elaine says. Her voice is steady, but an octave higher than usual.

I put her on speakerphone so Miles can hear better. "Where did he go?"

More silence. For someone who never seems to stop babbling, Elaine's lack of chatter is unnerving. "I don't know. He didn't tell me he was leaving... I was hoping he told you."

I gnaw on my lip and meet Miles's gaze. "He didn't."

"I'm sure he's fine. Elaine, are you at Aspen's house right now?" Miles touches my arm.

"I am."

"Okay, stay there in case he comes back. I'll call my family to see if they've seen him while Aspen and I look around town. He could be at the Manor."

"He's not," I grit, anger steaming in the air around me.

"What is it?" Elaine asks frantically.

Miles watches me curiously.

"Vanesa."

"She wouldn't do that," he assures me. "She may be over the top, but she would never do something like this."

I look at him sincerely, murder in my eyes. "You better hope the hell not."

CHAPTER 18

*O*nly *a deranged, psychopathic human being would kidnap my brother to force my hand.*

This thought swamps my mind with fear and adrenaline as I speed through the woods, remembering that Vanesa is by no means human, and her uncle is Ambrose Draven—a well-known psychopath in my household.

The tiny cabin she brought me to looms in the distance, looking ominous in the sun's retreat. I humored Miles. I searched the town high and low for Dallas while his family checked the Manor, and Elaine stayed put at my house. That proved to be a monstrous waste of time now that I'm right where I wanted to be from the start.

Vanesa was also conveniently absent from the search. Miles went to my house to check on Elaine, still convinced that it's Adrian who has taken my brother. Adrian doesn't strike me as the type to entertain a game of cat and mouse such as this. He has no reason to take my brother. If he wanted to talk to me, he would have sent someone like he has in the past. Kidnapping Dallas doesn't fit his usual habits. Then again, he did use my mom to get to me... I'd be a fool to assume he wouldn't go further than that.

But Vanesa has proven herself time and time again to be the sort of person who does what it takes to get what she wants, disregarding the consequences. And still, Miles denies the possibility of her involvement.

If she's laid a hand on my brother's head, there will be ramifications.

The cabin door is open when I arrive, and I storm through the tall grass, all but ready to rip her head off.

My chest starts to ache though, and I slow down, bending to my knees to catch my breath as sweat trickles down my face. I blink slowly, trying to rid the blurring of my vision when I discover the cause of my disorientation. Ash. Everywhere. Sprinkled into the grass like sand.

I fall backward, lugging my body back through the weeds and inadvertently bringing some of the ash with me. It's stuck to my palms and my forearms, and I claw at it vigorously, wiping myself down with leaves and dirt in attempt to dislodge the particles.

"Ash is a bitch, isn't it? Dallas put that there. Poor guy. I told him I thought he was in danger, and that we'd be safe inside if he spread it through the weeds." Vanesa's voice coos from the cabin and I look up to find her leaning in the doorway, a safe distance away from the poison. It's spread around the entire perimeter. If I could just push past the thick of it though, I might be able to make it inside without passing out. Then I could recover in there before beating her senseless. "I always thought it rather interesting that, when burned down, the thing that can kill us is still our kryptonite."

A nearby tree branch serves as my anchor when I stand,

shakily shifting my weight back to my feet. I'm far enough away from the ash now, but there must be some stuck to my clothes somewhere, because I still feel nauseated.

"Where is he, Vanesa?" I raise my voice, trying to sound braver than I am. She has my brother. My other half. The one person in this world I have always protected above myself, even when protecting him meant lying about what I am.

"He's in there." She points a thumb back into the cabin, but all I see is darkness. If it weren't for the second heartbeat, I wouldn't believe he was here at all.

The air is still, buzzing with electricity as it seems the gods are on the edges of their seats, waiting to see what happens from here.

Fear claws at my gut. Everything is *too* still.

Vanesa digs a heeled boot into the ground, lifting her eyes to lock with mine, and the sky flashes. "I thought about making demands, offering you your brother's safety, and in exchange, you change three new vampires—because let's be honest, we know you could. Rachel was still coherent after you bit her, which is more than I can say for the other poor saps I turned." She examines her nails, a look of pure satisfaction lining her angular features. "But that's a never-ending game, you know? Sure, I could milk that for all it's worth, but to what end? And when you're so reluctant? Besides, do we really want *you* to dictate the terms of every new individual we change? So, I thought this situation required a little more... handling."

"You bit him," I breathe, suddenly feeling lightheaded. "Mark my words Vanesa—" I clench my fists, nails digging in so hard I'm sure they've drawn blood "—the minute it rains, and all of this ash is washed away, I am going to kill you."

Thunder rumbles above, enhancing my threat.

She shrugs carelessly. "You left me no choice. You don't give in under pressure, and you've never let any of us talk you into doing something you don't want to—I mean, we're facing extinction and you won't lend a hand because what we need you to do is *immoral.* I had to make you *want* to help us. And it worked, didn't it?"

I grit my teeth, so angry that words won't justify what I'm feeling. What I want to do to her. How I want to tear her apart.

How could she do this? How could she bite my brother knowing full well the others are hardly surviving the venom coursing through their veins? She could have backed me into a corner, threatened him, beat him until I submitted and tested the change, but no. She had to change him on her own, despite the consequences, so that I'd have no choice but to help her. To break the curse for good. Because it seems even I don't have the power to reverse the effects of her venom.

If I want to save Dallas, I have to give Vanesa what she wants.

And every vampire in this town will then be free to kill whoever they want.

∽

Thunder rumbles as I hold my position outside of the cabin, impatiently waiting for the rain to fall. Once it does, once the ash is washed away, Vanesa will stop breathing.

Being a vampire intensifies everything, not just senses and hunger, but emotions like passion, hope, love, fury, and hatred. Right now, I'm feeling each of them at once, all intermingled and swirling from my chest to my fingertips, which itch to dive into her eye sockets and rip them out.

Vanesa has always tested my patience and made unforgivable mistakes, but this is far beyond anything she's done before. I never would have expected such an irrational decision from her, but I suppose that's what I get for underestimating her. I pushed her buttons. I denied her everything she thought she deserved, and this is her way of making me pay for it.

Miles was wrong. I do lose everyone I love. Regardless of this outcome, I'll lose my brother as I know him. And once I get my way with Vanesa, I'll lose Miles, too.

Two sets of feet move in my direction, and I'm almost relieved, thinking it's Miles and Elaine, until I realize they're trying much too hard to be quiet.

My fingers search the ground for something I can use as a weapon, when a booming voice cuts through the night, "Adrian would like to speak with you."

"Tell him I'm busy." I find a rock, tossing it between my hands carelessly.

The two men come into view, then exchange a look, moving to either side of me. "I'm afraid that is not an option. We are to return with you at once."

I stand, and they stiffen, clearly not as violent as the others Adrian has sent. Maybe he's attempting a different approach after our last encounter. It might have proven to be effective, too, if my brother wasn't facing imminent death, and I wasn't waiting out this storm in order to exact my revenge. "Tell Adrian I don't answer to him."

"We've been advised to use force if necessary," one man says, swallowing nervously. I see news of my last encounter with his vampires has gotten around.

"And I said I'm busy at the moment." They look between

each other. "My brother is in danger. He wouldn't be if Adrian would have removed himself from town instead of looming around like a threat. Except, it doesn't seem as though he intends to wipe out the Dravens just yet, so remind me again, why should I adhere to his requests?"

"He requires your presence, Ms. Troy." The bigger of the two grabs my arm. His grip is strong, but he still seems uncertain.

"I am not coming with you. So, either you leave without me, or I kill you both."

"I would listen to her, boys. She's a real maniac." Vanesa has appeared at the doorway once more, looking like death in the glow of the night sky. Their heads whip in her direction, and they move forward ever so slightly. Actually, if they moved a little farther…

"Tell Adrian if he and the Twelve want my family dead so they can keep their influence over our kind, then he should probably show his face occasionally. A shadow isn't much of a threat." She steps out onto the porch, away from the safety of the cabin, and leans against the outer wall, crossing her ankles lazily.

The vampires most likely perceive this as her arrogance, but I know better—the ash is stronger now that she's crossed the threshold, and it's more than she can bear standing up.

"How happy would he be if you brought back, not just Aspen Troy, but a full-blooded Draven?"

Adrian's men move forward, pushing aside the weeds as they navigate their way toward Vanesa, looking hungry for power.

She's right. If they return with not one, but two members of the Draven clan, they would be in for a generous promotion.

After a few steps, they falter, looking around hazily as their knees weaken. The bigger man grabs on to the smaller one, and they wind up falling to the ground, coughing. They crawl back toward me the same way I did only a half hour ago, and I stand above them, wooden stake in hand. I'd brought it with me for Vanesa, but in case these two have any bright ideas, it'll work just the same on them.

"Tell Adrian I am busy." I clench my knuckles around the wood. The two of them nod, stumbling and retreating the way they came.

"You should have killed them," Vanesa says. "Sends a louder message."

I just watch her, wondering why in the world she felt compelled to come out here and help me. I've made it perfectly clear that I will end her the moment I can reach her without crumpling in agony from the ash.

Reading my thoughts, she rolls her eyes. "Don't flatter yourself. I need you alive for this to work."

Several footsteps crunch through the woods, growing louder as they near where I'm sitting with my back against the tree, staring at the cabin door. My eyes haven't left it since Vanesa went inside, and I have half a mind to start pelting rocks at the windows in hopes of hitting her with one. If it weren't for the possibility of accidentally hitting Dallas, I would have done it by now.

The Draven siblings come into view, and once they get close enough, they stagger backward, green in the face from the poison on the ground. Vira latches on to Elliot's shoulder for support, coughing violently and turning away from everyone to catch her breath. "What the hell? Why is there ash everywhere?"

All five of them shift uncomfortably on their feet, looking wary. The only person unaffected is Elaine, who stands off to the side and watches them curiously.

"What is this? Why are we here?" Elliot asks, clearing his throat. He tries to mask his discomfort with irritation, but even he looks ready to pass out.

"And how are you sitting so close to it?" Lucas asks me, taking long, controlled breaths in attempt to help him withstand the pain.

My eyes drop to the grass. Four, maybe five feet away from me is where the ash line begins. I can feel its effects, but not nearly as much as the others clearly do. If I had to, I could probably move closer and still manage to stay upright.

"I found Dallas," I say hollowly, lifting my eyes to watch their expressions. Elaine and Miles immediately look relieved, but the others still seem confused, glancing between each other anxiously.

I texted both Miles and Elaine the coordinates to the cabin after Adrian's men retreated and Vanesa went inside. I wouldn't tell them why or if I'd found Dallas. I didn't even answer the phone when Miles called. If I had, I might have lost it, and I need them to see this firsthand—*see her*. What she's done. Who she really is. Otherwise, I'm not sure they'd ever believe me.

"Where is he?" Vira asks. She looks skeptical as her eyes roam the area around us, nothing but trees for a mile in every direction.

"In there." I nod toward the cabin, picking up a rock and

rolling it between my fingers. I'm afraid if I don't occupy them, I might hit someone.

The air around us is thick with silence. Our senses are weakened by the ash, so they can't smell Vanesa or Dallas, but their hearing should be working fine.

Elaine moves toward me since she's the only other person who can get this close to the ash without crumbling in pain. "Aspen, what's going on?"

"Why don't you ask Vanesa?" I cross my arms, squeezing the rock so tight in my hand that it slices my skin.

Miles shakes his head slowly. "Aspen, she would never hurt your brother. We don't even know where she is right now."

"Wait…" Vira says, but is interrupted by Elliot.

"Besides, kidnapping Dallas would only annoy her to death."

Miles nods along, and Vira orders her brothers to be quiet again, but Miles ignores her. "This must be Adrian trying to—"

"*Stop talking,*" Vira snaps, dipping her head with a look of concentration. She braces herself, taking two steps closer to the ash. "Do you hear that?"

"Two heartbeats," Danielle says in a short breath. She swallows hard and closes her eyes like she's in pain.

"So?" Elliot says. "What does that have to do with anything?"

Vira shakes her head rapidly, a horrified expression on her face. "I don't understand."

I look at her plainly. "Yes, you do."

"She wouldn't…" Vira looks at her siblings for backup, voice sounding shaky and unsure. "You can't be serious. She— she would *never*…"

"Ask her yourself." I raise my voice, getting to my feet. "Ask her if she *bit my brother* so I'd be forced to help you create more vampires. Go ahead. She's right inside."

"No," Lucas says, running a hand down his face. "She's done a lot of questionable things, but she wouldn't go this far."

Danielle is ghostly white, biting her lower lip and glancing nervously up at Lucas.

"How can you defend her?" I ask, shaking with anger. "You know her better than anyone else. Vanesa lives for taking things too far, and you're in denial if you think otherwise."

I take a step closer and Miles reaches for me, taking my hand and trying to tug me toward him.

I yank out of his grasp with so much force that I stumble backward toward the ash, but he grabs my wrist before I fall and jerks me back to safety.

The anger I felt earlier is fading now, and I'm suddenly really overwhelmed by everything that's happened. Pressure builds in my throat and my nose starts to sting, but I swallow the urge to cry. The last thing I want to do is get upset in front of the Draven siblings, especially when Vanesa is no doubt listening from the cabin, hanging onto every word. "Don't comfort me—*do* something. Help Dallas. I told you this was Vanesa's doing and you didn't believe me. He could *die*, Miles— do you understand that? My brother could die because of your stupid family, and I can't even get to him."

I can't hold in my emotions anymore and my tears fall freely. I wipe them away harshly with the material of my shirt, then clench my fists tight at my sides and take a shuddering breath, attempting to rein in my emotions.

No one knows how to react, and I can see how badly Miles wants to comfort me, but he doesn't know how. He glances hauntingly at the cabin and then back at me, distressed and heartbroken.

Finally, he purses his lips and closes his eyes. "Vanesa," he says in a low voice.

It's like time stands still as we all stare at the front door, waiting for her to reveal herself. A few seconds pass, and I'm suddenly afraid that she might cower inside to make me look like a delusional fool, but then the door creaks, opening ever so slowly.

Vanesa comes into view and doesn't appear to be the least bit remorseful for what she's done. Even still, the arrogance she wore earlier has vanished.

She looks at me first, tilting her head to the side in exhaustion. "Are you always this overdramatic?"

"I swear to God, Vanesa—"

"You bit Dallas?" Danielle gapes, on the verge of tears.

Vanesa licks her bottom lip and lifts a shoulder innocently. "It was the only way."

"What is *wrong* with you? Those other innocent people weren't enough? Being able to feed again wasn't *enough* for you?"

"Don't you dare judge me," Vanesa sneers. "We've all done terrible things."

"Not like this. Not to someone we care about," Lucas says. Tension rolls off him in waves as he grits his teeth, unable to look at his sister. "You've taken things too far, Van. Just—way too far."

"Maybe, but I don't *care* about Aspen or her brother. That's the difference. I care about our family, our clan—our survival. Nothing else matters."

Elaine scoffs, gritting her teeth. "You're sick."

"And you're pathetic," Vanesa says, unfazed by her meaningless insult.

"So are you," Miles says, putting his arm around my waist to guide me away from here.

I shake my head vehemently. "I'm not leaving."

"There's nothing you can do for him now. We will come back once the ash washes away, I promise."

I nod shortly. What I don't say is that I was already planning to come back—and he's not going to like what I have in mind for when I do.

Vanesa stomps her foot angrily and crosses her arms. "Would you all stop acting like this is the end of the world? Once again, I did what the rest of you didn't have the nerve to." When everyone simply stares at her like she's a stranger, she turns her attention to the only person who always agrees with her unorthodox methods. "Elliot—you know this was necessary. Everything I do is necessary for us to survive."

Elliot looks torn, and for the first time, he doesn't seem so sure of himself. "I don't know, Van. This is extreme."

"You're kidding me—she's gotten to you, too? You'd choose her over your own flesh and blood?"

"Of course not," he says instantly. "But all you've done is give us another mess to clean up. There are other ways."

"*All I've done* is ensure our survival. Aspen will never let her brother die—she has to help us now."

"I don't have to do anything!" I snap, wishing so badly that I could get my hands on her.

Vanesa pouts her lips sadly. "It's cute that you think you still have a choice."

Miles has his arms around me before I can charge at her, and Vira comes to his assistance, holding me in place as I struggle to break free. More than ever, I want to tear Vanesa to pieces.

Collectively, the siblings guide me away from the cabin, and the graphic images flashing through my mind are all that keep me from fighting them with everything I have. They're a promise of what's to come when it rains and I can finally get my hands on Vanesa's skinny little neck. They're a promise of revenge.

CHAPTER 19

"*J* don't care if you shove ash down her throat," I yell. "She took my brother. She *turned* him knowing he'd probably die. No punishment will serve her right."

Danielle gives my hand a squeeze. "We will make this right, Aspen. I promise. No harm will come to your brother."

"It already has," I exasperate, yanking my hand away. "His life will never be the same."

If he doesn't change, he will never be safe, and there's no precedent as to how long a transitioner can survive in that state, because any that avoid making the choice are killed first. And if he does change, no matter where he goes, he won't be able to hide from what he is so long as bloodthirsty hunger boils in his veins.

"And what of the others she turned? How are they?" I direct my question to Elliot, who drops his gaze, muscles flexing with tension.

Vira answers instead. "The woman had a seizure and died this afternoon. Look, you can do whatever you want to Vanesa

—at this point, I think we can all agree she has it coming—but you cannot kill her. We won't allow it."

"Fine," I relinquish. "But if you're wrong, if we can't fix this and Dallas dies, so does she."

"Aspen," Miles says, touching my wrist.

"A life for a life, Miles. Don't you always say there has to be a balance?"

Lucas looks intently around the room. The Draven siblings are all here—minus Vanesa—and Gwen and Owen are here as well, which Elaine was less than thrilled about when she arrived. "For now, let us worry about what we can control. Has anyone come to you with new ideas, Gwen?"

"A few," she says, though unenthusiastically. "Most are simple remedies—our blood, our venom. Someone suggested feeding them a human to test the full turn. But I doubt it's just the transition stage that's faltering. None of that can be done without experimentation, and the last man who drank our blood died, if I'm correct?"

"Yes, experimentation is out of the question." Elliot crosses his arms, and the vein in his thick neck pulses. "We only have one transitioner left, anyhow—two counting Dallas. If they are to die in experimentation, I'd rather it be because we thought we found a real cure, not because we were carelessly injecting them with our fluids. Our solution is not going to be basic. The curse itself has already proven to be more complex than we thought."

"Then how is it that one of you turned her without an issue?" Owen asks, tapping his fingers on the arm of Elaine's chair. She stares at them viscously, then rolls her eyes at his existence.

"We think my ancestor's blood was part binding agent of

the curse. He fled shortly after it was complete, so it would make sense that he was the key." Some of my previous anger at Vanesa simmers now that we're doing something other than talking ourselves in circles. It's not much, but it feels like we're getting somewhere now. "Elaine, didn't you say you found something the other night?"

Her eyes spark, and she stands, pulling her ancestor's journal from her purse. "Yeah. I noticed that two of the pages were stuck together, and this was in between." She moves toward the center of the room, and Elliot meets her, examining the page. "It looks like a riddle, but it's incomplete."

"A nursery rhyme isn't going to solve this, Elaine." Elliot dismisses her, leaning back against the wall. Her nostrils flare, and she clenches her teeth, slamming the book shut.

"We don't know *what* can help us. You said we need out of the ordinary. An incomplete riddle stuck between two pages in the journal my ancestor wrote around the time the curse took effect doesn't seem crazy to me. I found it between two entries in 1804."

"Did your little journal ever mention someone like Aspen coming along? Or his best friend Elijah Troy who fled the country, who was somehow involved in the curse?"

She quirks her head to the side, face souring at Elliot's bad attitude. "No, but—"

"Exactly. If he knew any more than the rest of us, chances are he would have mentioned it somewhere."

"Or maybe that was the point," she argues, settling back in her chair.

He sighs, cracking his knuckles. "You shouldn't even be here. Your ancestor specifically wanted out of our business for good reason. It is no place for a human."

"That was his choice. For his family at the time. Not mine. He helped a lot of people by protecting your secrets, and I want to continue that legacy." She crosses her legs, and a look of satisfaction dances in her eyes. "Besides, Aspen needs another morally right person on her side, or the lot of you will murder the whole town."

"Why don't we all get some rest and reconvene in the morning?" Vira eyes the room, daring us to question her. We don't. "Let's meet at Aspen's house around eight. If we keep piling in here Adrian is bound to think we're up to something. Besides, I'm sure you want to check on your parents, and we should probably compel them again since it doesn't seem to be working too well. I'd also like to stop at the cabin and talk to Vanesa in the morning. We can head to your house right after with an update on Dallas."

I nod, glancing at Elaine. "Did you clean the ash?"

"As much as I could while your parents were sleeping. There's bound to be some lodged in the hardwood, though."

Our little group breaks apart, and Danielle pulls me in for an unnecessary hug. "We will fix this, okay? We won't let him die."

I give her a squeeze and lead the way outside with Miles following behind me. I'm sure he didn't appreciate my promise to kill Vanesa any more than the rest of his family, even if he disagrees with her methods. At the end of the day, what she's doing is in their best interest, and what I'm doing is in mine and my family's.

He walks past me, opposite of where he parked his truck. "Miles?"

Reaching into his pocket, he pulls out a set of keys, tossing them to me. "You can take the truck. I need some air."

I call for him again, but his back is to me. He sighs, turning around and pulling me into his arms.

"I love you." He kisses my forehead. "I just need a minute."

Miles's truck is clunky, roughly bouncing over every pebble and pothole on the short ride to his house behind town, shielded by a mask of pine trees. I grip the steering wheel, cursing when I hit the unfinished driveway with my teeth rattling from the vibrations of the motor. I can't recall the last time I drove a vehicle, much less a truck this size. It's a three-seater with an open tailgate, but it's roomy and exceptionally high off the ground.

I was hoping Miles would be back by the time I got here—I even drove around in circles a few times—but it doesn't look like it. He said he needed some air, so I assumed that meant he would walk home. Except vampires are freakishly faster than, well, anything else, and he easily could have walked for five minutes and then hightailed it home, still arriving before me.

I lock the door behind me, throwing my purse on the counter and slumping into the couch. Did he mean for me to take his truck home instead of his house? I never said where I planned to go, though home would make sense given Elaine cleaned. But my mother is still a flight risk. She might try to hurt me again, and Dallas won't be there to stop her this time.

Leaning over, I thumb through Miles's record collection, admiring his taste in music. It's not often you find someone who enjoys the classics nowadays, though I suppose he lived through the debut of them all, so it makes sense that he would harbor a soft spot for them. Sighing, I slide a Bread vinyl out of its sleeve, placing the needle down on the fourth track, "Everything I Own."

I rest my eyelids, listening as the music ticks the time away. Every minute Miles doesn't come walking through the door is another minute I worry. Anything could happen out there. If he hadn't shown up outside my house the last time he was attacked, who knows what would have happened to him.

I turn the dial all the way up to fill the small house with music, then I make my way upstairs as I unbutton my shirt. In the bathroom, I undress, taking advantage of the scalding water that pours from the shower head. I haven't had a true shower since I lived in Colorado. It's hit or miss with the hot water tank in my house, and since I'm usually the last to shower, I never get the latter.

Sudsing up my hair, I run my fingers through it thoroughly, making sure I get all of the dirt and grime out from the past two days. When I'm satisfied, I turn the nozzle off, drying my hair and sliding into clean sweatpants and a t-shirt. After combing my knotted hair, I pick up my clothes from where I discarded them on the toilet seat before my shower, and whip open the door.

"Jesus," I gasp, almost dropping my dirty clothes. Miles is standing before me, ridiculously close to the bathroom door. If it opened the other way, I would have hit him square in the face.

He looks worn down. His eyes are far away, and his face sags tiredly. Even his shoulders are drooping like a wilted flower. His shirt is littered with small dots, which means the rain must have finally begun. I try not to think about what that means, because after taking a little time to reflect, I'm not sure what my next move is. What I realized during my hot shower is that if I kill a Draven, I might as well off myself next because they'd never stop hunting me.

"Come here." This time I do drop my clothes so I can wrap my arms around him. His warm hands circle my back, and his chin dips so his face can burrow in my neck. He shudders, tangling his hands in my wet hair.

"I won't kill her," I promise, very reluctantly. "I will make her wish she was dead. But I won't kill her."

"Why not?" he asks, baffling me. I try to lean back so I can gauge his expression, but he's firmly snuggled into me and is making no effort to detach. "I would if I were you. I wouldn't even hesitate."

"Killing her would only hurt you, and I don't want that." I sigh, shifting my feet against his weight. I'm basically the only thing keeping him upright. "And no matter how horrible they've been, I don't want to hurt your family, either. Killing Vanesa would punish everyone but her. She did this. She bit Dallas."

"I know. I'm so sorry." He kisses my mark, lifting me and carrying me to the bed where he nestles us under a quilt.

"Vanesa is not your responsibility." I touch his cheek, positioning my own so it lays on the pillow next to him. "I just... you say you choose me, and yet, you didn't believe me when I told you it had to be Vanesa who kidnapped Dallas."

His hair brushes my forehead as he shakes his head. "I didn't want it to be true. And I knew that if one of us was somehow responsible for Dallas getting hurt... then everything bad that has happened to you really is because of my family."

"Hey." I poke his ribs and he startles, bewildered eyes finding mine. "Elijah did this to me, not you. This is his fault if we're assigning blame. But even he was only trying to do the right thing by stopping your uncle."

"That doesn't change the fact that—"

"I'd be dead if you hadn't smelled my blood in the field that night? That you quite literally brought me back to life and continued to protect me and respect my wishes despite having every reason not to?" I poke his ribs again, and this time he grabs my finger, folding it in his hand. "Things are awful right now. And yes, a lot of it has to do with your insanely complicated family, but it's better than being dead, which is exactly what I would be right now if it weren't for you. So stop feeling guilty."

He looks at me then, his eyes serious. "Only if you do."

I sigh, turning my eyes to the ceiling.

"What's happening to Dallas is not your fault."

"I know that," I say, though it doesn't make me feel like any less of a terrible sister. My involvement with Miles unintentionally turned Dallas's life upside-down as well, and now he's in some sort of weird paranormal coma. "He's strong, he'll be all right."

Right about now, his strength is the only thing I'm counting on.

CHAPTER 20

*I*magining a world where there is hope and tranquility has grown increasingly difficult in recent months. For a glorious while there was silence—from the hunters, the clans, the police—there were no prominent reasons that forced us to look over our shoulders. If I could go back and sprinkle each of our current problems gradually throughout the past few months, I would, because it seems as though the universe is closing in on us all at once.

Every time I have a slight clue as to what is going on, as to who I am, something comes along and reminds me that I'm as lost in this world as I would be without sight. Sure, there are ways around seeing, but that requires learning—no, *relearning* the fundaments of living out your everyday life until it begins to feel normal again.

Dark clouds coat the blue sky above as a looming reminder that our troubles are only beginning. I'm worried about how my parents will react to seeing me again, specifically my mom after what she tried to do. And I know Elaine took care of the ash, but I still worry that all of us being in my tiny house together is a recipe for disaster.

Miles left early this morning to help his siblings with their research on the curse, but from what he told me, they haven't had any progress. He offered for me to come, but after I promised I'd murder their sister last night, I'm not sure that would be in my best interest. Besides, they're wasting their time. Elliot, however painful this is for me to admit, was right when he said an ordinary solution will not be the answer to our problems. We're missing something big, and until we understand how the curse was manufactured, we won't be able to reverse it. We're aimlessly searching for answers but haven't the slightest clue where to look.

With all of this on my mind, I plaster on a smile to greet my parents. Father sits on the couch, glasses I haven't seen him wear in months slid down to the tip of his nose, eyes looking over them as he reads a newspaper. He hardly looks up when I walk inside... that is, until he notices I'm not alone.

"Aspen. It's nice of you to come home," he remarks, turning the page. I waited twenty minutes for Miles outside before I would even consider stepping foot in this place. After last time, there's no way I was walking in here alone.

I stomp down my elevating irritation, holding a fake smile in place. At least he noticed I was gone. "Where's Mom?"

"Sleeping." He yawns and flips his wrist to check his watch. It's about seven forty-five in the morning, fifteen minutes before we're supposed to meet. "Who is he?"

"This is Miles. He joined us for breakfast a few months ago...?"

Father's eyes search the air, staring at nothing in particular while he tries to remember. After a few long moments, he shrugs, going back to the words before him. I shake my head, motioning for Miles to follow me upstairs.

"I have a few more friends coming, so you know," I say to my father, though I'm still not sure he's listening at all. I suppose some things even a two-hundred-year-old evil vampire can't change—my father's inability to pay attention when I'm speaking to him. Even when he was still himself, before Derek, before Ambrose, he never listened to a word I said. If it didn't involve one of my brothers, he was disinterested.

"The others were right behind me. They should be here any minute." Miles opens the study door for me, and we both slip inside as quietly as possible. "Elliot will compel your parents before we get started."

"Is Vanesa coming?" I worry.

He shakes his head. "She won't leave the cabin. Vira tried. Even Elliot tried to talk her down. He wants her to bring Dallas's body back to the Manor because they're both safer there, but she won't budge."

I shiver at his choice of words. *Dallas's body.* It makes it sound like he's a corpse that needs to be removed from a crime scene.

The floor beneath me groans when the front door opens— no knock, no warning. I hear their footsteps on the stairs and brace myself for what's to come. What Vanesa does is not their fault, and I momentarily forgot that. We are not the actions of someone we associate with.

They file into the room one by one, each looking exceptionally glib and weary, eyeing the room like it's filled with poison. I often forget they used to come here frequently as kids, while Edgar and Ambrose met with the other clan heads to discuss business. I've always gotten the impression that they held quite the influence with the clans, since the meetings always seemed to take place on their territory and no one else's. Though, I suppose that influence came from their father and grandfather, who were on the council first.

Elliot is the last to come upstairs after he reinforces my parents' compulsion. No one says a word, and I begin to wonder why we're meeting to begin with. I doubt anyone had an epiphany overnight. The only reason I'm sure they actually care what happens to Dallas is because I *know* they care what happens to Vanesa. Right now, my threat on her life is their only motivator other than their freedom. At least this way, I have the control—or at least, I have the illusion of control. When it comes to the Dravens, I'm not sure there's much anyone could do to overpower their will.

One last set of footsteps pounce up the creaking stairs and Elaine comes into view, looking refreshed but apprehensive when all heads turn in her direction. Her eyes skate the room and I know exactly who she's looking for, but Owen isn't here. Apparently, Elliot didn't think it was appropriate for the clan to be involved in every step of the research process, even if we are desperately relying on their help.

Danielle tilts her head to the side, staring at the wall behind me. Her eyes are fixated on something I can't see. I hope that means she's really thinking about how to save my brother's life, because I have absolutely no new ideas other than experimenting with what we already have and are almost positive won't work—with what could kill another human being.

"Anything?" Lucas asks, folding his hands in front of him as he leans casually against a chair. We each look around, and with every blank stare I meet, my hopes fall a little farther until I'm so discouraged I feel like crying.

How am I supposed to save Dallas? I've survived the impossible so many times by chance but have absolutely no idea how to possibly save my brother.

"I could have sworn…" Danielle drifts off, lost in thought. The others ignore her, rolling their eyes when Elaine suggests once again that we consider the riddle she found.

"For the last time—"

"Don't even call it a nursery rhyme," she warns, cutting Elliot off. "So help me. How can you turn down even the slight possibility that I might be onto something?"

"Because you're not. Your ancestor has yet to leave you anything of actual use, and suddenly you think he might hold all the answers?"

"It is doubtful," Vira agrees. "He wouldn't know a curse from a crystal ball. Not even our parents knew how the curse was orchestrated."

"But Elijah Troy did," Elaine argues, leveling with Vira's stare. "And Elijah Troy was best friends with my ancestor."

"Just let it go." Vira crosses her arms and rolls her dark-lined eyes.

Elaine looks to me for backup. It seems unlikely that her nurs—riddle—will solve anything, but stranger things have happened.

"Try to figure out what it means," I suggest. Her eyes light up, gleaming in satisfaction when she looks back at Elliot. He crosses his arms, biting his inner cheek. "Don't give it all of your effort, but if you can decipher it... who knows? Maybe it will be helpful."

Vira yawns and uses a purple nail to tuck a dark strand of hair behind her ear. "This is a waste of time."

I pin her with a stare. Her reacquainted attitude is not lost on me. "Have you got any better ideas?"

Her jaw tics, but she says nothing, turning to Elliot. "Maybe we should reach out to Adrian, convince him we're not a threat."

He looks at her stupidly. "We are a threat—or at least we will be."

"I know that," she snaps, hand on hip. "But it might buy us more time to figure out our little survival situation."

Her brother nods once, and Miles agrees. "We have to try everything we can. Reaching out to Adrian might give him pause."

"Or he'll see right through our ruse and execute us on the spot." Lucas puffs out his lips, giving a little shrug.

Danielle gives him a sour look, then takes a step away from our small circle, still studying the wall behind me. Her fingers slide along it, and she turns to her siblings, curiously eyeing the architecture. "I remember this room being so much larger," she says thoughtfully.

"We were a lot smaller back then, sister," Vira responds.

She shakes her head, not ready to submit her argument just yet. "No, I'm serious. I could have sworn... we used to run around here, remember? We'd play tag while Dad and Uncle Ambrose did business downstairs."

"Danielle—" Vira drags, looking tired.

Elliot steps forward, placing his own hand against the wall.

"I think you're right. Remember, there was a long structural beam along the back wall."

Danielle smirks. "This isn't that wall."

Elliot knocks on the wall, then pulls out a pocket knife and slides it between two wooden panels.

"What are you...?" Before I can blink, he's ripping it out of the wall and setting it aside on the couch. He peers through the opening, and then uses both hands to pry the next piece of wood away, discarding this one on the floor. "Elliot, you can't just take apart my house."

He grunts in response, continuing to work until there's a large enough opening to climb through. My annoyance is replaced with intrigue when I notice that the study extends about another six feet. Light spills through the hole, revealing a small space coated in dust and cobwebs. I can already tell there's a lot of water damage on the floor from before I had the roof fixed.

"Why was this blocked off?" Elaine asks, sticking her head between mine and Elliot's for a better look.

"Ambrose was busy," Vira says. Her heels click on the floor as she shoves us all aside, lifting a knee through the opening. "There's a desk here," she grunts, hoisting herself up and slowly easing her weight onto the probably very un-sturdy piece of furniture. She puts a hand up to her face, blinking rapidly as the dust she disturbed settles back around her.

"What do you see?" Danielle asks, rising to her tiptoes so she has a better vantage point.

Vira coughs, swatting the air and leaning her head backward before she walks into a cobweb. "Dust. Darkness. Some old furniture. So help me, if I crawled in here for nothing..."

"It can't be nothing if it was boarded up," Lucas points out. "Look for anything out of place, a loose floorboard, maybe."

Vira halts, swiveling her neck so she can see her brother. "They're all loose, Einstein. This room hasn't seen life in the better part of two hundred years."

She sidesteps the mush and sunken-in wood at the center and moves around to the far wall.

"Wait, why would Ambrose hide anything in here? He couldn't have known Aspen wasn't the answer," Danielle says.

I bite my lip, craning my neck to see more of the old room. "She's right. He thought killing me was the key, not changing me. I was his last chance at freedom."

"Elijah maybe?" Elaine suggests, but even she looks skeptical. He left in such a hurry, so suddenly and unbeknownst to anyone, that I doubt he had time to build a wall that hides a quarter of his study.

"Maybe it was Elaine's ancestor," Elliot offers smugly, shooting her a side glance. "He seems to be pretty important."

She smirks, then says as evenly as possible, "You know, with your charmed personality it's a wonder the clans held off on killing you for so long."

"Guys," Miles intervenes. "We're losing focus."

Elaine stares at Elliot for a moment longer, then tears her gaze from him. "What does it matter who put up the wall anyway? We just need to know if there's anything of use inside."

I shake my head, hoisting a leg through the opening and struggling to find my balance on the desk that sits below it. It's going to take me a while to get used to my vampiric abilities. Vira climbed through here with such grace, and I'm struggling to hold my own weight.

"It matters," I grunt, leaning on my hip before I ease my feet to the ground, "because whoever cared enough to hide this part of the room might know something more about the curse than we do. And if that's the case, then we at least have somewhere solid to start looking for answers, instead of searching cluelessly like we've been."

Elliot clears his throat. "For instance, if we found something that leads us back to Timothy Graves, then we'd know where to focus our energy."

"I get it asshat. You think I'm irrelevant."

"I don't *think*," he remarks.

"That part is obvious," Elaine quips before he can continue. "You know, you're so neck deep in your own—"

"Miles is right. This—" Danielle waves her arms around "—isn't helping anyone."

Vira sidesteps another weak spot on the floor—how she even knows where to look for them is beyond me, but it's as if she can tell how sturdy it is simply by pressing the tip of her toes to it. "A few lighthearted insults never hurt anyone."

"What about Emile?" I change the subject, moving carefully to a bookshelf on the wall closest to me.

Vira raises an eyebrow, looking displeased with my mention of her sister. Her eyes skate to my necklace, then revert back to the floor stretching before her. "What about her?"

"Who else had access to this house? Elijah lived here, Ambrose was banished here—"

Vira stops short, her neck snapping toward me. "You're not suggesting my sister did this."

"Between the two of you, the stupidity is astounding," Elliot mumbles, gesturing between me and Elaine. Lucas shoots him a disapproving look, and Miles clenches his jaw but says nothing, waiting for me to continue. But Elliot beats me to it. "Emile never saw Ambrose again after he was banished here. She wanted to remember him as the man he was, not the one he became."

"Yes, but you thought he *became* that man because of the curse. He did, I suppose, in a way, but you didn't know the full story. You didn't know about all of the innocent lives he took. There was no memory of his to preserve for Emile because he'd already tarnished it."

"Your point?" Vira asks, sounding bored.

I roll my eyes, hating that since she feels she no longer owes me, she's back to being her prickly self. I'm not looking forward to when I have both her *and* Vanesa in the same room again. Although, when that happens, I'm sure they'll be prying my thumbs out of Vanesa's eye sockets, so there won't be time for me to be annoyed by both of them.

"My point is that she knew more about the curse than you did, and possibly more than Ambrose himself. When he attacked me, he said that she's the one who turned him in. That Elijah caught him killing humans and confided in her. What if that's not all he told her? What if she boarded up this room after he fled in order to preserve any traces of the curse so that no one could ever break it? No one expected Ambrose to kill himself. He would have lived forever with plenty of time to explore the house."

"Why would Elijah leave anything behind that could help us?" Lucas asks, genuinely interested. "If I was in his position, I would have made sure to bury everything I'd done. Not just for the curse's sake, but for my safety. If Ambrose ever got out, he would have tracked Elijah down."

"Exactly." Miles grabs Lucas' shoulder. "Where would you hide something you never want found?"

"The last place they'd look," Danielle says, blinking rapidly.

"But that means nothing because Emile never came back here. She swore to me that she never visited him after they locked him away. She told me it was too hard." Elliot runs a hand down his face.

Danielle touches his arm, and her eyes soften. "Emile died here, Elliot—and yes, I know that's because she was lured by a hunter, but still. Ambrose died a long, *long* time ago. It only makes sense that she'd want closure. Maybe she came back here and found something. Or maybe she boarded up the room before the Twelve bound Ambrose to the house."

"There are a lot of maybe's circulating right now." Elliot clenches his teeth. "Emile may have been the reason we were cursed, but I'm sure she did everything in her power to find a way to break it, not conceal the answers we need."

"Mayb—*it's possible* that she thought it was for the best in case Ambrose ever escaped. Besides now, our lives have been fairly quiet since then, and other than the hunters, we haven't been bothered in a century."

"Stop making up excuses just to explain what you want to be true," Elliot says, then turns and walks out of the room, slamming the door behind him, and then our front door after that.

Danielle lowers her eyes, then looks helplessly at Lucas. He ruffles his blonde hair, heaving a sigh. "Just give him a minute. You know Emile is a touchy subject."

"That doesn't mean he can blindly ignore the truth—or the possibility of it, at least. It's a touchy subject for all of us,"

Danielle says, then excuses herself from the room. "Let me know if you guys find anything."

I nod, glancing at Elaine, who seems just as uncomfortable as me.

Neither of us have ever seen Elliot so... emotional. So... human.

CHAPTER 21

*V*ira and I explored the remainder of the small space but didn't find anything that seemed out of the ordinary. Just a lot of old trinkets and ancient books filled with dust and mildew from the leaky roof. We searched high and low for engravings in the walls or hidden compartments. Lucas even convinced us to check beneath some of the floorboards just in case there was in fact anything stored inside them, but we came up empty. Nothing but dust-coated surfaces and darkness lie within the hidden room, which doesn't seem right, considering it was boarded up in a way that makes me think no one was ever meant to discover it.

"That was an incredibly disgusting waste of time," Vira says, unhappily combing spiderwebs out of her thick hair. "Are we all in agreement that we should approach Adrian to buy ourselves time?"

Miles and Lucas nod.

"It's settled then. I'll send Elliot to contact him once he's calmed down."

"Are you sure Elliot is the best person to send?" Elaine asks, looking unconvinced.

"I don't recall asking for your opinion," Vira chides, brushing off her hands. "But yes, he's in charge of family ordeals when our parents are away, making him the acting head of our clan, and the sole person in the world with the power to negotiate for us."

Nerves flutter in my stomach at the thought of Elliot dealing with Adrian. I know I'm new around here, and I have complete faith that Elliot knows how to handle himself, but the clans have spent the better part of two centuries despising the Dravens and everything they stand for. I'm not sure Elliot is the best person to appeal to Adrian's empathetic side.

"I don't think Adrian will be willing to speak with him," I warn, but even Lucas seems to think otherwise.

"Elliot is smart. He watched our father handle affairs with many of the Twelve before the rest of us had even become vampires. He'll know what to do better than anyone else."

"We need Adrian to trust him when he says we're not a threat. Elliot is strong, capable, and undeniably confident, but these are qualities that are likely to set Adrian off and make him doubt our intentions," I reason.

If say, Vira were to speak on Elliot's behalf, there's a better chance he would believe her enough to hopefully second guess his plans.

"You shouldn't doubt my brother." Vira sighs heavily. Dark circles I hadn't noticed before deepen the black eyeliner around her eyes. "Being part of a clan means there are times when you must trust someone else to handle things instead of involving yourself. The chain of command exists for a reason."

"They are reasonable concerns, Vira." Miles steps in,

earning a long look from his sister. "It causes us no harm to listen to another's opinion."

"Until it costs us our lives. The faith of our people. I've been considering Aspen's for months because I owed her that much for saving my life and yours, but we are not a democracy, and if our followers see us scrambling to keep ourselves together, they will lose faith. If we're taking turns playing leader, who will they listen to when we tell them not to kidnap her, force her hand, threaten her family?" Vira pauses, looks at me, then says, "What Vanesa has done with your brother is not right. We don't partake in activities such as those, which the other clans build their livelihoods around. That is why they disliked us. Our leadership is what makes us who we are, and without my parents here to keep our people in line, I'm afraid sending in anyone other than Elliot will make us look unstable. With everything else, we don't need the loyalty of our people tested. It's crucial we remain united."

I breathe out and nod my head even though I still disagree. But who am I to argue with that logic? Vira knows better than I do the way their people will react, the chain of events that will occur if it looks as though Elliot's own family isn't standing behind him. It's funny though, Miles always seems to have such unwavering faith in their followers, and yet, Vira fears one slight change in regiment may be enough to upend their entire operation. Unless she fears that with all the dangers lurking, their clan may begin defecting to other clans, leaving the siblings alone to fight.

Lucas stands from where he's seated on the couch, silent and listening. He walks over to the window and slides it open to allow a cool breeze to float through the room, washing the tension away with it. I just hope that this plan to derail Adrian works, because frankly, I don't think he's stupid enough to believe we're not a threat so long as we continue to search for ways to demolish the remnants of the curse.

"Are we going to survive this?" Lucas asks, drawing us all from our thoughts.

Elaine blinks rapidly, ponytail swishing as she shakes her head in denial. "Of course you're going to survive this. You have to."

"We have no idea what we're up against." He sighs, massaging his temples with his back to the room. "We don't know where to start looking for answers about the curse. We don't have the numbers to fight a war if it comes to that. We probably won't fool Adrian for long. And the police are still pursuing the Aaron Anderson murder investigation because our compulsion isn't strong enough right now to convince them not to."

"It's like the walls are closing in," I agree, dropping my head onto Miles' shoulder, and he touches my knee for support.

Vira stands. "Then we push them away. We hit the walls so hard they crumble. We scale them and jump over to the other side, but this—what you all are doing—we don't give up. We don't give up until our bodies are decaying in the ground, do you understand me?"

"You're right." Lucas comes to Vira's side, resting a hand on her shoulder. "You're right, I'm sorry."

"All right then. Miles, Lucas, we're going back to the Manor to search through Emile's stuff, whether Elliot wants us to or not. Aspen, search Elijah's things, see if you can't find anything that alludes to our situation in any way, no matter how small. Elaine—" Vira eyes her up and down, flipping long strands of hair over her shoulder "—try to do something relevant."

CHAPTER 22

*I*t takes me the better half of three hours to sort through the mess of Elijah's things. I've gone through them before, but never to this extent. And any time I have, I've been looking for something specific and could have easily missed other items of importance in the process. Except now, I'm not sure what I'm looking for or if I'll even know when I find it.

Throwing down a pile of papers I've looked through more times than I meant to because, in my exhaustion, I kept putting them in the unread pile, I let out a frustrated growl and stand up so fast I knock over my chair.

"Do you want to take a break?" Elaine asks, setting aside her own pile. I had insisted she rest for a while since she didn't sleep much after she found out Dallas was taken out from under her nose, but she was determined to stay in case my mom decided to ash me again.

"No, I don't want to take a break. I want to break this stupid curse so my brother doesn't die," I yell, pressing the heel of my palm into my forehead, then run the hand down my face. "I'm sorry, I'm sorry. I'm just… on edge."

"And you're sure there's nothing else you can do to save Dallas besides freeing the demon family and their hell minions?" she asks, thumbing aside another page of paperwork. I'm not sure how she manages to talk and research at the same time. After so many hours of this, I don't have the energy for either.

I shake my head, pacing the room. "There's a reason I was able to turn but no one else can, and why the transition doesn't make newborns crazy anymore, but keeps them alive. It's like they're… waiting? I don't know—that's ridiculous, I'm aware, but I just don't think there's going to be yet another loophole. *I* am the loophole—why else did I transform successfully?"

"Maybe you didn't," she suggests, and I whip my head around, brows raised high. "What? You've said yourself that your balance feels off, and you're having a hard time gaining control of your abilities."

"That's typical when you first change, Elaine." I roll my eyes. I don't have time to start focusing on my inability to adapt. One issue at a time.

"I'm just saying."

"Maybe I'd be a better vampire if I had proper and consistent training, instead of being stuck on research duty." I vent angrily, looking up at the ceiling as if the Dravens are a God I'm complaining to.

Elaine raises her eyebrows then dips her head to continue reading, mumbling, "I think you're the one who needs a nap."

"I need answers, not a nap." I sigh, lowering back into my chair, which creaks in protest as my weight eases onto it. I close my eyes, hating that I'm taking my frustrations out on

Elaine, who has no reason to be here whatsoever. This isn't her world. She doesn't care about the Dravens. She could easily respect her ancestor's wishes to keep her nose out of the supernatural world and pretend she never found his journal, never met me. She doesn't, though. She stayed, and against her best interests, she's gotten involved in Draven affairs to help me. "Actually, I could use some food."

She bites her lip, twirling the tip of her hair around her index finger. "Fine. But you're buying. Consider it an apology for being so miserable these past few hours."

I laugh, dropping my head in my hands. "That's fair."

"And I want dessert."

"Okay, Elaine."

"Oh, and—" she starts, and I peek at her through my fingers, unamused. "Just kidding."

Shaking my head, I grab my phone and slip it into my jeans pocket, throwing on a fleece jacket before we head downstairs.

I open the study door quietly and glance around it to make sure my mom isn't hovering somewhere close by. I still haven't seen her since she hurt me, and I'd prefer to keep it that way. I don't think Adrian would use her to weaken me again, but I'm also not sure how long the effects of compulsion last. Will she have the urge to smear ash all over my face every time she sees me, or is the spell broken now that she's done it once? That's something I should keep in mind to ask Miles for future reference.

During the walk into town, my mind keeps wandering back to Vanesa and my brother, all alone in that cabin—him helpless, her predatory. She could do anything to him. She could kill him, cut off his arms, poke out his eyes. I know she won't, she can't, not if she does want to live, but nonetheless, she is in a position to do whatever she wants.

I'm itching to check on him, especially now that the ash has probably been washed away after the rainstorm last night. So many times did I contemplate showing up to give her a piece of my mind, but I didn't. I swore to Miles that I wouldn't kill her, and sure, I don't know that I actually have it in me to murder someone—although she's anything but human—but being alone in the middle of the woods with her and no one to play interference… well, I just might have broken my promise.

"Aspen?" Elaine nudges my arm, nodding her head toward a tiny cafe in town. I don't eat out too often, so I haven't tried many local restaurants, not that there's a wide selection to begin with.

"Oh, um, yeah. We can go there," I say, not sure that's what she was asking.

Elaine bites her lip, walking toward the cafe without another word—and Elaine not talking endlessly is rare.

"Sorry," I say shortly, feeling as though I'm being a horrible friend to her today. Not three days ago, I showed up at her house in the middle of the night asking for a place to stay, and here I am, treating her as if she's unimportant. It's horrible enough that Elliot constantly belittles her ideas, when in reality they're not as ludicrous as he makes them out to be. The last thing she deserves is for me to begin treating her as if she's merely an object in my way.

"Elaine," I call when she doesn't turn around.

She stops short, interlocking her fingers as she turns toward the breeze that's picking up, a sign that another storm is brewing. "I've hit a wall. I don't know what to do, and that's not your fault. I don't mean to be distant." I shrug my shoulders a little, unsure of what to say exactly. Her hair blows around her face, little strands slipping from her ponytail and dancing with the wind.

She crosses her arms, scanning the town square around us absently. She bites her lip and nods slightly, but the irritation in her eyes is still present. "Are you still having nightmares?"

"Not since I've been staying with Miles," I say, baffled by the realization. Ambrose could only invade my mind when I was in my house because his spirit resonated within the walls. When I left, he had no connection to me. But I had a nightmare when I slept at Elaine's, which means my house isn't a common factor. So why not when I'm with Miles? Do I feel safer? More guarded? Am I less vulnerable?

"Weird," she says thoughtfully, holding the strands of hair back from her face.

"Add it to the list," I say dryly, moving past her toward the cafe door.

Once inside, we grab a booth in the back corner and examine our menus, though I hardly read mine. I'm too distracted by the thoughts racing around in my head. So I settle for the first thing I see that looks remotely appetizing and set my menu at the edge of the table for the waitress to pick up when she comes to take our orders.

My fingers tap anxiously on the table, causing Elaine to peer over her menu at me, eyebrows raised. I inhale deeply, clasping my hands together and dropping them in my lap as my eyes skate around the busy dining area.

I do a double take when I notice a familiar face waiting by the counter where we're supposed to pick up our food after the waitress takes our orders. Most food establishments in Ichorye are short-staffed, so they find it's more efficient to take the orders and allow us to retrieve our own meals so that they can tend to other tables.

"What is it?" Elaine asks, eyeing me worriedly. "You have that look."

Thankfully, the waitress nears our table, pulling out a pad of paper and a pen before I have to elaborate. "It's nothing."

She opens her mouth to say something, but the waitress interrupts. "What can I get you girls?"

Elaine groans, giving me a look like I somehow compelled the waitress to come over at this exact moment so I wouldn't have to answer her question. "I'll have the BLT combo with a side of home fries. And a hot coffee. With hazelnut creamer. And a cinnamon roll."

I roll my eyes, knowing she purposely chose the most expensive items on the menu because I'm buying.

"And for you?"

"I'll have the turkey club sandwich, no mayo, and a hot coffee as well, please."

The waitress nods, gesturing toward the counter on the far side of the room, then to the number carved into our table. "Your order will be out shortly, just keep an eye out for your table number."

I mumble a thanks, hoping that Elaine's attention span is shorter than the amount of time it took to place our orders, but judging by the way she crosses her arms over her chest and leans back in her chair, I doubt it.

"Explain."

I bite my lip, glancing back up at the counter where Nadia Porter stands. My stomach churns with guilt. I clear my throat, lowering my voice in case anyone is close enough to overhear us. "Nadia."

Her eyes widen, knuckles grasping the side of the table as she leans forward. "Nadia Porter is here? Do you want to leave?"

Would I prefer to not be in the same vicinity as the woman whose fiancé I killed? Absolutely. Can I abandon every room I find myself in with her? No. "If she suspects I'm involved with Aaron's murder, it's better she doesn't think her presence bothers me. Let's just eat—moderately fast—and leave."

Nadia turns away from the counter just as our food is set out, and our eyes lock. I give her a slight smile to be friendly since we've talked once before, then avert my eyes back to the booth.

"Our food is ready. Can you...?"

"I got it." Elaine stands, understanding. "Stay here."

I watch as she walks away, her eyes scanning the small cluster of customers waiting on their food. But as soon as she's far enough from our table, Nadia leaves her spot leaning against the wall and walks straight toward me.

My heart skips, and my hands begin to sweat profusely while I try to act as casually as possible when she reaches me, sliding across the booth into Elaine's seat.

She smiles without humor, rubbing her hands up and down her arms, long black hair flowing over her shoulders like a river. "Aspen Troy."

I shift in my seat, crossing my ankles before I return her smile. I squint my eyes in mock thought. "Nadia, right? I thought I recognized you."

I close my eyes, praying my cover is more convincing to her than it sounds in my head. She blinks her wide eyes rapidly, stretching her lips, though they don't quite meet a smile. Her face appears thinner than the last time we met, and her eyes are sunken in, skin ashen and tired.

"How are you doing?" I ask, because that seems to be an appropriate thing to say after finding out she's lost someone she loved.

"I've been better," she admits. Her gaze never leaves my face. Not for a second. I tap my foot, glancing around to see where Elaine is with our food, but I don't see her anywhere.

"Your friend was talking to some guy," Nadia says, pulling my attention back to her. My breath quickens and I try to calm my nerves, hoping that's actually the case and not one of Adrian's men trying to lure her into a trap. "Anyway, what were we saying? Oh, I said I've been better. You see, I assume you know how this feels since you just moved here, uprooting your life from—where was it? Colorado?"

I swallow hard, sitting up a little straighter. She shouldn't know that. No one does besides Miles and Elaine, and I doubt they would tell anyone. Legally, I'm Aspen Troy from Chicago, Illinois, and not one single person on this earth should have the ability to make the connection between me and my previous identity. Destiny Wilson no longer exists, and Aspen Troy hasn't so much as vacationed near Colorado, much less lived there.

"I'm from Illinois," I tell her, forcing down my nerves. Before, I'd felt guilt, concern that she'd somehow connect me to her fiancé's murder, but now I'm incredibly scared. She doesn't just suspect me, she knows me. She knows things no one else could about my identity.

"Oh." She appears baffled. "I could have sworn it was Colorado. My mistake. Anyway, you moved here so suddenly, everything for you changed so fast, and I know our situations are polar opposites, but I can't help but feel like you might know what it means to have your world turned upside-down overnight."

"Moving was challenging," I agree, trying my hardest not to frantically search for Elaine. What could possibly be taking her this long? "Change is imminent. Good or bad, nothing remains the same forever. And you just might discover what you're really capable of along the way."

Nadia tilts her head to the side, assessing me. "That was really beautiful."

"My brother loves to write poetry," I explain, giving in to my urge to check on Elaine and preparing to make an excuse to go look for her.

"And here I thought you were just an old soul. It would make sense with the company you keep." Nadia stands, adjusting the scarf she always seems to have draped over her arms. She touches my shoulder, giving it an assertive squeeze. "Anyway, I'm glad I met you, Aspen. It almost feels like... destiny, wouldn't you think?"

I suck in a sharp breath, rigid in my seat at the mention of my old name. But it had to be a coincidence. Destiny is a common word. There's no way she could know... no way. How could she?

Except she seems to know about Colorado, too. It's impossible, yet I can't calm myself long enough to think straight.

She's gone before my mind can process any of our conversation, floating out of the cafe as if she's riding on a cloud.

After a moment, I realize she never got the food she was

waiting for, if she ordered any at all. Which makes me wonder —was Nadia following me?

"Hey, sorry about that," Elaine says, dropping back in her seat with two large plates of food. She slides mine over to me, tightening the top of her ponytail. "You missed Oliver. I ran into him up at the counter and we got to talking. I think this is the first time I've seen him in a month. Anyway, I told him to come say 'hi' since you guys *still* haven't met, but he left in a hurry. I swear, he's been acting so strange since—"

Elaine stops short, her eyes darting to me, noticing for the first time how ghostly pale I'm sure I am. "What's wrong? Did you talk to Nadia? I'm so sorry, I should have rushed back here, but I got distracted."

"Since when, Elaine?"

"Huh?" She looks at me in confusion, and I can see her trying to work out my intentions in her head.

"Oliver has been acting strange since when?" I elaborate, watching the door Nadia exited from.

She swallows, staring at the untouched food on our plates. "Since you got to town."

"You don't think he's... involved with any of this, do you?" I ask, hesitant to question her best friend, the boy who has had her back all her life, whose family took her in and treated her as their own when her parents couldn't be bothered.

Except Elaine was occupied just long enough for Nadia to subtly mention details about my old life to intimidate me. As much as I hope I'm wrong, such a coincidence doesn't exist.

"No. no. Oliver is my best friend. I would know if—I would know if he was..." Her voice falls off and uncertainty clouds her expression. "You know, I'm ready to go now. Thanks for lunch. I, um, I'll see you later."

Elaine leaves in a hurry, not bothering to take a bite of her meal. We haven't eaten since before we discovered the secret room in my house. There's no way she isn't hungry.

Thunder rumbles outside, followed by three bolts of lightning streaking across the sky, one after another. Through the tiny window adjacent to our table, I can see the tall trees bending to the will of the wind, and the few people outside with umbrellas are struggling to keep them upright, fumbling with the canopy as it folds inside out. It won't be long until rain starts pouring, unless the dark clouds hover like they often do, teasing the rain until the most undesired time to release it.

I eat half of my meal and half of Elaine's, then decide to box up the rest to take home to my parents. Since Ambrose's influence abandoned my family, Mom has been cooking less, and despite my father's restored coherency, he never cooks at all. Now that Dallas is incapacitated, I'm worried they might accidentally starve themselves to death.

If only Dallas had joined me at Miles's house. Then Vanesa wouldn't have been able to kidnap him so easily. He only stayed home for my parents, and now they're alone anyway, so it was for nothing.

Cupping my hands, I drop my face into them as a headache brews, spreading up my neck and across my forehead.

"You all right, hon?"

I look up to find our waitress eyeing me with concern. I sit up straighter, taking the container she hands me and dumping the leftover food inside. "Yes, fine. Long day at work."

I brush past her and out into the chilly autumn air. My head is still spiraling from my conversation with Nadia. How could she possibly know who I am? And if she knows about me, does she know about Rachel? If someone tracks her down, they'll know I'm the one who turned her, and that would be very bad for the Dravens, and by extension, me. It's a miracle Adrian hasn't killed me already, but I suppose he wants to understand what is happening before making any rash decisions, which seems a little too meticulously thought out for a vampire whose image has been made from horror stories.

Miles told me once that during his rise to the Twelve, Adrian wouldn't send men to take care of those who tried to cut him down in order to take power after the previous American clan leader died in a war against the hunters. Adrian would personally seek them out, without backup, and murder them himself. He would then take a small vial of their blood while it oozed out of their bodies and into the earth, as a token of his victory and proof to the others that he had, once again, bested someone who intended to oppose him.

So why he hasn't murdered me just on the suspicion that I can break the curse, I have no idea.

At every new turn, I feel as though I'm spiraling, tumbling down a dark abyss with no end in sight and no hope of being rescued. But I do know one thing. One increasingly concrete certainty that proves over and over again to be true.

In some twisted, miraculous, and intricate way, every single thing that happens in this death-ridden town is interconnected.

CHAPTER 23

J make my way to Draven Manor after lunch because I have nowhere else to go. Elaine bailed after I insinuated that Oliver may be connected with whatever Nadia Porter is involved in. And for obvious reasons, my own house isn't livable at the moment. Funny enough, it's more livable now than it had been when I moved in, since I had the leaking roof and our air conditioner repaired, except now I have a reason to sleep elsewhere.

"Are we taking in strays now?" Elliot glares at Danielle as she hands me a soft blanket to curl up with on the couch.

She gives him a pointed look, shaking her head subtly. This is the last place I want to be, yet it's the only place I have to go. Miles is in the armory researching ways to save Vanesa's transitioners, i.e., my brother, so unless I wanted to sit alone at his house for the rest of the afternoon, sulking and useless, I had to come here. "She has nowhere else to go."

"That doesn't mean she's permitted to waltz into our house whenever she pleases," he argues, snatching the brown blanket from my hands as I'm trying to open it up.

I grit my teeth, anger bubbling in my chest at his words. "You think you'd be a little more considerate of my situation given that you're the only reason I'm in it to begin with. Had it not been for Ambrose, I'd probably be living in Colorado right now, blissfully unaware of your existence."

Elliot smirks darkly, tossing the blanket on the couch across from mine. "I'll be sure to tell Miles you said that."

Vira walks into the living room, hips swaying as she moves effortlessly in her high-heeled boots, landline in hand. She sucks in her cheeks and purses her lips, unhappily holding out the phone for me. "It's for you."

I lower my brows, wondering who would be calling me on the Draven's landline of all things. "Hello?"

"It's me." Elaine's voice rings through the line, but the static makes it hard to hear her.

"We've become a human hotel," Elliot scoffs, shaking his head in disbelief before slamming the door to the kitchen behind him.

"Are you okay?" I ask, hoping I didn't upset her too much earlier. "About what I said earlier..."

"No need. I was a little too sensitive about the whole thing, and I'll admit it was sort of strange, him being there at the same time as Nadia."

"But?" I prompt, trying hard to ignore the impatient glances I keep receiving from Vira, who has her hand outstretched in wait of the phone.

"But... I'm going to choose to believe it was a coincidence. With everything that's happening right now, it's so easy to become paranoid and to begin suspecting every single person in your life of being something other than who they are. Oliver has always been there for me, and doubting his intentions is only going to create more problems, not solve the ones we have."

Vira clears her throat, a hint that I'm taking advantage of my phone privileges. "You're right. I can't talk right now, so I have to go. But let me know if you want to come by."

I hang up, just in time to hear Lucas let out a huff of laughter from Mr. Draven's desk. He's so quiet, at times I forget he's even here.

"How's the search coming?" I ask him, pretending not to notice Vira's annoyance. I stand, moving across the room to where Lucas is leaning a hip against the desk, thumb bookmarking one page in a book while his other hand skims to another.

"Not very well. I don't think Miles has had any luck, either." He slams the book closed, placing it back on the shelf behind him and dropping down into the desk chair, looking worn down.

"Is there anything I can do? I already searched my ancestor's files, but maybe I can help here? Make things go faster?" I offer, hoping he'll allow me to help in some fashion.

"I'm about done looking through these books. Danielle did most of them this morning, but I'm sure Miles wouldn't mind your help in the armory."

As if on cue, Vira snaps her neck to us, eyes wide. "We don't let humans into the armory, Lucas. They're not even supposed to get past our *gate.*"

Elliot told me once, the last time I insisted I help fix Vanesa's mistake in the armory, that not even the highest ranking (basically, the oldest) members of the Draven clan have access to the armory in times like these. He only let me in for a few seconds before deciding better of it. He called it a lapse of judgment right before he ordered me back upstairs.

"In case you forgot, I'm not human anymore, thanks to you." I mean that generally, because it is her family's fault I'm in this position, but I know Vira thinks of it differently. She's the only reason I had to kill the hunter that night. Had she not abandoned me to rescue her family instead of helping me fight him, I might still be in transition.

"You're not from our world. We haven't had a human transition in two centuries. Newborn or not, you're human in my eyes, and you are certainly not vampire enough to enter the armory. If our father found out, he'd cut off our heads and leave them on the side of the road until we learned our lesson."

I have so many odd questions about how that would even work, and what he'd do with their bodies in the meantime, assuming he'd sew them back together when their punishment was over. Either way, this takes child abuse to an entirely new level, and I can only hope she's being sarcastic. "I just want to help."

Vira purses her lips, eyebrows lifting as she says, "You know what Vanesa would say if she were here."

And I do. She'd tell me I could help by turning as many pathetic humans as I could to build them an army big enough to destroy the other clans. She'd also insult me plenty in the process.

"What will letting her into the armory hurt? You're starting to sound like Vanesa." Lucas stands up, and Vira resolves, shaking her head as though she still doesn't think this is a good idea.

"Fine. But if she is ever compromised, if she ever gives up

our secrets to another clan, it's on you." Vira turns, looking at Danielle as well. "*Both* of you, and my lovesick brother."

"It will never come to that," Danielle assures her, tucking her short, black hair behind her ears.

Vira props an arm on her hip, reminding me so much of the way she acted when I met her and she didn't trust me. "And if it's us or her brother? Who do you think she chooses, then?"

When Vira is gone, strutting out of the room like she owns it, the three of us are quiet, and I can't help but obsess over what she said.

If I'm ever compromised.

Does she really think that I would turn on her family? No matter how unbearable they may be, I wouldn't trade their secrets for anything. Plus, I doubt a few armory secrets could really destroy everything they've built. The hunters and clans are much bigger threats than I am, though I suppose if I were to betray them, I'd know exactly how to tear them apart. I know what buttons to push with each of them and exactly how to sever their relationships.

"Come on, I'll walk you down to the armory." Lucas puts his hand on my back, guiding me out of the living room and into the hall.

"Are you sure I should go down there?" I worry, hesitant to cause any further tension between the Draven siblings.

Lucas doesn't say anything, just continues leading me down the hall to a deep-brown door that opens to a spiral staircase. I peer over the railing. The air feels damp and cool compared to the warmth of the rest of the Manor, but I can't see anything beyond the darkness, which means it goes down quite a ways if even I can't see anything.

"It was intended to look that way so that no one can see

below." He moves around me, starting down the stairs, and if it were anyone but Lucas here with me, I might think this was a trap and that I was about to be executed.

My shoes echo on the metal stairs, my hand following the smooth railing as it twists around and around until my feet hit concrete. It's colder down here than it was above, and there's something wet on the pavement, which explains the humidity change I felt.

"Before I lived here this was an underground sewage pipe, but it collapsed during one of the wars." He leads me around the stairs to a door blended so well into the dank walls it's almost impossible to spot. I often forget that he hasn't always lived with the Dravens. He was once a part of another clan until he defected because of their inhumane behavior.

"Everyone thought it collapsed," Lucas continues, feeling around on the wall for something. "Only part of it did, though, leaving the rest intact. Then Edgar became a vampire around the time Elliot was twelve, and he, his father, and Ambrose built this place above it, using the salvageable parts as a secret tunnel into the armory. At first, it was just a room filled with information he collected on vampires before his change, but it's turned into much more than that."

"How did Edgar become a vampire?" I ask, curious. From the way Miles talked about it once, it sounded like his choice.

"That," Danielle appears behind me, and I suck in a breath, clutching my chest, "is a very dark and twisted tale."

The wall begins to shift as Lucas must find what he was feeling around for, and a concrete slab slides into a metal track on the ground, disappearing between the wall and a layer of brick that sits behind it to reveal a large room. Red brick lines the entirety of the armory, save for the concrete floors and ceiling.

Miles stands, bent over something on a long, metal table in the center of the room. His back is to the body of the only transitioner left, placed against the far wall. I scoff, unable to believe that Vanesa thinks Dallas is safer in a cabin in the woods than here, in a secret dungeon hidden in sewer tunnels believed to have been destroyed upward of two hundred years ago. Probably more, since Elliot was only twelve, at the time of the collapse.

"Does Elliot know you're down here?" Miles asks, raising an eyebrow.

Danielle lets out a short breath. "Oh, we will all know when he finds out."

"Maybe that will finally get Vanesa out of hiding," Miles says, and Lucas laughs.

"She won't be able to resist screaming at us for letting an outsider in on our secrets." Danielle rolls her eyes, tilting her head to the side, and for a moment, I see the resemblance between her and her sisters. Usually, Danielle is so sweet and humble that I have a hard time picturing her in relation to Vira and Vanesa. But for a second, I could see it in the way she upturned her eyes, and how her hair fell off one shoulder with her movement. She drops down in a little sitting area with three chairs and a coffee table, crossing her legs elegantly. "Anyway, Aspen was asking about Dad, and how he discovered vampirism."

Miles smiles fondly despite all of the torture and horror this long life has brought him, and a small part of me wonders if he doesn't resent what he is as much as I'd thought. I just assumed, with the way he was against me turning, and how he seems to dislike the lack of humanity his species possesses, that he disliked his fate. But after all this time, could he imagine his life in any other way when this is basically all he's ever known?

"Everyone thought my father was a madman. That he'd completely lost his mind when he first started rambling about vampires and the supernatural to the townspeople. Things had evolved past the ways of the Salem Witch Trials, but people were still close-minded when it came to otherworldly creatures such as us. They shunned him, threatened to fire him from his job at the mine, but it never discouraged him. He knew there was more to this world than ordinary people, and he was determined to prove so. He observed silently, watching those he suspected of inhuman abilities from afar, until he learned enough to face them on his own. Essentially, he became a hunter before we knew of such things. My father and grandfather captured several vampires by weakening them with ash, then begged them to turn my father. When they refused and tried to kill him instead, he drove a stake through their hearts. He tried threatening their families, torturing them, but vampires are resilient and don't take kindly to a human trying to force their hand. And then he captured Natalia. She refused, like all the others, but unlike them, she was kind, humble, and she didn't try to kill my father simply for seeking immorality.

"So he persisted. He never gave up, begging her to change him and swearing he wanted a way to protect his children should anything ever happen to them. And eventually, she gave in."

"But how did your father become one of the Twelve?" I ask, intrigued by their history.

This time, it's Danielle who speaks. "Ichorye's head vampire wasn't powerful. He was only in charge because he was the eldest and no one else wanted the position—until our grandfather. Our father turned him, and he gained the respect of the clans. Then when the current leader stepped down, he rose to power as one of the Twelve, until he died in the war with the hunters and our father was chosen to replace him over Ambrose."

"What became of Natalia?" I wonder, curious as to how things turned out for her after she essentially began a legacy by turning Edgar. This Natalia woman created the most revered—and feared—family in all of the vampire world.

"Our father married her," Miles says, eyes meeting mine.

My jaw hangs loose as I try to comprehend what this means. "W—but I thought...?"

"Our birth mother died four months after I was born," Danielle whispers, tears clouding her brown eyes. "The circumstances surrounding her death were strange, and our father was desperate to know the truth. That's how he discovered the existence of vampires. He was desperate to make sure no one ever got to us like they did our mother."

"After two centuries, the woman who cares for you, consoles you, and protects your life above her own... she becomes family. She's as much our mother as the woman who raised us," Miles explains.

"So your birth mother never knew what your father became?"

"It's for the best that she didn't. When we were all old enough, we changed too. She never would have chosen immortality over a happy, human life," Miles says, and I'm reminded of how Danielle had chosen to remain human until she met Lucas.

"He killed a lot of people to get us where we are today," Miles continues, looking ashamed of the things Edgar did in the name of power, "including a few of the hunters who got in his way and had tried to take out whatever vampire he was targeting at the time, but our father, despite what he did in the past, he's not a bad man. He just…"

"He wanted to live forever," I finish, understanding the desire to be more in order to protect those you care about. There's nothing I wouldn't do to prevent Dallas from the pain he's going through right now. The only difference is Edgar had a solution to his problem. I don't.

A strange emotion clouds Miles's eyes, but before I can interpret it, the inconspicuous door groans and parts to reveal Vira standing next to the only person on this earth that makes my blood boil on sight. Vanesa Draven.

I growl, clenching my fists at my sides, trying really hard to remember the promise I made to Miles. I will not kill her. I'm not that person and doing so would only hurt the people she loves and torture me in the long run, not punish her.

Her eyes widen considerably when she sees me, but not in fear. "What the hell is she doing down here? Are we just revealing our most sacred and confidential secrets to anyone with our bloody venom running through their veins?"

"Where is Dallas?" I clamp my teeth, and Miles lightly touches my wrist. That gesture alone is enough to keep me grounded and remind me yet again that ripping off her pretty little face is an exponentially bad idea.

Vanesa scrunches her nose, eyes dark with humor. "I left him at an impound lot. If you hurry, you might be able to snatch him before he's crushed to bits."

"Van," Vira warns, back to playing interference despite the

dislike she took of me while Vanesa was busy holding my brother's unconscious body in a run-down cabin. "Your brother is on the couch upstairs. We'll move him down here later."

"Why are you here?" I speak only to Vanesa. No one else matters right now.

She takes a long breath, thinking over her answer and severely ticking me off. "Elliot has gone to meet with Adrian. Vira came to tell me, and I decided that now would be the best time to transport Dallas and myself to the Manor. Most of Adrian's men will be at the meeting, guarding him in case of an ambush."

"Will Elliot be okay?" Danielle stands. Her voice is etched with concern for her brother. "How could you let him go alone?"

Vira moves across the room, clutching Danielle's shoulders. "It was Adrian's request. I insisted I go with him, but if Adrian's men sensed that Elliot wasn't alone, they may have killed him on site."

Danielle nods, but her shoulders sag low, hands clasped rigidly in front of her. "Do you at least know where they're meeting? In case he's not back soon."

Vira nods, stroking a strand of Danielle's hair and pinching it at the end. "At the lake near Aspen's house."

By "the lake" I wonder if she means the lake where her uncle famously got his title as the *Twelve Day Killer*. It's the only lake I know of in town.

"What happens if Adrian doesn't buy our ruse?" I ask, knowing for a fact he won't if Elliot is the one discussing terms.

"We just need to make him pause long enough to break the

curse. That's all we can hope for right now," Vira says, crossing her arms over her stomach and looking just as worried about this meeting as Danielle—Vira's just better at hiding her emotions.

"Lucas, will you help me carry Dallas down the steps?" Vanesa asks. She should be the last person on this earth who has the right to touch him after what she's done.

Lucas nods and follows Vanesa out of the armory.

"Elaine is here," Miles says. I'm not sure how he could possibly know that—I can hardly hear Vanesa and Lucas's footsteps on the landing above.

"I'm assuming watchers aren't allowed in the armory," I deadpan, looking specifically at Vira.

She blinks, squinting her eyes at me. "You're lucky *you're* making it out of here alive."

"You stay and help Miles for a little," Danielle says, moving toward the door and motioning for Vira to follow her. "I'll entertain Elaine for the time being—we really can't allow a human down here. They can be compelled by other vampires for information, and she's not strong enough yet to resist. It's too risky."

"Humans can resist compulsion?" I swear, every time I think there can't be anything else to learn, there always is.

Danielle nods. "A very select few, most of which come from long lines of humans involved in vampire affairs. They have to be trained to strengthen their minds, and Elaine doesn't have anyone in her family who can help her with that. I'll try, but I'm not equipped to do so any more than her clueless parents."

"If it's okay," Miles looks at Danielle before settling his gaze on me, "we're going to stay here tonight since it's getting late.

Besides, with Elliot meeting Adrian, I think it's for the best that we're all together."

"What about Elaine?" I ask, worried Elliot and Vanesa won't let her stay here, even though they did once before. "Her parents aren't home this week. She'll be completely alone."

Danielle sighs and the concrete door slides open as she nears it. "Elaine can stay. She can sleep in my room so you don't have to stay on the couch with her again."

"Thanks, Danielle," Miles says, and she gives him a small smile, gesturing to the books and papers stacked on the table.

"It's a good thing you had your date night when you did. I don't think you'll be getting another for a while."

$\mathcal{M}$iles and I pour over the armory files for what feels like hours, but as I feared, we come up with nothing. We're not going to find our solution in an ancient book unless we find one specifically written about the Draven curse, which is most unlikely.

The first volume I read through had to do with curses and how they're constructed, and typically, you have to reverse the process used to create the curse in order to break it. The problem is, there isn't a curse strong enough to remove the powers from a vampire, or so the book insinuates. Most of them can only bestow bad luck or restrict an intended person from doing a specific thing. The Dravens have been kept dormant for years, and nothing I read about curses describes what they've had to endure.

Although, I did find a potion that forces a person to do whatever you say, and I can't say the idea of using it on Vanesa isn't enticing. More and more I think about how beneficial it would be to have her on a leash.

"You're not thinking of using one of those to make my sister jump off a cliff, are you?" Miles asks, tapping the book of potions in front of me.

I bite my lip and run my fingers through my hair before tying it up in a loose knot on my head. "Oh relax, she'd survive."

Miles smirks dryly, thinking I'm only joking—and I am... sort of.

"Why don't you close your eyes for a little." He nods toward the chair Danielle was sitting in earlier. It must be close to midnight by now, if not later. Keeping track of time is difficult when your mind is lost in the pages of a book. "The exhaustion is giving you dangerous ideas."

I avoid looking at the bodies along the back wall as I make my way to the chair. Lucas and Vanesa brought Dallas down here a few hours ago after Danielle left, and I haven't been able to bring myself to look at him. I'm not entirely sure I have the strength to see him that way.

I curl up on the armchair, closing my eyes and trying to force the image of Dallas's mangled body from my mind. Every time I think of him, I see his death. I see blood pouring from his veins as Vanesa sinks her teeth into him, sucking out every part that makes him who he is.

With this in mind, I feel myself start to drift off, hands trembling and legs shaking as I think of the terrible things that could happen to my brother if we succeed in breaking the curse. He will become a transitioner, a drug to any vampire he comes in contact with. What sort of life is that to live? No better than mine, I suppose. If I know my brother at all, he will die before he became like the Dravens.

My leg jerks, and I startle awake just before I can fully coast into sleep. Sitting up, my eyes shoot directly to the white sheet covering his body. I stand and walk slowly to it. My fingers run along the seam, and I curl them around the material, ready to pull it back when my legs abruptly feel as though they're sinking into the ground.

Suddenly, I'm standing in water, in the middle of a lake. I'm no longer at the armory with my brother lying in front of me, awaiting his fate. I reach out for something to grab on to as I'm pulled under like quicksand. I try to take a breath, to swim to the surface, but I'm cemented in place. Water thrusts up my nose and down my throat, burning my lungs as I let out a scream, hoping someone—anyone—will hear me. But I'm mute. My voice won't work, and my flailing limbs refuse to cooperate as I try to dislodge my feet from the lake's bottom.

I don't know how I got down here so fast. Only moments ago I was standing with only my ankles submerged, and before that, I was at the armory with Miles.

Miles. He can help me. He can—

I choke, clawing at my throat as I try to inhale, only to swallow another mouthful of water. My body writhes and my mind shuts down. My eyes glaze over when I stop struggling, and I sink farther into the ground as the water rocks me back and forth in its current.

Just when I think my time is up, a blinding light beams through the surface, followed by a hand that reaches for my own. I reach for it, toward the light, and the hand grabs on to mine, freeing me from the silt that was holding me down and lifting me from the water.

∾

I squeeze my eyes against the light, bringing my hand up to shield my face as I blink through the burning under my eyelids. It feels as though I've been staring directly into the sun, and my head is buzzing with static, ears muffled. Groaning, I sit up, gripping the rough material of the armory chair beneath my hands as I shift my body, stiff from sleep.

When my vision grows used to the brightness of the room, and I can see better, I find myself surrounded by five figures staring at me as though I'm some foreign specimen in their basement.

"What happened?" I ask, clearing my throat and stretching my shoulders, feeling strangely foreign in my own body. The room is cool, but there's a layer of sweat on my upper lip and the back of my shirt is sticking to my skin uncomfortably.

Danielle is the first to speak, eyeing me up and down. "You were screaming in your sleep."

Miles moves from behind me, and I notice that he's touching my shoulder, which means he must have been the one to wake me up. Now in front of me, he bends, tenderly taking my hands in his. "Are you okay?"

"It was just a nightmare," I say and nod groggily, hating that my night terrors have disrupted all of them from whatever they were doing at this hour. I look around, searching for a clock, but there isn't one down here. "What time is it? How long was I asleep?"

It felt like mere minutes, but I'm not sure when exactly my exhaustion took over. Normally when I have nightmares, even with Ambrose, some part of me always knows I'm sleeping even if I'm not consciously aware of it. But this time… I didn't realize I was. The last thing I remember is standing up to go see Dallas, but even then, I'd felt completely awake.

Even Vanesa looks slightly taken aback by my screaming. Elaine stands off to the side of the Dravens, looking just as concerned as they do. They all must have been too entranced by my yelling to notice that she snuck down behind them.

I swallow. Their stares make me feel anxious, like I'm a parasite. "What is it?"

This time, to my surprise, it's Vira that speaks. Her face softens as she steps closer to me, shadowed by the lights overhead.

"Aspen..." she begins, looking at Miles for confirmation. "Vampires don't dream."

I blink a few times, not exactly sure what she means. "No, I-I've always had nightmares... they started before we moved here, and then continued because of Ambrose. It's nothing to be worried about—my brother gets them, too."

Vanesa and Vira exchange a look that makes my stomach sink, and even Lucas watches me cautiously. Nothing good ever comes from looks like those.

After Derek attacked us, and Dallas and I began having nightmares, Mom forced us to visit a doctor to see if there was anything they could do, short of prescribing us medication. My family had never been anti-medicine, but after seeing what Derek's addiction did to him, to his relationship, and to our family, both of our parents refused to allow them to prescribe anything to help us sleep. Short of weekly counseling, there wasn't much the doctor could do until we eventually "moved on" from the trauma. So for the past year, we've had to endure the hardships. My nightmares have gotten better, believe it or not, but they were also never as bad as Dallas's.

"We don't have a subconscious," Vira continues, looking at

her siblings for confirmation. "It helps to enhance our senses to keep us alert and undistracted."

Vanesa speaks next, and the lack of sass and irritability in her voice makes me uneasy. "Even when we're asleep, our minds are still wide awake. It's a weird state to be in because to us, it feels like sleeping—it's as though our bodies are resting, refueling, but we never actually fall asleep the way humans do. I don't fully understand how it works, I don't think anyone does, but I do know that no vampire dreams. Ever."

"Then how can I?" My voice comes out soft and breathy. I'm still reeling from my nightmare, and now I'm being told it's unnatural for me to have them at all.

Vira takes a deep breath. "I don't know, but we need to find out. It could have something to do with why you can turn people and we can't."

"Maybe she's a half-blood," Vanesa jeers, and it sounds as though that was supposed to be some sort of joke, except no one is laughing.

"What's a half-blood?" Elaine asks, looking at Danielle and Lucas because she knows no one else will warrant her with a response.

Miles clears his throat, pulls his hands from mine, and stands to face his siblings. "Why don't we give Aspen some space? We can discuss this further in the morning."

Danielle and Lucas nod, so do Elaine and Vira, but Vanesa doesn't budge.

"Did you know about this?" Vanesa asks Miles, stepping forward. The two of them haven't so much as looked at each other since Vanesa came back, so I don't think they've resolved their issues regarding my relevancy.

Miles doesn't respond, and the rest of his family watches him, waiting for a response.

Vanesa shakes her head, disbelieving. "Oh my God, you did, didn't you? You knew she was having nightmares and didn't bother telling any of us? Did you at least tell *her* that she's a freak of nature?"

"Vanesa," Miles says, and I can feel the anger radiating off of him in waves. Suddenly, I'd like to know what it is Miles hasn't told me more than I'd like to punch Vanesa in the face—and nothing's ever so important that I forget about my hatred for her.

My hands tremble nervously at my sides as I stand and repeat Elaine's question. "What *is* a half-blood?"

Not a single person speaks, all staring at Miles as they seem to have a silent conversation amongst themselves. Danielle is the first to step forward per usual, seeming disappointed in Miles. "A half-blood—"

"Danielle," he warns, clenching his teeth.

"She has a right to know, Miles," she says sternly, pursing her lips. "A half-blood is a type of vampire that isn't entirely, well, they're not completely inhuman. They used to be regarded as a stain on their clans' bloodline, and oftentimes were killed for their differences, but I haven't heard of one in upward of a century. Basically, they're the same as a transitioner, they're stuck in the in-between phase of the transition, just with a little more vampire than human."

"That doesn't make sense. I'm entirely vampire. I've been training, my senses are enhanced, I have all of the usual abilities…" I suppose I have yet to venture into the compulsion aspect, but meddling in a person's mind feels invasive, and I'm not sure I'm ready for that step quite yet.

"You reek of humanity," Vanesa argues. "Even Adrian's vampire noticed. It must be why he's so infatuated with you."

"You're also behind where you should be with training," Lucas says, glancing at me shyly.

"You didn't hear me coming down the steps earlier, either," Danielle says, referring to when Lucas was preparing to show me the armory. "I startled you when I spoke."

"I wasn't paying attention," I defend. Surely being focused intently on something allows me to slip up. It would be impossible to constantly be aware of every single surrounding.

"That's the thing," she continues without a beat. "With our abilities... you don't have a choice. Only the hunters and other vampires have the power to sneak up on you because of *their* abilities, but I hadn't been trying to. I walked normally down the stairs. You should have heard me. As a vampire, you hear and see everything, even if you don't mean to."

"How could you keep this from me?" I turn on Miles, and everyone else slowly starts to back away toward the exit. I don't understand. Adrian's vampires had been trying to catch me off guard outside my house, and I sensed them right before they were prepared to attack. Is it possible they were there longer than I'd realized, waiting for me to leave? Should I have known that? Is my weakness the reason I'm unsure?

"I wasn't positive, and I didn't want to worry you if I was wrong." Miles reaches for me, but I step away, furious with him for not telling me the second he suspected I was different.

Vanesa ignores Vira's tugs on her wrist, not ready to abandon this fight just yet. "You weren't sure? God, it took the rest of us thirty seconds to put it together after her screaming woke us up."

"Don't pretend like you're a saint here, Vanesa. You

kidnapped her brother and turned him. If he dies, it's on you. Forgive me if I thought telling her she's still slightly human should wait until things calmed down a little. Might I remind you that you're the reason she has one more thing to fret over."

"Amazing, isn't it? *You* mess up, and somehow I'm to blame. Your priorities are farther off than I thought. This *human* is in your head. She's changing you, and you can't even see it. She has you lying to your own family for God's sake."

"And that's my fault?" I challenge her, unwilling to stand by while she refuses to take responsibility for her own actions. "Miles's choices are not mine. And just because he cares for someone outside of your cult of a family does not mean he has abandoned you."

"Everyone needs to calm down," Vira interrupts, but Vanesa isn't finished yet. She never is.

"You are the only thing keeping us from becoming who we truly are, you—"

"This again?" I ask, moving toward her, and Miles grabs my wrist, holding me back. I shake him off, getting in Vanesa's face. "I've seen firsthand what you're willing to do to get what you want. You'll kill everyone in this town if it saves you."

"Turning them isn't killing them. That's what you don't understand. We're giving them new life. A gift greater than any you could imagine."

"What if they don't want it?" I ask, shoving her backward when she tries to grab my shoulders. "Everyone deserves a choice, and all you want to do is take that away from them for your own selfish gain."

"At least I'm trying to save my family. What are you doing, really? Besides driving a wedge between all of us." Vanesa's eyes trail down my face to Emile's necklace, her expression darkening. "You're even wearing her necklace. She was supposed to be buried with that, you know, and here you are wearing it around like some sort of consolation prize—"

"Enough!" Vira yells, yanking her sister back before she takes a swing at me. "I'm sick of this. We all want the same thing. We all want to break the curse for our own reasons, even if they don't align. We have enough enemies. Why are we fighting each other? We've already established that Aspen won't build us an army. The curse is our way around that. Aspen, you need to break the curse in order to save your brother. So let's do it. Let us stop this paltry arguing and figure out a bloody way to get us all what we want. Can we do that? Or should we just surrender ourselves to Adrian now?"

We're all silent as Vira makes eye contact with each and every one of us. She's right. The walls are closing in on all of us, maybe in different ways, but we're being smashed just the same. Yet we continue to bicker and blame one another instead of focusing on our objective.

With nothing left to say, Vira turns on her heels, but before she reaches the door, it groans, slowly opening from the outside. She freezes, and we all turn, waiting to see who's on the other side.

Elliot stumbles into the room, face bruised and arms slashed and bloody. Vira rushes to him with Vanesa not far behind her as Danielle, Miles, and Lucas bolt to the center table, shoving everything to the floor to make room for Elliot.

As a team, they lift his large, muscular body onto it, and he sits, leaning with his hands on either side of his legs, air coming out in short, shallow breaths as he tries to calm his heartbeat.

"What happened?" Vanesa asks, placing her palms on his

face to inspect the gashes in his skin. Miles is already across the room, fumbling in a cabinet for something he can't seem to find.

Elaine and I stand off to the side, watching as the siblings work together. I realize then that no matter how mad they get at one another, nothing could ever tear them apart, not really. Their bond is stronger than the trivial words they speak in an emotional outrage or disagreement. The six of them are family. Come blood or high-water they will never turn their backs on one another. In a beautifully disastrous way, they're condemned together by DNA and ineradicable history.

"I'm fine," Elliot says, though I don't think anyone believes that, judging by his poor condition.

"Did they poison you? Was there anything on the blade that made these cuts?" Vira asks, dumping the bottle of whatever Miles hands her onto a cotton pad, then rubs it on Elliot's skin.

It sizzles, causing him to grunt and scrunch his face in pain. Elaine grabs on to my wrist, hands clammy with nerves as we watch the scene unfold before us.

Once they've coated the majority of his wounds in the liquid, Vira begins drilling him on what happened.

"Who did this to you? Was it Adrian? Did you speak with him?"

Elliot shakes his head, and she stops talking at once. He stretches his back, motioning for Miles to hand him a blood bag from the fridge. The sight makes my stomach growl, which reminds me that I haven't eaten yet today. I wonder if I could sustain myself on food because I'm still somewhat human. I know the Draven siblings still enjoy it—taste buds are yet another enhanced sensation—but they don't need it to survive. Do I?

After a long gulp, he hands Vanesa his drink, and she holds on to it while he gathers his thoughts. "Adrian said that he does not do business with us."

"So it didn't work," Vanesa says, visibly vibrating with outrage.

Elliot shakes his head, which confuses all of us. He groans, shifting his body like he's unable to get comfortable, or it's possible he's simply in that much pain. "Not necessarily."

"What do you mean?" Miles asks, moving closer.

Elliot goes to speak, but his eyes are drawn to me, then to Elaine and back again, as though in all the commotion he's noticing our presence for the first time. Just that one glance shows how unhappy he is that his siblings have allowed us into the armory. He must decide it isn't an urgent priority, though, because he pushes through.

"I don't know if it worked or not," he says, and his eyes slice daggers through my skin.

"How could you not know?" Danielle asks, confused as the rest of us. "Things clearly didn't go well, why would you think we still have a chance?"

He looks at her fleetingly before his stare flicks back to me, revolted and irritated. "Because Adrian said he will only speak with you."

CHAPTER 25

"*A*s if they didn't already hate you enough," Elaine whispers, shooting a glance at the open bedroom door to ensure no one is eavesdropping. "Imagine Elliot, thinking he's all high and mighty, going to speak to the American clan leader with the intention of deceiving him, only to get his ass beat and told that Adrian will only discuss matters regarding the Draven clan with you. *You.*"

"Yes, I know, Elaine. I was there. I received all the disapproving stares and snide remarks. No need to remind me."

"You're right, sorry." Elaine clicks off the lamp in Miles's room, slipping under her covers. She refused to sleep in Danielle's room even though she trusts her most out of the Draven sisters. So instead of sleeping on the couch with her so she wouldn't have to be alone, Miles suggested she stay on the sofa in his childhood bedroom. We haven't talked since I found out he's been lying to me, and I'm not exactly thrilled about having that conversation, either. He's downstairs right now, probably talking with his siblings now that Elaine and I are out of the way.

None of them think it's a good idea for me to meet with Adrian, but I don't have much of a choice. If we want to delay his plans until the curse is broken, someone needs to convince him we're not a threat. And as I predicted, Elliot was not the right person for that job. That's not to say that I am because I know nothing about what it takes to lead a clan or negotiate terms properly. I'm probably the worst person to speak with him, but for some reason, he's intrigued by me, and I think I could use that to my advantage.

"Am I wrong to love how inferior that must make Elliot feel? He's typically such a jerk, and if you ask me, he deserves to have his feet glued to the ground before his oversized head floats him away." Elaine grunts, clenching the sheets between her fists and letting out a heavy sigh. "Do you think they have any wine?"

I let out a laugh. "Probably, but I'd be wary of any red liquids you find."

She makes a face, standing up from her makeshift bed. "Good point. White it is."

"You won't sleep in the living room by yourself, but you're willing to search the mansion for a bottle of wine to steal?" I ask, floored at her logic.

She shakes her head as if I'm dense. "When I'm sleeping, I'm vulnerable. Vanesa could smother me with a pillow, and I'd never even know it. At least right now I'm awake and aware of what's happening. I can scream. Besides, hopefully you and Miles will have worked out your issues by the time I get back."

"If you make it back," I tease, raising an eyebrow.

She ignores my comment. "Just forgive him, okay? The rest of them are overly concerned about you being a half-blood or whatever because it's different than what they're used to. They don't like anyone that's not themselves. Miles was right to keep it from you, and from them. Look what it's doing—you're worried, and I know you've already considered how this affects who you are, and it doesn't. So forgive him and thank him for trying to protect you so we can move on and save your brother."

"It's not that simple," I say, and receive a wry look from her in return.

"Is it? Or are you just complicating things because his judgmental sisters are making you feel like you're less because they're somehow *more?*"

I sigh, hating that she has a good point and that she was right about me beginning to obsess over how this affects my sense of self, when in reality, what does it really change? The only thing different is that I know about it now. Everything else, for better or worse, is the exact same as it was before I knew. So what? I'm not as strong or perceptive as the rest of the vampires? I'd trade that for my humanity any day. "Just go find your wine and try not to get smothered to death."

Elaine sticks her tongue out at me and exits the room just as I hear footsteps climbing up the stairs. Miles must have been waiting for her to leave, which means he most likely overheard our entire conversation.

"You were listening?" I ask, but already know the answer.

"It was about me. I couldn't help it." He smiles, dark and sexy. His cocky grin fades, becoming more serious when he says, "Can we talk on the balcony?"

He nods toward the glass door in the corner of his room. I

hadn't noticed it before, but it extends to the balcony off the living room that we talked on a few days ago. There's a set of steps that connect the two levels together.

I nod, wishing this wasn't necessary, wishing he hadn't felt compelled to lie to me in the first place. Does he think I can't handle it? That I'm imperfect, or that I truly am lesser than he originally thought me to be? I was special. I was supposed to be the answer to all of their problems, even if we didn't know it at first, and now I'm only somewhat a vampire, and the curse is still intact by some means.

"It's amazing," he says, and at first, I think he's talking about the view, hills stretching out as far as I can see. But as I start to agree with him that the view is gorgeous, I realize he's not talking about the scenery or the rising sun. "It's as though I can see your mind turning as you comb through all the reasons I might have kept this from you."

I lean against the railing, a cool breeze cascading over my skin and through the strands of hair falling out of my bun. It's almost morning, and I've yet to actually sleep. I shiver at the thought of my nightmare and hope I don't have another episode like that again tonight. "I don't like not having answers. And I hate being left in the dark even more."

"Stop worrying, beautiful." He moves closer to me as I shiver and wraps his warm arms around my shoulders. It clicks then—he's never cold. I always am. I still wear a coat outside—I don't think Miles owns one except to maybe wear for appearances in town.

"I don't know how." I swallow, inhaling slowly. "Am I broken?"

Miles tightens his arms around me, resting his chin on my shoulder. "No. In fact, it's sort of fitting that you're a half-blood, what with all of your faith in humanity."

"But I'm still not what I should be," I whisper, scared that I'll never be able to protect Dallas the way I want to, that I'll be sidelined from every fight because I can't measure up to the competition.

"You're exactly who you should be. *You* get to choose who you are, not the term that's used to describe you. Danielle told you the story that most think of when they think of half-bloods. But many vampires believe that although half-bloods are not as strong or perceptive as the rest of us, they're only deprived of those abilities because they have more soul than we ever will. I always say there must be a balance, and it's possible that in order to keep your soul, you had to forfeit a few other unimportant abilities."

"Did you just make that up?" I ask, because it sounds too good to be true, and Miles has an uncanny capability of making things sound poetic.

He laughs lightly, nudging my hair with his nose. "There's a book on half-bloods in the armory if you don't believe me. It's full of theories and stories of past vampires just like you."

"Do I need a library pass to check it out?" I ask, knowing for a fact that the majority of the Draven siblings will not appreciate me taking one of their possessions from the place they don't want me in to begin with.

"Maybe only read it when you're in the Manor—specifically the armory," he says, and I huff a breathy laugh.

"Am I like this because of the curse? Would I have been normal otherwise?"

"By societal standards, you're more normal than any of us."

"Answer the question," I coax, knowing this is one of those times he tries to sweet talk his way around the truth.

"I wish I knew." He releases his hold on me and moves to lean on the railing. I shift, resting my head on his shoulder, savoring the warmth on this chilly night. "I am sorry for withholding the truth from you. It changes nothing, and I didn't want it to alter the way you view yourself."

"From now on, I need you to be completely transparent with me. I cannot handle Vanesa discovering any more secrets about me I'm not privy to." Soft, golden strokes of light paint the sky, growing stronger with every passing minute. I should probably go to bed, but my mind is far too active to obey sleep, and thinking about my potential meeting with Adrian has me on edge more than usual.

"In the name of being honest," Miles says hesitantly, and immediately, I'd much rather him keep secrets, because the truth frightens me more than I care to admit. I hold my breath in anticipation, hoping my boyfriend doesn't have too many more shattering revelations up his sleeve. "I don't want you meeting with Adrian."

"Miles," I start, but he continues, interrupting my protests.

"I don't trust him, and I don't particularly appreciate the interest he's taken in you. He's not a respectable man. He cheated his way into power by utilizing intimidation and fear strategies to keep the clan members at bay. Why do you think he's here, and not the Twelve? I don't believe he's so intrigued by you that he didn't tell them, but they're not here. He is. Why is that? Why is he waiting on the outskirts to make his move? If he wanted to destroy us before we found a solution, his smartest move would have been to send in his men and wipe us out the moment he discovered we turned you. If you go in there alone… I don't know what he might do, or how he might proceed afterward. I can't protect you."

"There's only so much you can protect me from, and this doesn't qualify as one of those things. Besides, if buying us time buys my brother more time, then I don't really have a choice, do I? I have to go."

"Not alone," he says, his jaw ticking in finality.

"He requested Elliot come alone. I don't think he'll ask anything different of me." I place my hand atop his wrist, giving it a reassuring squeeze. "Would you stop Vira or Vanesa or Danielle from doing this?"

"Yes," he says, without hesitation.

"You would fight them," I agree, touching his chin so he looks at me. In that one glance, understanding passes between us. "But in the end, you wouldn't stop them from doing what needs to be done. If you forbid me from seeing Adrian... *that's* the difference. That's one more thing Vanesa can use against me."

"They don't think you should go either," he argues, but it's halfhearted at best. We both know that even though they agree, their reasonings are entirely different.

"Because they don't trust or like me," I point out the obvious. "I've made my peace with that. Your siblings—Vira, Vanesa, Elliot—will never completely accept me, and that's fine. But I need your trust. If you don't support me, then none of them ever will."

Miles's expression changes then. His eyes search mine, and he takes my face in his hands. "Always. And I'm sorry if I've ever made you feel otherwise."

Clutching his t-shirt, I shake my head, biting my lip as I say, "You haven't."

The sliding glass door to his room opens just then, and Elaine trots onto the balcony with a full bottle of wine in one hand and a glass in the other. "I'm assuming you two have made up?"

"There were hardly any amends to make," I say, a little annoyed by her intrusion.

"Good," she says, handing me the wine glass, "because I'm ridiculously bored, and being anywhere in that house alone makes me uncomfortable."

She tips the bottle of wine into the glass I'm holding, filling it a quarter of the way full. I furrow my brow when she doesn't take it from me. "Where's yours?"

Elaine smirks, touching the neck of the bottle to the tip of my glass, then raises it to her lips. "Cheers. May we live very long and vampire-free lives—well, oh. Sorry. That's just for me I suppose." She pauses, biting her lip. "How about... To lives that last the normal expanse of time and beyond."

"I didn't realize you loved wine so much." I take a long, slow swig of the tart liquid.

Elaine purses her lips, gazing out at the magnificent view. "I'm twenty-one now, so I might as well indulge a little, given I'll never have a normal life or normal friends, or parents who throw me a huge party for my birthday."

"I'm so sorry. I didn't realize. When was your birthday?" I ask, feeling like a genuinely awful friend. Birthdays and holidays seem like such an insignificantly mundane part of life now, and I'd never even stopped to wonder when hers was.

"Two weeks ago, but it's okay. You couldn't have known—I never told you," she says bitterly, taking a large gulp from the bottle. "Oliver didn't remember."

I close my eyes, feeling the light wind on my face as my heart breaks for her. Oliver is all she has. At such a stressful time, she needs someone to lean on. Except her best friend isn't there.

"That's horrible, Elaine. What about his parents?" I ask, knowing that they, too, usually make a big deal about it.

She takes another gulp, tears clouding her blue eyes. "His mom called, but she didn't invite me over. She dropped off a tray of cookies at my door, but I was here so I missed her. Part of me thinks that was intentional."

Miles reaches across me. He touches her hand affectionately, then takes the wine glass from my hand and taps it to her bottle. "Happy birthday, Elaine."

He takes a small sip, then hands it back to me.

A singular tear escapes from Elaine's eye, and she brushes it away quickly. I place an arm around her, leaning my head against hers. "Happy birthday."

"I'm so sorry," she says as another tear falls. "You guys were having a moment, and I just came out here and ruined it because I'm lonely."

"We have plenty of moments." I look at Miles for confirmation, and he agrees. I can see in his eyes how much he aches to take away her hurt. "Besides, who doesn't love a glass of wine with friends, huh?"

She nods, but I can tell our sentiment doesn't ease her pain.

"Are you okay?" I ask, wishing there was something more I could do or say to make her feel better, to explain away Oliver's change in behavior that doesn't insinuate he's involved with everything going on. "Tell me what you need."

She drops her head on her hands as she leans into the railing for support. "I just need a friend."

"You've got two," I tell her, pulling her up and hugging her fiercely.

Miles rubs her back soothingly as I rock her in my arms. My heart breaks for her.

"Why does this always happen to me?" she asks, trying to hide the emotion in her voice. "He knew what Owen put me through when he ghosted me, and now he's doing the same thing. He was my family. He was all I had. How could he just abandon me? It's like I don't know who he is anymore."

Her words strike deep in my core, and I remember feeling the exact same way when Derek attacked us. I felt lost, hopeless, like I'd done something wrong to make him turn on me the way he did. It's taken me a long time to realize that there's nothing I could have done differently to prevent him from becoming who he did. Most of that was because of Ambrose's influence, but the darkness was always in him. That couldn't be created out of thin air. Sometimes I even wonder who he would be now that Ambrose is gone—does he regret his actions, would he take them back, or did Ambrose unlock a deeply buried part of him that he will never manage to outrun?

"Having your heart broken is never easy," I say, stroking the back of her hair. And suddenly I remember what I told Nadia about change and moving on with your life despite its hardships. It was just something I said to distract her, to make her think more of me than she seemed to in the moment. But that doesn't make them any less true. Those words should have been saved for Elaine. "Sometimes, that change is what you need to grow, to move on and realize your true potential. Good or bad, everything that happens to you changes you in a way that you may not have realized you needed at the time. You just have to embrace the pain and find the beauty in it."

I feel her nod against my chest, and she lifts her head, eyes rimmed with tears. "I'm so glad I met you."

I laugh, removing the hair that sticks to her damp cheeks. "Even if it turned your life upside down?"

She smiles sadly, wiping the mascara from under her eyes. "Especially because it did."

CHAPTER 26

*M*y feet crunch on the dirt pathway as I move cautiously through the woods, flanked by Owen and Gwen. Miles—despite our conversation last night—still wasn't comfortable with sending me to meet Adrian alone. Adrian specifically said I was not to be accompanied by a Draven... technically, Owen and Gwen are not Dravens, although they are part of their clan. If he didn't want a single person to come with me, he should have been more specific.

A dark figure stands up ahead, shaded by the thick trees that block the rising sun. It's only seven in the morning, but Adrian was willing to meet, and I didn't want to put this off any longer. His tall figure shadows over me, intimidating and purposeful as he moves closer than I'm comfortable with. He demands a sort of attention and omits an urgency and darkness into the air around him that makes him someone worth respecting, but also fearing. And despite how still I hold my hands and how straight I stand, I'm utterly terrified.

"Aspen Troy," he says darkly. His eyes light up as they scan the length of my body. "I see you disregarded my request to come alone."

"You said not to bring a Draven. They're not Dravens," I say, tilting my head to the side, assessing him, as well. Four vampires emerge from the trees, apprehending both Gwen and Owen so that if I need them, they can't get to me. "If you hurt them, I walk."

"And what is to say we won't hurt you?" he asks, scrutinizing me with his gaze. His tongue trails along the tips of his teeth, then he bites his bottom lip. "What gives you the impression that anything you say carries any weight in this situation?"

"The same reason you haven't killed me yet, I presume. I'm not sure what it is, but I know it's why I'm alive." I force my hands to remain still at my sides. "Besides, this is not your territory. You hold no jurisdiction here."

"Intuitive," he remarks, lips stretching into a pleased line. "I underestimated your talents."

"We are not a threat to you," I say, desperate to get straight to the point before he sees right through my ruse. "The Dravens only wish to continue living as they have for the past centuries."

His eyes spark, and he spreads his arms in a warm greeting, but his intentions feel anything but welcoming. "Have you noticed that when you refer to *your* clan, you speak of them as if you are not part of it? Nothing but a bystander recruited to meet their demands. By blood right, you are as much a part of their clan as the very first member. I'm also assuming you were turned by one of the siblings, given that you reek of the middle child… Miles, is it? You must forgive me, I'm a little rusty on my knowledge of them after all this time."

I raise a shoulder, unwilling to confirm or deny any of his suspicions without knowing his intentions. "I think we both know you made a point to learn everything there is to know about the Dravens before you stepped foot in London. It's a bit dangerous of you to leave your own territory unattended. The only way you would is if you were certain another clan head wouldn't try to steal it from under you... and you could only be certain of that if what you were doing here was more important than one of them gaining more land and power."

Adrian's jaw tics and I can tell I've struck a nerve, which means I'm closer to the truth than he'd prefer.

"Anyway," I continue, satisfied that I made even the slightest of dents in his facade. "You've been wanting to speak with me for a while, and while I appreciate your last attempt being... civil, as I asked, I was busy at the time. But I'm here now. So, what is it you need from me?"

"Do you honestly expect me to believe the Dravens aren't working on a way to break the curse as we speak?" he asks, unfazed by my change in subject.

"I'm just here to do their bidding," I say, mimicking what he said about me previously. "What you believe is not up to me. You could have asked Elliot yourself, but you wanted to see me. So again, I wonder why?"

"'Why' is a very broad inquiry," he says, tipping his head up in superiority. "Try being more specific."

I think hard, not sure of how many free answers he'll offer without expecting something in return. So I settle on something that isn't quite so close to the curse that it will give him pause, but close enough that I can hopefully receive an answer that will help us in the long run. "Why haven't you killed me yet?"

He knows I've turned recently, that much is clear from his presence here, so why is he waiting? I could be turning humans left and right, but he doesn't seem concerned enough about that to end my life.

"If this is what you wish to understand," he says, seeming to weigh his options, probably filtering his response in his head. "Your ancestor and I took a blood oath two hundred years ago, in which I swore that I would not kill you until it was absolutely necessary."

"Necessary?" I ask, interest piqued.

He smirks, satisfied that he's dangled a piece of the puzzle in front of my face, but not enough for me to grasp on to. "I'm afraid that's all I can say. If I tell you more, then it would prove wiser to kill you now."

"Except... I'm still alive because of Elijah?" I press, hoping he doesn't shut down quite yet.

"I suppose you are, yes."

"And you have an alliance with the hunters."

"A temporary one," he admits, looking displeased about that.

"So why did you want to meet with me?" I take a step forward. Instantly, a few vampires move out of the woods, ready to come to Adrian's defense. He holds up a hand, and they fall back—which begs the question, why is he so cautious around me? A half-blood. Does Adrian even know about that?

"I needed to judge for myself how much you knew. Elliot... he's too guarded. Jumpy. He doesn't know the right questions to ask, and I'd never be able to read him like I can you." Adrian moves to me and traces a long finger around the edge of my jaw and up my cheek. He lingers at my hairline, gliding his fingers down a blonde strand. "It is a shame, too," he says more to himself. His gaze lingers on every detail so intently I have to fight the urge to squirm in my skin. "So much wasted potential."

I swallow, my pulse sputtering out of control. "It doesn't have to be."

"Even so, you will never stop your pursuit of the truth," he coos softly, seeming almost regretful. "In the end, you will give me no choice but to take your life. Curiosity—it's in your nature. You hold so many of your ancestor's qualities, more so than anyone who has come before you. It's no wonder it was you that was led here by fate."

"I'm not so sure it was fate," I say breathlessly, paralyzed by his touch and the cold air that surrounds us. It's as though his fingertips extract every ounce of warmth from beneath my skin and pull it to the surface, leaving me cold and empty in their wake. "What is it about the Dravens that has the most powerful beings in the world frightened?"

"Their influence is unlike anything the world has ever seen. They're a beacon of hope, survival. They show our people a different way. One without fear, and murder, and treachery. Without that, our seats hold no power. We rule by intimidation, but the Dravens... they rule by respect. If they are not incapacitated, the vampire world as we know it will be changed forever." Adrian stops abruptly, breaking eye contact with me as though he cannot believe what he's just admitted.

"Maybe it should be." My legs quiver as he circles around me, prowling like a predator, which consequently makes me the prey. "The Twelve have been in command for a long time. Maybe change is imminent."

"Only if we don't finish what we started."

"Eliminating the Draven clan." I piece together his meaning.

"It shouldn't have to be that way. You blamed the curse on a dead man's actions. There is no justification for killing them now."

Adrian blinks away the clouds in his eyes as though he's trying to see through a haze. "How is it you're doing that?"

"Doing what?" I ask, taking a step away and breaking whatever hold was keeping me rooted in place.

"Your purity," he says. His expression grows hard as he takes me in, and he places a hand above my heart. "I could feel it."

"I don't understand." I shake my head, backing away again as a hungry gleam takes root behind his eyes.

He blinks rapidly to rid whatever he was thinking from his head and takes a long stride forward, closing the distance I put between us. "No matter. Once you get close enough to the truth, I have permission to end your life."

Adrian says nothing more, just waits for me to leave. I nod once, not sure this meeting changes anything, and confused as ever on what his plans are.

Though, I suppose one good thing came out of this wasted time—so long as the curse remains unbroken, Adrian and the hunters won't attack, and I get to keep my life.

If only breaking the curse wasn't a crucial part of saving my brother's life—though, the Dravens would never settle for such an arrangement anyway. Now that they know hope isn't lost for their clan, they won't rest until they are free.

I steadily back away from Adrian, only turning away from him when I near Owen and Gwen, who are no longer bound by Adrian's men.

"And Aspen?" Adrian calls after me. "When I send my men for your audience, you don't refuse."

~

The three of us walk in silence back through the woods until we reach town, where Miles and Elliot await our return. I tried to convince them to stay at the Manor, but Miles insisted they be close enough to rescue us if things went awry. Elliot could care less about my well-being. If it weren't for the fact that I'm still the only means they have of creating more vampires, he probably would have left Miles to wait for me alone.

Vira seemed to want to come along too but decided against it in the end. I think that desire was mostly on principle, though—that, and Vanesa has been an earful since her return, so I'm sure she was just itching to be away from her. Besides Elliot, the rest of the siblings are still upset over what Vanesa did to Dallas. Me included.

It has only been a few short hours, but after my nightmare escapades, Vanesa has been considerably more annoying about how right she was about me since the beginning. I had hoped Vira's outburst would have reeled her in a little and made her reconsider what's actually important, but Vanesa can't stay dormant for long, even when it should be me berating her for hurting my brother. But in the name of more important issues, I've decided to set aside my hatred of her—for the time being—and worry about our current problems. I can off Vanesa any time I please.

"You're all right?" Elliot asks, looking both skeptical and surprised when the three of us return unscathed. Meanwhile, his bruises from late last night are still slightly visible. Vampires heal almost immediately, but no differently than humans—just faster. Bruises and cuts are still visible for a short time, and even a scar or two may appear before the skin properly heals itself—again, just at an accelerated rate.

Miles eyes us, checking for injuries, but there aren't any to be found.

"They hardly laid a finger on us," Gwen says, seeming surprised herself. She was highly nervous about walking into the lion's den without any weapons or backup. "It seems Adrian's only interest was..."

Both she and Owen look at each other, and then at me. Owen finishes her thought. "His only interest was with Aspen. He was hardly fazed that we accompanied her."

"In fact," Gwen continues, looking more perplexed as they further describe the events of our meeting. "He seemed almost impressed that she found a loophole in his request."

"Tell me you at least convinced him," Elliot says. I can tell he's perturbed that I didn't receive the beating he did.

I glance down at my shoes in the dirt and toe a little hole into it as I speak. "I didn't have to. He said he took a blood oath with Elijah after the curse was created. He can't lay a hand on me so long as we don't come close to breaking the curse."

"He alluded to it as a puzzle," Gwen adds. "Which is not at all how we've been approaching a fix."

"I don't care that *you're* safe," Elliot says bluntly, and I'm taken aback. He completely disregards Gwen as if she hadn't spoken at all. "What about my family?"

"I—" I start, but realize I never asked him for specifics. Adrian could easily have been pulling the same trick I did on him when I brought Gwen and Owen along. *I'm* safe, but are the Dravens? Though, somehow I find myself dismissing that thought. "He didn't say, but—"

Elliot scoffs. "Vanesa was right. You do only look out for yourself."

Owen steps forward, sensing the hostility in Elliot's words. "Adrian insinuated that he would not be advancing on our territory so long as we didn't pursue the curse."

"Basically, he won't be attacking us until we've discovered whatever it is we need to break it," Gwen says, stepping forward so Elliot has no choice but to acknowledge she's spoken. Still, he looks unsatisfied.

"You were supposed to negotiate with him and bargain for our survival." He grits his teeth, and Miles shoots him a warning glance, muttering his name beneath his breath the way he often does when Vanesa is about to take matters too far.

"She didn't need to," Gwen defends me, and suddenly, other than the added protection, I'm thankful for their presence today. Elliot may not trust me, but when both Gwen and Owen come to my defense, it's harder for him to deny that what I said is the truth. He's also more likely to believe what they tell him as opposed to anything that comes out of my mouth. "She's a natural leader. Truly. The meeting couldn't have gone better."

Elliot looks to Owen for reassurance. "You agree with this?"

Owen nods, looking uncomfortable with being singled out. "I do. Aspen handled herself exceptionally, especially for being a newborn. Your father would have been impressed."

Miles smirks, looking impressed himself. He shoots a smug glance at Elliot.

"You're welcome," I say, knowing I will never receive a thanks from him, even if I single-handedly brought him back to life. At least Vira was humble enough to acknowledge what I did for her and her family three months ago—Elliot will never have enough humility to acknowledge my importance.

"I will never thank you for putting us in this position," he says, then turns his back on us. As if he'd have known it was possible to break the curse without me.

Just to agitate him more, I say, "I know you won't. You're not evolved enough for that. But I will still assume your gratitude accordingly. So, as I said, you're welcome."

CHAPTER 27

*N*ow that we know Adrian isn't planning to wipe out the Dravens until he's sure we'll break the curse—or so he alluded—we can all breathe easier and search for a solution without looking over our shoulders every other minute. And so far, it's proven to assist with our productivity as a whole. Knowing we can put our imminent deaths on the back burner for the time being, we can distribute our undivided attention to the curse—how it was orchestrated, who created it, and how to reverse its effects quickly and quietly before anyone else figures out what we've done.

Sadly, we still haven't the slightest clue how to approach solutions to any of those issues. Honestly, it does feel like a hopeless waste of time. Except, if this waste of time gets me even the slightest bit closer to saving my brother, I won't hesitate.

Aggravated at our lack of progress, I grunt under my breath and exit the living room where everyone is working on their own individual research. I don't know where I'm going or why, but I find myself wandering the long halls of Draven Manor, aimlessly walking in and out of closed doors. I'm not sure if I'm looking for something—a clue, inspiration, blatant answers, because short of someone telling me exactly what to do, I'm not sure we'll ever find what we're looking for. Partly because we don't have the slightest idea what that is.

After the third or fourth door, I meander up a short staircase and stumble upon a small room. Air escapes my lungs at the mere sight of it, and I find myself in awe of the beauty before me. All around the room is glass that overlooks Ichorye. I can see the rooftops of most houses. Some, like my own, are covered by the thinning brush of trees as the leaves fall off in preparation for winter. The colors are immaculate—yellow, red, brown, orange, and some a golden mix of all four. I'd ventured up the cliff Miles took me to a few weeks ago for solace, and the view was unlike anything I'd ever seen. Until this.

I tear my eyes from the scenery to look at the sights to the right and left of me. One side shows the rounded loop of houses where the Draven clan lives, and the other is simply a thick brush of trees.

Turning, I find that the length of the wall behind me is covered in rich hardwood panels that match the rest of the Manor's woodwork, and a plush white carpet hugs my feet as I venture farther inside the room.

Elaine can never see this room. She will feel inferior as a watcher, because this view runs circles around the one she has at home. Although, I suppose she has a better view of people and their whereabouts. This is more scenic, general. Except there's nothing general about its beauty.

For such a dark and dangerous place, Ichorye resembles a fairytale landscape.

I hear the door open and close behind me, and sigh inwardly, expecting Elaine or Miles to have chased after me. Or maybe it's Vanesa, here to murder me in the most beautiful place imaginable. So I'm surprised when it's Lucas who speaks.

"I see you've discovered our hidden treasure."

"And here I thought the armory was the most sacred place in Draven Manor," I tease. "No one told me a room like this existed."

If I stay here long enough, I'm almost positive I could convince myself this is my life. I could pretend to be Rapunzel, without an escape. Except this wouldn't be my prison, but my sanctuary, protecting me from the dangers that lie below—not a hindrance keeping me from happiness.

I sigh, turning to find Lucas is just as entranced by the view as I am, and he gets to see it whenever he likes. "Why does someone always chase after me when I leave a room? Or is that a Draven fault I'll have to learn to accept?"

Lucas throws his head back in laughter. The sound isn't loud, but it echoes off the windows in the empty room. There isn't a single item of furniture in the entire space. "I'm afraid you'll have to adjust," he confirms my fears. "Don't be mad. We all care about you, Aspen. We've had hundreds of years to digest the insanity that is the world we live in. You've had approximately ninety days. And, if it's any consolation, I come here when I'm stressed. It wasn't for you."

"I can't recall the last time I was alone for more than a few minutes," I admit. When *was* the last time I was alone? When Miles was upset and I showered while waiting for him to get home? Even then I wasn't relaxing, but worrying about him, worrying about his safety. I never actually enjoyed the quiet.

Lucas grunts, his smile a little more cynical now. "Welcome to the life of loving a Draven."

And again, I'd forgotten Lucas isn't a Draven by blood or bloodline, which is weird because of his relationship with Danielle. It's weird of me to think of him as a sibling because he's not. And yet... he's one of them just the same.

"You're a Draven," I counter, smiling smugly.

"In all the ways that count," he agrees. "Which is all the more reason to believe me when I say, get used to feeling suffocated. And constantly bickering with Vira and Vanesa. Although, Vira has been better, and I think we have you to thank for that."

I roll my eyes. The second Vanesa kidnapped my brother, Vira slid right into her shoes, making snide remarks like she used to.

"Seriously," Lucas continues, seeming to pick up on my skepticism. "After so many years and so many hunters later, it's hard to maintain your faith in humanity. You'll understand one day. But you... you embody the best qualities of what it means to be human."

I don't say anything, mostly because I hardly talk to Lucas like this, but I also disagree. I just think he's spent way too much time around the wrong kind of humans. The ones out for blood. The ones who believe they're right above all else and refuse to do what's right, simply because it won't benefit them.

Vampires are like humans. They're not all bad, but they're not all good, and in your life, you're going to experience both kinds. Vanesa is the perfect example of someone who will do what it takes to get what she wants. But Miles, he's what it means to believe in others, to be kind, even when it's not always in his best interest—like taking my side over his family's, for example.

I don't think that the number of bad people who walk this earth should ever be a justifiable excuse to give up on the good, however few there are.

And despite how highly Lucas thinks of me, I can't be certain which category I fall into anymore.

Pale skin peeking out from beneath the white sheet is all I see as I stare at the lump on the armory table. I still can't bring myself to look at his face, so I touch his hand. It feels warm beneath my fingers. I'm not sure what else I was expecting. Dallas is still alive. It's just hard for me to believe that when he sits on a table like a lab rat, chest moving so slightly that at first glance, he looks dead.

"I'm going to fix you, okay?" I promise, and my throat constricts.

I'm not technically supposed to be down here alone. We came to an agreement that Elaine and I could enter the armory only if we were accompanied by *two* of the siblings. That was mostly so Miles couldn't bring me down here on his own. This way, we have to have someone else's approval as well.

It won't be long until one of them discovers I'm not in the bathroom where I said I'd be, but I couldn't fight the persisting urge to see my brother without a babysitter.

"If you want, I'll even let you kill Vanesa," I whisper, just in case someone discovers where I am and comes to scold me. "Or we could do it together as a form of sibling bonding."

My phone buzzes with a text from Elaine, warning me that

a few of them are going hunting for food, and that I should probably leave the armory before they figure out where I really am. How Elaine knows where I am… I have no clue. Maybe there's some validity to this watcher occupation of hers, after all. But it's also possible she's just nosy and pays more attention to my whereabouts than I thought.

Once I'm back upstairs, I haphazardly rinse my hands in the bathroom so they're damp when I return to the living room just in case Elaine isn't the only one paying attention. I shoot her a questioning glance, and she taps her eyes to insinuate that she was *watching* me.

I've been meaning to talk to her about Oliver again, but with all of our research, and my meeting with Adrian this morning, I haven't had a chance.

Owen and Gwen are here with us, too—much to Elaine's dismay. They stopped by to present another dead-end idea from a clan member, and Vira asked them to stay so we could get through our materials more quickly. I still maintain that a bunch of old books aren't going to help, but we don't have any other leads, so I'm just hoping we find something, however small, that sends us in the right direction.

Danielle slams closed the book she's been skimming and drops it to the floor with the rest of her discarded pile. "I can't wait any longer, I'm starving. Is everyone ready?"

Gwen sighs, and almost everyone else in the room follows suit, tired of researching. I think we're all itching to walk around a bit, and I know for a fact that I'm hungry, too. My stomach has been growling insistently for the past hour.

We all stand, including Elaine, which provokes an aggravated look from Elliot. "You are not coming."

She raises an eyebrow, and I already know she's waiting for

him to realize leaving her behind means giving her free range of the Manor. When they met with their clan that one time, they left us both here alone, but that was before even I knew what or where the armory was, or how to get inside.

He elaborates, as if he needs to establish his reasoning. "You're human."

"And you're a prick," she points out, and Danielle lets out a surprised laugh. I manage to hold mine in because I'm used to Elaine's candidness by now. "But I still have to deal with you."

"No," he says sternly, and Vanesa groans, knowing this will turn into an argument before the minute is up.

"That's the same thing you said when Aspen wanted into the armory, and now she's privy to all of our secrets," she says sourly. "Just face it. We've been overtaken by modern hussies, and our brothers and sister have fallen prey to their seduction."

Vanesa, as ever, is being overdramatic.

"No," Elliot repeats once again, and it's obvious he has no real argument. He doesn't want to leave Elaine here alone.

"Fine." Elaine sighs dramatically, plopping back down on the couch. "I'll just stay here. All alone. Sifting through all the dangerous poisons in the armory. I mean, how hard could it really be to use herbs to make someone bend to your every whim? I think I read something about that in one of your—"

"Just stay a safe distance behind us," he snaps, and Vanesa shakes her head, knowing he'd cave. Then he adds over his shoulder, "We wouldn't want to mistake you for a deer."

CHAPTER 28

*E*laine is still murmuring indecencies about Elliot under her breath as we burrow deeper into the woods. Everyone looks for their own meal, spreading out slightly as the trees thicken.

Owen and Gwen break off together, and I think I heard them say this is the first time they've hunted with any of the siblings. I find that strange for as often as the siblings call on them for assistance. I've only hunted with Miles, but that's because no one else likes me enough to invite me for dinner, and Danielle and Lucas typically go off on their own.

I catch up with Miles, and we veer off in the direction Owen and Gwen went. Basically, we go in the opposite direction as the rest of his family. Elaine follows, and despite her annoyance at Elliot's deer comment, she stays a safe distance back. Miles catches his meal quickly, but it takes me longer, and I know now that it's because I'm not a *real* vampire. I'm the cheap knockoff you buy at an off-brand store because the real thing is too expensive.

I groan, not even sure I understand my own analogies

anymore, and catch hold of something scurrying in my peripheral.

"That was a pretty decent grab," Miles says, nodding at the squirrel now squirming in my hands. Then he winks. "For a half-blood."

It's still hard for me to put aside my disgust when I sink my teeth into a warm-blooded creature, but it has gotten a little easier over time. More often than not, though, I find myself wasting half of my meal when I think too hard about what I'm eating, because I can't stand the vulgarity of it.

I touch Miles's chin, then nod to my meal versus his, both squirrels. "Mine is still bigger than yours."

"Only because I left the big one for you, beautiful," he says, and I'm once again reminded that we are discussing raw squirrels as dinner and feel the urge to vomit.

Before I eat, I glance behind me to check on Elaine. I can't imagine what it must be like to watch nine vampires indulge in raw meat. I just want to make sure she's not looking when I do —some things even a best friend should never see. When I look back though, she's not behind us anymore. She's quite a ways back, talking to Owen while he waits for Gwen to finish up her meal.

I smile fondly, but there's still a small pang of anger that pricks at my chest when I remember how he once hurt her, even if it was for a semi-decent, although senseless, reason. Just because Elaine's ancestor wanted his family far from vampire affairs, and the Dravens wanted to respect his wishes, doesn't mean Owen should have disappeared without an explanation and then pretend to not know her. He abandoned her for the right reasons, just in the wrong way, and it wound up hurting her all the more. The thought of him doing anything like that to her again, remembering her crying last night over Oliver's absence and how that pain stemmed from Owen's abandonment, makes my blood boil. I've never felt so protective over someone who wasn't my brother, not even Miles. Though, in a lot of ways, I suppose Elaine has become like a sister to me.

"You okay?" Miles asks, sensing my rise in resentment toward the men in Elaine's life.

Elliot is by us now, and he's also watching Owen and Elaine, mumbling on about how he doesn't understand the appeal of humans. Then he realizes who he's talking to—a newly turned half-blood, and her vampire boyfriend.

Ignoring Elliot, because I'm beginning to realize what a waste of breath it is arguing with his depreciating remarks, I turn toward Miles and notice a flash out of the corner of my eye.

"Yeah, I'm…" My eyes follow the movement. It's not fast, not like us, and definitely too slow to be any sort of animal. I blame my less-than-quality eyesight for the fact that I can't see exactly what's there.

"Aspen?" Miles follows my gaze, growing stiff.

Everyone else is still eating and completely unaware of an extra presence amongst us—too busy engorging themselves.

Actually…

"There's more than one," I whisper to Miles, and he nods stiffly, glancing casually around at his family. "Is Elaine still with Owen?" I ask, because if there's an attack, I want to make sure someone's close enough to protect her—God-forbid she's mistaken for one of them like I was.

Miles nods as his eyes roam the area around us.

"Hunters?" I gulp. The hairs on my arms stand up. I've yet to have a good experience with any of them. Not even when I was a human did I have a good encounter—mostly because he killed me, but semantics.

"Six," Miles confirms, keeping his voice low and me close to his side. "They know we've seen them."

I nod, figuring as much since I was trying to figure out what was watching us for so long. There's no way they didn't notice me staring.

"What do we do?" I ask, panicking as I grab his wrist. We have them fairly outnumbered, but I'm sure they're carrying weapons. Plus, they have a height advantage, given some of them are up in the trees. "No one else has noticed them."

"None of them have their weapons raised. They're only partially circling us, too."

"They're only watching," I say, not sure if I should take comfort in that realization or not.

Miles nods and places a guiding hand on my back. "I don't think they'll attack, but just to be sure, we should retreat home. Grab Elaine, Gwen, and Owen. I will gather my siblings."

"Are you sure *they* won't attack?" I press, worried that if Vanesa finds out we're being watched, she might provoke them.

Except when Elaine speaks, her surprised voice loud enough to get everyone's attention, none of that matters.

"Oliver?" She steps away from Owen, who is suddenly on guard and at her side, and peers into the trees. Sure enough, a man steps out hesitantly, eyes darting nervously from face to face. "Why are you out here?"

Oliver stands taut, shaking his head shortly, but it's not at Elaine. I look behind me where his gesture was directed, and see someone nod, lowering a crossbow. The rest of the Dravens are now taking notice of the extra pairs of eyes around us, craning their necks up at the trees. Vanesa growls, but Elliot holds up a hand, and she stays rooted in place.

"Ollie?" Elaine prods, though I suspect she already knows why he's here, and my heart breaks for her.

I never wanted to be right about him.

"My dog got loose, and I was searching for him," Oliver says, features stony. He's very attractive—light brown hair, golden skin that matches hers—and I'm sure when he smiles, his whole face lights up. Except I highly doubt I'll be seeing him at such ease anytime soon.

Elaine shakes her head, seeming confused. Maybe she doesn't realize why he's here. She can't see the five other men in the woods awaiting his instruction. "You live near me on the other side of town. Why would you be looking over here?"

"We were just leaving," Miles speaks up and moves slightly ahead of me. "If we come across *your dog*, we'll be sure to let you know."

"I appreciate that." Oliver nods, and it's clear how nervous he is. I don't envy his position. "We'll be going now."

Still stunned, Elaine shakes her head, stepping toward him. Already, I can sense the growing edge in her voice. "We? What's going on? Why are you here?"

Movement to the left makes her jump, and knowing that Gwen and Owen are on her right, her expression changes immediately, and she begins moving away from him.

"Elaine." Oliver reaches his arm out and completely lets his guard down, which I'm sure is not appreciated by his fellow hunters—not when he's surrounded by nine vampires. Ten, if they don't know Elaine is human. "They're not what you think."

"Neither are you!" she yells, jerking her arms. The

movement causes her to lose her balance, and she starts to fall backward, but both Owen and Gwen rush to catch her, grabbing on to either arm. I move around Miles and walk normally over to Elaine's side so as not to startle the other hunters around us. I don't have to turn around to know Miles has followed behind me, and not because of my heightened senses. I just know he wouldn't let me stand by Elaine's side alone. "You're one of *them.*"

"And since when are you helping the Dravens? You hate them, Elaine. We both do," Oliver argues. I'm assuming Adrian sent them to keep an eye on us, but Oliver slipped up when he saw that Elaine was here with us.

I can practically hear Elliot roll his eyes when he speaks. "Why don't you two finish this lovers' spat another day so we can get home."

"Humans make everything so complicated," Vanesa mumbles in agreement, following Elliot's lead as he begins walking in the direction of Draven Manor. They glance around to make sure the hunters remain where they are, and once they're content, Vira, Danielle, and Lucas follow behind them.

Meanwhile, Elaine is still fuming. "No, *you* made me hate them. Everything I thought about them was based on what you told me, and well, now I guess I know how you learned so much."

Oliver moves toward her, and this time she doesn't back away. She raises her chin, crossing her arms over her chest. "And it was all true. I'm trying to protect people."

"A vendetta isn't protecting anyone," she says. Her statement reminds me of the hunter who almost killed me over the summer. His hatred wasn't just of the Dravens, but of their kind, and the fact that I was affiliated with them was enough for him to want to take my life when I was technically still a human.

"Elaine," Oliver says, looking genuinely remorseful. Maybe it's possible not all hunters are as malicious as the ones I've encountered. For Elaine's sake, I hope that's true.

"You could have told me," she whispers. "I would have understood. You could have made my heartbreak much easier if you'd only told me the truth."

Gwen moves around us, sensing the finality of the conversation, and joins the rest of the Dravens impatiently waiting at the edge of the woods.

"It seems you recovered." Oliver glances behind Elaine at Owen, not buying her heartbreak comment. He then looks at Miles, lingering for only a moment before his gaze rests on me.

The wind picks up, a side effect of the pending thunderstorm still looming above us, and blows in my direction, dragging with it a metallic scent. It's a weird mix of blood, sweat, and dirt.

I study Oliver's eyes and feel a pang of familiarity when they meet mine, harder and colder than they had been when they looked at Elaine. Except I see a hint of fear buried deep behind the layers of revulsion and loathing he holds for vampires. It makes my skin recoil for some odd reason. How can a good person hold so much resentment toward someone they don't know? And even when he speaks to me, his tone is different, colder, as though he's been programmed to hate us since the day he was born.

"Your kind doesn't belong on this earth," he spits, and my blood runs cold.

Images from last July unfold in my head like a slideshow, blinding me to everything in front of me. I can no longer see the trees or my friends. The world spins, and images of me dying, screaming in pain, begging to be killed just to stop the suffering, replace reality.

Rage like I've never felt before explodes inside of me, and my skin feels as if there are flames erupting from it as I shove past Elaine and shake off Miles when he tries to stop me from making things worse for us.

"It was you," I growl, my voice low and steely as I squeeze Oliver's neck in my hand, backing him up against a tree. "You did this to me."

He claws at my wrist, but my grasp is too strong for him to breathe, much less fight me off. He was distracted by Elaine, by the memories of how he tortured me, and I managed to catch him off guard.

"Aspen." Miles is beside me now, trying to talk me down, but I can't hear reason. "If you don't put him down, the hunters are going to kill you."

He looks around anxiously, trying his hardest to stay calm. I risk a glance behind us and notice the hunters have moved from their hiding spots and are now standing around, all with their weapons pointed at me.

"Aspen, please. Don't get yourself killed over someone like him," Miles pleads with me.

Oliver is trying to move his head, and it takes me a moment to realize he's trying to communicate with his team. I loosen my hold enough for him to talk, but not enough so that he can tell them to kill me without me cutting off his airway first.

"Stand down," he rasps, his eyes wide and terrified. So unlike the stone-cold ones that broke my wrist, shattered my knee, and left me in the middle of a field to die. "The American vampire was very clear. We can't kill them yet."

The American. Adrian.

"Why are you working for Adrian?" I grunt, figuring I might as well get something out of him if I can't beat him to death.

"We want a town free of vampires. Once you discover how to break the curse, he helps us eradicate you," Oliver chokes on his words, and I realize I was unintentionally clamping down on his throat.

"Why doesn't he want us dead yet? Why not kill us right here and now?"

"He won't tell us, but without him, we can't win a war against all of you." Oliver claws at my hand on his throat, and Miles once again asks me to let him go. If it weren't for the five men with raised weapons around us, I'd be really irritated that he refuses to let me enjoy this.

"He's the one who killed me. Who *mistook* me for one of you." Oliver lets out a strange sound as my fingers crush his neck. Against my primal urges, I release him, and he drops to the ground, heaving for air. I look him up and down, malice lacing every word. "You deserve so much worse than what I could ever do to you."

In my furious haze, I'd totally forgotten about Elaine, about the bomb he just dropped on her, and that she's known him way longer than I have. What if she doesn't believe what I accused him of and thinks I've mistaken him for someone else?

"I'm so sorry," I say as earnestly as I can. Because I'm not really sorry, but out of respect for her, I am.

She clenches her teeth. Tears spill over her cheeks as she marches up to him, and I can tell it's taking everything in Miles not to throw us both over his shoulder and book it out of here right now. Owen is still standing by us, but he looks beyond confused and completely incapable of intervening in his shocked state.

"Is it true?" she asks Oliver, her lip quivering.

"They're killers," Oliver says, pleading with her to understand, and a part of me really does feel for him if he thinks that is enough to make her choose his side.

Because Elaine is stubborn and lionhearted. She twists her hips, tears and fury glistening in her eyes as she swings her arm, striking him in the face. "So are you."

CHAPTER 29

"You are frighteningly strong for a human," Vira remarks, tossing an icepack onto Elaine's lap, which she promptly wraps in a cloth and presses to her fist.

Elaine grunts, stretching her fingers stiffly. "My knuckles would disagree."

"He's a hunter," Danielle says, settling on the couch next to her. "They're incredibly strong for being mortal. I'm surprised the impact didn't shatter your hand."

"Maybe it's a watcher ability?" Elaine suggests, and Elliot lets out a groan from his chair in the corner, where he sits looking tired, miserable, and now thanks to Elaine, more annoyed than before.

"Watchers don't have abilities, stupid. You're entirely human." Vanesa deflates Elaine's ego, causing her to visibly sag.

Ironically enough, Elaine only wants to be special, to have a purpose, and here I am wishing I could give mine away.

"I should have listened to you," Elaine says to me, but the last thing I wanted was to be right about Oliver.

"You had no reason to believe me." I sit on her other side and take the icepack from her, pulling her fist into my lap and holding it on for her. "I wasn't sure he was a hunter. I just knew he was distracting you while Nadia talked to me for some reason."

Vanesa's head jerks up, and she shoots me an accusatory look. "You never told us that."

I swallow and force myself not to look at Miles. Because I told *him* my suspicions about Oliver, and I thought he told his siblings.

"I wasn't sure," I say, biting the proverbial bullet. "I didn't want to start an unnecessary investigation into some random person who may or may not be involved."

"If Oliver is helping Nadia, that means they've broken protocol and involved a human," Miles says. The hunters, much like the vampires, operate in the shadows. The more people who know about them, the harder it is for them to do their job, especially when their organization is immersed in the police force.

"That doesn't make any sense," Vanesa argues, twirling a long strand of black hair around her fingers. "How would telling Nadia her fiancé lied about being in the military, and was part of a vampire-hunting cult, assist them in any way?"

"By pointing her to his killer," Elaine says, sounding sure as the air we breathe. "They were hoping to use Nadia to distract us from their alliance with Adrian, or at least give us something to focus on while they spied on us. Nadia is furious and craving revenge. They've let her in, given her a purpose, and are expecting us to chase our tails trying to figure out how to cover up Aaron's murder."

I can tell Vanesa wants to argue with her use of "us", but she lets it go this time. "We've known this whole time, though, so they did a lousy job."

"Only because of Elaine's cameras in town," Danielle pipes up, crossing her ankles and leaning forward. "We only discovered their alliance when we saw that picture of the vampire and hunter. Otherwise, we still wouldn't know about it."

"Either way, Aspen killed Aaron. That doesn't involve us. If she gets caught, it doesn't affect us one way or another—they don't know we were there," Vanesa points out obviously, giving in to her desire to wash her hands of anything that concerns me.

Vira shakes her head, and to my utter astonishment, defends me. "Only because she was trying to save us, Van. As much as we might hate it, we're bound by that night, and I'd prefer that no one goes to jail for self-defense."

Vanesa still doesn't seem to care. Her lack of respect never fails to amaze me. "Okay, but if *she* does, then who cares? She won't rat us out because that would implicate Miles. All I'm saying is, if Nadia wants justice, I don't see why we all have to pay the price. Lucas and Elliot weren't even there."

"Are we not past this yet?" Lucas asks, and here we are, wasting energy on a past disagreement—*again*.

"I'm only trying to prove my point." She cracks her neck and folds her arms in front of her. Although even I'll admit her tone seemed accusatory when she mentioned their absence.

"Unnecessarily," Elliot interrupts, pinching the bridge of his nose. "Please, just give this a rest."

"You know what I want to know?" Vanesa continues, directing her words toward me. It's as though she's not content if she can't blame others for what has gone wrong. "How is it that you could turn, but your brother couldn't?"

Danielle sighs. Even in such dire circumstances, Vanesa always finds a way to view me as the enemy. "Vanesa, it's possible only one person in Elijah's bloodline could break the curse, and those after would be affected in the same way as everyone else."

"Was I asking you?" Vanesa snaps, eyebrows raised at her younger sister. "And she didn't break the curse, she altered it. We hardly have more freedom than we did before."

"You are so shortsighted," Elaine grumbles, but Vanesa doesn't hear her. She's too absorbed in her power trip.

I chuckle under my breath, whispering to Elaine, "And cold-hearted."

"And you know what else?" No one responds, so she takes this as a cue to continue. "We may have been unlucky because of the curse, but at least we didn't have hunters *and* vampires *teaming up* to terminate our existence."

"For the love of God." Elaine rips her hand from my lap, where I'm still holding the ice on her knuckles, and places her palms together. "We've all got problems, but at least we don't whine about them like spoiled children."

Once again, not a word is uttered, and we fall into a tense silence, and Vanesa quiets at last.

When Vira and Elliot begin discussing how to break the curse without drawing attention to ourselves, I clear my throat, hoping I don't sound selfish asking to sleep in a house his siblings don't occupy. "Are we going back to your place tonight?"

Miles looks at me absurdly. "Unless you'd prefer to lie awake all night listening to my siblings argue."

"Another time." I try to come off as sincere but fail miserably. I've never been one for acting. "Can—"

Miles stops me before I finish asking my question. "Elaine can stay in the spare room."

Elaine's inspecting her swollen hand, flexing her fingers stiffly, but I know she's listening because of the tiny smirk on her face. "You don't have to babysit me."

I bump her shoulder with mine and force the ice back on her hand to slow the swelling. Her knuckles have already morphed into a light shade of purple that continues up the back of her hand and to her wrist. "I'm not. Besides, Miles has quite the wine collection…"

"I'll even lend you a bottle," he bribes.

She perks up at this, a challenging gleam in her eye. "Do you have Château Haut-Brion?"

"I have three *bottles* of Château Haut-Brion," he confirms, looking pleased with himself. "From 1813, 1837, and 1973."

I blink, trying to figure out what in the world they are saying. Their words sound like nonsense to me. My mom only drank wine during family events because she claimed anything weaker wouldn't get her through the night, and anything stronger would make it so she didn't remember it. I was only a child then and didn't fully understand what she meant. Our families had a falling out many years ago, so I never had the opportunity to experiment with alcohol after that because Mom would only buy what my father drank—beer.

Whatever Miles said in wine language though, has Elaine eager to leave.

Vanesa starts intervening in Vira's conversation with Elliot, and their voices heighten. Miles and I exchange a quick glance, and I look over at Elaine, asking her if she's ready to leave. She nods and runs upstairs to collect the few items of clothing we left from yesterday. I hadn't known at the time that we would end up staying at the Manor, so my bag was still at Miles's place. Currently, I'm wearing a pair of his old sweatpants and a hoodie that looks so old I'm convinced it's from the nineteen-hundreds. I suppose it could be. I've never heard of the brand on the tag, or at least I don't think I have. It's somewhat hard to read since it's so faded from age. Danielle offered for Elaine and me to borrow her clothes, but Miles's old sweatpants actually fit me better. Danielle is curvy for her age—or her age when she became a vampire—so mostly everything of hers just fell off my slender hips unless I rolled it up fifty times. Elaine, on the other hand, was a better fit.

She returns after only a minute or two with our belongings, lingering in the hallway as Miles tells his siblings goodbye.

"You're leaving?" Vira asks, despite that Miles hardly sleeps here. He once told me stories about building his house, and from what it sounded like, it was a long, long time ago. I've often wondered why the others still live together. I know Danielle is technically young in the eyes of the law, but Lucas is old enough to live on his own. Why they all lodge under one roof is lost on me. Especially when the only thing this family does to bond is argue.

"Is there a reason for us to stay?" Miles asks, moving toward the hallway.

Vira and Danielle walked Owen and Gwen home after our encounter with the hunters, just to be sure they made it back all right, and they weren't followed, so I'm sure we're fine to drive back to Miles's house.

Vanesa shockingly can't help but comment. "They can go. But there's no reason for you to leave, brother. We have a lot to figure out."

Miles shakes his head, and I can see how much her words disappoint him. "When will you accept that Aspen is a part of our lives now?"

Vanesa scrunches her nose. "When she's dead."

"Just go," Vira says, looking torn between arguing and getting us out of here before another fight ensues. "I'll tell you if we find anything useful."

Miles, Elaine, and I leave the house without another word.

Miles is quiet as he helps me into his truck, where I slide to the center seat to make room for Elaine, who he helps in next. He's in the driver's seat in a flash, shifting gears and gunning down the road.

Looking at him, he's the picture of serene—his face is slack, eyes neutral, completely expressionless. Except his raging grip on the steering wheel and the sharp turns he barely makes exhibit entirely different emotions.

"Whoa," Elaine mutters, latching on to the edge of the dashboard for stability. His car is really old and doesn't have handles on the ceiling. Nothing but the window crank sits on the passenger side door.

My hand finds his knee, and I give it a squeeze, trying to tell him to slow down without saying it out loud. His chest heaves, and he obeys, meeting the speed limit and coasting around the curves a little slower. His jaw tics, and he shoots Elaine a remorseful glance. "I apologize."

She simply nods, face white as snow as she releases the dashboard and settles back in her seat.

"Everything all right?" I murmur, leaning close to his ear.

Miles nods shortly, but his shoulders are tense and his clenched fingers on the wheel don't release. He's holding it so tightly I'm worried it might snap in half. "I wish they would accept you. Both of you."

I struggle to explain away their behavior, but there truly is no excuse for it. Vanesa and Elliot don't have to like me—Vira doesn't, but at least she's not always a raging bitch where I'm concerned. She knows when to pick her battles, and when to ease off the pressure. Honestly, I think Elliot's position should be hers by right. Three months ago, I would not have thought a single one of them deserved any sort of authority in this world, but Vira is at least capable of putting aside her personal feelings for the greater good.

"Lucas and Danielle have never disappointed me, and as for the others, they're used to things being a certain way. With all the changes you're going through, it's natural for them to react poorly to new complications."

"That's exactly the problem," Miles grits, pulling into his driveway. "You're not a complication, you're my girlfriend. The fact of the matter is, after all this time, Vanesa refuses to come to terms with that."

"I, um…" Elaine clears her throat, popping open the door. "I'm going to give you two a minute. Is there a key to get in, or an alarm system I should be worried about?"

Miles turns off his truck, pulling the key out of the ignition and tossing the set to her. "It's the only silver one. Your room is straight up the stairs, to the right."

"Thank you."

The moment she's gone, he turns to me, a war raging in his dark eyes, the rims outlined with gold. "I thought it was just your paranoia talking before, but Vanesa's consistent hatred of you is tearing our family apart."

I swallow, suddenly a little concerned with where this conversation is headed. "I told you to choose them, Miles. There isn't another option."

"I won't," he whispers, and that's what I think his turmoil is really about—the realization that if he has to choose, and Vanesa is putting him in an impossible situation where he might, he won't choose them. "You have a choice of whether or not to turn people. You should never feel obligated to help us break the curse—except my own sister forced your hand by biting your brother."

"You can't abandon your family, Miles," I say, hating that I'm fighting for the end of our relationship, and not its continuation. "They're terrible and heartless, but I don't want to be the reason you go against them. You'll resent me for it someday."

"I won't abandon you."

"They are your blood. You have loved them, lived with them, gone through some of the most challenging times of your life standing beside them. You've known me for all of three months."

"And if you were in the wrong, I wouldn't have a choice to make at all," he says softly, leaning his forehead against mine. I breathe him in, hating Vanesa even more for putting her own brother in this position. "However, it's Vanesa who's wrong. Danielle and Lucas know that. Vira sees it, but she's having a hard time accepting that you're not the monster she originally thought you'd be. But Elliot and Vanesa... they will never understand what it means to cherish humanity, and it will be their downfall."

"People change," I say, pulling him to my shoulder where he rests his head. "Vira was a lot more like Vanesa when I first met her, especially when it came to me, but she's…"

Miles lifts his head, looking at me dubiously.

"… *a tad* more tolerable now than she was back then."

He rolls his eyes and places a long kiss atop my nose. "Thank you for trying to sympathize with them. It's more than they've done for you."

"Of course. They're your family, and you love them." I let out a sigh, driving my point home. "Besides, I do mean it when I say Vira has grown. You all have become so used to the unchanging life you live, it must be hard to let someone new in. Someone half human."

"You aren't half human," Miles says, and he reaches under his seat to pull out a book, the one he mentioned earlier in the evening about half-bloods.

I smile, knowing this gesture won't feel so special once Vanesa and Elliot find out he took it from the armory without permission. "I'm not a full vampire, either. So what I am then?"

"You aren't more or less of one or another, Aspen. You're fortunate enough to be both. Less and more, radiance and misery, blessed and cursed. I wish you'd appreciate that being a novelty doesn't make you any less of who you are."

His optimistic outlook brings me solace. I take the book from him, placing it in my lap and running my fingers over the beautiful cover with golden embroidery circling the title in the center that reads, *"Re Mala."*

"It means, 'impure.'" Miles explains, and I snort at the description. Of course it does. Because a specimen that possesses any type of human qualities must be considered unwholesome.

I hold his chin between my thumb and forefinger, bringing his lips to mine in a soft, slow kiss that warms my body from head to toe. His hands slide along my hips, and under his touch, breathing his air—I think I'm beginning to understand the symmetry of the good and evil tangled inside of me.

CHAPTER 30

*M*iles's wine cellar, hidden behind his fireplace mantle and down a narrow set of carpeted stairs, does not disappoint. The small room resembles an immaculate library with shelves stretching all the way to the ceiling, but with wine as opposed to novels.

I'm not sure what I expected, given everything the Dravens own is a higher level of quality than the rest of the world. The way the Manor is built, Miles's house, this room, their furniture... all of it was constructed with such attention to detail that modern homes no longer possess. Nowadays, everything is made as simply as possible so it can be mass-produced, overpriced, and shipped anywhere around the world. But here in Ichorye, everything is antique-like. Transcendent.

"Can you build me a room like this?" Elaine gasps, running her fingers over the wooden wine racks, creating a short trail in the layer of dust. She picks up a random bottle, rotating it around in her hands to read the label. "I have to be honest, when your fireplace started moving, I had high hopes that you were some sort of vampire-Batman configuration."

"All ideas come from somewhere," he says cryptically, earning a skeptical look from her in return.

"Are you insinuating," Elaine starts, disbelief threading through her accusatory tone, "that the idea of Batman's lair beneath Wayne Manor was inspired by you—this?"

Miles smirks, ducking his head and turning back toward the stairs. "I apologize for the lack of food in the fridge, but you're free to help yourself to anything you find if you're hungry."

"Do I need to worry about anything being laced with blood?" she jokes, although there's a slight note of concern in her voice.

He shakes his head, a rueful smirk on his lips. "If there's blood in it, you'll know."

Elaine doesn't seem convinced, but another bottle of wine nabs her attention, and she practically drops the one she was holding and lifts another delicately from its place. "1949 Château La Conseillante? How did you manage to find all of these?"

"I bought them when they were new."

Elaine pauses, pursing her lips sheepishly as she delicately places the bottle back on its shelf. "Right."

"It was actually Emile's hobby. She lived here with me up until she passed. When she defected to our clan, she had only just started collecting the most popular wines of our time. She was determined to collect as many as she could, knowing that someday they would be valuable, and we would be around forever. This room was technically hers, but I've continued to collect any I can find."

"There are so many," Elaine states obviously, but I know what she means. There are, without a doubt, wines in here that are the only left of their kind, and probably some that haven't been made in hundreds of years. Suddenly, I'm much more fascinated by wine and the various types aging from back in the 1800s. "Are you sure you don't mind me drinking this?"

"Not at all. Emile and Vira would occasionally sneak down here and drink a few bottles. I'm sure there are a handful empty on the shelves that I don't know about. Just be sure to put the bottle back when you're finished with it."

Miles and I head upstairs while Elaine further explores the wine cellar, and I can tell reminiscing on Emile has him reflecting on his family again. Most of the stories I've been told about their lives occurred so many years before me that I often forget Emile only died over a year ago.

My wounds still cut deep from Derek's attack. I can't even begin to fathom what it must feel like to really lose your sibling. If I lost Dallas, I'm not sure I would ever recover.

"I keep thinking about how alone she must have felt." Miles leads me into the living room, and I curl into his side as we settle on the couch. I'd much rather go to sleep, but neither one of us wants to leave Elaine until we're sure she's okay.

Since Oliver's confession, she hasn't shown nearly any emotion toward the situation at all. After how upset she was last night about her birthday, it's only a matter of time before her denial is washed away, and she has to face the reality of the situation.

"Finding out the truth about Ambrose was hard for me and my family to swallow, but knowing the guilt Emile must have undergone all of those years, keeping his secrets and listening to us gripe about the curse, knowing that she felt she was to blame for it…"

"You couldn't have taken away her guilt even if she had been straightforward with you. It would have eaten at her either way."

"Yes, but at least it would have been lessened." Miles runs a hand down his face and tips his head back so it leans on the large couch cushion behind us. "I don't know."

He's quiet, and I allow him to stew in his thoughts. There isn't much I could say to make him feel any less culpable for her mistakes, even though there's no reason for him to be. I do, however, understand the desire to reverse time so you can right something before it goes wrong.

After a long moment, he shifts, sitting forward on the couch and bringing me with him. "Do you mind if we go back to your house in the morning? I'd like to have another look around that hidden room just in case we missed anything the first time."

Apparently, Elliot hung a sheet over the hole and compelled my parents not to notice it, but given the fact that their compulsion isn't as strong as it should be, I'm a little concerned about them wandering inside and plunging through the ceiling.

"Whatever you need," I say, but instantly dread having to see my parents again. I went from refusing to leave them in case the hunters attacked over the summer, to completely leaving them to fend for themselves. Needless to say, I'm a horrible daughter. I'm also partly to blame for the fact that their son is currently in a coma-like sleep. "Has Elliot agreed to comb through Emile's stuff for clues about the curse?"

Miles bites his lip, shifting awkwardly. "No, but I caught Vira in the attic yesterday. She was unearthing Emile's boxes."

"I thought she was in denial about Emile's involvement,

same as Elliot?" I ask, confused. I know Vira said she *would* look through Emile's things, but I honestly never thought she'd do it. She'd still acted as though it was a ludicrous idea.

"She's desperate. Dallas's life isn't the only one on the line if we don't figure a way out of this."

"Do you blame me?" I wince at my question. Yet even though we've discussed the topic several times, I need closure. "For not turning people in town to help increase your numbers."

Miles shakes his head, not a flick of doubt in his eyes when he looks at me. "We would have taken a vote, just as we did when Vanesa didn't want creating vampires to be your choice, and *most* of my siblings would have agreed that anyone we turn should give consent. That requires us to reveal ourselves to those we want to turn and risk them not accepting us. Some of whom could be hunters for all we know. In the end, nothing would be different. Short of you waltzing into town and biting everyone with a pulse, Vanesa's grudge against you holds no weight because what she wants you to do simply isn't plausible. Her mind still works in ways that would make her revered if it were the 1800s again. Those strategies don't work here in the twenty-first century, where people stand up to fear, as opposed to bowing down to it."

Despite my desperate need for sleep, I stay up for hours reading the book Miles lent me on half-bloods. When I first saw the cover, dread rose deep inside me in fear of what I might find. Calling half-bloods *impure* didn't strengthen my wavering faith in the situation, but the information is actually intriguing. Basically, as Miles said, I'm both human and vampire, just like a transitioner, except I'm technically a vampire with some human qualities, which muddles my senses —as opposed to a transitioner, who is still human and only slightly advanced to give them a taste of what being a vampire would feel like should they decide to turn.

Before I'd made the decision to turn—or, more accurately, was forced to turn in order to save mine and my friends' lives —I had concerns about what becoming a vampire would do to me. How it would change and darken me. Recently, though, I'd begun to think that it doesn't do anything of the sort. Except, it does—sort of.

According to the *Re Mala*, upon the transition, human souls are altered, darkened in order to withstand the length of time that lies before them. In my case, however, my soul remains untouched, and other than my weakened senses, that is the only major difference between me and a full vampire. A human soul trapped within a vampire at full strength would become damaged over time. Eventually it would burn up, leaving the host to die slowly as the years pass by. But when those vampiric abilities are weakened, the soul remains intact and can withstand immortality without incident.

Around three in the morning, I start to drift off with my neck bent over the book, reading by the small lamp on the nightstand so Miles can rest. Watching him sleep is a strange experience now that I know he doesn't dream. If it weren't for his subtle inhales and exhales, he would basically look dead. He's been asleep for around an hour and hasn't so much as moved a muscle.

As I doze off, I immediately feel the pull of water, like I'm being sucked under a tide. This time, it's not a surreal experience like my other nightmares. I'm not confused or scared or fighting for breath, but coursing along the current and allowing the water to bob me back and forth like a rocking chair. Even still, in the gratifying whisking of the ocean, I feel broken, unearthed, inadequate, like there's a piece of me I lost somewhere along the way and I'm hoping the current will return me to it.

The sadness is overwhelming, pressuring me to fill the holes inside me before it's too late. Before my oxygen runs out and water punctures my lungs.

And all I want is to fill the growing void within me.

Someone calls my name in the distance. The voice is feminine, soothing, and the mere sound of it feels like a hand caressing my skin. Like I'm being curled in her arms like a baby.

I hear my name again, but this time, there's a seam in the blissful dream, and it keeps growing, growing, growing until the water parts, tearing a hole in the surface above me before it crashes down, waking me from the fantasy.

"Aspen." Miles strokes my cheeks, wiping his thumbs underneath my eyes.

I blink rapidly, struggling to see through my bleary eyes. "What's wrong?"

I try to sit up, but he remains where he is, so I can't go farther than my elbows. Propping myself on my forearms, I scan the room, worried that he woke me because something's wrong, or there's an emergency with his family and he needs to get to the Manor.

"You were crying in your sleep," he says tenderly, and I notice the wetness on my cheeks. This time, when I try to sit up, he doesn't stop me. I rub my hands down my face, damp with tears, and use my tank top to wipe them off of my chin and neck, too.

"Did I wake you?"

He shakes his head but looks concerned nonetheless. "I could sense your affliction. It was like you were in a weird hallucinogenic state. Is that how it always is when you have a nightmare?"

Besides, when I was screaming in my sleep at the armory, Miles has never been around me when I had a nightmare. "This was calmer than the others. I knew I was dreaming, but I was just coasting along with it. Normally I can't breathe and am scared out of my mind trying to inhale. This time all I felt was loneliness."

I blink in confusion, unable to process the sudden change in my nightmares and what it could mean. The sheer fact that it was based entirely on how alone I feel is interesting in itself, since I haven't had a moment to myself in so long. And even when I have, Miles, Elaine, and Dallas usually weren't far.

I take a deep breath, reminding myself that now is not the time to hate Vanesa. Once I save Dallas and hug him endlessly, *then* I will release all of my pent-up anger on her. I will make that woman's life miserable if I have to move Heaven and Earth to do it.

And if Dallas doesn't make it...

I won't think about how I plan to proceed from there just yet.

Someone pounds on the front door, startling both Miles and me. I glance at my phone and find that it's four in the morning. "Who would be here at this hour?"

"I have no idea. This is early, even for Vanesa." He stands, back rigid.

Elaine appears in the hallway, a thin blanket draped over her back that bunches the shoulders of her midriff nightshirt. Her bronze legs glow in the murky light from Miles's lamp, accentuated by the tiny material hugging her hips that she calls shorts. "It's four in the morning, who the hell is pounding on your door?"

Bang, bang, bang.

The pounding ensues, and a wave of panic rolls through me, vibrating my bones and freezing my blood. My heart rate increases, and before I know it, I feel like I'm on the brink of a panic attack as I remember the first time I ever heard a knock like that.

Sure, I've heard people knock on our door back in Colorado, and Elaine has knocked before she let herself in my house several times since I moved here, but it's different than the pounding downstairs—it's the pounding I heard in the first nightmare I had after we moved here, when Ambrose led me to Emile's necklace.

"Maybe you should answer it," Elaine suggests. I glance up at Miles, waiting for his reaction when I realize Elaine is looking at me. And so is Miles.

"What?" I blink, unsure of why they'd want me to get the door. I don't live here, and normally Miles would be doing nothing short of gluing me to the bed to keep me out of harm's way.

"What are you so afraid of?" Elaine asks, blinking slowly as she turns her head, looking me up and down.

"Nothing." I swallow and glance between them nervously. Something isn't right. "The sound just reminded me of the first time Ambrose invaded my dreams."

"Ambrose is gone," Miles says candidly. Elaine crosses the

room to stand beside him, and they both stare down at me. "It's time you stop letting a dead man dictate your life."

I shake my head, squinting my eyes at him. "I don't understand... Ambrose was one of the worst things to ever happen to me, but he doesn't dictate anything. He holds no power over me."

"Are you sure?" Elaine cocks an eyebrow, her voice strangely monotone. The pounding pursues almost as soon as she's done speaking, and my heart lurches into my throat. "That's what I thought."

"We have to break free, Aspen. Our trauma binds us, but we can still mend the tear it ripped into our soul."

"We?" I blink, and Elaine moves toward me, kneeling on the bed so our faces are inches apart. Her eyes grow dark, glowering at me until her face slowly morphs into Ambrose's— his decaying skin, rotting teeth, even the smell is the same. Death, horror, blood, vomit. Just by seeing his face, I remember the feeling of his hands on me, cold and rough, trailing up my skin, his teeth piercing my neck, the pressure of his body as he trapped me against him.

"Please stop," I beg with tears welling in my eyes. I thought I was ready. I thought I was no longer afraid of him. I reach for Miles, hoping he can save me. "Help me."

Miles just stands there, watching blankly. The pounding at the door grows louder and louder until it's all I can hear. Each time, the vibration sends a bolt of lightning through my bones, lighting me on fire until I feel as if I'm drowning in my own blood.

I cry out, trying to shove Elaine away from me. Her face morphs back into her own, but I'm still stuck. I'm suffocating. I can't breathe.

I close my eyes, attempting to even my breathing. "This isn't real. This isn't real."

"Oh honey," Elaine coos, and this time when I look at her, she's covered in blood—her face, her eyes, her teeth—everything is exuding the rust-colored liquid. The sticky substance drips off of her and onto me, its warm moisture trailing down my skin. "This may only be a nightmare, but the dangers here are much less than those you face when you wake."

CHAPTER 31

I'm thrust out of sleep so fast and so fiercely that I tumble off the bed and land on the carpet with a hard *thud*. The *Re Mala* falls with me and slides across the floor.

I cry out on impact, and before I can blink, Miles is beside me, looking slightly confused and even more concerned as to why I'm on the floor. He takes my face in his hands and brings me to his chest without having to ask what's wrong.

"Were you crying in your sleep?" he asks me. The words send a jolt of panic through me, and I shove him away, pressing my back against the mattress.

I touch the carpet, my skin, thread my fingers through my hair, and then touch Miles's hand when he reaches out to me, trying to find tangible evidence that I'm not still asleep. "Is this —am I awake? This is real?"

"You're awake, beautiful." He pulls me back into his arms, rocking me back and forth on the carpet. That one word, the nickname he refers to me by frequently, confirms that I'm no longer dreaming. "They're getting worse, aren't they?"

I nod, drying off the tear stains left behind from my nightmare—the only proof that it happened.

There's a soft rap on the door, and then I hear Elaine's groggy voice. "Are you guys okay? I heard someone scream."

Miles abandons me on the floor to open the door for Elaine, and then drops back down beside me, not bothering to move us to the bed.

"Nightmare?" she asks, standing awkwardly in the doorway in her cutoff shirt and shorts. The only thing missing is the blanket over her shoulders.

Biting my lip, I nod, and notice that she looks like she hasn't gotten a moment of rest tonight. Not that I can say I have. I'm not sure unsettlingly realistic dreams count as sleep.

"You can come in."

Elaine moves toward the bed and picks up the book I accidentally flung across the room. Smoothing out the bent pages from its fall, she sets it up by Miles's pillow and takes a seat at the foot of the bed.

"I didn't even know I was dreaming. It was much worse than yesterday. I had a dream within a dream, where I thought I'd woken up, but didn't. You were both in it, which is also new because usually it's only me. I can always feel another presence but can never see it. And everything is usually symbolic—although I don't know how yet. I just know that it means something." I take a long, shuddering breath and lean against Miles's chest, appreciating his solid comfort. "I even remember thinking about how much I can't stand Vanesa, and how angry I am at her for what she did to Dallas. It was so real. I don't know how to explain it."

"Honestly, you could break down every minuscule detail,

and it's unlikely anyone would understand but you," Elaine says, reaching over the bed to squeeze my shoulder.

As if my nightmares aren't embarrassing enough, I can still feel myself trembling from its intensity. There's sweat coating my upper lip and my back. My hands and feet are clammy, and even though my arms are wrapped around me and I'm sitting on my shins, I can't stop myself from shaking.

"Elaine is right. This is happening for a reason, and in all my years I've never heard of anything even remotely similar to what you're being put through." Miles rests his head against mine, defeated knowing he has no way of helping me through this other than to hold my hand when I need it.

"In all your years you've never known a half-blood," Elaine points out.

I think this over, not entirely convinced that it's a half-blood related issue. "Not even the book details nightmares for vampires like me. Technically, I'm still dead. Only my soul is different. Plus, I have this odd feeling in the pit of my stomach every time I wake up—this is something different, something much deeper than a faulty transition."

Miles sucks in a breath at the end of my sentence, and I appreciate him keeping his opinions to himself regarding my word choice of *faulty*. I'm just not sure how else to describe the differences in me.

I turn suddenly so I can see Miles's dark eyes and worried expression. "Can we go to my house now? While my parents are asleep? There's no way in hell I'm going back to bed after that nightmare. And even if I wanted to, I'm afraid my fear would keep me awake anyway."

I also can't help this persisting urge I have to go home. Like I need to be there right now. It's important.

Miles shrugs, un-opinionated, so I turn to Elaine. "We're going to do one last look-through of the hidden room to ensure we haven't missed anything. You can come if you want, but I understand if you would rather catch up on sleep."

Elaine scoffs, already heading back to the guest room. "I'll just lie awake staring at the ceiling, wondering why every man in my life tends to choose their relations with the Dravens over me. Just let me change really quick."

Ten minutes later, we're standing outside my run-down shell of a home. It's sad to say that even after I tried to salvage some of it, but it's true. My family is broken and has been for some time. The people inside of my house are no longer whole, and even if they were, it'd be filled with so many lies that it'd be pointless to call us family at all—other than being blood related. But I'm also bound by blood to Miles. There's more to blood and the continuance of love than the liquid that runs red beneath our skin.

"Are you sure we won't wake up your parents?" Elaine whispers, even though we're not inside yet.

I'd love to tell her that I'm positive we won't, but it's been a while since I've snuck through the house—I'm a little rusty on where the squeaking parts of the floor are, and I have no clue if Father sleeps upstairs or downstairs nowadays. "Let's just pray my mom hasn't lined every room with ash."

Elaine sighs and crosses her arms over her stomach, shivering in the cold. "Reassuring, thanks."

"We'll be careful," Miles says, walking up to the front porch and glancing behind us. "I think we were followed here."

I nod in agreement. I thought I felt someone tailing us a little way back, but no one engaged or got too close. "Probably the hunters."

"Should the fact that they haven't attacked reassure me, or should I be concerned that they're stalking us to begin with?" Elaine asks.

I shrug, glancing behind me. There's definitely someone down the road waiting in the trees. Two, maybe three men? "I think they're mostly tracking Miles and me, so I suppose you don't have a reason to be concerned. Besides, you're human. They'll hopefully give you some leeway."

"You were human."

"I was also wearing Emile's necklace." I step up to the porch and twist the old, rusted doorknob, which creaks throughout the entire motion. "Ready?"

They both nod, and I push open the door. The lights are all off, which is usually how my father likes to sleep, but I don't see him on the couch as we snake our way through the room. Elaine is behind me, and Miles brings up the rear since I know the terrain much better. Elaine is the only one who can't see in the dark, so Miles is also back there to make sure she doesn't misstep and bump into anything.

It's freezing in here, and from the sound—or lack thereof—I figure the fireplace has burned out.

I reach behind me, tugging Elaine's wrist when we're at the stairs so she knows to turn. I go first, and Miles holds on to her so she doesn't trip and wake my parents up.

The trickiest part is getting past the bed, where they're both sound asleep on their respective sides, and to the study door. But once we manage to do that and ease the door shut, I breathe a sigh of release.

I feel along the wall for the light switch, hoping at some point the power came back on. With one flick of the switch, I gather that it hasn't. Looking at Miles, I shake my head, and he pulls three small flashlights from his jacket pocket and gives them to Elaine and me.

Stripping off my winter jacket, I stick it at the base of the door in case either one of my parents gets up to use the bathroom. This way they won't see the light beneath the door. Now if only I could soundproof the room, though I don't see a reason for much noise to be made—after all, Vanesa isn't here, so it's unlikely there will be several minute intervals of time wasted on arguing.

"Exactly what do you expect to find that you didn't before?" Elaine prods, sinking down on the couch, setting the bag she always carries at her hip.

"A sign from God," Miles says tiredly. It seems even he thinks this is a pointless errand, but nonetheless, what does it hurt to have one last look around?

Thunder cracks and lightning strikes across the sky, brightening the study. The overhead lights flicker, dimming and brightening occasionally, then burning out. At first, I think I must have left the switch flipped to *on,* but one glance at the wall tells me otherwise. Goosebumps surge up my arms, and I shiver, moving to the far wall.

The wooden floor creaks beneath my feet as I grab the cloth covering the hole Elliot made and yank it down. Lightning strikes again, this time so close that I'm almost convinced it touched down on the grass in my front yard.

"Did you see that?" I ask, and on cue, the sky lights up again.

"This storm has been brewing for days. Of course it chooses now to start raining." Elaine peers out the window, and another bolt of lightning causes her to jump back. And sure enough, when I move closer, I can see raindrops slowly beginning to fall. They gradually pick up their pace until it's a complete downpour.

I move back to the hidden room, placing my hands in the opening and hoisting myself onto the desk inside. "We'll need to move quickly. If it storms any harder my parents might wake up."

There are two light fixtures on the ceiling, and I wish the power was on so we could have a better look around. Though, I'm sure the bulbs burned out a long time ago.

Miles and I search the room while Elaine keeps an ear out for movement from my parents' room. Besides the same dust and cobwebs Vira and I braved the last time, we don't find anything new.

A loud bang from downstairs makes all three of us freeze. Elaine backs away from the door immediately, almost tripping over the hems of the sweatpants she borrowed from Danielle. All at once, we switch off our flashlights.

Footsteps creak up the stairs from below, slightly quieter than their bold entrance had been.

Slowly, the study door creaks open, moving with it the coat I laid down to block the light. Miles and I move to either side of the hole in the wall so the intruder can't see us, and Elaine stands rigid in the corner parallel to us. I peer through a slit between the wood panels, waiting to see who's there.

We all relax as Vira eases the door shut behind her, raven black hair soaking wet, the same as the clothes suctioning to her skin. She crosses her arms, waiting for us to step away from our hiding spots.

Miles climbs through the hole, and I follow, cringing at the wet puddles Vira is dripping onto the floor. Sure, they're hideous and need to be replaced anyhow, but I'd rather they not get any more destroyed in the meantime.

"Answer your phone once in a while, would you?" Vira grits, squeezing the tips of her hair and maneuvering out of her sopping leather jacket, draping it over the back of a chair. Her heeled boots *cluck* as she moves farther into the room, and she scrunches her nose each time the material squeaks. "Leather is not meant for rain. I called you at least five times, why weren't you answering?"

Miles slips his phone out of his pocket, lowering his eyebrows. "Three. And I have spotty reception up here."

"Apologies, the five was counting the two stops I made before I figured out you had to be here, because otherwise you must have been kidnapped. I went to your house first and then Elaine's. Why in the world are you here anyway, and why didn't you tell anyone?" she demands, propping a hand on her hip.

Miles looks contrite.

Vira has a point. We should have told someone where we were going.

"It was a last-minute decision. None of us could sleep," I explain. Well, Elaine couldn't sleep because of what happened with Oliver last night. Miles was sleeping just fine until my nightmares woke him up.

"Vanesa's right. You're going to get one of us killed," Vira says offhandedly, catching me by surprise. Vanesa accuses me of their ultimate destruction, but she's never insisted my actions might get someone killed. I suppose she does say more about me behind my back than she does to my face, but with the way she insults me on a regular basis, I didn't think that was possible.

To my dismay, Vira texts Elliot, telling him where we are.

"The others are on their way," she says, and for once, I'd much rather we go to the Manor instead. At least there I can leave. There are enough rooms in that place to disappear into, but here, this is the only place we can congregate in case my parents wake up. The rest of the house is pretty much an open floor plan besides my bedroom, which is too close to the fireplace. Either way, I would never leave the Dravens in a house alone with my parents. "If you would pick up your phone now and then, you'd know that Oliver showed up on our doorstep around forty-five minutes ago."

"Why?" Elaine steps away from the corner she was still standing in, giving Vira her full attention.

"He was beaten to an inch of his life. He couldn't stand much less get there on his own, so someone must have dropped him off." Vira looks indifferent, but I can tell she's not comfortable with a hunter being battered and left on her doorstep.

Elaine purses her lips, clearly torn between feeling sympathy for him or proceeding with hatred. "I—is he going to make it?"

Vira shrugs a shoulder. "If we help him."

"Then help him, goddammit!" Elaine yells, then quickly lowers her voice. "You have to help him. You have to."

"She's right. This could be a test. The hunters may want to see if you're decent enough to save his life, even though he poses a threat to you," I say, brushing a cobweb off my arm.

"What's more likely is he's undercover." Vira rolls her eyes, seeming tired of such frivolous conversations.

Elaine scoffs, anger coloring her soft cheeks. "You think they'd beat him to death just to send him undercover? Who would do that?"

"Morally, believe it or not, the hunters are probably less human than we are. They put the cause before their lives. So yes, it's possible that after it was made clear you have an attachment to Oliver, that they'd send him to spy on us, using your connection as a weakness."

"Isn't it possible something really bad happened to him after we left, and the Manor was the closest place he could run to?" Elaine asks, sounding hopeful. "Did he even say what happened?"

Vira sighs, giving in to her discomfort and stripping off her black long-sleeve shirt to reveal a black bra. I bet if she took off her shoes, she'd be wearing black socks, too.

"Do you have a shirt I can borrow?" she asks me, and I can tell the request makes her miserable. When I nod, she answers Elaine's questions. "He can hardly speak. His left eye is swollen shut, and it looks like one arm is broken. All he said to us though, was that he wouldn't talk to anyone but you."

"Then what are we still doing here?" Elaine asks, ready to jump out of the window in anticipation.

Vira shakes her head when Elaine moves to the door, grabbing her shoulder to keep her in place. "On the off chance our theories are wrong, the last thing we want is the other hunters to think that we've kidnapped him, or worse, that we're the ones who beat him up—"

"Or both," Miles adds what we were all thinking.

"So it will be better for all of us if they go searching for him and he's not at our house," Vira says, and her hard eyes meet mine.

"No. No, no, no. What about the armory? Or that cabin in the woods? Gwen, Owen? *Somewhere* other than here," I beg desperately.

"Those places are too affiliated with our clan. And if they've been watching us for a while, they'll know that Vanesa stayed in the cabin for a few days. They'll look there, too."

"Even the armory? No one knows where it is. I bet they don't know it even exists," I argue. I don't care if Oliver is in a coma—he *killed* me. Left me for dead. Betrayed Elaine's trust. No way in this world am I letting him camp out in my home. "And won't the hunters look here? I'm part of the clan now, too."

"Yes, but you have a secret room *nobody* knows about." Vira's logic trumps my own, and I realize that if the hunters find the armory in a search for Oliver, they have more to worry about than their accusations. Not to mention Oliver himself being in there could prove to be catastrophic. I've read maybe one percent of the research they have down there, but even I know that, in the wrong hands, that information is ruinous. If Oliver is a spy, and even if he's not, he shouldn't have access to such information—or anything in their house, really. It's too dangerous, and the cabin is also easily escapable.

"Aspen." Elaine takes my hand, squeezing it in hers. "Please. I know he doesn't deserve it. I just can't let him die."

"For how long?"

Vira rolls her eyes, glancing at Elaine. "Until he's better, I suppose. Then we find out what he knows and release him. The only, *only* reason he gets our attention at all is because we need to know exactly what Adrian is planning."

Elaine looks satisfied with this, and I can't tell if she's dreading seeing him again, or anxious to get closure. Because whatever the Dravens have planned, I already know Elaine will have her own interrogation questions prepped and ready for asking.

CHAPTER 32

The thunderstorm rages on outside, and the lights have been blinking sporadically since the Dravens arrived with Oliver, making me even more uneasy about what we're doing and how it will end.

Elliot and Miles carried my mattress up from downstairs and placed it on the floor in the hidden room—they had to widen the hole in the wall, which I wasn't particularly happy about, especially when the movement started tearing a rip in the ceiling. It seems that after so many years, this wall has become a sort of support beam, and I'm afraid of what might happen if it breaks.

Two syringes are in Vanesa's hand, and she moves toward the door leading to my parents' room. They woke up frightened and confused when the boys were transporting the mattress from downstairs, so Lucas had to compel them to stay put on their beds until we were finished. At first they obeyed, but after around ten minutes my father started getting antsy, barking commands at the siblings to stop what they were doing, asking where Dallas was, why I'm not staying at home, who the man was who broke in a few months ago—though it's clear from their confused states that they don't realize how much time has passed since Ambrose attacked us, because my mother referred to it as a recent event.

"What the hell are those?" I demand, latching on to Vanesa's wrist as she heads into their room. She tears away from me and sneers when my nails slice her skin in the process.

"It's a sleeping potion. Herbs and some other stuff. It's harmless. It'll keep them asleep until this afternoon." She bites her lip, raising an eyebrow as if to ask if she can continue or if I'm going to stand in her way. Then to further convince me she says, "Danielle made it."

Letting Vanesa anywhere near another member of my family requires a lot of trust, and I have next to none left for her. I would rather it was Elliot sticking needles in their necks than the devil herself.

"We're out of options," Danielle says suddenly, sounding tired and desperate. I watch as a needle is injected into each of my parents' necks, but neither of them squirm to get away.

"We're not out of options," Miles assures her, placing a kiss on the top of her head. "We just haven't found the right ones yet."

"Because there aren't any!" she complains. Lucas puts a hand on her knee. "I suppose if we never break the curse, they'll let us live."

"Maybe for a month," Elliot retorts. "They've wanted us dead for centuries, nothing will change that."

"Way to look at the bright side, brother." Danielle's eyes narrow. I've never seen her so on edge. Even when she argues with Vanesa, she's usually not this sarcastic.

Miles runs a hand down his face and Lucas meets his eyes.

Understanding passing between them. It's looking more and more like we won't find our way out of this mess. But that means my brother dies, and I won't let that happen. "Then we try everything we can think of."

"We already have," Vanesa drones, reentering the room and dropping the needles into a trashcan by the door. She and the others drove here because of the rain and having to transport Oliver, so Vira is the only one that's still wet. I considered giving her an ungodly pink shirt, because I can't even picture the sight in my head, but I opted for a light gray one instead. Sure, I have plenty of black tops, but I don't like her quite that much. She looks foreign in the color, though. The contrast lightens her features a little, which makes her look slightly younger and softer, smoothly blending her usual sharp edges.

"Not everything," Elaine pipes up. She hasn't said much since they carried Oliver in, and even I will admit I feel bad for the kid. He looks the way I felt when he left me for dead last summer, and it's not a pleasant feeling. He passed out soon after he told Vira he'd only speak with Elaine, so we're still waiting for him to come to. Hunters heal at a slightly faster rate than humans do, so he won't be on bed rest for as long as he should be considering the beating he took.

Elliot presses his palms into his eye sockets and I'm afraid he might knock them loose. "For the love of God, stop with your stupid nursery rhyme."

"*Riddle.*"

"You are insignificant. How many times do we need to spell it out for you before you finally get it?"

She cocks her head, not taking well to the insult. "Is the man in that room *insignificant*? Because if it weren't for little irrelevant me, you wouldn't have someone to beat for information. Oliver is useful, and by extension, so am I."

Elaine stands, migrating over to the desk where Elliot stands with Vira, Vanesa, and Miles. I follow behind her, but Lucas and Danielle stay seated on the couch.

"Humor me, will you?" Elaine persists. Elliot begins to argue, but she cuts him off. "Sorry, do you have something better to do? Stronger leads to follow? Any other tangible evidence on the planet to analyze that will help with your predicament?"

"You are tiring," he grumbles, seeming to have no argument to that.

She smiles darkly, opening her bag and pulling out her ancestor's journal.

Vira blinks, tongue sweeping across her lower lip before her teeth nag and drag across it. "Do you just carry that around with you…?"

Elaine shrugs, unfazed. "I've been waiting for my moment."

I close my eyes, willing away a growing headache as Elaine opens the journal, flipping through hundreds of ink-covered pages detailing her ancestor's life, until she finds what she's looking for. "Here, see. The other half is missing."

I lean over the journal, and contrary to everyone's belief that this is a waste of time, they do the same. The journal looks ancient, and although I've seen it before, its fragility never fails to take my breath away. Elaine carefully presses her hand across the wrinkled page to make it easier to decipher.

At the bottom are four phrases, written in a column on separate lines of the paper. Next to them is a tear, and in the spot where the page breaks off, there's a smudge of ink. As if reading my mind, Elaine points to the ink smear. "There had to have been something else written here. I've tried to figure out the remaining words, but it's nearly impossible without knowing if this was meant to be a sentence, short phrase, idiom, some kind of poem…"

I read the phrases, slightly intrigued myself.

> *One half of a*
> *Put together is*
> *It takes*
> *To come*

"This is a waste of time," Elliot complains, but his eyes continuously read then reread the incomplete lines. However unimportant he thinks this is, it's a puzzle, and he'll be damned if he doesn't find every piece. "How are we supposed to make sense of a jumbled mess of words?"

"Does that mean you want to?" Elaine asks, which she probably shouldn't do so he doesn't refuse his help out of spite.

He growls. "Only to prove how pointless you are."

Elaine starts to turn the page, and I notice a stain on the bottom edges of the journal, so light it's barely noticeable after all the years of wear.

"Hold on." I latch on to the journal and examine the writing. After a closer inspection of the way the words glide effortlessly across the page, my mind keeps catching on one singular thought—the penmanship looks familiar. "I've seen this before."

"You have?" Elaine asks, sounding surprised. "When? How?" Then to Elliot. "I told you it meant something."

He bites his lip. "Don't waste your excitement—you still haven't the slightest clue what it means."

I shake my head, trying to keep my thoughts in a row. "Dallas found a note." I point toward the hidden room. "I think he said it was lodged under a baseboard."

Lucas removes himself from the couch immediately, and I'm right there beside him, directing him to where Dallas was standing when he picked it up. Lucas kneels on the ground, his fingers running along the stretch where the baseboard meets the floor. "There's a small gap here. Something could have easily slid underneath if there was a draft from inside the room."

"The leaky ceiling?" Danielle suggests. I suppose it's possible, with all the mood swings in Ichorye's forecast, that a gust of wind through the faulty roof could have blown the piece of paper underneath the gap. It just seems unlikely, and a bit farfetched.

"Where's the note now?" Miles asks.

I don't bother to respond, just bound down the stairs and into Dallas's room, ignoring the pang in my chest when I see his unmade bed and sketchbook lying haphazardly on the mattress. Vanesa never said how she kidnapped him, but I know it was willingly. She probably knocked on the goddamn door claiming to need his help, and he fell for it.

I rummage through his drawers, trying not to choke on the ash buildup from the fireplace. My parents did let it burn out, but its remains are still there, and there's enough of them to weaken my knees and cause sweat to break out on my upper lip.

With nowhere else to look, I move to his bed, flipping through the pages of his sketchbook until a small piece of paper slips from between two pages. I pick it up, and sure enough, the handwriting is identical to Elaine's riddle.

Bolting back up the stairs, I trip, winded from the ash, and stumble into the room. Miles tries to grab my arm, but I make no effort to stop myself when I fly into the desk, shaking it as I catch myself. I set the paper down next to the phrases, and like they were made for each other—the piece fits perfectly in the tear.

> *One half of a whole*
> *Put together is one*
> *It takes two*
> *To come undone*

"I still don't understand," Vira says, the wheels in her head turning. "'It takes two to come undone?' What is that supposed to mean?"

"I doubt it has anything to do with the curse," Elliot says, and I think he's only disregarding the possibility because it's all thanks to Elaine that we have another avenue to explore, even if we don't know what exactly that is yet.

"You don't know that," Vira argues, and Elaine looks stunned. This is the first time she's truly been defended by one of them.

I touch my thumb to the corner of the loose piece, toggling it a little in thought.

Vira leans to get a better look, and a tiny droplet of water rolls down her nose, dripping onto the bottom corner of the page.

Elaine goes mad, frantically shooing Vira back with a waving hand. "Watch, you'll smudge it."

She wipes her thumb across the page, then continues pressing the damp spot to ensure the words don't start to bleed. But when she touches the page for longer than a second, a jolt of something shoots down my spine, and I jump, gasping loudly.

No one seems to notice my reaction in their pursuit for answers, too engrossed in the mysterious riddle and what it might mean for their future.

"Elaine," I say slowly, almost accusatory, then remove my thumb from the paper. "Do that again."

She looks at me, confused, and raises an eyebrow in question. "Do what?"

"Touch the page." My eyes shift to the paper as though to confirm my request.

Her lips slack, and she touches the tips of her fingers to the parchment unsurely, never separating her gaze from me.

"Not like that." I demonstrate with my own thumb, pressing it down exactly where it had been before. "Like this."

She looks wary, undecided as to why in the world I'm requesting she touch a piece of paper with her thumb, but obliges, nonetheless. The moment her thumb makes contact, mine starts tingling, and the sensation spreads up my arm and down my spine, softer and less energized than the spark I felt before.

"What is that?" Elaine's eyes widen, and she gasps as the adrenaline races through us. The pad of my thumb starts to burn, and slowly, my piece begins to mend with the original page, glowing gold at the seam.

Vira breathes shallowly, this time careful to hold her hair back when she moves for a closer look. "It was spelled."

"Spelled?" Elaine cries, fear coating her voice, but she doesn't remove her hand. Something is rooting us in place like gravity, and all I want to do is get closer. Learn more, become one with… I'm not sure. Myself? Elaine? I have no idea, but I know I'm not supposed to become one with the paper. "Why is my body tingling?"

Black spots cloud my vision, and the tingling comes to a halt. I back away quickly, as does Elaine, and notice two thumbprints have appeared on either side of the paper where we touched it. They're black, like we dipped our fingers in ink before pressing them to the page, but they're much too large to be ours.

Upon a closer look, through the splotches growing larger in my vision, I notice two smaller thumbprints inside the large ones, these ones outlined with what looks like blood.

"Aspen?" someone says my name, but I can't tell who, and my vision blurs in and out as I stumble on my feet, trying to catch my balance. Flipping my hand over, I inspect my thumb. The pad slightly buzzes, and the lines of my fingerprint are stained with blood as though a carbon copy of it was transferred to the page like a tattoo.

My eyelids droop heavily, and the raindrops on the roof grow louder, sporadic, and it's the only sound I hear as I'm pulled under, crashing to the ground like a tidal wave.

I'm in my living room—but it's not my living room.

The walls are repainted, the furniture is brand new, and a large, deep red area rug sits in the living room. There is a large painting of a birch tree hanging on the wall where we currently have our television. I'm across from it on the couch, which is soft and warm compared to the one we have.

Smells of cedar and oak flood my senses, and I notice the

back door is open. Beyond it is a family, but I can't see them clearly with the way the sun shines in my eyes, but they don't seem to notice me. Heat radiates inside from the open door, and I'm reminded that it's not summer right now, but mid-October.

I wander to the kitchen, where there's a freshly sealed countertop, shiny sink, and a fridge with a singular picture taped to the surface. I recognize it almost immediately as the picture I found with Elijah's belongings—the one of the Draven family that features the mirror my mom loved. The mirror that Ambrose had somehow attached his spirit to and used to control my family's decisions.

Back in the living room, I look out the front window. The yard is beautiful. The porch is intact and visibly new. It's such a dire contrast from the house I live in now, but I guess time ages more than just people.

"Beautiful, no?" a melodious voice asks from behind me.

I startle, coming face to face with a girl that looks to be a little older than me. It's her attire that gives me pause—she's wearing a flowery pink dress that accentuates her dark bronze skin and curly hair. Her eyes are soft, expression kind, although she's not smiling. She almost looks sad, yet she's so bright and so lovely, that it's hard to imagine such an emotion being part of her make-up. She moves aside, gesturing to the couch. "Sit, Aspen. We have much to discuss."

I obey, not seeing a reason to deny the request, and she takes the seat opposite mine. With ankles crossed, knees pressed together, and a back straighter than I would think possible, her chin lifts as she takes me in, lips upturning in the slightest of smiles. "I have been trying to reach you for some time now."

I look around, feeling as though I've been transported to a dreamscape. This place is nothing more than a delusion, yet the air, the furniture—it all feels so real.

"I'm afraid I don't understand…" I eye her, taking in dark eyes and small lips, a glowing complexion. "… You look so familiar."

"I would hope so. You're wearing my necklace."

CHAPTER 33

"I do suppose it was foolish of me to think you would recognize me from such an old photograph." The girl leans forward, extending her hand to me in greeting. "My name is Emile."

I can't help the gasp that escapes me.

So as not to be rude, I take her delicate hand in mine before she retracts it and laces her fingers together in her lap.

"Where are we?" I ask in fascination, though I suppose I know the answer. I just don't understand what I'm seeing—Emile, my house, the summer heat, the family outside... it's like I'm experiencing the collision of multiple worlds.

"I'm in your head at the moment. I can project whatever it is I want us to see, and this is your house restored to its original condition."

So this is what it looked like after Elijah moved in. Actually, I think I recall finding a blueprint in some of his things... he didn't just move in but designed and built this place. My eyes are drawn back to the immaculate painting above where Emile sits, and I find myself wondering what happened to it after so much time. She shifts to admire it as well.

"Elijah was quite the artist," she murmurs, teeth grabbing at her bottom lip as she turns back to me. "I want to begin by sincerely apologizing for your recent nightmares. They were only intended to show you the way to freedom. Until now, I haven't been able to make physical contact with the living. I expended all of my energy on the note I placed for you to find under the baseboard, and that was weeks ago."

"You're the reason for my nightmares... and the note...?"

She nods, and I feel a surge of nausea. "The nightmares—I couldn't always reach you. The connection was strongest when you were here because it's the site of my death, but the necklace was a beacon for me to latch on to when I needed. It connects us the way Ambrose was connected to your family through the mirror. Though, I had a harder time reaching you when Miles was near because you're less susceptible to your vulnerabilities around him. So when I did finally manage to contact you, the dreams were more scattered. I lost control a little bit, and your own fears bled with my intended message, which alternated into the strange nightmare you had this morning."

I take a long breath, allowing this information to digest. "So the dreams were symbolic. They were trying to warn me...? Show me something...?" Except I could never figure out what that was, which almost makes the torture I endured because of them seem pointless.

"I was trying to tell you that the curse is only partially broken. The nightmares were meant to show you that you're being suffocated, and you need to take the necessary steps to free yourself, which requires the help of another."

I think back to all of my nightmares. I did always feel suffocated, and several times I felt as though I was looking for someone who would pull me out of the water. In fact, a hand *did* reach for me when I was drowning one time.

"How do we break the curse?"

Emile ducks her head sheepishly, tucking her hair behind her ears. "I wasn't privy to that information."

I shake my head. She has to have more for me than *the curse is partially broken.* Sure, we weren't looking at it as an extra step to take, and more of a hiccup that needed smoothing out, but this still isn't enough to go off of. We already know it's incomplete. "My ancestor told you this much. You must know something."

"Elijah and I were friends, yes. He had enough confidence in our friendship to entrust me with the other half of his note when he left. Even though he was responsible for the curse, he had a soft spot for the Dravens and didn't want the truth to be lost somewhere in America when he died."

"Responsible in the same way you are..." I pry, knowing that together the two of them turned Ambrose in, which resulted in the clan leaders cursing the Dravens.

"Oh dear, you truly don't know much, do you?" Emile purses her lips, uncrossing her ankles and sitting forward slightly. "All curses must be bound by blood. And usually, human blood is a stronger binding agent because of their life force. The Draven curse was bound by Elijah Troy's blood."

"That's why I was able to turn."

"Yes, but only one person of your bloodline can trigger the loophole, and until you unlock the second half, everyone else in your bloodline will experience the same effects as the rest of humanity does."

Just as Danielle suspected, which explains why I could turn, but Dallas couldn't. "And the rest of the curse? The second piece—how am I supposed to figure out what I need to do?"

I tap my foot anxiously and chew on my lower lip. Suddenly, I'm panicking. Not once did I think our solution involved me performing another act of some sort. Now I'm afraid it's going to be a blood sacrifice or a ritual that forces me to adhere to all of the Dravens' wishes.

Emile smiles knowingly and stands, floating up the stairs to the study like she's riding on a cloud. I follow, noticing the floors don't creak quite so loudly, that they're flat and smooth. If I didn't know any better, I would truly think I was in a different century.

The study is gorgeous. A large chandelier hangs from the ceiling over Elijah's desk, and the room is long and wide, not yet blocked off by a wall in the center, which all on its own makes the house feel so much larger.

To my utter bewilderment, Emile begins organizing Elijah's desk, placing bookmarks in open novels, then piling them neatly off to the side. She sticks a letter opener in the top drawer and tidies the scattered pieces of parchment, as well. A newspaper sticks out from the pile that reads June 1802.

Once the space is cleared, I notice a singular piece of paper I hadn't before… or maybe it wasn't there at all until she finished organizing. Emile picks it up, humming softly as she makes her way to the back of the room. Dislodging one of the wood panels from the left wall, she sticks the paper inside a small slot beside a well-used journal, then puts it back as if it was never removed. The space would be nearly impossible for anyone to locate if they don't know it exists.

"You shall find what you seek," Emile says meaningfully,

reaching out to touch my hand. I squeeze hers in return, and then remember something Vanesa said to me not long ago.

Releasing her hand, I reach around my neck to open the fragile clasp that holds my necklace together, then hold it out for her. "I believe this belongs to you."

Her eyes cloud with a look of longing as she takes it from me, holding it close to her heart. Tears sheen over her eyes as she watches me.

"Ambrose led me to it," I tell her, in case she doesn't know.

"Then he did one good thing for this world." She grabs a hold of my shoulders, and the space around us starts to flicker with images of what it is now—old, rundown, broken. Her ruse is fading and reality is moving in and out of view. "Take care of my brother. You fill a void in his life and bring out a passionate and unmistakably human side of him I feared he lost long ago. And as for my sisters... they've never known a human they trusted. Once they open their eyes and see you for who you are, they will understand the light you shine upon them."

I open my mouth to thank her, but the two simple words don't reflect hers with the sincerity they deserve.

She understands my dilemma somehow, removing her hands from my shoulders and enclosing them around my own. "Thank me by ensuring they never feel regret over the secrets I kept from them. I may not have been blood, by bite or DNA, but I was the oldest all the same, and sometimes as the oldest you must make sacrifices and bear the weight so the rest don't have to."

Emile fades away, smiling through her tears, and I can't help but wonder if now that her necklace has been returned, she can move on at last.

~

Miles hovers over me with his hands on my face and a cold compress pressed to my forehead. I groan. My entire body aches from hitting the ground when I passed out. In a room full of vampires, you'd think one of them would have quick enough reflexes to catch me.

I sit up rather quickly, forcing Miles to move away so I don't ram into him. I look around the room and find that almost everyone is standing where they were when I fainted, which means not much time has passed, thankfully. Other than Miles, only Elaine and Danielle have moved. Elaine is sitting on the couch with her head between her knees, looking nauseous, and Danielle is pestering her to put a cold washrag on her forehead.

When everyone notices I've come to, they start bombarding me with questions, and from what I can gather, I'm the only one who passed out. Elaine just became really dizzy and needed to sit down.

Without a word, I wobble to my feet, stumbling toward the hidden room where I practically dive headfirst through the entrance. Moving to the left wall, I shove aside a rickety chair, which breaks on impact, and attempt to move the standing bookshelf. It never occurred to any of us when looking behind it that there may be a hidden compartment in the wall. Frustrated with my limp arms and trembling legs—a combination of my nerves and fainting—I latch on to the top of the shelf and pull it over with all of my strength. Luckily, it doesn't land on Oliver, who's still asleep on my mattress in the corner, though it comes fairly close. He lets out a groan but doesn't so much as flutter his lashes.

The siblings all crowd around, watching me with a mixture of disturb and perplexity.

"Has she lost her mind?" Vira asks at the same time Vanesa says, "I think she's gone mad. Can we put her down now?"

I feel around the wall, unable to recall exactly which panel Emile put the letter in, and when I finally find it, I push up on the bottom, just as she had, and toss it aside. Relief swamps me when I find the letter is still there, and in great condition for how long ago it was written.

I find that there's more than one journal in the snug space as well, which confirms my suspicions that Emile merged images and events from several different decades into a few short minutes. Otherwise, the timeline wouldn't add up—the young Draven siblings playing in the yard, a full refrigerator before its time. Even the date on the newspaper was a few years before Elijah would have known about the curse—assuming the paper Emile hid details it.

"I was right," Lucas utters, astounded.

Vira rolls her eyes. "You were not. You told us to look under the floorboards."

He shrugs a shoulder, unbothered by this fact. "Close enough. I still predicted a hidden compartment."

After a short inner-debate, I decide to leave the journals be. From this angle, only I can see them, and I'm not sure I want to share with all six of the Dravens before I get the chance to thoroughly read them myself. Besides, Emile drew attention to the letter, not the journal. If this turns out to be a dead end, then I will consider revealing the rest of Elijah's artifacts.

As I reenter the main room, I'm met with multiple questions regarding what I found and how I knew where to look for it.

"Emile," I respond, which causes them to fall silent. "She's been trying to tell me this entire time with the nightmares. There's nothing wrong with the curse. It's incomplete. There's another component other than me, and I think this letter might tell me what that is."

I unfold the paper, carefully smoothing it down on the desk as we all circle around it, eager with anticipation.

My dearest Descendent,

I am deeply sorry for all you must have endured in the time since you discovered your fate. It is not a life I would have chosen for myself, much less for someone I love. Your life, if it hasn't already, will soon become unfathomably complicated, and I'm sorry I have nothing more than this letter and my journals to guide you.

I am responsible for not only setting the Draven curse into motion but setting it in stone by binding it with the very blood that flows through my veins—through your veins. But I did not act alone.

If you have been unfortunate enough to find your way back to Ichorye, and back into the Draven circle, then chances are, fate has already begun working. It was necessary that I flee Ichorye. I had to be as far from the other blood agent binding the curse as possible, and if we both left, suspicion would be drawn. Besides, and though I hate to say this, it is more probable that during the consideration period, where you decide whether vampirism is what you desire, one of the two of you will perish before both completing the turn. If this happens, it cannot be undone, and the curse can never be broken.

All of these precautions are to ensure the Dravens will be unable to create more of their kind. If only one of you becomes a vampire, as I said, then it is only that person alone who can create more vampires. This is to ensure the clan is unable to dispose of you once you set them free. It gives you a purpose and allows you to live freely without fear of being killed once they think you've done your part. If only you have the power, then they still need you alive.

I have faith that whoever you are is strong enough to resist their pull, and that you will not share their bloodthirsty ambition in creating more of their kind to exact revenge on those who have wronged them. Besides Ambrose, I truly trust the Dravens, but I do not know who they will become in the years that follow me. Deprivation can change a man.

If you are lucky, and yes, there are a lot of ifs in this terrible situation you've befallen, the other bloodline mingled with the curse will not exist where you are or will be too far from Ichorye to be of any use. This is why I will not tell you the surname—to be sure that the curse remains intact, and so as not to give you another secret to keep.

But if you aren't lucky, then the other family never left. To break the curse, you must both live in Ichorye and be bitten by a member of the Draven clan. Then you must both complete the transition to become vampires. Only then will the curse will be lifted.

The blood that binds is the blood of the curse's demise.

Ridiculous as it sounds, I saw a palm reader today in the hopes of learning about the future and who you may be—if you exist at all. It was rather unhelpful, as she only provided me with a single word —destiny.

I have the suspicion that I was played for a fool, but I'm hopeful that someday you will read this, and that word will have meaning to you—if for nothing else, so that I didn't spend eleven pounds for nothing.

I haven't the slightest clue how long it will be, if ever, until you are reading this. I don't know where life will take our family from here but promise me this—remember that you are always and forever a Troy. Not a Draven. And although their intentions are pure, and only ever out of love for one another, darkness can find even the brightest of souls.

Best wishes,
   Elijah Troy

Each of us finishes reading around the same time, and when I'm done, I let out a heavy sigh, my throat feeling dry and my tongue thick.

"He could have been more helpful," Vanesa remarks, unsatisfied with our solution being laid out on a silver platter. The blood of *two* humans was used to bind the curse, not just Elijah's, so the transition of an individual in each of the bloodlines will be what reverses it.

A part of me is proud of him for what he did, giving up his life and his friends, abandoning his home, all to protect the people in this town from Ambrose. Then there's me, who unknowingly upended everything he strived for. He'd even thought far enough ahead to make sure that whoever in his bloodline became a vampire couldn't be killed, because only they have the power to create new vampires—so long as the other bloodline doesn't transition as well. Plus, he took a blood oath with Adrian so that even he couldn't kill me until he was certain the curse was about to be broken...

With this revelation, suddenly I'm not feeling entirely safe anymore. The siblings may not understand what this means, but unfortunately, I do.

"My ancestor just gave you everything you need to break

the curse." I scoff at Vanesa's absurdity, nausea making me feel like I'm going to vomit.

"A name would have been nice," she counters.

The fact that she read that letter at all is precisely why he didn't include one. Except... he sort of did. He mentioned his flee from Ichorye, as well as someone who stayed. The way he worded it almost gave me the impression that they were close enough to have joined him if it were safer, but because of the circumstances, he had to leave them behind.

"But now we have somewhere to start," Lucas says, hope laced in his words. "All we have to do is figure out which family."

"Oh, yes, and convince one of them to become a vampire and take a human life to complete the transition," Vira says plainly. She crosses her arms, leaning against the wall.

"Unless we don't ask. Make it look like a fluke. If they don't see who bit them, they'll never know we were behind it," Vanesa suggests, and it's scary how serious she is about this. She would be willing to put on an entire ruse and play into a person's fear just to break this curse. "There were dozens of families that lived here during that time, and a lot of them *did* move away. Whoever it is would have been smart to leave if they didn't want us to find the truth. I say we track them down and get to biting."

"There's no way to know that for sure, and we're not going to start biting anyone who has a connection to the people who lived here in 1804." Miles reaches for the letter, then scans it at an insanely fast speed. "There is another key out there just like Aspen, we just need to figure out who—" His words fall off, eyes inconspicuously finding mine.

Elliot says something, Danielle responds, and they continue

discussing the predicament back and forth as I hold Miles's gaze. Biting my lip, I drop my eyes, still reeling from Emile's visit, and now this huge chunk of the puzzle that's been neatly pieced together for us.

From the way Emile spoke, I was under the impression that just because Elijah didn't specifically tell her who the other key was, didn't mean she was unable to figure it out on her own. Just like us, she had all of the pieces, but much more time to decipher them. My ancestor trusted her though, and despite the love she holds for her siblings, she respected his need to preserve the curse.

Now all that's left is a name.

I can't help but feel like a colossal disappointment. I should be protecting his legacy the way Emile did, not willingly handing over the instruction manual to the Dravens' freedom. Except I have to save my brother if it's the last thing I do. And it sickens me to know that I'm choosing the few over the many. In choosing Dallas, I could very easily be condemning every soul in town to a more gruesome fate than his.

Vanesa looms over me suddenly, and she locks her hand on my shoulder, giving it an unnecessarily painful squeeze. She moves her face closer, whispering suspiciously in my ear. "You're awfully quiet."

"I didn't realize my opinions were appreciated now," I say, forcing myself not to cower away from her. Vanesa craves control. Dominance. And I refuse to ever give her such power.

I can't see her face, but I know she rolls her eyes when she says, "They're not—only when I think you're holding something back."

"I have been completely transparent with you since the beginning, Vanesa. Do you think you were ever meant to read that letter? I could have waited until you left to retrieve it, but I didn't."

"You lied about your little trip to America to test the change. You didn't tell us about your nightmares, or that you met Adrian."

Of course Vanesa would remember everything I didn't tell her, instead of considering how much I have. How much of myself I've given up to help them. She of all people should recognize that, especially when considering that she's currently using my brother as a bargaining tool. If I could, I would set the Draven clan free and keep her bound to the curse for all eternity so she could never know peace. That may be a cruel thing to want, but it's the truth. Besides, it would be better for my conscience than killing her—and I already promised Miles I wouldn't do that.

"Your point?" I turn, clenching my teeth as I glare up at her.

"Tell me what *destiny* means." Her tone is cool, and I'm slightly relieved that she's focusing on the wrong aspects of the letter.

Except I don't want to tell them. I never planned on explaining any of my life before now to them. Not about what happened with Derek, and not about who I used to be. I don't trust Vanesa not to bring him here just to spite me. But I don't have another option. I need time to think about what I've read and consider how to move forward in the most appropriate manner. "My real name is Destiny Wilson."

"What?" Danielle is the first to speak, looking shocked at my revelation.

"It has nothing to do with breaking the curse, other than the fact that Elijah wasn't conned—the psychic was genuine. He just didn't realize Destiny was a name. My name." I swallow, feeling like I'm betraying Dallas by speaking of our past. Yes, I told Miles, but that's because I trusted him and felt as though he was someone I could confide in. That's not the case for everyone here. Even Danielle, as much as I love and appreciate all she's done for me, doesn't need to know the disturbing details of my past. "It's complicated, but all it means is that even back then, I was destined to be the key, or part of it, at least."

"Aren't you just full of surprises," Vanesa coos, tapping a sharp nail on my shoulder.

Danielle twirls a strand of her hair nervously, biting her lip. "Why did you change your name? And how did you end up choosing Troy in the first place?"

"Ambrose influenced that choice. He thought it would be ironic since I actually am a descendent of Elijah Troy," I say, interlocking my fingers nervously and hoping she doesn't notice how I skipped over her first question—*why*.

Miles closes his eyes, and I know he's figured out the same thing I have. The others are too blind to see it. They can't read between the lines. Elijah gave me everything I need to figure out who the other key is, but I suppose only Miles and I have talked about it before, so the others wouldn't think of the obvious solution so readily.

I'm not sure what he's going to do now. How can he not tell his siblings? How can he not disclose what we both know to be true when it makes perfect sense? If he stays quiet it's for no one else but me, and I can't have that… but I also can't disclose the sort of information that could potentially ruin another person's life.

Tears cloud in my eyes, and I try my hardest to hold them back because I have to save my brother. I have to make sure he survives the hell I introduced him to. I just don't know how to do that now.

"I don't know what to do," I tell Miles, whispering softly once the attention is off of me and back to their many theories.

He starts to say something but is interrupted by Elaine, who is all too eager to assist. And to my surprise, not even Elliot belittles her suggestions or tells her she's irrelevant now that she's provided the biggest lead any of us have had in months. "Now that we know what we're searching for, I can read through my ancestor's journal again to see if anything catches my eye."

"Wait, what was your ancestor's name again?" Vira asks, touching the journal thoughtfully.

Elliot straightens his back, flicking his gaze to his sister and then back to Elaine, responding before she has a chance to. "Timothy Graves."

"Hold on, Timothy Graves." Danielle rolls the name over her tongue, trying to remember. "That sounds familiar. Wasn't he...?" Her eyes widen, and she glances at the journal, where the two pieces of paper have mended at the seam by our touch, then looks straight at my best friend.

"Elijah Troy's best friend," Lucas finishes for her, and suddenly every single person in this room is staring straight at the descendent of Timothy Graves.

Elijah's best friend. The man he was inseparable from. Who was deeply involved in Draven affairs but withdrew his position after the curse took effect. Who *stayed behind* when his best friend moved away.

Vanesa drops her head to the desk with a thump, groaning in agony. "Bloody hell."

CHAPTER 34

For all of five seconds, Elaine is incredibly ecstatic over this new development, eager that her newfound relevancy proves false Elliot's claims of her insignificance. Until she fully comprehends what this means.

The Dravens need Elaine to become a vampire.

To do so, Elaine must kill someone to complete the transition.

She will essentially be dying for the clan her ancestor wanted her kept away from, although his wishes seem slightly more meaningless now that we know he only wanted to keep his bloodline from intermingling with theirs for fear someone would turn her and set the curse-breaking into motion.

Worst of all, if she doesn't choose to turn, if she doesn't choose to murder someone in cold blood, Dallas will die.

As horrible as my situation was, at least the man I killed was trying to kill me. Despite how bad I feel about what happened, and about what Nadia and Aaron's family have gone through because of my actions, he wasn't a good man. That's no excuse, but in a way I was lucky. If not for him, I might still be a transitioner debating my fate—or worse. I could be dead.

"Holy mother of evil." Elaine rubs her head, messing up the smooth ponytail she put her hair into before we left Miles's house. "There has to be some mistake."

"I don't think there is, Elaine," Miles says in a low voice, sounding regretful.

I move around Vanesa to where Elaine leans on the desk, head sagging between her shoulder blades. I place my hand on her back, and she turns to me on the verge of tears.

But she's Elaine, so she straightens up and holds them in like a pro. "How is this possible? It doesn't make any sense. Why me?"

"Elijah and Timothy were best friends—my family moved away, yours remained in Ichorye. Then there's the riddle we both have pieces to, and you also possess an odd amount of strength."

"Maybe I'm just freakishly strong," she suggests, sounding unconvinced.

Vira steps in, assessing Elaine in a new light. "Is there a specific point in time when you noticed yourself getting stronger?"

She looks down, and though she doesn't want to say it, we all know the answer. When I became a vampire, she grew stronger because of our bond with the curse. We're connected. Unbeknownst to anyone, our families have been intertwined for two centuries.

In one way or another, *all* of our lives are tied together by this curse.

"You knew, didn't you? You figured it out, and you weren't

going to say anything," Vanesa accuses, shoving me with her hands as she gets in my face.

I knock her arms off, too tired for her anger. It's as though she doesn't have an off switch. "I knew for all of five seconds before you did. I was processing."

"I knew," Miles speaks up, earning a furious glare from his sister. "And I wasn't going to tell you."

Vanesa shakes her head, appalled. "I don't know who you are anymore. *My* brother used to choose his family over everything else. Not one day in your life have you put a single thing above us, and yet here you are."

Her insults don't bother him, and he counters her statement with his own accusations. "I could say the same about you. Is this who we are now? Putting other lives in harm's way to fix our own? We were happy. We were content. We accepted our fate a long time ago. Just because we've found a way to get back to who we used to be doesn't mean we should take it. Not at the expense of someone else."

"And what of your little infatuation?" Vanesa gets in his face, clearly not in any place to accept these terms. She begins shoving him one after another until he grabs her arms, holding them in front of her chest. "How long do you think you and your princess will last once you stand by while her brother dies?"

"That's not up to him," Elaine cuts in, grabbing Vanesa's shoulder and spinning her so they're face to face. "The choice is mine. Even if Dallas dies, it won't break them up, but nice try."

"Why don't we take a vote," Danielle says, and Vanesa purses her lips, nodding in understanding.

"I see how it is." She blinks, shaking her head as she moves backward, looking at each of her siblings as she does so. "One needless human life is more important than all of ours."

"We've lived more than enough lifetimes," Lucas says, dipping his head in surrender. "Elaine only gets one. She should decide what is to be done with it."

Danielle takes his hand, and together they stand their ground. "I agree."

Elliot brushes past us, exiting the room as he says, "I don't."

Vanesa looks at Miles. "Don't even respond. You're pathetic. V?"

Vira lets out a shuddering breath, looking torn between saving herself and saving a singular human. "If we don't break the curse, we won't have to go to war..."

Vanesa takes a long breath, and I can see the respect she has for her siblings diminishing with her hope, her strength. Already she knows that, once again, she's going to be outvoted. "It's never been about the curse, you know that. They're going to attack us either way. One way, we break the curse and have an army to defend ourselves, the other, they kill us all in ten minutes because none of you could be bothered to do what is *necessary.*"

Then she turns to me, even though my vote, no matter what it is, won't change the decision in the slightest. The scale has been tipped. "And you? You're willing to let your brother perish? Vampirism isn't the end, it's only the beginning. Dallas will still be *alive.*"

"Your family gave me a choice once. I'd be a hypocrite not to do the same." I choke on my next words, tears welling because of what this means for my brother. "Elaine has the right to choose."

"Fine." Vanesa's almost to the door now, shaking with anger and resentment. "You win."

But I know Vanesa too well. And she will try to turn Elaine, just like she did Dallas. I'm not even sure she cares about her family anymore, not when they've all expressed their contentment with this plan—minus Elliot. It avoids a war with the clans—though we still need to have faith that they won't kill us anyway—and it protects the people in town.

The only person Vanesa looks out for is herself—an admirable quality if she didn't maim others in the process.

Danielle and Lucas leave, offering to drive us back to Miles's house since the storm outside is still severe. The thunder and lightning have dissipated, but the rain is pouring down harder than it was when Vira got here.

"Go ahead, I'll catch up."

Miles looks unsure, but I insist he go with them and promise to be safe. Besides, Oliver is still out cold in the hidden room, and I'm not comfortable leaving him here with my parents. I don't know if the hunters are above harming unsuspecting humans as leverage to get to me, but I don't want to take that chance. Anyway, it's almost dawn, so we can figure out what to do with him once everyone calms down from tonight's revelations.

"If you're sure." Miles pulls me in for a hug, kissing my forehead.

"I am. Go be with your family. I'll get some rest and then find you later. Plus, someone needs to be here in case Oliver wakes up."

"You aren't going to murder him in his sleep, are you?" he asks, teasing.

"No." Then I lower my voice. "I need to talk with Elaine. She has to know I will understand her final decision, whatever she chooses."

Miles is distracted from our conversation though, and his eyes are drawn to my chest where they linger on my necklace. He scoops it into his hand to inspect it closer. "It's different."

I blink, unsure of how that's possible. When I look down, sure enough, it's no longer the mix of brown and gold it once was, but pure white, almost like a milky crystal.

"The necklaces made for the women in my family are sculpted from clay, but when finished and placed around the neck of its owner, the colors dissolve into one another, representing the shade of your soul." He sets it back on my chest, but his eyes remain glued to the pendant. Even the vines are silvery now, as opposed to the gold of the others'. "Yours is… pure. How did this happen?"

"Before Emile and I parted ways, I returned it to her." Knowing how strange that sounds, I elaborate. "Everything felt real. I could touch her, I could feel the summer heat from outside, I could hear laughter. I think it was your family, actually, when you were still human. I don't know how I know that, but Emile projected herself as a human despite coming to you guys after she turned. Anyway, I thought she should have it back. I thought the gesture was purely symbolic, but I suppose not."

"Incredible," he breathes in astonishment.

"What does this mean?"

He bends, pressing a kiss to my lips. "It means that, for better or worse, you are a Draven."

The Dravens haven't accepted a member into the family since Lucas… and I'm not sure how I feel about that.

Elijah's words come back to haunt me, burned into my

memory. *Remember that you are always and forever a Troy. Not a Draven.*

"I'd much rather just be yours," I say, then pull his lips to mine one last time before he goes.

Miles strokes my cheek, moving backward in his departure. "As fate may have it, we were always going to find one another."

"Hey." I stop him, brushing my fingers to his. I've been too scared to face the intensity and weight of what my next words mean for our future. Afraid they'll further deepen the rift between him and Vanesa. But suddenly, in this moment, they feel right. "I love you, too."

A tender smile forms on his lips, and he squeezes my hand.

"You can go without me," Vira says, still entranced by my ancestor's letter. She's bent over the desk, reading it a third time.

Miles nods, then heads downstairs to meet Danielle at the car, and I watch through the window as they drive off into the rainstorm.

"I think I want to go home," Elaine says from the doorway, where she's been standing ever since the unofficial vote was taken.

"You can stay here if you want," I offer. Her parents won't be home for another few days, and I'm not sure it's the best idea for her to be alone at the moment. Not only did she just find out she's the other half of an ancient curse, and that she's essentially my blood-sister, but she also discovered that her longtime best friend is a hunter who's vying to destroy the people she could help protect if she chose. Becoming a vampire would result in her losing him forever if she hasn't already simply by working with us.

She shakes her head. "I want to sleep in my own bed tonight."

Hesitant, I nod. Arguing this won't make her change her mind and will probably just upset her further. "I'll walk you."

She shakes her head again. "Then you have to walk back alone. You're in more danger out there than I am."

I can't argue with her there. Vira sighs, and runs a hand through her wavy hair, folding up the letter and tucking it in the top desk drawer. "I'll come to make sure she gets back all right."

"You will?" Elaine asks doubtfully.

Vira steps away from the desk, stripping off the shirt I lent her and replacing it with her damp one. It's mostly dry by now, but her leather jacket is still dripping with water, so she drapes that over her arm. Distracted, she pulls her phone out of her pocket and reads a message before slipping it back in, seeming troubled by whatever it was.

"I was wrong about both of you, and I truly am sorry for the petty way I've acted. We are bound together, have been for two centuries now. You both were meant to become part of our lives since before you were born. And although I don't always agree with you..." She takes a deep breath, struggling to admit her faults "...I disagree with Vanesa more. And, Aspen, I cannot stand your self-righteousness, but you are good for my brother. For a long time, all we've had was each other, and it is a lonely place to be."

I bite my lip, feeling as though I might be able to level with her for once. "Even I find it hard to understand at times, but I am on your side, and not just because I want to save my brother."

Vira nods, and the three of us head downstairs, out into the rainy night. I hadn't thought this part through—we're going to be drenched by the time we get back.

Vira pulls the phone out of her pocket again, still looking conflicted, but doesn't respond to whoever keeps texting her. She moves ahead of us, not seeming to care about the rain since her hair is still damp from earlier. She scans our surroundings, then nods to insinuate we're in the clear, but something in her expression worries me a little.

Before I have time to consider my gut feeling that something isn't right, Elaine distracts me by grabbing my wrist, inhaling shakily.

"I love this life, Aspen. I love the danger and the mystery and feeling like I'm a part of something bigger than myself... but I don't want to be *part* of it. I-I like the sidelines. I like the research. I like bickering with Elliot when he doesn't think I'm smart enough and then proving him wrong every time." Tears stream down her face, and my heart breaks for two reasons— one being the anguish she feels, and the other for my brother, who I swore I'd protect above anything. "But I don't want to be like them."

I cup her cheeks with my hands, wiping away the tears that intermingle with the rainwater dripping from the porch awning. "I will never blame you for that. Ever. I understand what it's like to be in your position more than anyone. I don't envy you."

"At least I understand what I'm up against. You were never given a choice. Ambrose took that away from you." She closes her eyes sadly, staring out into the rain. "It's not fair."

"No," I agree. "But neither is life for putting you in this position, too."

"I don't particularly enjoy standing in the rain for fun," Vira calls, crossing her arms over her chest. "Hurry up."

Elaine rolls her eyes, and the reaction eases the tension in my shoulders. Part of me is scared that, just like Dallas, the darkness of this world will overtake the light within her, making her a smaller version of herself. That little eye roll tells me it's not too late to replenish her spirits.

We step vigilantly down the two front steps, careful to avoid the spots that are too broken to support our weight. Vira stands in the center of the grass, rain soaking through her clothes. In the chilly air, the rainwater is even colder, and I shiver, wrapping my arms around myself as we walk to meet Vira in the grass. She doesn't move when we reach her, and I raise an eyebrow, wondering why she complained about the rain if we're just going to stand here anyway.

"I truly meant what I said to you before." Vira moves away from us, and I notice a figure standing off to the side, near the shed behind my house. "But this needs to be done."

Before I can comprehend what's happening, Vanesa is running toward us at full speed, shooting straight past me and to Elaine, whose wrist she takes forcefully and brings to her lips.

CHAPTER 35

*S*napping out of my daze, I lunge at Vanesa right as she's about to sink her teeth into Elaine. Both of us stumble to the ground, but when she lands on her back, she uses all of her strength to throw me before I fall on top of her. I go flying across the lawn, dropping hard on my side, and if it weren't for my enhanced strength, I probably would have broken several bones in the right half of my body.

What's worse than my pain is the second of hesitation I had before stopping Vanesa from biting Elaine. Because the horrible, monstrous, disgustingly inhumane part of me wanted to let her.

In a flash, I'm lunging at Vanesa again, and this time when she tries to catapult me off of her, I'm ready. I latch on to her arms, and when she shoves me away, I just fall back onto her, bringing my elbow down on her throat. She gags, choking as I cut off her airway. She recovers quickly though, and grabs my neck, bowing her back and rolling me off of her, only to straddle me and squeeze my throat between her slender fingers. She pulls a wooden stake from the inner pocket of her leather jacket and holds it between us.

Curling her fist around the wood, she rotates her wrist and punches me. I taste blood immediately. Enraged, I spit it in her face, smiling like a lunatic. "You can't kill me, Vanesa. This will all have been for nothing if you do. You'll never break the curse."

Vanesa removes her hand from my throat, transferring it to my face where she crushes my cheeks, digging her nails into my skin. "I can still make you wish you were dead."

She stabs the wood into my stomach, not close enough to my heart to kill, but still in a near enough proximity to make me see stars. She stands, towering over me, and finishes the job with a cowardly kick to my ribs.

Limping, she makes her way back toward Elaine, who is rooted in place. She knows running isn't an option, not when vampires are involved. I tear my eyes from them, grunting as I pull the stake from my stomach. Searing pain sends blotches across my vision, but I can still make out Vira standing off to the side, shoulders stiff and eyes boring into the scene before her.

If she's going to betray her family's vote, the least she could do is help Vanesa. She doesn't, though.

She stood and watched us grapple with each other when she so easily could have bitten Elaine while I was distracted. I used to have some ounce of respect for her, for the way she could command her siblings to listen, the way she spoke to her clan. She's even taken my side a few times, and I know that was only because she felt indebted to me, but it took courage, nonetheless. She and Vanesa seemed so close when I first moved here. It couldn't have been easy for her to go against her sister, for me of all people. And now, watching her stand there like a coward, I realize that she is just as pathetic as Vanesa, if not more.

Vanesa may be a venomous cockroach, but at least she's honest about what she wants and has the drive and guts to attain it.

I force myself to my feet, throwing the stake as far as I can so Vanesa can't use it again, and so I don't use it against her—because right now, I don't trust myself not to do something I'll regret later.

She has a hard time moving fast with the limp I gave her when we fell to the ground, and when she attempts to use her speed, she stumbles, giving me the time I need to catch up.

I latch on to the back of her hair, yanking so hard she falls backward, collapsing onto her knees. "This is her choice, not yours. I won't let you take free will from anyone else."

"You are like a sad and pitiful broken record," Vanesa spits, breathing rabidly.

I tug harder, gaining the upper hand—or so I thought. Vanesa places both hands on the ground, leaning into me and lifting her leg. The toe of her boot scrapes across my jaw, and the power of her kick forces me to release my hold on her hair. I regain my composure and lift a knee, connecting it with her chin before she can get to her feet. I'm about to follow up the favor by kicking her in the ribs when Elaine screams.

"I'll do it," she erupts, voice piercing through the tense silence like a gunshot.

Vanesa stops her efforts to stand, turning slowly toward Elaine with a strange admiration in her eyes.

"Elaine…" I can hardly breathe. My lungs are on fire and

there's blood actively leaking from the stab wound on my stomach.

Again, a selfish part of me is thrilled, because horribly enough, I want her to turn—but I don't think she's aware of the choices she will have to make moving forward. Whatever she does following this moment will haunt her for the rest of her life. Her next words determine everything, and the weight they hold affects more lives than just her own.

She shrugs, and I can see in her down-turned lips and glassy eyes that she's only doing this out of obligation. "Dallas will die, Aspen. And I won't let you do something you're going to regret in the name of my conscience—Vanesa's a cold-hearted bitch, but she doesn't deserve to die. I will become a vampire to end the curse."

The moment she's done speaking, there's movement in the woods. Vanesa springs to her feet, and I curse her for being so reckless that we wasted most of our energy on each other instead of the enemy. Also, we might have noticed the hunters creeping up on us if we hadn't been so busy fighting.

Then there's the problem that the second Elaine revealed her involvement in the curse, they emerged from their hiding spots.

Eight hunters appear, crossbows in tow, surrounding us like people at a campfire.

"For the love of God," Vanesa cries, throwing her head back. Her ruby lipstick is smudged down her chin and a little around her mouth, giving the appearance of dried blood. When she sneers at our company, she looks lethal. Then her glare turns on me, dead serious. "We're not finished here."

Not by a long shot.

Vira is by my side in an instant, the three of us moving so

Elaine is protected by us at all angles. At least we have one common goal—keep Elaine safe.

The hunters shoot their arrows first, and Vira and Vanesa expertly grab and swat them out of the air, leaving me speechless at the sheer smoothness of their motions and the confidence that oozes from them despite our odds. The hunters outnumber us eight to three, and the sisters don't seem the least bit concerned. I only hope they haven't already sent a messenger to Adrian.

All at once, they charge at us. Vira and Vanesa break off, each running in opposite directions, then jump and fly at the men, taking out two of them at a time. Vira knocks one out, and snaps another's wrist, then turns to a third who was about to charge at me, sweeping his legs from beneath him. Vanesa's not as quick on her feet, though, weakened from our fight. This means the last three hunters are gunning for me, each with their own weapon in hand.

I avoid the first swing easily, ducking under his arm and punching him in the ribs. Then I turn toward the hunter who's heading for Elaine, and the distraction gets me kicked in the ribs. The man who swung at me tries again, and this time, I block his arm, twist his wrist, and knee him in the groin, narrowly avoiding getting stabbed by the second man in the process.

They're all large. So much so that in the human world, they would be assumed to be on steroids. I take out the second hunter easier than the first, and head for the third just as he reaches Elaine. He's much quicker than the other two and immediately grabs my throat instead of leading with his weapon.

After knocking my legs out from under me, he kneels on

my ribcage, attempting to drive his stake through my heart. I cross my wrists to block it, then wrap my hands around his to keep them from moving. He thrusts his hips forward, pushing his weight farther into me until I think I hear the crack of a rib breaking. A sweat breaks out across my skin as I fight against him, losing the battle. The tip of his stake pierces the skin above my chest. I try to shift, looking for Vira or Vanesa, and to make sure that Elaine is still okay, but I can't see any of them. The movement causes me to lose my leverage, and the blade drives deeper into me.

"Let me go!" I hear Elaine scream, and when I finally catch sight of her, she's being dragged away by Vanesa. "Stop! We have to help her. Vanesa!"

I grunt, noticing this hunter has not said a word to me the entire time we fought. Last time I was in a situation like this was with Aaron, and he wouldn't shut up about how much he hated the Dravens. This man is gruff, older and stronger than Aaron was, and well-practiced. Negotiating with him is pointless. I can't use humanity as my defense now that I'm not human, so I try for the next best thing.

"If you leave me here, you will lose Miles forever," I yell at Vanesa. The effort it takes to do so wanes my strength. Hunters have no empathy, no soul. I'm better off appealing to Vanesa's twisted mind instead. "You'll still be cursed, and it will all be for nothing."

Vanesa sneers a dark smile that elicits chills down my spine. "I've already lost him, thanks to you. And I realized while watching you lie there, struggling—just to see you dead, I'm willing to take that chance. Both of them."

"Vanesa!" I scream, struggling harder as the hunter fully gains the upper hand. The point of the stake scratches the surface of my heart, and I close my eyes, not wanting to die to the image of this stranger's face, or Vanesa's.

Without warning, the pressure is lifted from my body, and the stake is yanked out of me as the hunter is thrust to the ground where Vira stands. She punches him twice, and he slumps over almost instantly, unmoving in the grass.

Vira holds out her hand to me, and I curl my lip, standing up by my damn self.

She clears her throat and tosses me a stake from one of the hunters' bodies that I catch in midair.

Vanesa jeers from the road, holding both of Elaine's arms behind her back, furious at her sister for helping me.

"Now we're even," Vira says to me, and the ludicrousness of such a statement threatens to send me on a rampage, but I stamp down my anger because she did just save my life.

"Your family ruined my life. We will never be even." That may be a tad overdramatic, but other than Miles, all the Dravens have done is destroy me. Even if we survive a war and make it out the other side of all of this, how could I ever lead an ordinary life afterward?

CHAPTER 36

*E*veryone's on their feet the instant we walk into the warm living room at Draven Manor. Their faces mimic those of horror when they take us in—drenched, sopping with blood, covered in bruises, and limping across the slippery hardwood. Little do they know, most of these wounds are from my fight with Vanesa.

Vira is virtually uninjured, meanwhile, it looks like Vanesa and I were hit by a truck.

Elaine collapses to the floor and drops her head between her knees, unable to make it to the couch. She had a panic attack on the way here, and we had to stop several times so she could calm down and catch her breath. Vira and I practically carried her most of the way.

"You're dripping blood on the floor," Vanesa informs me, and I physically have to interlock my fingers to keep from poking her eyes out.

"You look like you've been mauled by a wild animal," Danielle gasps, and Miles bolts to the kitchen, grabbing several towels for our wounds. He tosses one to Vanesa, but she's not bleeding nearly as badly as I am.

"Take them to the armory," Miles says to Danielle, running back for more towels when I soak through the first ones immediately.

Someone scoops me up in their arms, and I realize after a beat that it's Lucas. He carries me down the spiraling stairs and the others follow behind. Elaine, shell-shocked and terrified, follows as well, and I'm not sure she even realizes it.

"Who did this?" Miles growls, stripping the shirt from my stomach and pulling it over my head while his five siblings and my best friend watch. I'm in too much pain to care, though, and I lay back on the silver table in an attempt to even my breathing.

"Vanesa," Elaine says, her voice stony and cold. "She and Vira ambushed us, and Vanesa tried to bite me and kill Aspen. Twice."

"Danielle," Miles grunts, and his fists turn white over the cloth he's pressing to my stomach. "Stitch Aspen up, please. She will heal faster if you do."

Danielle nods hesitantly, then grabs a needle and begins to work on the wound, first flushing it out with the same liquid they used to clean Elliot's injuries. I let out a groan as it singes my skin, but after that, I notice I'm too numb from the cold to feel much of anything. I stare at the needle as it weaves in and out of my skin with precision, but it's as if I'm watching it be done to someone else.

"Leave," Miles says, grabbing Vanesa's wrists. She flinches, and for the slightest of moments, I think I see genuine fear in her eyes. "And don't ever come back."

"You don't have the authority," she hisses and tries to escape his grip, but can't.

He laughs without humor, and it's a frightening sound. "And where do you get off giving yourself the right to hurt other people? We took a vote, and you lost."

"Only because you're so biased you can't tell the clouds from the grass!" she screams, voice echoing off the brick walls. "One day, you are going to see her for what she really is, and it will be too late. Is she really worth all of that? Is she worth losing our lives over, Miles?"

He expertly avoids her question. "There is no us or her, and until you understand that, I want you gone."

"You—Miles, you can't kick me out. You're not even in charge."

"But I am," Elliot says. He's on the other side of the room, bandaging up a cut on Vira's hand. "I'm on your side, Vanesa, but this has gone on for far too long. I will not cast you out, but if you don't stop these childish games of revenge—" His sentence falls off, leaving the rest of his threat to be determined.

Miles releases Vanesa. She looks straight at me with a bloodthirsty expression that sends chills down my spine.

"Fine, I'll behave," she lies, and I can see right through her, clearer than ever before. "However, when you all wake up and decide to choose blood over water, I want to be the one to drive a stake through her heart. Deal?"

No one responds, and she struts out of the room, disappearing behind the concrete wall.

Miles is at my side again, hand grappling for mine. "I never should have left you. I never thought—" his eyes slide to Vira, and he must remember that she too, is to blame for what happened to me.

"What's your excuse?" He nods toward her, ice in his tone.

"I want our people to be free," she says softly, but she can't bring herself to look at him. "Vanesa texted me that she was outside before we left... I knew I should have told her to stand down—" She drops her head into her hands, and I'm floored to see her look so small. "I tried to convince myself that it was Vanesa who was in the wrong. That I was merely a bystander."

Her words fall off, and she raises her swollen and defeated eyes, but still won't look at us. I'm not sure what compels me to justify her actions, but I find myself coming to her defense just the same.

"She had my back when it mattered," I say. "And she's going to help me with something else I need, too."

This time Vira does meet my eyes, and a troubled expression takes root. I don't elaborate on what I mean, and she doesn't ask. We both know she owes me that much. Despite how angry I am with her, I think a part of me has always known gaining her trust and respect isn't one large battle, but accumulates across the small ones. The first step was saving her life over the summer, then by not holding it against her, and now defending her to Miles. We've reached common ground, whereas little things such as those wouldn't phase Vanesa in the slightest because she doesn't know loyalty if it's not to herself.

Instead of continuing the conversation, Vira looks at Elaine and asks, "Are you ready?"

Elliot furrows his brow, as does Lucas. Danielle is so concentrated on stitching me up with her small, nimble fingers that I don't think she's paying any of us a lick of attention.

"To join the clan," Elaine elaborates and stands so she's closer to Elliot's height. Her hair is down now, and slight waves pattern her long, auburn hair. "That is, if you don't mind putting up with being lesser than me for all of eternity."

There's a slight twinkle of a response in Elliot's usually blank stare, but he covers it well. "I'll kill you well before we near eternity."

Vira actually laughs at that, the sound sending strange shock waves flitting about the room. Before I know it, she's dropping her head into her hands, laughing hysterically as we all stare in awe. Hearing Vira laugh, seeing even the resemblance of a smile that isn't sinister or mocking upturn her lips is the most jarring experience.

Elliot raises an eyebrow, and Lucas asks him if he gave her some sort of anesthetic for her hand that's making her loopy.

"Sorry." Vira coughs, trying to catch her breath. She drags her fingers through her hair and gives it a tug. "I'm sorry. I'm just so tired of being *mad* all of the time. It's exhausting."

"Imagine how Vanesa feels," Elaine grumbles.

"I truly can't fathom it." Vira cackles deliriously. Her face is beat red now, and even I'm beginning to think she's been drugged. The sight, however strange, brings an amused smile to everyone's lips, and I suddenly wonder how long it's been since she truly laughed at something. Since they all have.

"Okay," Elaine says after a few minutes when we finally recover from Vira's rapid mood swing. "Let's get this over with before I change my mind."

Danielle finally finishes stitching me up and drops the needle with a sigh, wiping the back of her wrist on her forehead to dab away a few beads of sweat. "Elaine, you know you don't have to do this if you don't want to."

Elaine's gaze travels to Dallas's body lying limply on the table behind me. "I know."

"Who will she kill?" Elliot asks, and Elaine physically flinches at the words.

Vira nods her head as if to gesture outside, where there's a body tied up on their porch. "Vanesa brought one of the hunters home with us. He won't survive his injuries and is only suffering. Nothing short of our blood could save him."

"But you could still save him," I state, knowing that's not what Elaine wants to hear, but needs to if she's going to make peace with this choice.

Danielle disagrees. "Hunters refuse to drink our blood. It goes against the oath they take upon becoming part of the organization. I promise you, that man out there would rather die than drink from any of us."

"But wouldn't he rather live than help make another vampire?" I counter.

"I'm doing this, Aspen," Elaine says, pursing her lips.

"I'll go get him," Lucas says after a moment, and then exits the room.

After Vira saved my life, she and Vanesa rounded up the hunters, disposing of the ones who had died and moving the ones who hadn't into the woods so they wouldn't draw attention before they came to. Not including the one who almost killed me. Vira injured him beyond saving when she punched him in the side of the skull. It was Vanesa's idea to use him to complete Elaine's transition.

For the first time, I allow my gaze to travel to Dallas's body. I can almost reach him from where I sit, but my stitches protest, as does Danielle. "I am not redoing those."

She moves around the counter, then gently pulls the sheet off of Dallas's face. He looks pale, and the only indication that he's alive is the weak sound of his heartbeat. I have to look away, unable to witness him like this.

"So, who's it going to be?" Elaine asks, placing her hands in her pockets to hide her nerves.

Danielle immediately rejects. "I will not play any part in this decision or its process. I'm merely moral support."

Miles declines, too, claiming he's afraid if he changes both of us, something might go wrong. Elijah's letter never insinuated anything of the sort, but I don't think he feels right changing the both of us. It's an intimate bond. And one that the two of us share. As far as I know, he hasn't turned many others before me, if any. Danielle has never turned anyone because of how long she waited to complete the transition. The curse took effect not long afterward.

"Lucas won't do it either," she adds. "He's scared to be a mentor. His father was a despicable man, and he's worried about inflicting the same neglect onto a protege."

Elaine grits her teeth, rolling her aqua eyes when she realizes who it's down to. Vira and Elliot—though I'm sure Vanesa would still be eager to turn her if she wanted.

Vira smirks, raising an eyebrow. "I think Elliot should take this one. I would be a lousy mentor as well. Aspen got lucky with Miles."

"And you think dark and broody over here will be much better?" Elaine gapes, appalled by this turn of events.

Elliot looks her up and down, seeming just as displeased with this arrangement. Though, a distorted part of my brain finds the idea of Elliot and Elaine being bonded for eternity unbelievably hilarious, given their dislike of one another. "Vira..."

His sister shrugs, pursing her lips. "You're the only one left who didn't automatically decline."

"Because I never thought I'd actually be the one to do it," he gripes, shifting awkwardly on his feet. "Why doesn't Aspen?"

"She's part of the key that unlocks the curse. Why would we ever risk anything else going wrong? For all we know, having her turn Elaine could kill us all." Vira sighs heavily at Elliot's apprehension. "Stop this childishness and turn her."

Elliot bites his lip, sliding his gaze to Elaine hesitantly. "Fine. Let's just get this over with."

"Agreed." Elaine turns toward him and holds out her wrist. She braces herself, squinting her eyes and turning her head away so she won't have to watch him bite her.

Elliot leans forward, taking her wrist and placing it back down at her side. This surprises her—all of us, actually—and she watches him with wide, fearful eyes as he cups one side of her neck, brushing the strands of hair off the other to reveal the tan skin covering her carotid artery. She visibly sucks in a breath, tilting her chin up as he lowers his lips, and exhales sharply the moment his teeth sink beneath her skin.

A couple seconds longer than necessary go by, and when Elliot releases her, a trickle of blood runs down her neck that he catches with his thumb. His eyes are glossed over, and it's as if he can see her, yet isn't really seeing her at the same time. He looks different somehow, like for the first time since I met him, he's actually alive.

His voice is hoarse when he speaks, chest rising and falling with deep, heavy breaths. "I haven't tasted a human's blood in far too long."

Lucas finally comes back with the hunter's body, but Elaine is none the wiser, staring at her arms as if they're some foreign entity. "Does it always feel so…"

"Invigorating?" I supply and find myself smiling even though I never wanted this for her. Because I know what it feels like—electricity coursing through your veins, flooding your body with life and energy and awareness like you've never felt before.

Elaine nods, keeping her eyes trained on her arms.

Danielle smiles in spite of her reservations. "It never gets old."

"And now neither will you," Lucas adds, and it's evident then, that in this moment, each of us is living through her.

Coming to her senses, Elaine kneels beside the hunter and presses two fingers to his wrist, checking for a pulse. He's unconscious, so he won't see or feel a thing.

"I can feel the blood pumping through his body." She stares wondrously, lowering her mouth to his skin and enveloping her lips around his arm.

As we stare, watching her suck every last drop of blood from his body, my own blood begins to hum. I feel as though I'm being cleansed, washed clean of the death on my hands and stripped of the darkness in my soul. The lights in the armory flicker wildly until Elaine lifts her head, blood smeared across her lips and eyes glowing a deep, rich golden color. When I look around, I notice that just like Elaine's everyone else's eyes are glowing, too.

Miles slips his hand into mine, and I latch on to his arm. This feeling of freedom, of strength, is so much more than I ever expected. Truthfully, I didn't expect to feel anything at all when Elaine changed, but I do. We all do. And for the first time since I turned, I feel like I'm a part of something bigger than myself. Like I'm no longer disconnected from the Draven clan. I feel the siblings as I feel the oxygen flowing in my lungs.

"We actually did it," Vira breathes, looking up at the ceiling. "We're free."

"How do we know for sure?" Danielle asks.

Vira snorts, but even the wondrous look in her eyes can't be masked by her sarcasm. "Were the flickering lights and glowing eyes not enough of a sign for you?"

A cold hand touches my arm, startling me, and I spin around abruptly, my heart lurching at the sight of sandy curls and lively eyes before me. I cup a hand over my mouth, and a strangled sound escapes me before I can stop it. "You're okay."

I lurch into my brother's arms, and he lifts me up, crushing me in the biggest bear hug ever. I can't help the tears that prickle in the corner of my eyes. For a brief while earlier, I thought I might never see him again, and hell if I'm not relieved to have been wrong. "I'm so sorry. I'm so, so sorry, Dallas."

The other transitioner begins to stir as well, groaning and stretching restlessly. I'm not sure exactly when Vanesa turned them all, but I'm assuming he was one of the last ones before Dallas, given that the other women didn't survive. Luckily, we solved the problem before we had to worry about a timeline.

Dallas sets me down, but I'm not ready to let go, so I just hang on to him as he takes in the room—the body on the ground, Elaine's bloodstained lips, Vira's rat's nest hair from the rain. After a moment, I realize I still haven't put a shirt on since Danielle finished with my stitches, so I grab it off of the table.

Dallas sighs uneasily, his expression only growing warier when he notices the stitches and dried blood on my stomach as I pull the shirt over me. "I get the impression that I've missed a lot."

CHAPTER 37

My feet trudge through the muddy path that leads to where I last met Adrian. Vira is on my heels, the both of us eager with anticipation as we near the spot where we're to meet the American vampire.

I'm still so pissed at her that I'm not sure what to do with myself. But she's practical, and I need that from her right now. I need someone with me that can keep their mouth shut when necessary, and she owes me.

Adrian stands in the center of a small clearing, surrounded by a handful of men and women. I can't tell if they're all vampires, or some hunters, as well, but just the same, they look ready for battle.

"Aspen Troy," he drawls, glowering. "I hear you failed to heed my warning," he pauses, noticing Vira, *"and* you brought a Draven along."

I skip the pleasantries, getting straight to the point. Earlier when I mentioned needing Vira's assistance, I had been working up a plan in my head—a way to avoid Vanesa killing every soul in sight in the hopes of winning a war against the clans, and in the process, hopefully a way to keep the Draven clan alive. "That's why I'm here."

"Is that so? You needn't come all this way to tell me you've broken the curse. We would have been seeing each other soon enough." He moves closer to me, and his men straighten, ready to defend him if it becomes necessary. "I suppose you're simply trying to make it easier for me to end your life. Though, it never needed to come to this."

"We both knew that it was inevitable." I move toward him and a few of his followers raise their weapons—so vampires *and* hunters. "I have a proposition for you—if you would be interested in such a thing."

"Bargaining for your life is not going to work with me. I'd thought you were smarter than that."

I raise an eyebrow. "Thinking so little of me already? I'd thought more of *you*."

He leers, and despite his duty to eradicate any and all Dravens, he can't help but listen to what I have to say. Exactly as I predicted. Vira had been worried he'd kill us on sight, but I knew better. Despite his reputation, Adrian isn't necessarily rash, but calculated and meticulous. His inquisition is also his weakness, and he can't help his curiosity when it comes to me. "You have my attention."

"You think you're destroying an entire clan of vampires for power, but you're not. You're doing it because the Twelve, besides Edgar Draven, want to protect themselves from the risk of other vampires seeing a better and brighter future under the Draven name. I'm assuming you were sent here to assess the situation because the others couldn't be bothered to and think we're harmless. You want the legacy of exterminating the Draven clan to yourself because you think it will give you power, but it's the opposite. If you kill us, you're giving *them* the power. You're being controlled by them, played a fool, and honestly? I wouldn't have pegged you for one of those. Menacing, deliberate, cruel—yes. But foolish? A puppet? That surprises me." I start to walk around, goading him like he did me the last time we spoke. It's a bold move, and I can tell I have Vira scared beyond comprehension, but she doesn't bail on me like I thought she might. Ever since Elaine broke the curse, I've felt a new sense of strength, and this newfound courage just might get me killed. But if I'm to do this right, I need it.

I've made a lot of baseless assumptions, but at some point, I must have struck a nerve. Adrian grabs my arm, halting me in place, then yanking me closer. "You are not doing yourself any favors by insulting my intelligence."

"You must be mistaken," I assure him. I'm sure my mysterious and power-hungry ruse is blown by the erratic beating of my heart, but I'm trying my hardest to mask it. To hold myself together. "Things are changing, and sure, you can kill every vampire that resides in Ichorye, but it's not going to change anything long-term. Once the Dravens are gone, you'll still be one of eleven clan leaders. Sure, the Twelve has power, but the Draven name is known by vampires around the world. If you want real power, you're not going to obtain it by being the man who slaughtered an entire clan. And yes, that will be a legacy you'll have for eternity.

"Just imagine, for a moment, what that legacy would look like if you were the man who brought down a government of the most powerful vampires in history. What is one measly clan compared to that? Because it's not a matter of whether or not you attack us today, tomorrow, or in a year. There will be a war, with or without us, and the real question is whether or not you want to be on the winning side of it."

He thinks this over, his face sculpted so meticulously out of stone that if there's a change in his expression, I don't see it. "And what is it you're vying for?"

"You want power. The Dravens need time and an army for when the clans attack—because once the Twelve discover we've broken the curse and you did nothing about it, they will take matters into their own hands. And you have one of the largest territories of vampires in the world—"

"You misunderstood me." He leans close, tapping the underneath of my chin. "I asked what it is *you* desire from this arrangement. I know you don't care about a war that will rage due to a sequence of events set in motion over two hundred years ago, and my dear, you don't care about my status. So, I will ask you once again, what is it *you* are vying for?"

I take a long breath and force myself to stay rooted in place instead of jerking away from his touch. "The townspeople. I don't want them to die to serve in an army, and I don't want the clans marching into Ichorye and wiping them out in a turf war."

"So you want to war on my territory? Destroy those human lives instead?" He cocks an eyebrow, starting to understand my angle. Adrian has enough members in his clan that we wouldn't have to turn anyone, and if we merge for the purpose of overthrowing the Twelve... well, no one in town has to die in a war, either.

"Of course not," I say, almost losing my patience, but I rein in my anger. I've gotten much too used to releasing it when Vanesa pushes me over the edge. I need to practice control. Before I turned, I never had to worry about such things. "Your territory is larger. There is more open space for a war that won't inflict pain on others. The Twelve have to come to us for a fight, but it doesn't have to be in Ichorye."

"Human casualties are inevitable."

"Since when do you care for the minuscule lives of humans?" I mock, matching his confidence.

"I don't think you understand what an unfathomable request this is."

"You want power? Command? It's not much to ask at all. I'm even allowing you to work from home."

His eyes grow dark, the rims lined with liquid gold, and he extends his hand to me. I take it hesitantly, and he hovers them between us, pending like our agreement. "You have a deal. I will keep the status of the curse a secret—for now. But I need assurances that once we rip the ground out from under the Twelve clans' infrastructure, you won't murder me next."

I nod thoughtfully. It makes perfect sense. Throughout this process, we could easily recruit Adrian's followers out from under him, and then stab a stake through his heart. "I'm listening."

"The American girl," is all he says, and I draw my brows together. I'm the only American here. For the most part, the rest of the Dravens were born and raised in Ichorye. When he realizes I don't understand, he elaborates. "When we first met. The girl you went to see. She has been creating more of you in search of someone, a man I perceive. You're close with her, no?"

I swallow hard. Rachel. He's talking about Rachel. She's turning people? Why hasn't she tracked me down yet? I guess I did set her free in the wild with the complicated task of finding and killing my brother, but still. "What about her?"

"She was causing quite the commotion by creating more vampires like you—the clans are calling them the *tainted,* but no one knows where they originated—yet. I had my men lock her up because of the trouble she was causing, and she has been asking for you, and only you. I have no desire to harm her, but I would like to keep her as assurance—a token of good faith."

I feel sick. How many people has Rachel turned to exact revenge on my brother? I hate leaving her with Adrian, but if she's out in the world, there's no telling how many people will get hurt on her path of destruction, and that blood will be on my hands. Not to mention, if any of the Twelve get to her, they'll know she was turned by someone of the Draven bloodline, and we won't be able to keep the state of the curse a secret from them any longer.

"You won't hurt her?" He nods, and I squeeze his hand in a firm shake. "We have a deal."

He doesn't release me just yet, leaning closer so I can feel his breath on my face. "How am I to know that the Dravens will adhere to these terms? You are not their representative."

"I am here on behalf of Elliot," Vira speaks up, lying through her teeth. If Elliot knew where we were, what we were doing, he'd quite literally kill us. We planted the idea in her siblings' heads a few hours ago, and most of them were wary. So, we're giving them time to think it over, and this way, when they finally agree, it won't be too late to strike a deal because it's already been done.

And if they don't agree... well, that's a problem for another time.

"Very well, then." Adrian smiles a ghastly grin, then speaks over his shoulder. "Amell? Tell the hunters to stand down and remove our soldiers from Draven territory. Also, tell the clan representatives that Adrian Hayle will no longer be in attendance."

The man nods, but Adrian has yet to let go of my hand. I swallow hard, some of my confidence waning at the look of pure evil in his eyes, and it occurs to me then that I may have just made a deal with the devil—and he's always one step ahead.

"You want something else in return," I realize, clenching my teeth.

He lifts a shoulder, expression unchanging. "Just a simple favor."

"Which is?" I stutter. This time he notices me falter and strokes his fingers beneath my chin.

His lips stretch into a deadly grin. "That is to be determined. But whenever I decide I need something, you must fulfill it."

"Aspen…" I hear Vira's warning voice from behind me, and I close my eyes, knowing if I don't agree, if I deny him this, he will tell his men to march on Ichorye right this instant.

"I won't harm anyone for you."

"I would never expect you to," he says, raising an eyebrow and glancing between us at our hands.

I swallow hard and stamp down my apprehension, tightening my grip around Adrian's hand to show him that I cannot be intimidated, no matter if that's actually true at the moment. "Deal."

"You must oblige me when the time comes. As you know, I take my promises very seriously." Adrian releases my hand, but the adrenaline coursing through my veins prevents me from moving. This may not be a blood oath, like the one he made with my ancestor, and I may not be physically bound to him, but this deal feels like more than owing him a favor in the future. Adrian will collect on his half of the bargain, and I just pray that somewhere along the line my soul isn't tarnished in the process.

～

I find Dallas later tonight on the Draven balcony, staring out at the evening sky. He doesn't remember much about what happened before he fell into his coma, but the moment he woke up, he said he felt different. Not good or bad, just different than before he'd fallen asleep. Part of me had hoped he knew what happened, that way I'd be spared the horrible task of breaking it to him. He didn't take the news as horribly as I'd feared, but he already said he won't complete the transition. He said he would rather die.

It's admirable, really. I once said the exact same thing. But his blood is sweeter now, and we live in a town infested with vampires who haven't tasted human blood for two centuries and are now free to feed at their will. After Elaine's sacrifice to save my brother, it seems so fruitless for him to die that way.

Right now, Elliot is on his way to the police station to compel each and every one of them to drop the investigation into Aaron Anderson's death, and then he and Vira are going to compel Nadia to forget everything new she's learned about her fiancé, only allowing her to keep the memories she had of him pre-death. Half of me feels guilty that she will never learn the truth, but the other half is relieved that after tonight, I won't have to worry about her anymore.

"You know," Dallas says thoughtfully, neck craned toward the sky. "I never used to believe in God."

Taken aback, I look at him, surprised he even heard me coming. When I first walked out here from Miles's room on the balcony above, I couldn't believe how small he looked. How lost and far gone the old Dallas is, the boy I used to rock to sleep at night because our mother didn't, too lost in her grief to notice her last living children were dying inside—and that was only a few months ago. "I don't understand."

"After Derek... I just thought, how could someone so good and so powerful, let such bad things happen to the world, to the innocent people who live in it. It's tragic and pointless. Pain and heartache are pointless." He licks his lips, motioning for me to join him at the railing. "I just mean that I understand why people believe now. When there is so much bad in the world, how can you go on without something to put your faith in? Because believing in yourself isn't always enough."

"So..." I say slowly, a touched smile stretching my lips. "What you're saying is, this entire experience has made you... believe in God?"

"If you believe in the devil, you believe in God, right?" he asks, and suddenly I understand.

Both of us have seen the devil wear many faces. We've looked him in the eye and stood face-to-face with his demons. Despite our best efforts, we couldn't stop the darkness from latching on to us as well—how could we when it's everywhere?

How do we stop evil from stealing our souls when it's in the air we breathe? And how do we stop the devil from claiming us when his influence stems from the darkness within?

WANT MORE OF THE DRAVEN FAMILY?

Order the next book in the Nightfall
series, **Until Daybreak.**

ABOUT THE AUTHOR

Lexi (J.) Kingston started writing when she was fifteen years old solely because she was obsessed with the idea of creating fictional worlds like the ones she lived through growing up. There was this thrilling allure to writing characters that you can relate to and find pieces of yourself within that she couldn't shake, and this eventually drew her to fiction writing. She wanted to create a world people could get lost in—a fictional safe haven, if you will. A place filled with endless possibilities, where you can lose yourself, yet find yourself within the pages.

You can find Lexi's contemporary romance titles under "Lexi Kingston."

LEXI KINGSTON ONLINE
INSTAGRAM: instagram.com/l.kingston.books
FACEBOOK: fb.me/l.kingston.books
TWITTER: twitter.com/Lkingston_books
GOODREADS: goodreads.com/lkingstonbooks
BOOKBUB: bookbub.com/profile/lexi-kingston
WEBSITE: https://lkingstonbooks.com